Bindings

Jenny Kalahar

Book 3 in the
Turning Pages Series

Special note: One character's name was the result of a charity auction to benefit the National Foundation for Ectodermal Dysplasias. Kim Lau won the right to name a character for inclusion in this novel, and she selected Dontae, her son's name. The character has nearly the same ED conditions as Dontae Lau. No other comparisons to the real-life Dontae are implied herein. There are over 150 types of ectodermal dysplasia, and all are very rare. Please see www.nfed.org for more information.

Bindings is dedicated to all those who tirelessly, patiently and lovingly protect and serve the emotional and physical needs of animals and people everywhere. Thank you to my dear husband Patrick, who makes my writing possible. Thanks to Last Stanza Poetry Association members, Poetry Society of Indiana, ICHC friends, and to everyone who helps and encourages any author along their creative way.

Chapter One

Kris Dehlvi sat on a plush chair with his back to the windows holding Lila Pearl, watching sparkling dust float in the strong afternoon light. His right arm supported her, but it was starting to fall asleep right along with the baby. Not wanting to wake her, he stayed as still as he could, and soon his breathing matched hers.

Nearly hypnotized by the sunlit dust, he eventually closed his eyes, letting the soothing classical music from the stereo in the rare bookshop's main room calm his thoughts. Tatyana, his girlfriend, was leaving for Botswana once school ended for the summer.

"I'm going home," she said as she'd stood on his front porch the day before. She was clearly upset as she held his hand and looked at their feet.

"Okay, but you just got here."

"No," she said, pulling him with her as she sat on the cushioned bench. She kept her eyes on the pots of red and pink geraniums hanging above the railing. "My parents and I are going back to the country of our birth. We had planned to stay there for a month or two to visit family like we did when I was eleven." She'd paused, her head bowed. "Lately, though, my mother is hinting that she might want to stay there forever."

Kris replayed that scene over and over to the rhythm of L.P.'s soft breathing and the gentle music, his eyes still closed. He remembered feeling relieved, but then guilty that he'd felt relieved. He had wanted to pull away from her for weeks, ever since the picnic at the Cumber's celebrating the grand opening of their new antique shop. Nothing had happened, and they hadn't argued, but being around all the loving couples at the party made him realize that he didn't have that same kind of bond with Tatyana. They were good

1

friends, but nothing more. It hadn't been fair to her to pretend it was something more.

Mrs. O'Malley leaned against the doorway and watched Kris and her grandniece resting. She sighed almost noiselessly, but it was loud enough to rouse the boy, who opened his eyes and smiled.

"Could you take her, Mrs. O? My arm is getting numb," he whispered.

Mavis O'Malley pushed her glasses higher onto her nose before crossing the room to lift the baby into her arms. L.P. yawned and sleepily asked, "Mama?" even though she could see that it was her great-aunt who was holding her.

"Your mom had to go away for a little while, Lily. Want to go back to sleep, or do you want Kris to take you to the front room to pet Buglit?"

L.P. twisted around until she found Kris, who was standing nearby in front of a showcase shaking the numbness from his arm. She grinned and opened and closed her hand toward him.

Mrs. O'Malley gave the baby back to Kris and watched as the boy carried her to the main room in search of the shop's resident calico cat.

"L.P.—where's Bug? Can you find Bug?" coaxed Kris.

"Bah!" called L.P., using her name for Buglit. She didn't see the cat, but she did spot Mack O'Malley at the far end of the room where he was shelving books in the science fiction paperback section. She smiled, showing off her four new teeth.

Mr. O'Malley placed a stack of paperbacks on the end table near the bookshop's big red sofa. "Well, Lila Pearl. Did you enjoy your nap with Kris?"

She yawned a long, slow yawn. "Ba-ah!" she called again, and Buglit dashed into the room from the hallway.

"There's Bug," Mrs. O'Malley said. She lifted the calico cat and hugged her to her chest. The older woman then stood

2

close to L.P. so the tiny girl could pet her favorite cat with one outstretched finger.

"That's nice, sweetie," said Mack. "Soft. The kitty has *soft* fur, doesn't she?" He then looked at the boy. "Hey, Kris—what's going on at your house? Any news?"

Kris scratched Buglit under her chin with his free hand and answered, "Mom and Dad are thinking about taking in another kid."

"I knew they were talking about fostering again, but I didn't know it would be this soon. Are they going to get a boy or a girl, do you know?" asked Mrs. O'Malley.

"I'm not sure. And they aren't going to foster at first like they did with me. I think they want to adopt from the start."

L.P. squealed, making Kris and the O'Malleys laugh. Buglit had licked her finger.

Mrs. O'Malley said, "Well, that is kind of them to want to help out another child, Kris. This will be a big change for you and your brothers. Are you excited?"

Kris paused, taking in a slow breath. "I'm not what you'd call *excited,* but I think adopting again is a good thing. I guess I don't know if I want so many things to change all at once." He looked down at the baby shyly as he said, "Tatyana told me yesterday that she's moving back to Botswana."

The O'Malleys each looked for the other's reaction to this announcement.

"She is, huh? Her parents, too? I thought her dad was enjoying his professorship," said Mack as he walked toward the science fiction paperbacks again, scooping up the stack on the end table on his way.

Kris shrugged. "They plan to go back for only this summer, but Taty thinks they might stay permanently. Her mom's family has been putting pressure on them, I guess. They don't want Taty to be a young woman away from her home country. That's a part of it, anyway."

"Hmm. Well, I'm sorry to hear this, Kris," said Mrs. O'Malley, frowning. "I know how close you two are. You're sure going to miss her, aren't you?"

Kris shrugged again and looked only at Buglit. "I guess."

His answer seemed strange to Mrs. O'Malley, but she let the topic drop. Buglit jumped to the floor from her arms, so she took L.P. from Kris, who then went to the science fiction section.

The Mary twins—so-called by the O'Malleys because the friends look alike, both have gray hair, and usually dress alike—came in to browse for romance novels. "Hello, everyone. Nice to see you again, Kris. My, how tall and handsome you're getting to be," complimented the older Mary.

"Hello, Marys," said Kris.

"His voice! I can't get used to that grown-up voice coming out of him, can you, Mary?"

"No, I can't either, Mary."

"He's like a young Cary Grant, don't you think so?"

"Oh, no, dear. Definitely more of a Paul Newman type with his sandy hair and those piercing blue eyes."

"I once saw Paul Newman and his wife in person. I'll never forget that day in New York. Have I ever told you about meeting Paul Newman, Mary?"

"Yes, yes. But now that I look at Kris closer, he's starting to resemble my cousin Melvin. When Melvin was much younger and still had hair, of course. Melvin was a looker. He eventually married Ethel Ramsbacher, which was unfortunate. Did I ever tell you about Ethel Ramsbacher?"

The ladies chatted some more about unfortunate Cousin Melvin before switching to a discussion of the high price of saffron as they headed to the far end of the main room to look at the recently-shelved romance paperbacks.

Sighing and stretching, Kris told Mr. O'Malley, "Well, I should get home. I need to study for a final exam. I can't wait until I can get back to working here every day. It seems like a whole decade has gone by since last summer."

Mack nodded, feeling the same way. "Are you doing anything this Saturday? Oh, and do you know if Matt is doing anything Saturday?"

Kris shook his head. "I don't have anything going on. I'd have to call Matt to ask him if he's got any big plans. Katrina is taking piano lessons now, and I think Saturday is one of the two days of the week that she has 'em, so I don't think she's available."

"No, I only need your help and Matt's. There are two auctions in two different towns taking place simultaneously on Saturday, and I'd like to go to both of them. Since I'm only one tall, plaid-shirted fellow, I can't manage to cover both by myself. Mrs. O should stay here to run the shop, and that puts me in a bind."

"Oh, yeah—I can do one of them for you, Mack. I've gone to a few auctions, and I know how they work."

"Thanks, kiddo. The ads for both state that they'll be selling a lot of old books. Neither has a preview before the morning of the sale, so I don't know if one will be more worthwhile than the other, if both will be great, or if both will be a wash. You'll definitely need Matt along. Trying to keep track of what you've bid on and how much you've spent is hard. I hate to go without Mavis as my helper, but we can't afford to be closed on a busy Saturday. Do you think Matt would want to go with us? I can drop you boys at one auction, get a bidder number for you, then go to the other sale."

"I'm sure he'll want to do it," Kris said from his seat atop a short, white stepladder.

"Listen—and no arguing about this: I'm going to pay you kids. I know you're planning to work here again in exchange for so-called 'book-dealing lessons' this summer, Kris, but this is a different situation."

"Okay. Want me to try to get Matt on the phone now?"

Mack nodded. "Yes, please. Mavis and I are headed to Jack and Darla's for a supper party. We're going to shoo everyone out right at closing time to give us a chance to get back to our apartment to clean up and put on our going-out clothes. Danny, the Cumbers, Jack's folks, and a couple of others will be there, too."

"Oh, I thought you two have L.P. because the Jacksons went somewhere for the afternoon," Kris said.

"No," said Mrs. O'Malley from the computer chair where she was sitting with the baby on her lap. "Darla wanted some uninterrupted time at home to cook and clean."

Kris walked to the counter and reached for the telephone. "Matt? Hey, are you—wow! What is that awful noise in the background? ... It *is?* Oh, man! Well, she's just beginning. Maybe after a few more lessons, it won't sound like a horror movie soundtrack. Anyway, are you doing anything special on Saturday? I have a job for you if you want it. A *paying* job for Mr. O. We'd go to an auction, bid on books, and then wait there for him to come back from another auction to pick us up. ... You will? Great! Okay, I'll talk to you later about what time and all that stuff. Bye!"

"I take it Matt isn't too excited by Katrina's piano practicing," said Mack as he straightened the small, colorful area rug in front of the sofa.

"No. I don't know how Browser can stand it. I wonder why he wasn't howling. Maybe he's in the yard with his paws over his ears."

Mrs. O'Malley said, "I took lessons for a while when I was a girl. I couldn't make both hands do different things at the same time. I'm sure Katrina is already doing better than I ever did."

Mack, who was wiping dust from his glasses with his shirttail, asked, "So, is Matt on board for the auction?"

"He said he'll go."

"Great!" He looked at the clock. "Mavis, you should probably carry your little miss next door to Jack. I'll close up shop while you're gone."

Mrs. O'Malley frowned. She snuggled the baby higher into her arms, not wanting to let go. "In a minute, maybe. I don't see why there's some big rush. She still wants to cuddle."

"Or *you* do," Mack said.

"Darla! I love it!" Mrs. Cumber said after slipping off her coat in Jack and Darla Jackson's living room that evening. She crossed the orange shag carpeting to stand in front of a dazzlingly lit-up blue and red 1970s jukebox.

"Here it is," Jack said proudly. He lifted a soda can and made a toasting gesture to the machine. "Fully restored. My folks gave it to us as a surprise a few days ago."

"Wow! That is something else!" said Mack as he held the door open for his wife.

Mrs. O'Malley stopped in surprise when she saw the strobing machine in the corner. "Oh, Jack! I have the strongest urge to do the Hustle right now. Wasn't there one almost exactly like it at the Dairy Deluxe about a million years ago?"

John Jackson called from the kitchen, "That's *the* very jukebox, Mavis." He stepped into the living room to join Danny, Lisa and Sonny Smith, the Cumbers, the O'Malleys, and his son Jack. "It was put into storage for twenty-five years after the Dairy closed, but then it went up for auction this past winter when the Douglass estate was sold. You should have seen all the middle-aged people bidding silly high prices for anything at all having to do with their old hangout. Even ice cream dishes brought big bucks. I was lucky to be able to get this tugboat for the price I did.

Probably because it didn't work, and it was dirty." He finally looked away from the jukebox to his company. "Hello, everyone! Nice to see you all. Darla and Ruthie are still getting supper ready, so go ahead and have a seat wherever you'd like."

Mrs. O'Malley went to stand in front of the jukebox, looking over the song selections and the details of the machine. "I can't *believe* it. I never thought I'd see this one— or one like it—again. I wonder if it recognizes me in my old age."

"Should I have it play?" asked Jack, smiling. "And you're hardly 'old,' Mavis." He looked around at the gathered group for suggestions. "What should I put on? Disco? Country? Blues? I have it all loaded up."

"Have any Lawrence Welk?" Sonny asked.

"Liberace?" tried Lisa.

"Um, no. Sorry. And you two should clearly enter the modern age—at least a little bit."

"Well, put on some blues," said Mack.

Jack snapped his fingers. "Blues it is."

Danny took a seat on the center of a vintage orange and black tuxedo-style sofa, his long legs in black jeans stretching out in front of him.

Jack pressed a selection, and the record played without being paid to do so. "Didn't It Rain" by Sister Rosetta Tharpe splashed out of the speakers. "I can't have the volume too loud," he explained. "It would hurt the baby's ears."

"Weeee!" squealed L.P. as she crawled from the kitchen to look at the lights and hear the lively music. Jack lifted her to his chest, pushed his glasses higher on his nose, and danced energetically with her as she laughed and laughed, her eyes shining.

Mrs. O'Malley removed her jacket, slung it on the arm of a chair, and patted Danny's knee to greet her brother before taking Mack's offered hand. The O'Malleys swiveled and jumped, clapped and sang along with the words they knew, their own singing volume about the same as the recording.

The Cumbers took a seat on either side of Danny and clapped happily, and Darla and Ruthie Jackson stood in the kitchen entranceway, smiling. Lisa pulled her husband from a purple-striped armchair and moved all around him as he stood nearly still, uncertain as to how to dance to anything other than a polka or a waltz.

A swanky song called "Bumble Bee" by Lavern Baker started. The two couples danced with the same enthusiasm the whole time that second song played. Mrs. O'Malley accidentally ran into Lila Pearl's playpen, but she quickly recovered and found the beat again.

When that record ended, the world was suddenly silent. L.P. wanted down from her father's arms. She crawled to the jukebox to try to pat it into playing another tune, but just then Darla announced that supper was ready to dish up.

"Sissy, you and Mr. Bookstore dance *deliciously*. You should go out dancing now and again. I never hear about you two dancing anywhere," said Mrs. Cumber as they stood in front of the pizza casserole on the kitchen table.

"We're too tired by the end of the day to do anything terribly exciting," said Mack as he buttered a thick slice of warm bread.

Mrs. O'Malley nodded. "I like to bowl, but I go with the ladies. I haven't even been bowling in quite a while, now that I think about it. I don't know, Mack. Maybe we should go out more together. What do you think?"

"We're partying right now, aren't we? And we had the picnic at the farm a few weeks ago. Why, we're practically party *animals.*"

"No. We're not," countered his wife flatly, shaking her head.

Darla and her mother-in-law, Ruthie, had made two casseroles, a ham, barbeque burger bacon beans, potato salad, a grape and melon salad, mixed cold greens, and candied yams.

"What are we celebrating, exactly," Mack asked Jack as he spooned up a serving of the savory beans.

"Mom and Dad's anniversary. It's their fortieth."

"What?" asked Mrs. O'Malley, who had overheard.

"It is?" asked Elwood Cumber, his plate already full. He stopped on his way to the dining room to look at the Jacksons in surprise.

Mr. and Mrs. Jackson both nodded.

"Forty years ago today. I know—we don't seem old enough. We were mere children when we married," said John Jackson.

"Well, happy anniversary, you two," said Mrs. O'Malley, all smiles. She put her plate down before giving Ruthie a hug. She then squeezed John's arm. Her face was still a little flushed from dancing, making her smile extra radiant.

"Congrats!" said Lisa, setting her full plate next to her husband's. "I knew about the jukebox. I assumed this was a party to christen it."

"Ba-baa!" said Lila Pearl, adding her congratulations to the round of handshaking and hugging going on above her head.

"So, let me get this straight," said Elwood. "It's *your* anniversary, but you buy a great, expensive present for your kids? How's come *that* is, John?"

"Um ... Ruth wouldn't let me have it at *our* house."

"I *thought* so," said Elwood, continuing into the dining room again. He let loose and loudly laughed once he'd set his plate safely onto the table.

"How goes the antique biz, Quaintance?" asked John, scooting his chair closer to the table. "Any interesting customers come in lately? I know you haven't had your Barntiques open for very long, but you must have *some* stories to tell us by now."

10

"Oh, you betcha!" she answered. "Last week I had a lady in there named GillyAnn—she must be eighty-five or ninety—and she wanted to know if we had any old legerdemain supplies. You know—things for a magic act. She used to tour with her husband when they were young, and now that her husband has passed on, she wants to go back on stage. She sold their trunk of tricks decades ago and always regretted giving them up."

"A magic act?" asked Darla as she put L.P. into her highchair. "Fabulous! So, did you have anything?"

Quaintance nodded after swallowing a sip of water. "A top hat. She bought it. And some old white handkerchiefs, and a very slender walking stick that she said she'll have sawn in half and painted to make a wand. She left happy. I've been checking the newspaper every day to see if she's advertised her show yet."

"Ha! It sounds like you're having fun, Quainty," Mrs. O'Malley said to her sister. "If you see her again, tell her we've got a few vintage magic books in stock."

"Oh, yes! I should have thought to send her over to you and Mr. Bookstore. Well, I wasn't thinking along those lines when I was scrambling around trying to find magical tidbits of my own."

When everyone had settled at last around the table with full plates, Mrs. Cumber began to sing "Happy Anniversary." It was a solo at first, but then the others joined in as the elder Jacksons held hands under the table and looked happily embarrassed. L.P. clapped her hands a few times, not caring in the least that she wasn't exactly on the beat.

Glasses of water and iced tea were held high as Jack gave a toast. "To Mom and Dad, the best ... well, simply the best. May you have another forty happy years together."

Ruth raised her glass and replied, "Thank you, Jack. And, since the jukebox is over here and not in *my* living room, I'm sure they'll be very happy years, indeed."

11

"Oh, you love that jukebox, too. Admit it, Ruth," said John.

"I love that it's in Darla and Jack's house."

"Well, if I ever go missing in the middle of the afternoon, at least you'll know where to find me."

A dog barked in the back yard.

"Jack, why don't you invite Patrick to join the party? It seems strange not to have him in here with us," said Ruth as she cut into her slice of ham.

"He's afraid of the beast in the corner."

"That dog? He's survived storms and floods and L.P.'s teething tantrums. How can he possibly be afraid of a jukebox?" asked Mack.

Jack sipped his water and said, "Pat bumped into it yesterday while romping around with the baby. It started playing Little Richard's 'Tutti Frutti,' and it scared the heck out of him. I'm not sure if the hackles on his back have settled down even now. He hasn't wanted to come into the house since."

Chapter Two

"'When I first open a book, I don't want to be shouted at. I don't want to hear the screaming of a damsel in distress, the trumpeting of a charging elephant, or the banging of a nightclub drum. I want there to be whispering at the beginning. Very, very interesting whispering, but whispering all the same,'" read Mrs. O'Malley from a book she was holding in one hand. She supported her grandniece on her lap with her other arm. The afternoon sun was too weak to make its way through the clouds, so the late spring day felt cooler than it should have for that time of the year. But it was warm inside the bookshop, and the overhead lights and table lamps gave enough yellow glow of their own to make anyone browsing the bookshelves feel golden.

A rush of wind tangled and detangled the green leaves of a small maple tree outside the display window as Mrs. O'Malley held Lila Pearl. She adjusted the baby into a more upright position on her leg, and Buglit extended a paw from under the counter where she had been snoozing on a stack of folded paper bags. A rollicking piece by Bach had started on the stereo a moment before. The cat had never liked Bach, so she woke up in a cranky mood. When she spotted the baby, however, her spirits improved.

"Mrrew," Bug called. She sniffed the light, powdery scents that came from freshly changed L.P. and decided to join the baby. Bug purred and climbed onto the one still-vacant and irresistible leg.

Mrs. O'Malley closed her book, lifted the cat, and turned her around so they all faced the cash register and computer. There the three friends companionable sat together as Buglit tried hard to ignore Bach's harpsichord pounding away from the speakers overhead, and Mrs. O'Malley tried hard not to doze off from pure contentment.

All three roused as Darla Jackson pushed in through the glass front door, bringing a rush of cool air in with her. Dressed in sweatpants and a dust-covered hooded sweatshirt, bits of dirty hay clung to the folds of her hood where it met her neck and brown ponytail.

"Shh!" Darla said, holding up one hand to motion for Mrs. O'Malley to stay just as she was. She took her cell phone from a pocket, stepped around the counter, and took a photo of the trio as they snuggled together. She then admired the resulting shot.

Mrs. O'Malley grinned as Darla showed her the screen. Buglit jumped to the floor as L.P. was handed to Darla.

"Bug—don't jump in the bassinet again," Mrs. O'Malley warned, sending the cat in the opposite direction.

"I thought Bug hates Bach. How'd you get her to tolerate being in the same room with the stereo while her least favorite composer was on?" Darla asked as she pulled L.P.'s striped shirt lower over her tummy.

"I guess the temptation of a triple cuddle was too much for her to resist. She sure loves your baby." Mrs. O'Malley stood, stretched, and yawned. "It's been quiet in here today. It felt good to have a slow business day, though. We were working so long to get Elwood and Quainty's antique shop open—while also working full days here—that Mack and I were worn out. It's been weeks, but I can't seem to rest enough now. I was sitting here thinking about the party at your place last night, and about the Cumber's party in April. Wasn't that grand opening picnic something else?"

Darla nodded as she lowered the baby into her portable bassinet beside the computer chair. She then opened the mini refrigerator and pulled out a bottle of orange juice. Mrs. O'Malley handed her a clean cup. "It was … it really was. I can't get used to seeing Kris holding hands with a girl. He's growing up fast!"

14

Mrs. O'Malley sighed. "But Kris told us that Tatyana is leaving for Botswana when school lets out. He said that she and her family may stay there longer than this summer."

"Poor kid. I remember *my* first heartbreak." Darla drank, then added, "I hope he's not too upset."

"Actually, I got the impression that he wasn't. Oh, well. Teenagers are full of ups and downs. It's hard to tell *what* he's feeling. Maybe he's still holding out hope that she'll be back when the new school year starts again this fall."

Darla finished her drink. Some hay from her sweatshirt dropped to the floor.

"Don't bother picking it up, Darla. I need to clean and sweep this afternoon, but I keep putting it off. Now that you're taking L.P., I no longer have an excuse. There's hardly been anyone in the shop all day. I think the gloomy weather has everyone staying inside."

Buglit rubbed Darla's legs in greeting. "Hiya, kitty. Been taking care of L.P. and Aunty Mavis for me?"

The calico squinted up at Darla, enjoying being appreciated for all her hard work. Buglit then left them to visit the litter box in the cats-only room at the far end of the hallway.

"So. How'd you do at the auction?" asked Mrs. O'Malley.

"Good," Darla answered, pouring herself more juice. "I won't really know until I get them next door where Jack and I can go carefully through them. The records I did manage to examine there seemed to be in nice, clean condition. I didn't see any rarities, but they should sell all right in our shop. I like selling online, but it's much more fun to talk to people in person about the music and performers they love and to recommend others that they might never have heard of before. Jack has taught me so much."

Mrs. O'Malley nodded. "You don't miss your life as a parking meter reader, then?"

"I thought I might, but I don't. Running the record shop with Jack is fun. He teaches me the business and all about music and musicians, and I'm teaching myself how to sell our rare records online. I love having the baby with us day and night, and I don't have to worry if I have to leave for a while to take L.P. to her appointments. You're always here for me to visit or to watch the baby, too. The boss is Jack, and he never cares if I need time off. Also, he calls *me* 'the boss,' to keep emphasizing that we're in this together now."

"I feel the same way with our store. Owning a business is a big commitment and a lot of work, but with Mack, it's a lot of laughs, too."

"Where *is* Mack? In the storage room?" Darla asked, glancing around the empty main room and down the hallway.

"No. He's at your other aunt and uncle's place. They bought the contents of a farm shed in Patience a couple of days ago. Elwood finally has everything loaded into their antique shop except the salamanders and cobwebs. El said they'd gotten about twenty boxes of old books with the vintage automotive parts and tools, and Mack volunteered to sort through the group for ones that they should keep to sell. The rest can be donated away, or we can take them here and put them outside on our windowsill as freebies. If there are any rare or valuable books, we'll list them on the internet for Quainty."

"Sounds good. I was thinking of doing the same thing if they buy a group that includes records. Jack can sort through them and, if they like, we can list the more exciting ones online for them." She looked at the time on her phone. "Well, I suppose my little girly and I should get over to the shop. Jack's dad dropped off Mrs. Jackson—and yes, I'm still calling her that—at home before bringing the truckload of records here. It was nice of them to take me with them today. He parked in the back alley and is helping Jack unload

16

everything into the office. I think I'll see if I can get a ride with Mr. J back to our house so I can clean up and flop onto my cushy chair for a nap before dinner. Jack can bring L.P. home later. Auctions wear me out."

"Oh, me, too. I hardly go to them anymore, and we went to one practically every week when we were first married." Mrs. O'Malley wrapped a white knitted blanket around L.P. and lifted her into a goodbye hug. She kissed the baby's cheek and got a dimpled smile and a giggle in return. "I can keep her longer if you'd like. She gives me an excuse to avoid cleaning."

"Nah. Jack misses her. And me, which is very sweet."

Mrs. O'Malley nodded, giving her a wink. She touched L.P.'s nose. "Thank you for an entertaining visit today, Lila. Buglit and I both hope you'll come back soon."

"Bah!" replied the baby.

As she took L.P., Darla asked, "Are you getting a new cat from the shelter soon? It seems strange to see Buglit wandering alone among the bookcases."

"One is coming in a few days. I told Doris to wait since I knew I was going to be tied up with our little punkin' all day today. And then there are the two auctions tomorrow that Mack, Matt, and Kris are going to. The place will be very crowded if we have to haul in a bunch of boxes. Buglit seems a bit lonesome for her next companion, so we'll all be glad to have a new feline roaming the aisles and sitting on the sofa." Mrs. O'Malley touched the tip of the baby's nose and smiled, enjoying L.P.'s brown curls and pink, round cheeks. "Oh! I forgot to tell Bug that 'her' baby is leaving. She'd never forgive me. Bug," she called. "Buglit! L.P. is going next door now."

In a flash, the calico cat sped into the main room. She bounded onto the computer chair and stepped onto the countertop. She sniffed the baby's sock-covered toes one last time as she purred a goodbye of her own.

Mrs. O'Malley put on a CD of rockabilly music and turned the volume louder when she was alone. She wiped dust from the small tables, lamps, and knick-knacks in the main room, all the while half-dancing.

When she'd finished dusting, she re-shelved books that had been left on a cushion of the big red sofa that faced the counter and tidied the rest of the room. After a short break, she swept each room that had a wooden floor.

At nearly closing time that late afternoon, Mack entered the shop backward, carrying a cumbersome load of two cardboard boxes that he placed on the countertop.

"Hello, Mack," said Mrs. O'Malley cheerfully from her computer chair. "Are those the books we're going to sell for Quaintance?"

"Are you still sitting there? That's where I left you this morning. Lazy thing!"

She playfully threw her dusting cloth at him.

Mack picked it up. "Yep. There are some dustjacketed mid-century cookbooks in one of the boxes, and about five math books in German that I think might be valuable in the other. I put several interesting oddities in that box, too."

She yawned. "I can barely keep my eyes open. Well, if there are more books to bring in, bring them in now. I piled a group of flattened boxes here behind the counter for the auctions. Speaking of auctions, Darla went to one today. No big, exciting finds for her, sadly. I hope you have more luck tomorrow. We could use some new, interesting stock." She turned on the monitor and checked her email. "Looks like our internet sales are humming along. I should concentrate more on online selling."

Mack opened a box and pulled out a 1950s cookbook by a Cajun chef. The book's spectacular orange and yellow dustjacket showed abstract vegetables and fruits holding spice bottles and dancing toward a cooking pot. "How does this one grab you?"

18

"Nice! Are there more like that?" Mrs. O'Malley asked, standing for a closer look.

"This box is full of culinary delicacies, plus there are one or two more boxes full of them still in the van. I think most of the rest of the group contains math and science books. I'll try for a closer parking spot to make it easier to unload. While I do that, would you call Kris? I'll pick up the kids at about seven-thirty tomorrow morning. Have Kris call Matt with that info, please."

She nodded once, distracted by a small, orange booklet titled "Crickets in the Rain and Other Poems" by Lottie Gunn Russell. "Why does this seem familiar, Mack?"

"Oh, yeah. Quainty sent that to you. That's the booklet she was telling you about, the one with the 'ooze and slime' poem in it. She said that her neighbor friend Richard gave it to her years ago, and now she's passing it on to you."

Mrs. O'Malley opened it and read two of the poems.

"What's wrong?" Mack asked a few minutes later when he'd brought in another box from the van and lifted it to the quickly-crowding countertop.

"Everyone seems to have an art thing except for me. Katrina's taking piano lessons. Darla and Kris write poetry. You repair books like a master. Quainty paints. Danny has his excellent woodcraft and carving, and Jack sings beautifully if you can talk him into a song. I don't have a single artistic bone in my body."

"Hmm," said Mack. "Well, have you *tried* to paint, write, or sing? Have you taken music lessons?"

She thought. "Well, I have tried singing, but you know how terrible I sound. I joined the elementary school band in the fourth grade. My flute was mighty sorry I ever blew air through its mouthpiece. I tried piano lessons. I can't draw a stick figure without throwing it away from embarrassment at my lack of artistic talent. Nope. I'm stuck without one hope of living the life creative."

"How about writing? You love Darla's poems, and Kris is very good at coming up with poems, too. How about trying to write?"

She sat on her chair, frowning again. "I could, but I hated writing in school. I've always loved reading, though."

"Well, that's important, too. Where would writers be without appreciative readers? Where would artists be without admirers? Why give a concert without an audience to hear the music?"

Mrs. O'Malley tried to smile at a woman and little girl who had entered the shop. "Maybe I *will* write something," she said to Mack before she stood again to ask the customers if she could help them find a book.

Chapter Three

The next morning, Kris raced from his front porch carrying a small cooler, a notebook, and a jacket. He swung the van door open before hopping onto the cracked vinyl of the front seat next to Matt, who moved closer to Mack to make room. Kris lowered his visor to block out the bright morning sun.

Mack said, "I'm bringing you kids to the McAlister sale where I'll register for a bidding number. I'll tell the auctioneer that you'll be doing my bidding for me while I'm gone." At a stop sign, Mr. O'Malley continued, "I'll then drive over to Laurie Parks' auction. She usually puts the books up for bids during the first part of each sale, but I can't count on that. If the crowd is small, she'll probably stick to the high-priced antiques and furniture for a long time, letting the books and household items wait until the end."

Matt, always hungry, was chewing on a granola bar before they had even gotten halfway to the sale.

"If I'm not back until late afternoon, are you kids going to be okay?" Mr. O'Malley asked as they followed the road that ran along the lake. "And thanks, Matt, for helping Kris and me. It's terrifically hard to handle an auction alone. Normally, I would have picked one or the other to attend, but they both sounded equally interesting and mysterious."

Kris nodded. "We'll be okay. We each have a cell phone with your number in our contacts. We both have some cash and food for a long day. Well … I do. Matt's already eating his lunch." He shook his head at Matt, who kept chewing. "Oh, and my mom said to tell you that she'll come out to the auction if we have any kind of a problem before you can get back." He glanced at Mr. O'Malley. "The only thing I'm nervous about is keeping under your five-hundred-dollar spending limit if the books are super good. I brought a notebook and pen for Matt. He'll keep track of the money amounts as I bid, and he'll keep track of the books we've bought so I don't have to worry about them while the rest of the books are still being auctioned."

Mack rolled down his window. "Mr. McAllister often has his sales in his big auction house in Anders Lake, but lately he's been conducting two sales each weekend. One on-site—like this one—and another auction that his employees set up in his building throughout the week."

Matt directed Mr. O'Malley from the notes the man had written on a scrap of paper, leading them far away from town to an area the boys had never been. After nearly an hour of driving, it was clear that they'd reached the auction site: cars, trucks, and moving vans clogged both sides of the country road. Mack pulled as far to the right into the cattails as he safely could before parking. He and the boys got out on the driver's side to avoid the marshy ground on the shoulder.

As they neared an enormous, ornamented Victorian house, Matt stepped aside as a pair of little girls wearing matching blue spring jackets raced between himself and Kris. The peach and burgundy-painted mansion's lawn was full of people. Various household and farm goods were jumbled together in old cardboard boxes. Sofas, tables, lamps, and tools were set out in rows that covered much of the grass or were on wide, worn boards raised on sawhorses.

Mr. O'Malley took out his wallet. He handed Kris several small bills that totaled fifty dollars. "That's for any emergency." He slid his driver's license from its slot as he stepped to a table where two elderly auctioneer's assistants were still setting up to start assigning bid numbers.

"This is some house!" one of the women remarked to the other as she took Mr. O'Malley's license and entered his information into a laptop. "I wonder what its story is, and why the contents of the house were locked in the farm's outbuildings for over a decade. Every time I drove past here,

22

I felt sorry for this place. It should have had new occupants long ago."

Kris stared at the large, lonely house and the scraggly bushes around its open porch. Two of the dust-caked windows on the main floor were the only ones that still had remnants of curtains. One of the upstairs windows was cracked. Leaves and debris were compacted against each of the rungs of the railings all the way around the porch.

Mack left the registration table to walk over to the auctioneer who was hooking up his microphone to a portable amplifier at the open entrance to a faded barn that sat at the end of an overgrown driveway. While the two men spoke, Mack pointed to Kris and Matt, and the auctioneer nodded. After they shook hands, Mr. O'Malley scanned the side yard and saw that the books, all in boxes, were in a U shape at the far edge of the property near a rusty wire fence.

Kris and Matt joined Mack, and all three of them went to inspect the loosely-boxed books. After a few minutes, Mr. O'Malley sighed and stood straighter, holding his back with one hand. "I absolutely have to get going to the other sale, or I'll miss those books if they're auctioned first. You have my number. Call me if you need me. Do what you can, but please don't go over the budget or I'll have a problem if I spend too much at the other auction." He scanned the boxes one final time. "I can't make a judgment on these in a hurry. Kris, it's up to you to look through them before the bidding starts. Rely on your experience and instincts. You've got a notebook. You know what we usually do during the preview when we're together. This time you'll take the lead and use Matt as your assistant."

Mr. O'Malley left them, cutting across the yard at a diagonal in his long, quick strides. It looked to Kris like the books were getting more attention at the sale than anything else, and it made him nervous that he'd have competition.

Matt flipped to a clean sheet of paper in the notebook and clicked the end of his pen, ready to write.

"We need to look through the boxes exactly in order, so we don't get all mixed up. But don't write down a box number. Note the advertising on the outside of the box, or what it looks like. Sometimes the boxes are moved, which means our numbering would get screwed up. We'll start here and then go along this row and around again to the opposite end," Kris said, pulling on Matt's sleeve with one hand while holding his jacket and cooler with the other. "By the way ... where's your sack lunch?"

"I already ate everything except half a sandwich, and that's in my sweatpants pocket," Matt said, clicking the pen again. "I got hungry."

"You're *always* hungry."

"I smell food cooking. Suppose there's time for a hot dog before we get started?"

"No. There's got to be a hundred boxes to look at. Come *on,*" Kris said, pulling Matt along again.

When they stood in front of the first box, Kris whispered that Matt should mark a 0 in his notes with "Pepsi" as a box description, as it contained a mix of badly worn romance paperbacks and a few *Reader's Digest* anthologies. At the second box, Kris knelt on the slightly damp lawn and carefully lifted out a few hardbounds from the early 1900s. Nothing looked to be in good condition or very interesting. He whispered for Matt to write down a 1 and "Parker toilet paper." The next few lots also had nothing of much interest, so he had Matt write 1, 2, and 0 in his notebook, along with a note beside each that described their box.

Once they'd reached the tenth box, the books looked much more valuable. When they had gone through and had written notes for only twenty boxes, the auctioneer's voice announced over his loudspeaker that the sale was about to begin and that he was going to start with the books.

"What? No way! Is it nine o'clock already?" Kris whispered. He stood and brushed the dirt from his palms onto his jeans.

"Oh, geez, it *is!*" Matt groaned as bidders crowded around them. "What are we gonna *do*? We've got like *no* idea what's in those other boxes."

Kris exhaled slowly, determined not to panic. There was nothing he could do except try to peer into each unfamiliar box right as it came up for bid. He took his coat and cooler and walked back to the first box they'd looked at, hopeful that the bidding would start there.

The auctioneer and his young woman assistant arrived at the same moment Kris and Matt did. The woman's hair was in a ponytail, but the rubber band holding it had loosened and her hair was hanging sideways. Mr. McAllister's shirt was untucked and dusty. It appeared that they'd already put in a long day's work to prepare the sale.

Leaning on a rickety wooden stepladder with his foot on the second rung, Mr. McAlister cleared his throat. Raising the microphone, he said, "I don't want to take all day with these, folks-a-folks-a-folks. Let's get going and get these gone. We have a barn full of smalls and loads of furniture and household good and tools in the yard and in the house. The real estate itself is sold, but everything else has gotta go. Gather round and come in close, now, folks-a-folks."

Kris looked at the long, U-shaped row of book boxes. Bidders appeared to have stationed themselves in front of the boxes that they planned to try to buy. A lot of the boxes had no one near them, including the ones near the auctioneer at the start of the line. Kris whispered to Matt to pay very close attention to what was going on and to what the auctioneer was going to say. He would need to add their bids together as the auction went along so Kris could know at a glance of the notepad how close to their budget they were.

Matt nodded but frown appeared between his eyes and at the corners of his mouth.

The auctioneer cleared his throat again, and his assistant rested a clipboard against her waist, pen at the ready.

"Okay, ladies and gents and young lads all gathered. Let's go-a-go-a-go! Here's what we're gonna do today-a-day. I'm gonna to start at this end. We'll follow around with the boxes in order as they come. No skipping. No bids for something over in the right quadrant or outfield, ladies and gents. I'm going to start with this box and wrap around the yard in order. Bid on one or bid on more in order. Here we go, with this box of romance paperbacks from the glorious nineteen-seventies era. What am I bid? Five-a-five-a-five dollar bid, am I five-five-five? No? Start me off then. What'll ya say, what'll ya bid? Two? Two-a-two-two-two. I've got one dollar from the younger gent here. Any advance on one dollar? No? Going once … going twice … gone!"

Matt had raised his hand. *He* had done the bidding.

Kris scowled, his mouth open. He was about to protest when Matt suddenly pushed him aside a little roughly and told Mr. McAlister, "We'll take them all. We'll take all the boxes in order, right down this row, around the corner, and over along the next row to the end."

The auctioneer heavily slid his foot from the stepladder, obviously stunned. Recovering quickly, and looking relieved to be done-a-done-a-done with the whole mess of books in only a few seconds, he told his assistant to "Add 'em up, Margo. One dollar times the count to bidder number … what's your number, son?"

In shock, Kris was unable to react. Matt took the bid number card out of his friend's back pocket and held it up so the assistant could write it in her ledger before she started to take a count of the boxes.

Kris grabbed his friend's sleeve. "What the …? Matt! What did you *do?* Matt! *What?"*

Matt looked pleased with himself. "I listened carefully like you said. We're *super* under the spending limit, and we bought all the books so we don't have to compete with those other bidders on down the row. *That's* what I did."

Kris scanned the people still gathered at the boxes they'd intended to buy. They hadn't heard or hadn't understood that Kris and Matt had bought every last one of them already. As the assistant counted, she explained to each bidder or small group of bidders what had happened. Dirty looks were shot at the boys every time the assistant revealed that the books were no longer for sale.

"They think we've played a rotten trick on them," gasped Kris, slapping a hand to his forehead. "Oh, *geez,* Matt. That was the most brilliantly awful thing you've ever *done."*

Matt plopped his jacket over the first boxes protectively. "I'm supposed to, like, gather these into one spot now, right? Where do you want them?"

Kris peered around again, a little afraid of the people who had been robbed of their turn at bidding. His cheeks reddened.

One man of about fifty years old with a bald head and oversize muscles walked up to them. "I gotta hand it to you, kids. Pretty swift! I never, ever would have thought of doing that. We all heard McAlister, but none of us really *heard* McAlister. Pretty swift, all right. Ha! I bet he'll never start off the bidding on a group like *that* again. How are you boys going to get all these home? Did you drive here yourself?"

Matt explained that they were waiting for their ride.

Kris' stomach dropped even farther toward his feet. Mr. O'Malley! How was he going to take this news? Would he be angry that they hadn't played fair? He pulled his father's cell phone from his front jeans pocket. No service!

He nudged Matt as the auctioneer was starting his patter near the front of the barn. "There's no cell service out here. We'll have to wait for Mack. We'll tell him what happened when he gets here."

"Maybe there's a phone you can use inside the main house," offered the muscular man.

"There's no phone here. There hasn't been for years," said a middle-aged woman in a purple pants suit as she passed them. "No one's lived here since … forever. The parents died about a dozen years ago, and the son passed away in prison. All these goods have been in locked sheds on the property. There's been a buyer for the house and barn now. He doesn't want the contents, so that's why this auction of the things that were left in the shed, house, and outbuildings is finally happening. They'll have a *job* fixing up the house. I remember when the family still lived here. The home was supremely beautiful, with lovely gardens in front and acres of corn in the fields. They kept the place in top condition for decades. The son turned out to be a ruffian, though." She took a breath. "Oh, boys—I overheard at the cashier's desk that if there's an emergency, we should drive to the nearest house about a half mile away on the right and use their landline phone. Do you have an emergency, young man?" she asked Kris.

Kris hesitated. "No. Thank you. I guess our plans are the same either way."

Both the man and the woman left, but several of the bidders who'd wanted books still stood in their places. Kris stuck the phone back into his pocket and walked to the closest of them, saying, "It just sort of happened. Sorry for how weird this is."

"I want to buy these two boxes full. How much do you want for them?" called a man of about forty years old who was standing several feet away, his legs planted firmly in place. In a rumpled jacket and tweed pants, he looked perfectly dressed for a country auction. His lips smiled, but his eyes seemed intensely unhappy as he kept pointing at the boxes that contained the books he wanted.

Sighing and motioning for Matt to join him, Kris said, "We can't sell *anything* now. If you go downtown in Anders Lake, you'll see a used bookstore on Main Street across from a bank. I bid on these for the shop's owners. They'll all be out for sale soon." He walked away. "Matt, let's start to pack the books now. Have them lie flat in their boxes so they'll travel safely back to town."

"*No,*" the man said sternly. "I'll give you twenty dollars for these alone. I'm from upstate, and I'm leaving the area today. I need to buy them now."

Kris inhaled to brace himself as he turned toward the man again. "Sorry, but I honestly can't do that." Part of him felt guilty, and part of him felt defensive at being bullied.

"Fifty, then. Fifty bucks. That's probably half of what you paid for everything."

Kris shook his head. "Check later at the store."

"A hundred. One hundred dollars cash. Come *on!*" the man insisted, a dangerous edge to his voice. He paused to reach into his rear pocket. "*Two* hundred. I have it right here in my wallet. You won't even have to tell the bookshop owners that we did this deal. Two hundred bucks, all for you two boys to split. It'll be our secret."

"Is there a problem, kids?" asked someone behind them. It was the muscular man. He'd been by the barn looking at tools but walked toward them when he saw that they were being hassled. "Is this guy bothering you?"

Matt looked relieved that they were getting some help, but Kris felt that he needed to handle it himself. "No. He wants to buy some of the books here at the sale, even though I've said I can't do any selling. We bought them for a friend."

The muscular man gave the other man a hard look. "That's right. You can't. Don't you know that it's against the law to collude?"

"I wasn't doing anything of the sort," growled the other man. "I was swindled! That was no way to conduct an auction. I should call the police and claim *robbery. I was robbed.*" He swore under his breath, balled his fists angrily, and stomped away toward the lines of parked cars and trucks.

Kris raised his eyebrows at Matt, looking scared.

"What's a 'collude'?" Matt asked as he watched the tweedy man until he was out of sight.

"That's when bidders don't bid against each other. By pre-arrangement," the muscular man said as he put some stray books into a box that had "So-P-Suds" printed on its side. "Doing that keeps the price down. Then they both reap the profits when the sale is over, with one buying the bidder out for an item or a share. It works if no one else bids them up very high."

During the argument, all the other auction-goers had wandered away from that part of the yard, understanding that the boys wouldn't be letting them buy the books they wanted, either. Mr. McAlister's humorously repetitive voice over the loudspeaker was clear and melodic, calming Kris at last. Another assistant had joined him since Margo was busy counting the boxes of books.

Matt and Kris thanked the man who had come to their defense, and when they were alone again, Kris said, "We're probably going to be waiting for Mack for at least a couple of hours. I'll use that time to pare down the heap. The cruddy books I'll put beside this tree for boxing up quickly when we're done with the rest. The ones I think are worth the most I'll re-box myself as carefully as I can. Those that I think the O'Malleys would want—but aren't very valuable—I'll stack behind me. Once you've got all the boxes in one group

30

together for me to go through, you join me in repacking, okay? You don't need to be super careful, but make sure they all go in flat. If you have loose space on the sides, fill it in with softcovers, spine-side down. Got it?"

He nodded. "How many boxes are there? I didn't hear a final count."

Just then Margo passed them, answering, "You've got eighty-eight times your money. This buy sheet will be at the checkout desk whenever you're ready to pay."

While Kris did a first glance at the books, Matt brought the farthest boxes to the center bend of the U-shaped arc, the most out-of-the-way place to stack them while the auction was still going.

Kris tugged at an earlobe as he decided which box to start working on first.

And that's when his world suddenly went dark.

He awoke to the sensation of lying on his back, dizzy, and with a queasy stomach. He could smell rose perfume as he felt someone softly holding his hand.

"He's awake! He's awake now," that someone called loudly.

Kris moaned. His head and eyes hurt horribly. He kept his eyes closed and felt himself start to drift off to somewhere beyond the clouds.

Matt was beside him a few seconds later, taking over for the woman who had been with him. Kris only heard him. Even when he'd finally opened his eyes, he didn't see Matt or the woman or the pure, blue sky above.

"Someone drove down the road to call for an ambulance, buddy. Kris? Can't you answer?" Matt asked. He was on his knees near Kris' chest, one hand on his friend's shoulder.

"I can talk, but I can't *see*. What ... happ ... happened?"

"What do you *mean* you can't see?" Kris heard Matt's voice move higher above him. He must have stood up. "Mister, my friend can't *see*. He said he can't *see!*"

31

Kris squeezed his eyelids shut, took a few deep breaths, and opened his eyes again.

When Matt asked, "How about now? I'm waving. Can you see me?"

Kris moaned again and tried to sit up, but hands held him down. Someone put a long coat on the ground beside him before two people lifted him onto the top of it so the damp grass wouldn't make him cold. Someone else put their coat over Kris like a blanket.

"I still can't see. What happened? I feel like my head got cracked like an egg."

A strange man's voice answered, "Someone threw a baseball from the direction of the road. It hit you hard. You fell even harder. How's your arm? It looks like it might be hurt, too."

"A baseball? What road? Where *am* I, Matt?" Kris asked, his voice rising fearfully.

Sitting on a folding chair that Margo had brought for him, Matt said, "We're at an auction way out in the country. Remember? There's a whole bunch of old books. I bid on 'em, and we were waiting for Mr. O to come back from another auction."

Kris squeezed his eyelids together, then opened them yet again. "I don't remember anything other than I think we were going to go to a sale together. My mind's fuzzy. I'm not sure what the last thing is that I know."

"Well, that's where we're at. I bid a dollar and got every box here for that same dollar each. There are eighty-eight boxes. I was starting to get them moved to one spot together, and you were going to go through the books, when whammo-blammo! I saw you fall over like a swatted piñata!"

After another deep breath, Kris sat on his coat bed and let the one covering him fall onto his lap. He heard the auctioneer announce to the crowd through his loudspeaker that an ambulance was coming and that the "kid would be fine" and they should continue the sale with a collection of old board games.

"Here's some water in a cup," said Matt.

Kris' left arm vaguely hurt. He took and held the cup in his right hand, but he didn't drink it. "I'm not worried, really. Don't you worry, either, Matt. I just want some water. Can I get some water?"

"Where's that ambulance, anyway," asked Matt under his breath. He glanced around and saw that most of the crowd that had been gathered near Kris were walking to the barn to take part in or watch the bidding. Two more minutes passed without the sound of a siren in the distance.

"Where are we? How far from Anders Lake, I mean," Kris asked after finally taking a sip of water.

"Maybe fifteen miles. I don't know what town we're near. Kris? When the ambulance does get here, I'm not going with you. I'll stay behind here and re-box the books so they'll ride flat. I'll guard them, all right? I'll tell the medical people to call your mom, and she'll call Mrs. O. Even if your mom or Mrs. O can't get ahold of Mr. O, I'll be okay here alone waiting for him. I have money for food, and I'll have plenty of work to do with these boxes. Oh, and I took the cash and phone and bid number out of your pockets. I'll give them all to Mr. O."

"What cash? Ambulance? Is it nighttime? Why don't you have a flashlight? I can hear people, but I can't see anyone. Matt? Where are we? Turn on your flashlight, okay?"

Matt frowned. It was becoming clear to him that Kris couldn't remember anything he'd just been told. Matt kept one eye on the books and the other on Kris as he retold his friend a shortened version of the story of the auction, again and again. After what seemed like hours, he heard a siren wailing in the distance.

"They're coming!" said a stranger's voice.

Matt moved his chair out of the way. A middle-aged woman ran across the yard, jumped into her pickup truck, and then drove it away. The ambulance backed a short way onto the lawn near the apple tree.

Soon Kris was complaining that people were touching him. He frantically called out for someone to stop them. One of the medics, a young, friendly-looking red-haired lady with a short ponytail and glasses, signaled for Matt to hold his friend's hand. She put a blood-pressure cuff on Kris' other arm. "He's confused. No use talking sense to your pal right now. What happened, do you know?"

"He got hit by a baseball. Now he can't see. He doesn't remember anything from today, and he keeps forgetting what I tell him. Is he gonna be okay? I need to have somebody call his mom. There's no way to call on cell phones out here. Can someone write down her number?"

Three minutes later, Kris was in the ambulance next to the medic. The white doors closed, and, nearly before Matt could think about what was going to happen next, Kris was being driven away along the narrow, crowded gravel road.

"Do you need help with all this?" asked the tweedy man who had been talking to them earlier. He was brushing his hands on his pants and smiling strangely. "I want to make it up to you for the way I acted earlier. I shouldn't have gotten upset over a few old books."

Matt sighed. He was probably going to have two or three hours to spend until Mack arrived, so there was no rush.

"Naw. I can do it. Thanks. I guess I could use a lunch, though. Would you take this five and get me a couple of hot dogs and a drink?"

The man's face became a strange mix of disappointment and humor. He took the money, went to the tent where ladies were dispensing sandwiches and desserts, and quickly returned with food.

"I have a big van. See that black one over there? I can load these for you and bring them wherever you need them to go. No charge." The man handed Matt the food and drink.

"I think it's terrible that your friend was hit. Did you see who threw it?"

Matt shook his head, glancing at the van after he'd taken the two hot dogs and can of soda. "No. I wasn't looking toward the road. And I'd better not have you help me take the books away. I'm going to repack them to make sure they won't get damaged during the ride. My friend will be here in a little while, and he and his workers can get this done in no time." He felt that he needed to pretend he would soon have help and protection. "He's got a big cargo van. So ... I guess I'm all set. Thanks for lunch, though."

The man paused and seemed to be struggling for something else to say. Finally, he forced a smile and said, "Okay. I'll leave you to your lunch and work. My name's Charles, by the way. What's yours?"

"Matt. Matt Templeton from Lamarr," he lied again. "We came up for the auction." Matt had had a sudden memory of his mother telling him never to give a stranger his name and address, especially in a situation where he felt there might be some suspicious reason someone wanted to know personal things about him. Templeton popped into his head because his favorite literary character was the rat from *Charlotte's Web*.

"Lamarr, huh? I'm from Lamarr, too. Maybe I'll see you around there, Matt. And I hope your friend that got hit will be okay. At least he wasn't unconscious for very long. That's a good sign."

"I hope so," Matt said, a little less suspicious. He took a giant bite of hot dog as he watched Charles leave to go and look through some record albums that were on top of a wooden trailer on the other side of the yard. The boy ate, watching the stranger a few minutes longer. As he was about to crumple the wrappers from his lunch, he saw the man pull a cell phone out of his rear pocket, clearly using it to take photos. One of the photos he shot was of Matt, himself.

He suddenly realized Kris had told Charles that he and Matt had gotten the books for the O'Malleys' bookshop in Anders Lake! Why hadn't that man reacted to his lie about being from Lamarr? And *why* was he taking his photo?

Matt looked around, wishing with all his might that he recognized someone in the crowd, someone who could protect him. He considered finding one of the auction assistants, but then, as he thought about what exactly he might say to them, he realized that he was overreacting, imagining sinister things and people because of what had happened to Kris. He was, he decided, being a scaredy cat.

The bright sun finally burned away the haze of the morning, and the temperature seemed to rise quickly by twenty degrees. Matt took off his sweatshirt and worked fast and hard in his t-shirt, getting all the boxes into one area before packing the books flat. By consolidating them, the volumes took up fewer boxes than before. He didn't know a good book from a bad book and decided he should pack every last one of them, even if they were ragged and torn.

Two and a half hours later, when he had nearly finished, he heard Mack calling to him from across the yard.

"Matt! Oh, I am *so* sorry -I didn't check for cell service out here before I left." When he reached Matt, he added, "I'll never get used to modern technology and all the little details you have to think about. Mrs. Dehlvi called Mavis, and Mavis called me with the news. Your mom knows, too. She offered to come here to get you, but I knew I was wrapping up my auction and could get to you sooner than she could. The Dehlvis are all at the hospital. Let's load this stuff and get out of here."

Matt seemed to have suddenly gone wobbly in relief now that Mr. O'Malley had arrived.

Mack patted the boy on his back, realizing what he's had to go through alone since Kris had gotten hurt. "How many of these did you boys buy? I need to settle my bill."

Matt leaned shakily against a short stack of boxes. Looking a little sheepish, he said, "All of them. Every book that was here at the start is yours."

"What? I thought there would have been at least *some* competition. They looked good, and a lot of them still have their dustjackets." A thought then occurred to Mack. "Unless … Matt, I hope you and Kris didn't go over the budget. I spent more than I planned to in Ankalow. And wow—I hope we can stuff all these into the van. I bought at least these many books at the other sale."

Mr. O'Malley helped him finish repacking the last of the boxes while Matt told him what had happened when the books came up for bids, about their encounter with the angry man, and most of the details about what had happened to Kris.

"Well, this sure has been *some* day for you two," Mack said, bending to grab a few stray papers that were about to blow away. "Stay here. I'm going to get the hand-truck. I'm parked beyond that group of bushes. Do you need to eat or go to the bathroom?"

Relief at having Mr. O'Malley there with him after he'd been worried about Kris, and about anyone touching the books while he was packing them up, hit Matt more fully. He found that he couldn't say anything; he could only stare at the ground.

"Oh, Matt," Mack said. He realized then that Matt was still mostly a boy, even though he'd already gotten to be the size of a man. "Come here and sit on this stump for a minute. I'm going to get you a drink. I'll be right back. There's no hurry now. Kris is in good hands, and I'm here to help."

The boy did sit down. Mr. O'Malley was soon back with a bottle of water and a sloppy joe. Matt drank but merely held the sandwich loosely, feeling the meat's warmth through the bun.

"He couldn't *see,* Mr. O. He couldn't remember anything from today, and he even forgot the stuff I'd been telling him like a minute before."

"He'll be okay."

Matt took another long drink. When he looked toward the barn, he saw Charles staring at him.

"Mr. O, could you ... could you look over at the barn? There's a man there. He's wearing tweed. See?"

"I see him. He's looking at us, too."

"Could you do me a favor and remember his face?"

"Sure," Mack said without asking why.

"I'll tell you about him later, on the way home. I wouldn't ask you to remember him if it wasn't for an important reason. I wish I were brave enough to take his photo. He took mine."

Mack stared at the man intently for a moment. Then he faced Matt and winked, lightening the mood. "Eat. You'll need the calories to help me get *all these boxes* into the van."

Matt laughed before biting into the messy sandwich. While he chewed, both he and Mr. O'Malley took another look at Charles, watching as the man headed for the lines of parked cars at last.

When they had the boxes loaded behind the books that Mack had bought and had paid the auction bill, Matt put Kris' cooler and jacket on the front seat, and they set off for Anders Lake again.

Chapter Four

"Any news about our Kris?" asked Mrs. O'Malley on the telephone the next afternoon. After a minute or two of conversation, she replaced the phone onto its charger.

"What did she say?" asked Mr. O'Malley.

Mrs. O'Malley swallowed. "Mrs. Dehlvi said that Kris *still* can't see. He seems to be over his short-term memory problems, but he doesn't remember anything about the auction. She sounded fairly calm, though, and said that the doctor assured her that Kris could regain his sight very soon. They've done all the usual tests, and he should be fine and dandy once some more of the swelling goes down."

Mack frowned, looking stricken.

"Now, Mack ... I see how you're feeling. Don't blame yourself. Take your mind off this for a while. Go clean the litter box or something fun like that. Stop worrying. Daya said he'll be fine."

Mack stepped back and sat down hard on the red sofa.

"Mack, this isn't *like* you. I'm telling you—he *will* be okay."

"He wants to be a bookseller. A book restorer. I tell him all the time how tight our funds are all the time, but he doesn't care. He just wants to work with old books. What if—"

"Snap out of it. That is ridiculous. Two of our regular customers are legally blind. How would they feel if they heard you going on like this?" She then added firmly, "When Kris comes back to work in a couple of days, I want this place to be ready for him. All the boxes of books you and the boys bought yesterday are still stuffed inside our van. I'm going to call Matt and have him come to help you unload. If you're upset, think about how upset Matt likely is. Take some pity on him and put him to work so he's not at home doing this very same wallowing in woefulness."

Mack unexpectedly chuckled. He sat straighter and took one of her hands. "'Wallowing in woefulness.' That sounds like a poem title. There you go, Mavis. That can be the title of your first poem."

She smiled, relieved to hear him perk up at last. "I'll tell you what—you let me call Matt to come and unload the van with you, and I'll write that poem. Deal?"

He nodded.

Darla stepped into the shop with L.P. in her arms. The two were wearing nearly matching light blue shirts and denim shorts. "Sitting down on the job?"

"We were just talking about Kris. He still hasn't regained his sight," explained Mrs. O'Malley as she stood up.

Mr. O'Malley stood, too, and softly brushed his thumb against one of the baby's rosy cheeks. Hearing Kris' name again took all signs of humor from his brown eyes.

Darla raised one eyebrow. "He *hasn't*? Oh, that poor kid."

Mack ducked his head and walked outside.

"Hold on, Darla. I need to call Matt to ask him if he can help unload the books from the auctions. That boy could probably use a little distraction, too. Oh, I wonder if he might be at the hospital visiting Kris. Hmm. Well, I'll call and find out. How are with you and Jack and the baby?" she asked as she reached for the phone book.

Darla gently bounced Lila Pearl in her arms. "We're fine. But worried, like you are."

The baby twisted, trying to reach Elephant Gerald. Darla picked up the vase and held it close. L.P. patted at its glass trunk and ears and made what almost sounded like baby elephant trumpets.

"Katrina? This is Mrs. O'Malley at the bookshop. I did hear something, yes. He still can't see, I'm sorry to have to say. He has his short-term memory back, thank goodness. I

40

know. We *all* were. I know. Kat, is your brother there? Can I please speak to him? Thank you. Matt? This is Mrs. O'Malley. Are you busy today? Can you come to the shop to help Mack unload the books? Mack said he never paid you for yesterday, so we'll add that to the wages for today. I won't hear of it! Well, we'll argue about it when you get here. And bring your sister if she's sitting around worrying. We'll put her to work, too. Okay. Thank you, Matt. See you soon. Oh, and ask your mom if it's okay first, all right? See you in a bit. Bye."

Darla put the vase back and shifted L.P. to her other hip. "So, tell me more about Kris. What else do you know?"

"Not much more than what I've said. Daya said that the doctor thinks he will be able to see very soon. They're sure that more swelling will subside over time, and that his vision will eventually return to normal. They're keeping him there again for one more night, and if he doesn't improve significantly, they'll send him to Lamarr for more testing at a bigger hospital."

"Is Mack blaming himself?" Darla asked, looking through the door at the tall man who was leaning slackly against the maple tree with his back to the bookshop.

"He is. That's why I called Matt. Those two can help each other keep busy."

Five minutes later, while Mr. O'Malley was still outside, Katrina and Matt slid out of their mother's car at the curb. Katrina wore her blonde hair in a ponytail, and Matt's darker blonde hair looked messy, as if he hadn't combed it after a rough night. He held a pair of work gloves under his arm.

Mrs. O'Malley watched as Mack spoke to them a moment before going out of sight, most likely to drive the van around to the front parking spaces. Katrina and Matt stood in the empty spot near the front door to reserve it. She said, "Darla, we can't let those two know that we're worried."

She looked at the clock on the wall. "They'll know. And I hate to say it, but I can't stay. I've got a ton of work to do at the record shop. Someone brought in three big boxes of CDs this morning. I need to check them over before the seller comes back this afternoon."

"Well, thanks for coming by. I always love seeing my two best girls." She hugged Darla and L.P. together.

Soon the old, blue cargo van was maneuvering into the spot. Matt slid on his gloves, and Katrina walked into the bookshop. The girl almost always looked sunny and happy, but right then she seemed as downhearted as Mack had a little while before.

"Oh, Kat," Mrs. O'Malley opened her arms, offering a consoling hug.

An older man came into the shop with a full paper grocery sack while Mrs. O'Malley and Katrina were hugging. "Put your books on the counter, Cecil."

"What's the matter?" he asked, looking concerned.

"It's Kris," Mrs. O'Malley said with a sigh, letting Katrina go. "He had an accident yesterday, and he's in the hospital. His mom said he should be fine, but we're all very worried." She rolled her eyes. "And here I vowed to Darla that I wouldn't let on to this girl how upset I am. I am a failure at hiding my emotions, it seems."

"Oh, that *is* sad news," said Cecil as he lowered his sack of books. "Want me to come back with these some other time?"

"No. I need a project. Mack and his helper are going to be bringing in boxes from the van, so I'll have those books to look at a little later. I'll play around with yours now. Go ahead and browse."

Mack opened the door to ask, "Where's Bug?"

Katrina and Mrs. O'Malley looked for her. After a few seconds, they found the cat under the counter.

"On her bags, fast asleep. I think it's safe to leave the door open."

"Matt and I will be hauling in the fresh catch, keeping ourselves busy, as ordered. Where do you want the boxes?"

"In the back by the gardening section." She peered at the open doors of the van, dismayed at the vision of the many heaps of boxes. "If I get overwhelmed, you might have to keep most of them in the van for now, until we can get the first bunch priced and on the shelves."

Mack waved his acknowledgment and stepped back outside as the phone rang.

"Oh, hello, Doris. You have a cat for us? That's wonderful, but … can you hold off bringing him or her to us for about a half hour or so? Okay. See you soon."

"Was that about our next foster?" asked Mack when he went through the propped-open doorway, his arms full of two small boxes. He was hauling in from one end of the van and Matt from the other so they wouldn't collide.

She nodded at him and then asked Katrina, "How would you like to help me package the books I need to mail out tomorrow?"

"Sure, if you show me how to do it, Mrs. O."

They went to the end of the long front counter, near one of the large display windows. "It's easy, really. First, look over each one carefully to see if there are any problems like a broken hinge—a hinge is the place where the front or rear cover attaches to the rest of the book—folded page corners, pencil marks, dusty dustjackets, stickers, library pockets, and so forth. I can take care of some repairs and cleaning, but Mack handles the more complicated or delicate work. After a book has passed inspection or has been fixed up, the dustjacket is put into one of these clear mylar protectors. They're kind of like the sleeves the library uses. We, though, don't tape the protector to the book, and no tape touches the jacket itself. Now, if there is no dustjacket, or if it's a

43

paperback book, obviously you skip that step. Next, put the book into a protective plastic bag and tape it closed snugly around the book. That way, even if a book is delivered on a rainy day and the box gets soaked, the book won't get wet. Then we choose an appropriate shipping box."

Katrina looked under the countertop. "These?" she asked, pointing.

"Yes. They're arranged by size. If there's extra space around the book, we fill it in with packing peanuts or bubble wrap. Booklets and paperbacks—unless they're high-priced and fragile or very thick—get packed into these bubble-lined mailers. Thin booklets get a rectangle of cardboard on top and bottom for support. Once a book is packed with care, the package gets marked with this rubber stamp that has our name, address, and logo on it. The recipient's address is taped on, and, finally, if it needs an insurance slip, foreign address form, or any other sort of postal form, that goes on last."

"I didn't know No Page Unturned *had* a logo. Why don't you have it on your windows or door or anywhere?" Katrina asked, examining the stamp. She found a scrap of paper in the trash can and pressed out a red ink impression. "Cool! I love that it's a cat reading a book."

"I created our logo about a month ago, when I needed to order a new address stamp. I hadn't thought of ordering a decal for the windows. Do you really like it?"

The girl nodded. "I wish I could make out the title of his tiny book."

"Well, maybe he's reading ... *How to Save Your Human from a Deadly Chicken Salad Sandwich and Get Adopted in Three Easy Steps.*"

Katrina squinted, trying to read it. "I don't see how that many letters could fit. Are you sure?"

Mrs. O'Malley winked. "It's a long story. I'll tell it to you while we're wrapping. But, since you like that logo, I guess I might have it made into a decal for the door sometime." She stepped around her computer chair. "After I look over Cecil's books, I'll help you get started with this project."

Thirty minutes later, the stack of sold books that had been near the printer had been wrapped, many of the books from both auctions were out of the van and in the shop's main room piled in stacks four boxes high, and Doris from the cat shelter was parking in the spot Mack had vacated a few minutes before.

"Mack, Doris is here," said Mrs. O'Malley. She and Katrina were talking to Matt about the kids' summer vacation plans, which mostly involved the lake.

While Mack was glancing through the windows to wave to Doris, he had a terrible surprise. He called to Matt and had him look where he indicated. "Across the street. Is that the guy from yesterday? There, between the bank and the gift shop."

Matt took in a breath, startled. "That's him! Oh, *geez,* Mr. O. What is he *doing* here?"

Mrs. O'Malley couldn't hear what the two pointing toward the window were saying because Doris and Katrina were enthusing over the new cat who had stepped from a carrier, but she knew from their expressions of shock that it wasn't a casual conversation.

"Oh, what a gorgeous, *huge,* fluffy kitty," exclaimed Katrina as she took the long-haired black and brown cat from Doris. "I love the white pluffiness under his chin and on his neck." She then looked at the shelter volunteer, a question in her eyes. "Why does this cat's type seem familiar? Is he a particular breed?"

"I don't want to say that he's a Maine Coon since we don't know that for sure, but he sure does look like one," said Doris

45

as she slid a sheet of paper onto the countertop with the cat's details. "His name is Haiku. He came to us about two months ago. I thought he'd find a new home right away, but I guess he's too much cat for most households. He weighs a startling twenty-two pounds, so he's about five pounds overweight for his overall size. You'll have to stick to a strict diet with this guy, Mavis. Mavis?"

Mrs. O'Malley had only been partially listening to Doris and Katrina. She was also trying to hear what Mack and Matt were saying.

"Um ... what?"

"Haiku—you know, your new cat—will have to be on a strict diet until he loses a few pounds. The vet has examined him thoroughly twice to be sure he's hefty and not sick. I've brought some weight loss formula food for him. It's fine if Bug eats some, too, but it would be best if you fed them separately somehow. Even if he doesn't stick to a diet here, we won't be too concerned. A routine will be easier to manage once he has a new home. Okay? Mavis?"

"I'm listening. Diet food. Separate feedings. Not to worry if it doesn't work out while she's here," Mrs. O'Malley said distractedly.

"*He.* This is Haiku. He's a tomcat. Why are you looking off in that direction when this beautiful cat is over here?" asked Doris, getting exasperated.

Mrs. O'Malley grinned apologetically. "I'm wondering what those two are talking about. Something is going on outside. Hey, Mack! What's so interesting?"

Mr. O'Malley stopped talking mid-sentence. He walked over to the ladies, saying, "I don't know."

Something in the way he answered, and in the meaningful look he gave her, made Mrs. O'Malley drop the subject until they were alone. "Well, since you don't know, how about saying hello to our new feline friend, Haiku?"

46

Mack held the cat's front paw. "Heya, Haiku! How's it shakin'?"

This odd greeting made Matt and Katrina giggle.

"Well, here's Haiku's paperwork. His stats are on his collar. I'm going to get the diet food from my car so I can take off. I have a ... a date tonight, and I need to get gussied up," said Doris as she nervously pushed her cats-eye glasses to the top of the bridge of her nose.

Typically, that kind of statement would mean that Mrs. O'Malley would have to know all the romantic details, but she was so eager to be able to talk to Mack alone that she didn't ask a single question.

"How nice, Doris! Well, we won't keep you, then. Mack, will you pay Matt for the work he did yesterday and today? Kat—do you want to call your mom for a ride, or are you two kids going to walk home?"

No one replied, momentarily stunned by how obviously they were being shooed off. Doris and the kids glanced at each other, shrugging. Soon all of them had made their way out of the shop. Matt was paid and left to walk home with his sister, Doris brought in the food and took the pet carrier with her as she waved goodbye, and, finally, the last customer of the day, Cecil, left with a bag of books.

The O'Malleys sat on the sofa after most of the lights had been switched off, and the doors were locked.

"Okay, now tell me. What did you see through the windows that got you and Matt all shook up?"

"With the rousing excitement going on yesterday, I forgot to tell you that the boys had a head-butting with another auction-goer after the bidding was over. A man wanted to buy several books from Kris, but the kids wouldn't do it. Kris knew that I wouldn't want him to make any deal like that before I'd had a chance to see the books."

"Right. That's what I still do, too. When books come into the shop, I don't price them until you've seen them. Okay. That doesn't sound so bad. What else happened?"

Mack tugged at an earlobe. "I guess this man didn't want to give up. He tried bribery—up to two hundred dollars for two boxes of books. When Kris still said no, he started shouting at the boys. Another man jumped in and defended Matt and Kris."

"Well, that's good."

"Yeah, but that wasn't the end of it. I suspect the first man is the one who hit Kris with the baseball."

"What? Do you really think someone did that on purpose?"

"Yes. He'd volunteered to load all the books left with Matt into his own van. Matt suspected something was off and said no, that I was on the way. He told the guy a false name and town, but I'm afraid Kris had already told him to come here after we put the books out for sale. Matt and I saw that same man across the street when Doris came in."

"Mack! Why didn't you call the police?"

"About what? I have no proof that he did anything wrong. It's suspicious that he didn't come into the shop if he merely wanted to buy the books Kris wouldn't sell at the auction."

"I'm scared, Mack. What should we do? Is he still out there?"

Mr. O'Malley stood and walked to the front door. Except for two near the movie theater, no cars had parked on that part of the downtown streets. He shook his head.

"Should we call the Dehlvis?" Mrs. O'Malley asked as she powered off the computer. She then closed out the cash register, scowling as the machine noisily printed out a long end-of-day receipt.

"No use adding to their problems, Mavis. I think I'll talk to Jack about this, though. He might have some ideas."

48

Mrs. O'Malley watched the register spit out the receipt. "Matt bid on the whole yard of books before the boys could look them over. Since Kris was hit on the head, Matt did the re-boxing. What if there's something very valuable that the mystery man is after? Matt wouldn't know, and we haven't seen most of the books from that sale yet."

"That's a good point. I don't suppose the guy was angry because Kris wouldn't sell him a Dick and Jane reader." Mack flipped the door sign to read "closed" from the street. He went to a stack of boxes and opened the flaps of the top box. "Are you willing to pull an all-nighter here to go through these with me? Or, do you want to head home and leave me here?"

She swept her short, gray hair from under her collar. "I'll stick. And it shouldn't take all night. You and Matt unloaded only about seventy boxes. Together we can pore over them in three hours or so."

"That's optimistic," said Mack, pulling out a handful of hardbounds. "Put some of the lights back on, will you? I'll order a pizza in a little while."

"No mushrooms on my half. They look like salamander eyeballs. Ick."

"You and your wild imagination."

She flipped on two of the four light switches. "That's good. Maybe it will help me in my poetry-writing career."

"Oh, it's a career, now, is it?"

She smiled and held Haiku's shelter paper as if it were a certificate. "Pushcart Prize in poetry to Mavis O'Malley for her fabulous and brilliant 'Wallowing in Woefulness.'"

"I can see that happening," Mack said.

She put the paper down again. "I actually have no creative goals other than to write one decent poem."

"You've read thousands of them. You know how they flow, and you know which ones appeal to you. I'm sure if you try, you'll come up with a fine poem."

49

Mr. O'Malley sorted the books stacked at one end of the room, and Mrs. O'Malley worked on the other end, near the sofa. They stopped for a dinner of pizza without mushrooms. Every few minutes, one or the other of the O'Malleys would glance through the windows until the evening was too dark to see well beyond the reflection of the lights inside the shop.

"Oh, no!" Mrs. O'Malley said at nearly nine o'clock that night. "We forgot to send flowers and a card to the hospital today."

"Well, Kris couldn't see them any—" He stopped himself from finishing that sentence.

Mrs. O'Malley, exhausted and worried again about Kris, said, "I'm too tired to finish this job. I'm going to sit for a while." Buglit, who had been sitting atop a cushion, climbed onto her favorite person's lap to console her.

Mack wiped his dusty hands onto his tan slacks. "I know there are a lot more to go through, but I wonder if we've already missed whatever it is that's tremendously valuable? Are we reading doom and menace into what might be the innocent actions of that guy? I mean, some of these are mighty nice old tomes, but there's nothing here worth hitting a kid on the head over. I feel foolish. I guess it was a good thing that we got through these tonight so our work won't be as hard tomorrow, but now we're exhausted and still clueless. Want to go home?"

"While we were busy, I wasn't thinking about Kris. Now that I'm sitting down, that's all I can do."

"Let's go home," Mack said gently, reclosing a box lid. "I'm making the decision for us. Come on. I'll feed the cats and get the cash from the register. You get the lights."

When they were leaving through the rear door that led to the parking lot, they heard a loud *crack* and the shattering of glass. Mack pulled Mavis back into the shop from where she stood on the outside steps and motioned for her to be silent and not to move. He paused, listening. When he heard a book stack fall over, he slowly made his way along the hallway to the front room.

A small end table lamp was lit.

Stepping closer, Mack saw that the door had a large hole in it, and glass shards were gleaming faintly on the wooden floor inside the shop. A metal pipe had landed just past the coat rack. The man from the auction that he and Matt had seen outside earlier was rummaging through the piled-up books, quickly but neatly.

Mack held his breath as he returned to the hallway, silently pushing Mrs. O'Malley through the back door again. He followed her, calling the police on his cell phone as soon as the door had closed behind them.

Two patrol cars and four officers arrived within a few minutes, and the man from the auction was arrested before the O'Malleys could believe what was happening.

"Did he think he was going to casually paw through our books all night long?" Mack asked a police officer.

She shook her head. "I don't know. Most criminals don't think ahead. I have the number of a company that does quick glass work, even this late at night. Give them your insurance information when you call them. Or, will you board the door for now and worry about the replacement tomorrow?"

"I think it would be a hard job to board it up securely, and I'm dog tired from a long day and night. I'll call them. Thank you. And Mavis—you drive yourself home. I'll stay until the job is done."

Mrs. O'Malley looked alarmed. "I couldn't *possibly* drive now."

"Okay. I'll call Jack or Danny to come and get you. Want to stay with Quaintance tonight? It could be a few hours before I can leave here."

"We can drive you home, ma'am," said the officer.

Mrs. O'Malley swallowed, trying to decide quickly what she wanted to do. "I think I'll call Danny, but thank you, anyway." She touched Mack's arm. "I'll see if I can stay here in town with him. He has a fold-out couch. Come and get me when you're done here. I'll snooze at his place until you get there. Or, maybe you can stay at his place, too."

"Sounds fine, Mavis," Mack said with a smile. He then said to the officer, "I'll take that phone number for the glass company. After the door is taken care of, I think we'll be fine. Do you need any more information from me?"

"Not right now, sir. But we'll want to interview at least one of the boys tomorrow. I know that you said Kris Dehlvi is in the hospital, but the other boy will need to be interviewed." She swept her bright flashlight around the stacks of books, the countertop, and the bookcases, even though all the shop's lights were on again. "Doesn't look like any damage was done except to the door. Is that right?"

"Yes," said Mack.

"We can easily charge him with breaking and entering and property damage, but I, too, think there's more to the story. He hasn't done anything too criminally serious. I want to keep it that way." She nodded after writing down the repair shop's number on her card and handing it to Mack. "I'll keep in touch. Goodnight."

The O'Malley's linked arms, watching as the last of the police cars pulled away from the curb. Mack could feel his wife quivering.

She pulled away from him to step into the bathroom for a broom and dustpan.

Mack took the broom from her. "I'll do that. You call Danny, then I'll call this number."

She nodded, leaning the dustpan against the back of the cash register before heading for the phone. That's when she saw a frightened, large, and furry cat partially hiding behind the mini refrigerator. She tugged the cat out with some difficulty. As she sat on the computer chair with Haiku on her lap, she said, "My, you're a monster of a kitty, aren't you? Mack, did you see how huge this guy is? He's huge!"

She pressed the speed-dial for her brother. "Dan? This is Mavis. I'm over at our shop. I know. Very. We had a break-in while we were still here. We were working on the auction books. I know, I know. We're fine. *Really.* Mack, too. The front door. Nobody's hurt, no. He's sweeping it up right now. The police just left with the culprit. Yep. Caught in the act. Anyway, Danny, could you maybe come here to pick me up? Mack has to stay and wait for the glass people to fix the door. No, don't call Jack—you'll wake the baby. Mack said he'll be fine here by himself. Now that the fellow has been carted off to the pokey, I think it's safe to leave him here with only the cats for protection. I do *so* say words like 'pokey.' I think I said it once last month. Okay. I'll be by the front door. Thanks."

"I don't think I've ever heard you say 'pokey,' either," said Mack, broom in hand. "Or 'hokey,' for that matter. 'Folky,' 'jokey' ... now *those* seem like Mavis words. I think you should call him back and admit your error."

She didn't reply, but instead closed her eyes to rest them. It felt good to tease with Danny and Mack after such a frightening ordeal. Buglit leaped to the top of the counter, rousing her into action again. She let Haiku step to the floor and brought the phone to Mack.

Chapter Five

Kris kept his eyes closed, clinging to the fuzzy end of his dream. He felt the softness of his own pillow under his head and the second one covering his forehead. He soon remembered that he'd been in the hospital for two days and that he'd regained his vision the evening before and been allowed to go home. Fear that he would be blind again thumped in his chest.

He had a flashback to a few years before, when he was being fostered for the first time. He had hidden under the bed he'd shared with one of that family's sons, listening to the father and mother argue loudly. He knew he was going to be sent away.

At that moment, cramped beneath the bed frame, he had flipped a switch in his heart. He'd made himself be glad if it happened. If he were sent away, that might mean he would be fostered by a kinder, happier family. He'd focused on that possibility so wholly that the sounds of the arguing hadn't affected him anymore. It became nothing but noise, as if a TV were too loud.

In those frozen moments there in his bed, in his adopted, happy home, he again made himself flip a switch in his heart. It would be all right if he were blind, he told himself. He would learn to read with his fingers. He could still breathe, still talk, still hear, still hug, still laugh. He recalled Katrina smiling at him, Matt laughing, and L.P. holding onto his finger. He thought about his parents. The O'Malleys. The bookshop.

The scent of his mother's flowers along the edge of the house and in the front yard garden reached him. Their colorful petals seemed to bloom inside his head. He pushed the pillow from his face, and morning sunlight pressed against his eyelids.

He opened his eyes. His room was almost exactly as he remembered it. Now, however, there was a vase of long-stemmed flowers and several unopened greeting cards on his desk, and white flowers in a bud vase sat on his bedside table. As he sat straighter, Stomper pushed open Kris' door, and he leaped onto the end of the bed.

"Mrrooowwl!" exclaimed the cat. He stretched his legs before padding across the blue-patterned comforter to sit close to his boy.

"Good to see you, too, Stomps. I sure missed you while I was away. Were you here with me for part of last night? I must have been asleep already when you came into my room."

"Krissy? You awake?" asked a voice at the door.

"Yeah. Come on in here, Bijay. Let me take a look at you."

His littlest brother then raced into the room, followed in a few seconds by Dev, who was holding a contented Pip in his arms.

Pip, a cat with white fur and a patch of black over one eye, was one of the kittens Bijay had spotted behind the grocery store the year before. After the shelter cleared Pip for adoption, Bijay and Mrs. Dehlvi went to bring him home.

"You guys are getting big," said Kris as the boys sat on the edge of the bed facing him. "Pip, too."

Stomper dropped to the floor on the opposite side of the bed and bounded onto the window ledge where he pretended to be very busy washing his front legs and stomach. Stomper, at first, hated to have a frisky kitten bounding and scrambling around the house like a wild animal, bopping him on the forehead when he wasn't expecting it, and going after his tail when he was trying to nap. Many months later, he and Pip were slowly coming to an accommodation.

The three boys sat smiling at each other.

"Can you still see us?" asked Dev. He made waving motions with his arms, prompting Bijay to do the same thing. Kris joined in, laughing.

"What are you silly boys doing now, with your arms waving waving like that?" asked Mrs. Dehlvi in her light Indian accent.

"A vision check, I think," answered Kris, putting his arms down but still smiling.

"And so, what is the result of this arm-waving vision check, Kris?"

"I can see. Stomper came in first. He's sitting over there pretending to be all ho-hum, but I think he was glad that I was in my room like usual this morning." Kris slid out of bed and stepped over to the cat to scratch him under his chin.

"Well, then, very good, Doctor Stompercat," she said to the cat, who paused mid-lick to blink at her. "Thank you for checking on the patient during your early rounds this fine, sunny morning. Boys? Shall we have blueberry pancakes today to celebrate?"

"Pancakes!" cried Dev and Bijay together, getting up from the bed to run past their mother to get dressed for breakfast. Pip scampered after them.

"Pancakes!" said Kris, imitating their same enthusiasm.

Mrs. Dehlvi sat on the bed and patted the top of the comforter, motioning for her son to sit again.

"You have acquired a hint of some sad expression in your eyes today, along with those dark circles. Are you very sure you have your normal vision returned to you, little Kris?"

He swallowed. "I'm sure."

"What is it then?"

He wondered how to tell her what he'd been feeling. "Oh, it's … I had a bad memory of my first foster home when I was waking up. I think, though, that I used it to help me in case I couldn't see again when I opened my eyes. I'm okay now."

"Kris," she said, her tone of voice changing. "Would you help me, please? Would you help me in a way that might be very, very difficult? I only ask you to do this because of your past life. You are very, very strong. But, me? I don't know. I will need your help."

He wondered what she could possibly be talking about. Stomper left the windowsill and jumped onto the bed again, rubbing his round cheeks against both Kris and Mrs. Dehlvi in turns.

"Um, I can try," said Kris.

"Good."

Kris swallowed again, feeling his face grow hot. "What are you talking about, Mom? Is this about my accident? Did the doctor tell you something that they didn't tell me?"

"No, no. This is not about that. Your doctor—and Doctor Stompercat—both think you are fine and will be fine. Maybe a headache or an eye ache for a while. But, no. This is not about the baseball. This is about a little boy your father and I met several times, and who we visited again yesterday. We left your brothers with the Hawns while we had been in the hospital with you, and before we came home, we went to see this other boy again. There has been a lot of talking with the state workers. Lots of home study. Much planning. Some of this you know, of course, but you were not told that we have decided that he will be the one we would like to add to our family. We have now only to talk to you and your brothers."

"Oh," said Kris, shifting his thinking away from his own troubles. He breathed easier.

"His name is Dontae. He is from Jamaica. Do you know where that is? Good. He is living in a foster home here in town, but it is a crowded home. We are trying to have him come to live here with us."

"I knew you and Dad were getting serious about adopting again." He hugged Stomper for protection against the uncomfortable feelings that were rising in his chest. "I just didn't think—"

"This boy is not much like you. He was a long time in a Jamaican orphanage. He never has known his birth mama or his daddy. A couple nearly adopted him three years ago, but ... well, they returned him to state care almost right away. He needs a permanent home and family at last."

Kris stared at the vase of flowers, not speaking.

"There is most certainly a lot to know and to understand about Dontae. He has some physical differences from you boys, and from most everyone else."

"Oh," said Kris, his mind swirling. He pictured a boy in a wheelchair, and he wondered if his father would have to construct a ramp at the front door.

"This boy has a medical condition. It is very, very rare. I had never heard of such a condition. We will have to learn about it to take proper care of little Dontae."

Kris noticed then that his mother hadn't used the word "if."

"Oh," repeated Kris, letting Stomper loose from his grip.

"Your father is taking the summer semester off this year. He wants to be here at the start of our time with Dontae. We will talk about this over breakfast. I'm letting you go back to school today, but we have a bit of time to talk with you boys before you leave."

Kris nodded.

Mrs. Dehlvi leaned forward and gave him a brief hug over the top of Stomper.

"Get dressed. I will go to make the pancakes, and we will talk a little more about this decision."

Kris glanced up. "I don't think you and Dad will need my help. You'll have it—that's for sure—but you can handle anything." He paused. "You've faced coming here from India, not knowing anyone or how this country works. I can see why you'd want to help a boy from Jamaica with, like, medical problems. I'll do whatever I can to help." He paused, thinking of how to put into words what he wanted to say. "I have some feelings that I can't understand, though. I think it might be that I'm jealous. But it's more than that. I feel ... proud of you and Dad, too. This must be what Dev and Bijay felt when you were going to take *me* in. Part of me doesn't want to share the family with someone new, but part of me is super proud that I have parents who are eager and nice and kind, and who are going to help out a kid that really, really needs a good home."

Mrs. Dehlvi twisted away from Kris and stood. She wiped her eyes, leaving the bedroom without replying.

When Kris had washed and dressed, Dev and Bijay were at their places at the dining room table eating their pancakes. Mr. Dehlvi sat with them, but his pancakes were still on the griddle. Mrs. Dehlvi was in the kitchen waiting for bubbles to form before flipping that batch.

Kris filled a bowl of water for Stomper, who sat in the kitchen doorway waiting for breakfast, his tail swishing with slight impatience. "He still won't share his food and water with Pip."

"Give it time," his mother said, peeking under one of the pancakes with a spatula. "Sometimes adopted siblings take a while to warm up to each other."

Pip, hearing his name, raced into the kitchen from somewhere along the hallway. Stomper crouched and closed his eyes, preparing for a playful tackle that didn't come.

"I'll make our cakes next."

"Thanks. I feel like I'm too nervous to eat, though."

Mrs. Dehlvi flipped the pancakes. "I feel nervous, too, Kris."

She loaded a plate with three thick, hot, blueberry-filled circles and carried it into the dining room. Kris fed Stomper and Pip at opposite sides of the kitchen, washed his hands, and sat at the table.

Mr. Dehlvi sprinkled sugar and more blueberries over his pancakes. "Your mother tells me you are soon to be a single man again, hey?" he said, concern in his dark eyes that appeared slightly magnified behind his black-framed eyeglasses.

Kris had to think for a moment. Oh. Tatyana was leaving. He shrugged.

"Well, you were not ready for a girlfriend, I always thought. Such a young boy to be thinking of girls already! No. You are better off staying a bachelor for another ten or twenty years. Thirty, even. No use rushing things."

Mrs. Dehlvi called, "I am standing right here in this kitchen, hearing these words, Mr. Dehlvi who insisted we be married before you had finished at the university."

"I was forced to do so," he said calmly after swallowing some tea and placing his cup on its saucer.

"You were never, never forced! How can you sit there at the table eating pancakes and saying you were forced? *Who* forced you?" she demanded, playfully glowering through the glassless window between the two rooms.

"It was the only way I could have kept the other young men who were circling your front door from taking you home to their mothers. I had to marry you quickly, or you would have found out how rich they were, and then all would have been lost in my heart."

"Are you calling me a gold-digger, then?" She shook her finger at him.

Mr. Dehlvi picked up his fork, pausing before he somberly answered. "No, no, no. But I worried that your father would have tried to sway you away from a poor student like me. What life could such a poor man give to his only daughter? I was very, very worried. He did not vote for me as a son-in-law. Your mother took pains to change his mind. I think now she must have done a little fibbing on my behalf. Remind me to write a card of thanks to her sometime, please. It is so little to do for my rewards."

Mrs. Dehlvi carried two plates into the dining room. Before sitting, she squeezed her husband's hand.

Kris wanted to find out more about their courtship, but when pancakes were in front of him at last, and when his mother had joined them at the table at last, he knew that the talk about Dontae was going to start.

"Boys, while you eat, your father and I want to tell you about a little boy of about seven years old. His name is Dontae," said Mrs. Dehlvi as she looked back and forth between her three sons.

Bijay's eyes grew enormous with excitement. He clinked his fork noisily onto his plate. "Is that the name of our new brother? Mom! Why didn't you *tell* us?"

Dev looked at Kris as if wondering if he had already known this news. Kris shrugged at him.

Mr. Dehlvi swallowed and said, "Dontae, yes. He is a little boy from Jamaica. We'll find it on a map later. Your mother and I have been to see him several times now."

Dev stopped eating. He again looked with alarm at Kris before turning to his mother. "Why? I didn't think you were actually going to *do* that. I mean ... again. I just want Bijay and Kris. Do we *have* to have another boy in the house?"

Kris poured syrup over his pancakes. "What if you like him as much as we like each other, Dev? As much as I ... you know ... love you?"

Dev took a deep breath, speechless.

Bijay looked deflated that his brother wasn't as excited as he was about Dontae.

"Now, Dev. We haven't signed any papers. I think we should let your father tell you all about the boy. Then we will have a whole day without saying another thing about this adoption. We will talk about him later, after some time for

61

thinking has passed. Yes? Yes," said Mrs. Dehlvi, putting her slender hands on the center of the table, palm-side up. Kris had long ago learned that it was her sign that she wanted everyone to be reasonable and calm.

Mr. Dehlvi had another sip of tea. "He has had a hard life, this Dontae. We do not even know what sadness he has had to endure. We weren't told much of his story. At this point, it is not our place to ask too many questions. Others might use his past to rule out an adoption, but we will not. We do know that this boy needs special care. He needed a lot of surgeries; he needs to have more. Some people would not want that—to take a child in who needs too much. And some are not up to the task, let us say, of loving someone who looks too different from themselves. We don't understand that, do we, boys?" asked their father, looking at Dev.

Dev eyed Kris, a boy who did not look like the rest of the family. Kris' darkening blonde hair was nothing like the other Dehlvis' nearly black hair, and his blue eyes were not brown with dark eyebrows and lashes like the other Dehlvis'. He shook his head as he speared a last bite of pancake with his fork. "I get it, Dad."

Mrs. Dehlvi smiled and touched her son's back.

"Good," said Mr. Dehlvi. He finished his tea, made a gesture of thanks for the meal to his wife, then continued, "He has been a lost boy ever since he was a baby. He had what is called a cleft lip and palate. One of my childhood friends had a cleft lip. It is easily fixed when very young, but it can leave a noticeable mark. He has two fingers on one hand and three on the other, but the pinky and the one next to it are fused together. He has three toes on each foot."

"I've never heard of that," said Dev. "Can he stand up? How does he eat?"

"We've watched him do so many things with his hands that you'd be amazed," said Mrs. Dehlvi. She poured herself a cup of hot tea. "And he is very talented in karate."

The three boys looked at each other in disbelief.

"There is more to tell, boys," said their father, pushing himself away from the table to cross his legs. "He has a condition known as ectodermal dysplasia. He was born with it. It is very, very rare, and there are many different types of ED. Dontae is missing a lot of his sweat glands. Instead of sweating when it's hot or when he runs around, he overheats."

"I get hot, too," said Bijay earnestly. "A lot hot!"

Mrs. Dehlvi shook her head. "No, no, Bij. It is different for Dontae. You can perspire normally. You can overheat, too, of course, but it would take much more for you to pass out from heat. This boy must be very careful on hot days or when he exercises. Sweat comes out of your pores, and when air passes over the sweat, you are cooled. Dontae, however, stays mostly dry, and dry skin does not cool itself down."

"So, how can he do karate?" asked Kris. His last pancake sat ignored on his syrup-smeared plate. "How can he do anything very active?"

"With care," said Mr. Dehlvi. "Dontae wears a cooling vest when necessary, and he can exercise in a pool or in air conditioning. He may play outside in the summer if he doesn't overdo it. He is able to tell when he's had enough. No one—do you understand, boys?—no one should ever force him beyond what he knows are his limits, even when you are only being playful."

Dev didn't nod, but Kris and Bijay did. Dev seemed to be wondering if they were truly going to have to remember these things. "I don't get it," he said. "Are we taking him home, or are you only *thinking* about taking him home?"

"That is to be our discussion later," said his father calmly. "Now. More about Dontae. He will need to have some bone put into his jaws and a few dental implants since he is missing teeth. Most of his other surgeries are behind him."

"You said he's seven?" asked Bijay, his eyes disappointed. "Couldn't you get a boy two years *younger* so I can be a *big* brother this time?"

Mrs. Dehlvi pushed back her chair and went to kneel on the floor beside Bijay's chair to hug him and laugh. "Bij! You sweet boy! All this talk of sweat glands and hands and feet and lips and teeth, and all of those are fine with you. You just wish he were a little bit younger. Oh, this is a sweet boy we have here." She laughed again, and Bijay giggled. *"All* of my boys are sweet. Dev, you will be very close to him in no time, I know you will. And Kris, you have been in his position as a new family member. You will lead the way. I am proud of you all. But, as your father has said, we will think on this until tonight at dinner time. And then, if we all say yes—*all* of us—we can go to see if he will have us, too."

"Now, get busy and be on your way," said Mr. Dehlvi.

Kris hurriedly finished the remainder of his breakfast while sitting alone at the table with his mother, who ate her meal at a slower pace.

"Dev might not agree to take in Dontae," whispered Mrs. Dehlvi, sadness slowing her movements even more. Her hand rested near her tea saucer, the one with daffodils painted delicately around the outside.

Kris swallowed his last bite. He wiped his sticky mouth with a napkin and stood. "He will. Things are changing all the time. For everyone. He'll be okay with the new adoption. You'll see. Things are changing all the time."

As he started into the kitchen from around the corner, Kris saw Pip drinking from Stomper's water bowl while Stomper watched resignedly from two feet away.

Chapter Six

"I'm going to Round Theater," Kris announced as he clicked his blue metal locker shut to stand with his back against it. "Anyone want to go with me?"

Steve shook his red bangs from his eyes as he closed his own locker. "Mom and Dad and I are going to Leslie to visit my grandma. Mom is going to stay with her for a week or so, but Dad and I are driving home again after dinner. Grandma gets lonesome now that Grandpa is gone."

"I've got to go home and pack some more," said Tatyana softly, looking at the floor. After a few moments, she pushed her very long, black hair over her shoulders before lightly waving to Kris, Matt, and Steve as she swept down the long high school hallway.

Kris stared at her as she walked away, wondering if he should have walked her home.

"I'm taking Browser to the vet for his checkup. Katrina will go with you, though," Matt said, tying his shoelaces tighter. He stood and scanned the crowd of kids still walking out of classrooms nearby. "There she is. Hey, Kat!"

Katrina was headed toward them, anyway, but she grinned and raised a hand to her brother to make it clear that she had heard him. When she reached her locker, she asked, "What's up?"

"Go with Kris," her twin brother said with no explanation.

"Sure," she said, her blue eyes sparkling. She didn't need to know where. She put away a textbook. She noticed again that there were dark circles under Kris' eyes.

The sun was warm on their shoulders as they crossed the teachers' parking lot and turned toward downtown. After they had gone a full two blocks in silence, Kris explained, "I'm going to the theater where my parents worked. My birth parents, I mean. It's about a half mile ahead, then a block down Carter Boulevard."

"I know it, of course. I love that place. I saw *Hamlet* there a couple of years ago. We've got tickets for *The Pirates of Penzance* when it opens next month."

"I haven't been in a long time," he said. "I haven't even gone past it."

Katrina wished it could be five miles that they would be walking side-by-side. The air was fragrant with lilacs and various pink and white tree buds, newly mown grass, and the slight sandalwood fragrance that Kris' mother always sprayed on his shirts after folding them.

Kris moved closer and linked his arm through hers. "You didn't even ask where we were going to go. I wanted some company, and you came with me. Just another example of how nice you are."

"Am I?" she asked earnestly, glancing away to the line of houses nearby that each had fraternity letters on or above their doors. "Sometimes I don't feel all that nice."

He stopped walking and faced her, his eyebrows slightly raised. "You're the nicest kid I know. Well, my brothers are great, too, but I'd say you're at least tied with them. I know that if I ever need to count on someone, you're the girl for me."

He didn't link his arm through hers again, but they walked only inches apart for the next few blocks until the sidewalk ran out and they had to maneuver single file for a short way along a narrow path at the edge of the road.

Katrina purposely stayed behind him, her face red while his compliment replayed in her mind. "You never said, Kris. Why are we going to the theater? And why were you back in school so soon after getting knocked out and blinded?"

He shrugged. "I'm fine. I had a headache before lunch, but I went to the nurse, and she gave me a quick once-over and said it was probably a regular headache and not a dying-

66

at-any-minute headache. After I ate, I felt better. And I want to go to the theater because my folks are adopting another boy soon."

"Wait, wait, wait, and wait!" she shouted, pulling him to a stop and making him look at her.

Kris smiled, liking what the breeze did to her hair. Liking her face, the way it looked as sunlight flashed through the leaves above them.

She tried to ignore his sudden smile, asking earnestly, "What's this about another boy? And how come you never told me? And how in the world does adopting someone lead to us walking to Round Theater?"

"I kind of thought that Mom and Dad were getting serious about fostering or adopting, but today is the first time it's been ... real. And today was the first time I'd heard anything about Dontae. That's his name. He's from Jamaica. He's seven, and he has some sort of a medical condition that's super rare. I thought that would mean he'd be in a wheelchair, but no. It means he gets hot and needs dental work. Maybe some other stuff. Oh, yeah. His hands and feet are different, but I forget how they're different. We have another family meeting tonight at dinner. We're going to vote to say if we want to go ahead and adopt him or not."

"Well, what if the vote isn't—you know—unanimous?"

"If it isn't unanimous, I guess we don't take Dontae in."

"But that's not fair to that kid."

"I don't think there's anything to worry about. Dev wasn't too happy this morning over his pancakes, but I'm sure he'll say yes when we vote."

"You still haven't answered my other question. Why are we going to the theater?"

Kris started forward again, and soon they were back on a sidewalk. He leaped over a part of the walk that lifted into a peak from a large tree root. Katrina leaped, too, before falling into step beside him.

"I've been thinking about my birth Mom and Dad a lot today." He sighed. "I did a dumb thing when I left my last foster home. I didn't take anything with me except clothes and my toothbrush. I don't have *any* photos of my life before the Dehlvis. My first mom and dad used to work at the theater. I'm hoping they might have some behind-the-scenes photos I can see. So, that's why I'm going there. Plus, I'm in the mood to walk around after spending days stuck in bed and then in school."

A thought occurred to her. "Kris, are you and Taty having a fight? It seemed like you were ignoring her in geometry."

He kicked a small stone. "I did? I didn't mean to. I must have been thinking about Dontae. Or, I might have been ignoring her because it already feels like she's gone. She told me she and her parents are going to Botswana for the summer. She warned me that they might stay there forever."

Katrina stopped walking again. "She *is? What?* Why am I always the last one to know things? Taty's nearly my best friend! Why didn't she tell me? Why didn't you? For gosh *sakes,* Kris! You never tell me *anything* unless I *drag* it out of you!"

Kris had kept on walking, so Katrina sped up to reach his side again.

"I found out a few days ago. Then I got hit on the head. I don't know ... I don't know if I care what she does all that much."

She dropped back a half step, hiding the fact that she was beaming with joy that Kris was going to be without a girlfriend for at least all summer. Katrina then sobered, realizing that Kris' freedom also meant that she might never see her friend Tatyana again. Maybe Kris *did* care, she thought, but he was trying to keep himself from getting too hurt.

When they arrived at the Art Deco-style theater, they found that it was locked. No one answered when they pounded on the curved metal and glass doors. "Rats," said Kris, leaning against the doors in defeat. "Oh, well. It was only an idea. I wonder if there's an actors' entrance in back we can try. Mom and Dad always brought me in through these doors or the service door."

Katrina walked to the unmarked brown-painted door near the ticket booth and tried it. "Locked."

Just then Darla waved to them from in front of the pharmacy. They watched as she jogged across the street.

"Hey, kids. Kris! You give me a hug right now, mister. Don't *scare* people like that! What in the world are you doing walking around like nothing happened, anyway? Shouldn't you be recuperating at home in bed? Your eyes look sore. How are you?"

After their hug, he said, "I'm okay now. The bruises on my head and arm hurt, but that's about it."

Darla pressed her lips together, looking him over carefully. She then glanced at the theater doors. "What's up? Trying to get in early for a show?"

"No," said Katrina, cupping her hands around her eyes to peer through a round window. She gave up. "Looks like no one's in there. Kris wanted to talk to one of the workers. He thought maybe the theater would have photos of his birth parents. They used to work here. He ... he doesn't have even one photo of them now."

"He *doesn't?*" Darla asked, surprised.

"Left them behind at his last foster home," Katrina said as she looked at Kris, who was staring at the sidewalk.

"I know I shouldn't have," he said, not looking up. "That was a bad idea. But ... I just wanted to get out of there. I didn't pack anything at all. The Dehlvis had to buy me pajamas and underwear, even—right on the first day they took me in."

Darla checked the time on her cell phone. "Aunty Mavis is watching the baby. I'm done running my errands. Let's go

69

over to the newspaper office together. There might be photos on file from your mom and dad's accident. I mean that they usually print a photo of the people from before the accident. How does that sound, Kris?"

He didn't reply for a while, but then said, "I guess that's a good idea. Thanks, Darla."

They crossed the street at the light and walked two blocks to the newspaper's gray, hulking building where they were told at the front desk that any available archives are searchable on the internet.

Darla led the kids to a group of padded chairs near a desk that had a computer the public could use. She did an online search for Kris' parents. The only result was an obituary for both, without photos. Their names were too common for a general search engine to lead them to easy results.

Outside, Darla held up a finger, signaling she had a brilliant idea. "I know what we'll do! The library has all the old Anders Lake newspapers on microfiche. We can search for the accident report that way."

"What's micro-whatever?" asked Katrina.

"They're tiny filmstrips that have archives of newspapers and documents recorded on them. You read the film in a magnifying machine. Haven't you kids ever used one before?"

Kris shrugged, and Katrina shook her head.

"They're disappearing from libraries now, but maybe we'll get lucky, and ours will still have the machine and films."

The three-story brick library sat very nearly right across the street from the newspaper office. They asked a librarian for help, and after a few minutes, they were seated around an aging microfiche machine on the third floor near a bust of William Shakespeare and a poster advertising a retro magic show to be performed by The Great GillyAnn. Sun streamed through the tall windows, lighting the shelves of classical literature on the wall opposite.

Darla operated the machine as Kris and Katrina leaned forward to look at the screen.

"Are you ready, Kris? Remember, there is no guarantee that we'll see your parents' photos. There might only be a brief mention of the accident."

"I know. I'm ready." He glanced past Darla to Katrina, who smiled nervously at him.

After a minute, Darla announced, "Here it is!"

Kris and Katrina leaned forward even farther.

"That's Mom and *Dad,*" Kris said. He stared at the dot-matrix photos for a full minute. "I wish it showed them in color, and I wish they'd had better photos to use. My parents were a lot older than this when they died. I don't know where the newspaper got them. Oh, well. At least it's something. Can we ask for a print?"

Darla didn't reply. She was staring silently at the images on the screen. Her breathing seemed oddly loud to Kris.

"What?" asked Kris, looking at the photos of his parents again, wondering what it was that Darla was seeing.

"Kris? *These* two are your *parents? Your* birth parents, I mean?" Darla asked, staring at the images.

"Yeah."

Darla blinked.

Katrina and Kris both took another look at the article.

"We'll ask for a print," Darla said without explaining her reaction to the photos. Even though the library was cool, she was perspiring. She wiped her forehead on her t-shirt sleeve.

"Darla?" asked Katrina worriedly as they stood. "Darla, what's going on? You look like you've seen a ghost."

Darla stood, her chair's legs scraping the floor loudly. "Kids, I ... well, I can't talk about it now."

"Can't talk about what?" asked Kris, confused.

Darla wiped her face again on her other shirt sleeve. "N-nothing. I'm fine. I'll get the microfiche. Let's go."

Kris decided not to try to ask her anything more until they'd left the library.

Downstairs on the main floor, Katrina and Kris glanced through the new arrivals bookcase while Darla quietly asked the librarian for two copies of the film, paying for both hers and Kris' before they all left.

They paused on the concrete steps near the twin porpoises in front of the library, and she gave Kris the print of the news article. "I have to get back to Aunty Mavis' shop to get Lila Pearl now. I'll see you both later." She swallowed and looked sweaty again. "Everything's fine, but I have to run now. Bye."

Before Kat and Kris could protest, Darla was off, jogging away from them toward Main Street.

Katrina slowly sank onto a weathered wooden bench at the bottom of the library's staircase. Kris joined her after Darla was out of sight. The breeze picked up, rattling in the leaves of the oak tree above their heads. A group of students with backpacks went by, talking loudly and happily. Cars drove by, and another minute passed before Katrina finally broke their silence. "She's certainly got me spooked."

Kris raised his eyebrows. "That's one way to put it." He glanced at the large clock on the front of the library. "It's five already? I have to get home. We're having that meeting at dinner about Dontae. About adopting him or not."

She leaned back. "What do you think will happen?"

"What I said before. We'll probably adopt him. He's missing fingers and toes, did I tell you?"

Katrina stood and started to walk in the direction that led to both of their houses. "No, you didn't. You said earlier that you'd forgotten what the deal was with his hands and feet. Missing fingers and toes? Can he walk?"

"I guess he's doing fine. He even does karate."

"Wow," Katrina said, impressed. She lowered her gaze shyly. "I love it when people overcome tough times and bad problems. I love people who put their heart into life and try hard. Um, Kris? That might be why I love—"

"Look! It's Matt. Hey, Matt!" Kris called, holding up his hand. "And hi, Browser!"

"Duuuuuuude!" Matt called back. He made Browser sit while he checked for traffic before crossing to their side of the street. "Hey, Kat. The vet says Browser's doing great. He got his shots and new tags. Want to take his leash for a while?"

Katrina wasn't pleased to have her brother along on their walk, but when she took Browser's purple-spotted leash, she couldn't help feeling happy again. "Heya, pups. Don't I get a kiss?"

She knelt on the grass and let the black and white terrier lick her cheek. "Oh, thanks, Browsie. Bet you're glad to be done with all that poking and prodding, right?"

Browser yip-barked his joyful reply, his brown eyes seeming every bit as happy as his voice.

"How come you two are here? And what's that, Kris?" asked Matt as they began to walk together.

Kris glanced at the rolled-up paper in his hand. "It's a copy of the news article on my parent's car accident. We got it at the library. Darla saw us trying to get into Round Theater. I thought maybe they'd have some old photos of my mom and dad that I could have. I don't have any, myself. They were locked and no one answered, but I still want to get inside to ask them sometime. This print is okay, but the photos the newspaper used with their story were so old that my folks look like kids, practically. I sure hate that I got rid of everything when I moved the last time."

Katrina had a thought. "Why don't you go back to your former foster family and ask if they kept anything for you? It's worth a shot."

"Nah," said Kris, bending to pat Browser on his spotted back. "They weren't the type of people who would hang onto some foster kid's things. Besides ... no. I never want to see any of them again. None of the kids stuck up for me when I was being yelled at by the father and mother." His voice had cracked. After a full minute, he said, "I mostly can only feel sorry that the kids weren't taught to be kindhearted. It wasn't their fault that they were too scared to defend me. I've never thought of it that way before. I never realized that I should have seen that *they* were scared, too."

They started walking together, Browser in the lead.

Katrina wished that she was alone with Kris to console him with a hug. "Well, maybe we can get you into the theater on a Friday or Saturday when they have shows. Is anyone there who would remember you and let you in without having to buy a ticket?" asked Kat.

All four stopped when they reached the corner where they would part ways. Browser tugged, knowing the way, but then he got distracted by a fluffy-tailed brown squirrel that jumped to the side of a tree, chittering and teasing him from a level just above his head.

"Maybe. Good idea. I wasn't there very many times, but I think I remember the janitor, so maybe he'd remember me, too. Okay. I need to get home for supper. Thanks for helping out today, Kat. Bye, guys. Bye, Browser."

A half a block along State Street, Katrina said, "I haven't, but I suppose you've probably heard about his life with that other, awful foster family."

Matt sighed. "No, I haven't. He doesn't talk about his past. Makes you wonder what else we don't know about our friends. I should be nicer. I'm kind of a doofy oaf a lot of the time."

"No, you're not. Well, not a *lot* of the time, anyway." She wasn't smiling.

Matt looked at his sister, getting a strange feeling from her. "I just got done worrying about my best friend being

74

blind forever, and now I'm sure there's something you're not telling me. What happened today? What's up with you two?"

Katrina switched the leash to her other hand and pulled a windblown strand of her blonde hair from her mouth. She looked at him. "Matt, it was super weird. Darla about had a cow when she saw Kris' parents' photos in the news article. A cow!"

"She did? Huh. Did she know them all those years ago? Did she say anything?"

"She got hyper, sweaty, and nervous. I've never seen her that freaked out. But, nope. No explanation. She said she had to get L.P. from Mrs. O'Malley, and that was that."

He put his hands in his pockets, thinking. "Did Kris tell you about the new kid they're adopting? Or that they might be adopting?"

"Some. I was trying to imagine our lives if Mom decided to foster or adopt anyone, let alone someone with a medical thing going on with them. I guess it would be all right. But hard."

"I think this summer is going to be strange. There's this vibe in the air." Matt wiggled his fingers in front of Katrina. "And I keep looking around for that man from the auction— the one Mack and I saw across the street from the bookshop, too. I didn't tell him my real name or where I live, but I know I remember Kris telling him to go to No Page Unturned in Anders Lake. It would have been okay to say that to a nice person, but I think he's the guy who threw the baseball at Kris. So now ... ugh."

Katrina felt like changing the subject to make her brother stop worrying. She also felt the old twin closeness that they used to have before they were teenagers, and before they drifted a little apart. On a whim, she confessed, "I almost told Kris that I love him."

Matt stopped walking. "You did *what?*"

She shrugged and kept going, Browser pulling harder as they turned the corner onto their home street. "Well, it's true. Why not? Tatyana is leaving for Africa for at least the summer, and Kris basically said he doesn't even care if she goes."

"Since when do you *love* the guy? And in what way do you *mean* that, anyway?"

"Oh, cut it out, Matty. You've probably known as long as I have that I've got this mad crush on him. Stop acting surprised."

She started to run toward their house, a 1960s brick ranch in the middle of a neighborhood of much older Victorian homes.

"No, I did *not* know that," he said, running behind her and passing her. On their front step, he took the dog's leash from her. "I had zero clue. He's like a brother to us. Why on earth would you want to have a crush on *Kris?*"

"I just do."

"Well, at least don't *tell* him!"

"How am I going to get him to be my boyfriend? How will I get him to marry me in a few years if I don't tell him how I feel?"

Matt shook his head, not believing what he was hearing. "I need a drink of Kool-Aid to wash down all this stupid."

He unlocked their door, and they went inside and into the kitchen. Katrina removed Browser's leash and let him outside to the fenced back yard. The terrier ran eagerly to the white-flowering bushes that lined the far edge of their property.

She closed the patio door and played two one-handed chords on the old, upright piano that hugged the wall.

"Here," Matt said, offering a drink to her while holding one for himself. "Kat, is that all you're going to practice today? Not that I'm complaining or anything."

She laughed.

"What?"

"I remembered that one Saturday when Mom and I left you here alone while we went shopping. You had strict orders to do at least some of the laundry and dishes. When you heard us pull up outside, you took dishes out of the cupboard and put them in the drying rack, and you pulled clean towels from the wicker shelves and put them on the sofa as if you'd just gotten done folding them."

"Hey—it worked. For a few minutes, anyway."

She laughed again and played another chord before finally taking the offered purple drink.

Matt looked through the window at Browser who was running after birds that had landed on the feeder. "I guess you and Kris are okay as a couple, but geez, Kat—wait until you're out of high school to jump on him. Don't do it now."

"Why?"

"Mom would tell you the same thing. She married her high-school boyfriend. They'd dated since they were fourteen. They got married right after graduation. She once told me that it's a big mistake to latch onto one person when you're a kid. You haven't heard her say that, too? Mom said that she felt like if she'd dated around, she would have gotten to know exactly what sort of a guy she *did* want to spend her whole life with. And maybe it would have been Dad, and maybe it wouldn't have been. At least she would've been sure. And she would've grown up more in between boyfriends. Dating is what you do to try out different people. See how they fit. If you marry the first pair of shoes you put on in high school, how do you know they're still going to fit when you're … like … an old lady of forty?"

"Yeah, well, Mom wouldn't have had a couple of kids named Kat and Matt, then, if she hadn't married those shoes. I mean Dad." Katrina went into the living room to sit on the couch. She kicked off her sandals and put her feet on the cushions. "I get what you mean, though." She sighed, taking a drink. "Okay. I'll save Kris for later. But what if he falls in love with someone else in the meantime?"

"Then he does. I think you shouldn't be boy crazy, Kat. It makes the whole family look bad," he teased, throwing a small pillow at her.

"Hey! Watch the Kool-Aid! And oh, God. 'The whole family' is *so* not going to look bad if I go after Kris Dehlvi. *Puh-lease.*"

Matt laughed, throwing another pillow that barely missed her glass.

"And what about you and that Keylee girl?"

"Who?"

Katrina stuffed both of the tossed pillows behind her head. "Keylee. Your own little love interest."

Matt suppressed a smile as he walked down the hallway to the bathroom. "I have no idea who you're talking about. By the way, there's a note on the fridge about the casserole."

Katrina sat up. She took another long drink before walking to the kitchen to put dinner in the oven. She had a flash of a future life with Kris, of putting dinner into the oven before he came home from work. Or, of *him* putting the dinner into the oven before *she* came home from work. He was taller with darker hair, he had a mustache, and was wearing a business suit with an apron over it. She imagined him taking off the apron, his jacket, and his white shirt before sliding a meatloaf into the oven, his book-reading arm muscles bulging.

"All right," she said out loud to herself. "I'll wait, Kris Dehlvi. I'll wait for you. But *you'd* better wait for *me,* too."

An hour later, as Matt, Katrina and their mother were eating the last of the casserole and salad, a police car pulled into their driveway.

Chapter Seven

Earlier that afternoon, Mack pushed through the front door of the bookshop. "Whew! That's that. They're all loaded in now." He and Mrs. O'Malley had re-boxed all the auction books so Mack could put them back into the cargo van. Later, he and Jack's father, John, unloaded them into John's storage unit at the north end of Anders Lake.

"I'm happy we confided in Jack and Darla about the break-in last night. I never would have thought about someone being able to find our books if we rented a storage unit in our names," said Mrs. O'Malley, looking relieved.

"Good thing John had the space for them, now that the jukebox is out of there."

"Are we going to go through the books right there in the storage unit, or do you want to take them back here a few boxes at a time?"

Mack crossed his arms. "I think I want to leave them alone for at least a week or two until we see what's going to happen with that character who broke in. I'm glad that the books are out of here for now. This experience puts me out of the mood to go to another auction, I'll say that."

Mrs. O'Malley frowned in agreement. "It is strange, though. We've never had trouble like this before."

Mack said softly, "I'm worried about the boys. I wonder if the police have talked to Matt yet. This whole confounding situation is bizarre. What *is* it that we don't know about those books?"

"The new glass door looks nice, though," she said, trying to sound happy about something. "I like that it's tinted that pale, rosy color. It stands out when you're walking along the sidewalk or driving by. Thanks for getting artistic at eleven o'clock at night, Mack."

He looked at it. "I didn't choose the color, you should know. That was all the repair company had in stock in the thickness I wanted."

"Oh," she said, laughing. "Well, then ... it's a good thing I like it."

Mack laughed lightly, too.

"Ahhh, ah!" said L.P. from her bassinet behind them.

"Shouldn't Darla be here for the baby by now?" Mack asked as he stepped closer to L.P. He grinned at her and let her have his finger to hold.

"I thought so, but she didn't give me a definite time when she'd be back."

"I guess if she's not here soon, one of us can take her over to Jack. He should be done with the record dealer by now."

Mrs. O'Malley swallowed some of her cooling coffee. "That's the guy who's buying a bulk lot from them for his flea market in Lamarr?"

Mack nodded, still standing over L.P. He then straightened and pushed his nearly gray bangs from his forehead. "Jack has his inventory color coded by the month that he adds each record to the bins. If they don't sell in one year, he calls in the flea marketers to clear them out. It takes all day to go through each and every record to look for a particular color label, but at least it frees display space for new stock."

Darla, red-faced, sweating, and breathing loudly, pushed into the shop looking as if she'd been running in fear and had at last escaped into a place of protection.

"Darla, are you okay? Mack, get her a drink. Darla? Is there anything wrong? Is it Jack?" Mrs. O'Malley asked.

"I'm fine, I'm fine, Aunty Mavis," Darla assured her. She took a deep breath, wiped her face with a tissue, and tried to smile. "I know I shouldn't scare you, especially after your terrible break-in last night, but I did have a real fright this afternoon, myself."

Mrs. O'Malley tugged Darla to the sofa and made her sit down. Mr. O'Malley handed her a cup of water.

Darla took a long drink, resettled more comfortably on the cushions, and glanced around the shop to see if they were alone, moaning, "I don't know *how* to say this, or *if* I should say it, or if I should tell *you,* or tell someone *else,* or tell someone else's *parents,* or ... *what."*

Mrs. O'Malley went into the bathroom, where she soaked a clean washcloth with cold water. Bringing it to her niece, she said, "That *is* a dilemma, sweetie."

Darla wiped her face gratefully. "It's so hot out, and it isn't even summer."

"No, not really," said Mack. "It's maybe only about seventy-five degrees. Are you sick, do you think?"

She shook her head. "No. Overwhelmed. Oh, gah!" she exclaimed into the washcloth.

The family who had been in for a short time came from the hallway to the front to check out, each with a single book in hand. Mack rang up their sales while Darla and Mrs. O'Malley sat on the sofa together in silence, attempting to smile casually as if nothing were out of the ordinary in the bookshop. The baby sat up, and Mack lifted her from her crib and brought her to his wife before he bagged the family's purchases.

"Hi, baby!" said Darla, the hair around her face very wet. She smiled brightly and touched L.P.'s tiny nose in greeting. "It's delightful to see your little toothy smile. Did you have fun with your Aunty Mavis here this afternoon?"

The baby laughed and gurgled as the customers left with their purchases.

Darla watched them leave, letting L.P. tug on the washcloth. "It's seems highly unlike you, Mack, to buy a pink door. Was that a present for Mavis? I like it. I'm kind of jealous."

"It was all they had in stock in my preferred thickness," Mack said again, still ambivalent about the rosy glass.

"I'll have to get the number of the company that installed it." She looked again at her aunt as another wave of panic hit. "So. Back to my problem. On top of your problem. On top of worrying about the boys. Oh, wait. We're not necessarily going to go back to my problem. I have to think about who to tell this to first." She patted her face with the cloth again, watching Mrs. O'Malley fuss over the baby.

"I think you should tell us," said Mrs. O'Malley. "We need a distraction. Besides, we're family. Right? Family helps family. You and Jack asked John to help us this morning. It's only fair that *we* should help you with *your* troubles."

Darla shook her head. "No. I need to calm down and think for a while. It's not a big emergency. In fact, maybe I'll decide to keep mum about it forever."

Mrs. O'Malley stood with the baby in her arms and protested, "That's a *terrible* idea."

Mack took L.P. from her and said, "Mavis, you don't even know what she's talking about."

Mrs. O'Malley put her hands on her hips. "I know my Darla. She wouldn't be all red in the face and this upset if it weren't about something I should know about so I can help."

"You're just nosy."

"I am not."

"Are so."

"I am *not.*" She sat again, putting a hand on her niece's. "All right. I am so. But Darla, don't you think you should tell us what's going on? Or, at least tell us vaguely what it's all about. Or *who* it's about. Can't you do that?"

Darla looked into their faces, thinking. "Let me bring the baby next door to Jack. I'll come right back."

Mrs. O'Malley nodded to Mack. "Let your uncle take her. You sit here and calm down."

"Afraid of an escape?" teased Mack as he backed through the door with L.P.

"Exactly," said his wife, waving him away.

Mrs. O'Malley walked to the front of the shop to flip the open sign over. She switched off the overhead lights and the stereo, leaving only the small lamps lit. She called out in case there were still customers in the shop that may have been forgotten. She then sat again and took Darla's hand. "If I know Mack, he'll stay with Jack for a while to give us time to talk on our own."

Darla closed her eyes, relaxing. "I love your relationship with Mack, Aunty Mavis. I hope when Jack and I have been married for as long as you have that we'll glow, too."

"Glow? Do we glow?"

"Well, you know what I mean." Darla settled against the cushions.

Haiku was startled awake by the sound of a motorcycle revving. He had been sleeping on the cushioned wooden chair by the door. It was the first time he had slept out in the open since he'd moved into the bookshop. He trotted to the sofa to squint at Mrs. O'Malley.

"Hello, Haiku. Glad you're not hiding anymore. Have you met Darla?" She lifted Haiku and put him between herself and her niece where they could both pet his long, downy fur.

Buglit leaped up to sit next to Elephant Gerald, seemingly pleased that her shop-mate was getting attention.

"I ... don't know where to start," said Darla as she scratched Haiku under his chin. The cat purred in appreciation and lifted his head higher to encourage her.

"At the beginning?"

Darla frowned. "There are two beginnings, though." She concentrated on petting the cat's stomach for a moment before saying, "I ran into Katrina and Kris in front of Round Theater."

"You did?"

"Kris was there trying to get inside. He said he wanted to find some photos of his parents since he'd left the ones he used to have behind at his former foster home."

Mrs. O'Malley nodded and adjusted her glasses. "I think I remember that he told us he'd left everything behind. He must have been distraught and eager to get away from that place."

Darla exhaled, feeling calmer now that she was talking about her experience. "We couldn't get into the theater, so I suggested taking the kids to the newspaper office for a look at the report on the accident. His mom didn't die in the crash, but there was a chance the story would have included photos of both his parents."

"That sounds like a very good idea."

"We didn't have any luck there. We went across to the library to look at old papers that had been put on microfiche. There, we did find what Kris was looking for: photos of his mom and dad on the front page on the day after the accident. The article called his mom a 'survivor' at the time. It's unbelievably sad that she didn't make it."

Mrs. O'Malley looked confused. "But surely seeing the article wasn't what made you this upset. You knew all that, right?"

Darla nodded, petting Haiku on his neck after he had shifted positions. "I did."

"Well—what, then?"

"Aunty Mavis, I *knew* those faces in the photos. I'd seen them before. It was a long time ago, but I'm *positive.*"

"Okay, so you knew them. I don't understand why you're acting this way, Darla."

"I didn't know them, no," Darla said, looking away from petting the cat. "I just said that I knew their *faces.*" She paused to stare through the door at the street before saying more. "When I was a teenager, after I got furiously angry and left Aunty Q and Uncle Elwood's farm, I got a job as a waitress at this small family restaurant in Silverton. At that time, there was this girl a little older than me who also worked there. Her name was Ricki, I think. She was hugely pregnant and shouldn't have been on her feet carrying trays all day."

Mrs. O'Malley couldn't see where this story was going, but she nodded.

"Well, we got to be pretty good friends. I asked her how she was going to take care of the baby—you know, money-wise—and she said that she was going to sell her baby."

"What? That's outrageous!"

"I saw how determined she was, so I didn't say anything against her idea. I had no way to stop her or help her, and I felt a little glad that that baby was going to be raised by people who could afford to take care of him or her."

"You could have *reported* her. Darla, why didn't you?"

"I was young, and I was a weak person, truthfully." She got up to put the wet washcloth on the edge of the sink and to refill her cup of water. "I went with her one time when she met with the couple who were going to get her baby. We all went to dinner together at a café. I think Ricki wanted me along so she could convince me that she was doing the right thing. I sat right across the table from that couple for two hours."

"I don't like where this is heading, Darla. Do *not* tell me what I think you're going to tell me," warned her aunt miserably. A chill ran along her spine.

Darla took in a ragged breath. She stared at her knees, swallowed, and looked at Mrs. O'Malley. "It was them. They were the ones I saw in the accident photos. I'm certain of it. Kris' dad had a very conspicuous left eye. Here, look for yourself," Darla said, taking the folded print-out from her back pocket and giving it to Mrs. O'Malley. "He must have had an injury to it at one point. There was no eyebrow on that side, and his lid opened only halfway. His mom was super beautiful with her long, buttery-gold hair. And you know, of course, that I'm saying 'dad' and 'mom' in quotes now. Kris *must* be the baby of my friend Ricki."

Mrs. O'Malley looked at the faces smiling at her from the past, trying to get answers from the dots of ink. "You can't know that. What if they didn't go through with it? What if Kris was their own, natural baby? Maybe that friend of yours changed her mind and kept her child."

"I guess I can't be a hundred percent sure. I never saw Ricki after I went with her to that meeting. I think they took her with them. It's not a clear memory. They seemed lovely and were very ... soothing, I guess you'd say. Heck, *I* wanted to go home with them by the end of that long talk. Maybe that was a big part of the reason why I quit the restaurant a week later and moved back to the farm."

"Oh, *no.* Oh, *no.*" Mrs. O'Malley stared at the ceiling.

"Ricki planned to stay with them to breastfeed after she had the baby in their house. They were going to support her ... give her five thousand dollars for the baby when she left them after a few months. She'd have time to recover from the pregnancy while staying with them. That was what they told her. I honestly felt like they were telling the truth. I *did* wonder how they were going to get a birth certificate and what they were going to say to people, but I let it go out of my mind after a while. I was ... not the same person I am now. I was a wild mess, as Aunty Q probably told you."

"And this was in Silverton?"

"Yes. I don't know if they lived there then, or if they merely met at a café there but lived here in Anders Lake."

Mack appeared at the door. Mrs. O'Malley emphatically shook her head. He shrugged and went back toward the record shop.

"I know for sure that those two were raised here," Mrs. O'Malley said, looking at Darla while pointing to the printed article. "How did they get away with all these shenanigans? Did she lose a baby and then pretend to be pregnant until Ricki's delivery? Was she never pregnant herself? None of this seems real. Darla! This could mean that Kris never met any of his *supposed* parents' family because they hid him ... no. That doesn't make sense. Kris was a customer of ours with his mom. They weren't sneaking around. Oh, I'm *confoundedly* confused. No *wonder* you ran in here like you'd flown in from Fresno on the back of a vampire bat."

"What should I *do?*" Darla asked, her face reddening again.

The older woman could only shake her head and stare through the shop windows. "Oh, look. Here come Mack, Jack, and L.P. We'll stop talking now. You tell Jack tonight, and I'll talk to Mack. We'll come up with a plan of action together. All right?"

"I guess so."

"Hello, ladies," said Jack. "L.P. has gotten a change, and now we've come over to say goodnight."

"Oh, baby-babe! Goodnight, Lila Pearl," said Mrs. O'Malley as she stood. She wound a bit of L.P.'s hair around her finger. She gave the print-out back to Darla, smiling at the baby again. "Such a *good* girl for me today."

Lila Pearl grinned, but then hid her face shyly against her father's shoulder.

"And the new kitty likes her, too. Don't you, Haiku?"

Haiku, still stretched out on the sofa in a comfortable state of relaxation after receiving pets and scratches, lifted his head and opened his eyes—his only response to Mrs. O'Malley's question.

Jack noticed his wife's face was flushed and that the collar of her brown t-shirt was wet, along with a lot of her hair. "Darla? Is everything okay?" He bounced L.P. tenderly, his eyes full of concern.

"No," she said, then sighed. "We'll talk about it later. Mavis is going to talk to Mack tonight, too."

"Oh, no. Is this about Kris?" he asked, looking back and forth between Mrs. O'Malley and Darla.

"No. I mean *yes,* but not in the way you mean. He's physically okay."

Jack shifted the baby to his other shoulder, not happy with Darla's reply. L.P. fussed and frowned, suddenly also a lot less happy than she was a moment ago. She grabbed her father's brown hair and mussed it, frustrated. "She's getting a little grumpy. Want to go? I forgot to get kibble for Patrick yesterday, so we need to stop for some on the way home."

Darla stood, sliding the folded newspaper article into her back pocket again. She hugged Mrs. O'Malley tiredly and patted Mack on his arm as she passed him. "I'm grumpy, too. I feel all … wrung out." She sighed. "I've *had* it, and yet we *do* still need to sit together to discuss things. I hope there are leftovers to heat up."

Jack patted the baby's back. "There are. That noodle concoction with the green beans in it."

"Maybe you can find a soothing song to play on your new toy when we get home. I need soothing."

"Okay. D-seventeen is nice."

"Good old D-seventeen," Darla said, taking the diaper bag from Jack and kissing L.P.'s cheek. "By the way, what *is* D-seventeen?"

"A rockabilly version of Rock-a-Bye Baby."

Darla closed her eyes contentedly. As she opened them again, she said, "Perfect."

The three of them went through the rose-tinted door for home.

Chapter Eight

Knock-knock-knock

"Who could that be?" asked Mrs. Karlsson from the dinner table. She wiped her mouth with a napkin and pushed away from the table. She pulled back the burgundy-checked curtain from the long window beside the door and was shocked to see a policewoman and man standing on the welcome mat.

"The police," she whispered to Matt and Katrina, looking startled. A second later, she remembered why they would most probably be knocking, and she quickly opened the door. Browser barked and barked in the back yard.

"Ma'am? Is this the Karlsson residence? We're here to interview Matt," said a stocky, black-haired woman in a dark blue uniform. "Are you a parent or legal guardian?"

"Yes. Come in. Matt? Matt, come here. Katrina, do you have homework?" Mrs. Karlsson called to the kids who were still in the kitchen putting their dinner plates in the sink.

Katrina took her mother's hint and walked shyly past the officers before continuing along the hallway to her room. The girl liked to take over for or talk over Matt when she was nervous, but in this case, she knew her brother needed to do the talking for himself. She didn't have homework—she hadn't even brought home any schoolbooks since she had only one final exam left that she knew she'd ace. The next day was their last day of school before summer vacation.

After ten minutes, Katrina heard the crunch of gravel as the police car backed out of the driveway.

"So, how did it go?" she asked as she entered the living room, her thumb holding her place in a paperback mystery novel. Browser was already in the house, eating his dinner in the kitchen.

Mrs. Karlsson, her face looking more cheerful than Katrina expected it to look, stood up from the wooden chair near the door that no one usually sat in and said, "Matt did fine. I hadn't heard the whole story before. You did all the right things, Matt. I'm very happy to hear that you remembered what I told you about talking to strangers in that sort of a situation."

"But we probably have a problem now," Matt said to Katrina, who took a seat beside him on the sofa.

"What?"

"I thought they were here because Kris got hit on the head. Well, they *were* here for that, but something else bad happened last night."

Katrina faced him more directly. "Is … is Kris okay?" she asked, her stomach tightening.

"They didn't say anything much about Kris. But, well, the O'Malley's shop got broken into last night by that auction creep. I think *he* was the one who threw the baseball at Kris and blinded him."

"But … how did Mr. O know who broke in?"

"Because he and Mrs. O were still in the shop last night after working on the books until late. They were at the back door when they heard glass breaking in the main room. Mr. O'Malley snuck to the front and saw that guy going through the auction books. He called the cops, and they arrested him. *That's* why I got questioned just now. Since no one saw who threw the baseball at the auction, it could have been an accident. Someone could have been messing around, and the ball found Kris' head by mistake. But now, after the break-in, probably that man who broke in—and who was at the auction—*meant* to hurt Kris."

Mrs. Karlsson took in a long breath before heading to the kitchen to fill a tub with soapy water. The kids followed her to help finish clearing the table.

"Are the police going to talk to Kris, too?" asked Katrina.

"I doubt it. I told them that he lost his memory from that day," answered Matt. "Mom? That creep wouldn't do anything more to Kris, would he? The man wouldn't need to go after him again, now that the books are in the bookshop. Right?"

"I don't think anything more will happen to him, no," said their mother. She wiped her hands on a small towel. "I *am* worried that he might try to break into the shop again. I hope Mack and Mavis are being cautious."

Katrina knelt to Browser's level, hugged him, and then stood to carry him to her bedroom to have company while she read.

The twenty-fourth verse of the fourth chapter of the *Bhagavad Gita* was read before dinner, and dinner was eaten before the Dehlvis discussed Dontae again.

"So, family. We are all agreed," Mr. Dehlvi said, looking proud of his sons. He adjusted his dark-rimmed glasses, folded his cloth napkin, and stood to take his plate into the kitchen. Walking into the dining room again, he said, "Very good. There are more steps to take, but we are nearly done, as long as we have five yes votes."

Bijay ran around and around the living room, around the television, coffee table, sofa, out to the kitchen, down the hallway, into his room, and back again, shouting "Yippee!" every three seconds. Dev carried his plate and glass into the kitchen, his face unreadable.

"I've been thinking," said Kris to his parents once they were alone at the table, even though the conversation seemed to be over.

"What is it?" asked his father, pulling out his chair at the table and sitting again.

"Um … you know that I am more than fine about your Hinduism and prayers and food. And the music and everything. But will a boy from Jamaica feel the same way that I do? Will it feel all weird for him?"

Mr. Dehlvi rested his hands in his lap. He stared down for a moment, thinking. He then looked at Kris, saying, "This is our home. It will be Dontae's home, as well. Never have we asked you to become one of the followers of our religion, and that will also be the case with the new boy."

"I know. But … what if he has a strong feeling *against* Hinduism? What if it makes him uncomfortable to be around it all the time? I see how some people look at Mom and you when we're out together, how they look at Bijay and at Dev. One woman in the grocery store even pulled me aside once to ask me why I was hanging around with you. Yeah, I know. I never told you that. Even when those sorts of people don't seem particularly *unkind* when they eye us, I can feel that it must be hurtful to you to get stares. What if this boy is prejudiced? I worry about a stranger coming into the house who … oh, I don't know what I'm trying to say."

Mrs. Dehlvi reached across the table to squeeze Kris' hand. "Dontae and the two of us have spoken a little about religion. He is very wise and mature for a boy of seven, you'll see. He has no problem with throwing his arms around anyone who will love and accept him. I think once you meet him, you will stop having a worry in your heart about these things, Kris."

"I can't help but feel all … protective of you."

Mr. Dehlvi stood. "That is because you truly feel like our son now. But Dontae is not a boy to protect us from. Don't fear this wise and loving boy who will be coming. He has large eyes that see right through to a man's heart. You will not feel so protective and guarded once you have met your new brother."

Mrs. Dehlvi stood, too. She finished clearing the table while Kris stayed seated, thinking over what was said. Dev joined him again.

After several moments of silence, Kris moved his chair closer to Dev and put an arm over his shoulders. He hoped that Dev and Bijay hadn't overheard what he'd said to their parents. "I'm glad. Be glad, too. It'll be a change, but a good one. I've been worried, but I'm sure everything will be fine. *Better* than fine."

"Yippee!" cried Bijay as he pulled to a stop in front of the older boys. He'd been running around again after taking a rest in front of the TV. "I did it!"

Kris winked at the panting little boy and said, "Yep. That's right, Bij. If you hadn't brought that extra chair out of the closet to the table last year, we wouldn't be getting Dontae."

Dev shrugged off Kris' arm and stood, carrying away the last remaining bread plate that still had a slice on it.

"You'll see, Dev," said Kris to his brother's back. "*I'm* not terrible to have around, am I?"

Dev put the plate in the kitchen beside the sink where his mother was scrubbing a pan. He then walked back to the dining room and sat again. He pulled his chair away from the table a couple of feet and leaned forward toward Kris, putting his elbows on his knees. "I want you here. I've always wanted you here," he said sincerely, just above a whisper even though the television was fairly loud, and water was running in the kitchen sink. "I'm afraid that this won't be the end of things. If it goes well with this new boy, what makes you think Mom and Dad won't take in another kid? And then another?"

Kris watched Bijay lift Pip so he and the cat could watch TV together in the next room. "I super doubt that'll happen."

"Well, I worry. And I worry about how much work there is for Mom with three boys and Dad. And what will she do if there are four boys ... or more?" Dev pounded his fist on his knee.

"You're acting like an old man, Dev. Since when do you worry about how much work there is for Mom?"

"Since ... since I talked to her a month ago or so. She told me that she was getting more tired than she used to get. What if she's sick? She's only in her thirties. Why is she getting so very tired now?"

"That was one day and one bit of tiredness. Isn't she allowed that? Geez, Dev!" Kris said, also whispering. "How often have *you* casually said that you're tired or have a stomachache or a headache? Are we supposed to rush you to the hospital every time? No. She wouldn't be all revved up about adopting again if she knew she was sick. Stop your worrying, okay? Be happy. Mom and Dad and Bij are happy. *I'm* happy. Relax!"

Dev closed his eyes, opened them again, and nodded in the way that his father did when he wanted someone to know that he was convinced. He went into the living room and sat on the sofa. Stomper jumped up to knead the cushion beside him. After a moment, Dev looked back to Kris and smiled a weak smile, his lips pressed together.

"Good," said Kris, joining him on the sofa. They both petted Stomper, who purred with pleasure. Pip was on the floor with Bijay, washing his paws.

"Look, look, boys," said Mrs. Dehlvi as she came into the room with a tray of cupcakes and napkins. "Celebration time, yes? Do you three boys want a little tea or milk?"

"Milk, please," said Bijay with a bouncy wiggle from his place on the floor. Pip looked pleased with his boy's choice of drink.

"I'll get it, Mom," offered Dev as he started to stand up.

"No, no. You boys sit and sit and sit. I'm going to dump out the water and clean the sink. Shout out your drink wants, and I'll be back with them in two minutes and fourteen and a half seconds. Okay?"

Dev raised his eyebrows at Kris and rolled his eyes. "See? She does too much," he whispered.

Bijay spun around on the floor and grabbed a butterscotch cupcake. Before long, he had smears of light-brown frosting on his nose and fingers.

Kris wiped his little brother with one of the napkins and sat again, frowning as he realized how many times had he let his mother wait on him instead of doing something for himself. Well, he thought, that wasn't going to happen again. With a new boy coming into the family, he was going to be as much help as possible. Maybe he wouldn't even go back to work at the bookshop for the summer.

As soon as the thought had surfaced, though, he regretted it. Would he really not go back to the bookshop for the summer? And maybe never?

"Mom, let *me* get the milks," said Kris after he appeared in the kitchen doorway. "I should be doing more around here. I'm away too much. I'm the oldest. I can do more stuff now."

She wiped her hands before looping the towel back through its hook near the stove. "Little Kris. Or, should I say 'Kris who is not so little.' I can see already what is in your head. You are thinking that a new boy will mean new work. And you are kind and want to help me, and feel like you should start today. Am I correct?"

Kris blinked in surprise.

Mrs. Dehlvi took a gallon of milk and a pitcher of iced tea from the refrigerator before going on. "Kris Dehlvi, you are not yet a man, but you are becoming one quickly." She reached into a cupboard for glasses. "How many for milk?" she called loudly without leaving her spot.

"Two in here!" Dev answered.

"How many for tea?"

"One," called Mr. Dehlvi from the hallway. He then came into the kitchen, rolling up the sleeves of his colorful robe. "No ice, Daya. I need a dentist, I fear."

"Oh, no. Is it that tooth again?" Mrs. Dehlvi asked, pouring two milks and two glasses of tea.

He took his tea, grimacing. "Yes. Call for an appointment tomorrow, will you? I would do it myself, but I fear even hearing the receptionist's voice on the telephone. Your father is a big chicken, Kris. Sad. Sad."

"Kris wants to help me more," said Mrs. Dehlvi. "He thinks I will need more help now that Dontae is coming."

"Well, that is true," said Mr. Dehlvi as he left the kitchen to pick out a cupcake to go with his evening tea.

"I think we can manage. We managed when we took you in," Mrs. Dehlvi said.

"I had a few problems, I guess, but taking in a kid with ecto-whatever is a different, bigger deal."

Mrs. Dehlvi put away the milk and tea. Carrying two of the glasses to the boys, she said, "We will have a time of adjustment, but we will be fine, little Kris. Which reminds me—do tell me to stop calling you 'little Kris' from now on, please."

Kris smiled. He'd grown to love being called 'little' by his parents. "Speaking of taking in a new kid—where will Dontae sleep?"

The boys stopped chewing to look at their mother for her answer.

Mr. Dehlvi said, "In with you, Kris, if that is satisfactory. Otherwise, we can split up Dev and Bijay, and put one of them in your room and Dontae in the other room."

"He can live with me!" said Bijay, bouncing on his knees on the floor.

"I'll share with him," said Dev, glancing at Kris and then down at the sofa cushion.

Kris smiled at his brothers. "I think it might be the best thing if he *did* share my room, though. At least at first. Maybe—eventually—I can move to the basement," he said hopefully.

"We shall see," said his mother.

"That is very kind of you to take him in," said Mr. Dehlvi.

"Not nearly as kind as you and Mom are for opening the house to Dontae. And to me, of course."

Mr. Dehlvi closed his eyes and silently nodded to Kris. He sat on his paisley-covered recliner and placed his cupcake and tea on the end table at its side.

"And that's all I know," said Mrs. O'Malley. She sat on the edge of their bed, nervously smoothing the patchwork quilt with both hands.

Mack, in his brown plaid pajamas, sat beside his wife. He stilled one of her hands with his. "Boy, oh, boy. Well, Darla will have to tell the Dehlvis, naturally. I don't see that there's any big rush. I did wonder why there weren't any blood relatives available to adopt Kris after his parents died. He doesn't seem to know why himself. Apparently, he had nothing to do with any relatives even when his folks were alive. It doesn't make sense somehow. And to think—Kris is adopted, but maybe his first parents weren't his real parents, either. Weird."

"It's more than weird. It might possibly be criminal. Huh. There's that word again coming out of my mouth. Like we don't have enough going on already?"

Mack yawned, long and loudly. "I should have found out if that character is being held at the jail, or if he can get let out on bail or his own recognizance. I did press charges, but no one called us about his status. I wonder if he had any criminal record. I wonder how he knew that something *in* the books or *about* the books made them valuable enough to be worth stealing. I wonder about a lot of things." He walked around to his side of the bed, pulled back the covers, then sat against his pillows. "Let's stop talking for the night. Do you want to read for a while? Or put on a movie?"

She shook her head. "I feel like calling the Dehlvis."

"Don't. It's after midnight."

She stood and walked to her antique dressing table to apply lotion to her face and elbows. The scent of lavender reached Mack, and the familiarity of the nightly routine calmed him enough to make him feel he might be able to get some sleep.

"Come on to bed. We'll figure this out in the warm light of day. Okay?"

She nodded, switching off the hall light and a cat-shaped bedroom lamp that sat atop a low bookcase. Getting into bed, she said, "I think it's supposed to rain tomorrow."

"Naw. I'll make it sun, instead. You just watch." Mack slid his long legs under their sheet and thin quilt. He then rolled onto his side to hug his wife goodnight.

"I almost believe you when you say lovely words like that," she said, enjoying the feel of his comforting arms. "And I *do* believe that you'll find a way to make all these troubles come out all right in the end."

Chapter Nine

"Darla? It's Mavis. How's your dad doing? I woke up thinking about him. He wasn't very talkative when I was with him after the break-in."

"I saw him recently at the grocery store. I think he's dating someone, but he's being mysterious about it. You know, when I saw that it was you calling, I honestly never thought you'd open the conversation with a question about Dad."

"I know. I spent the night tossing and turning, and Danny is one of the things I was tossing and turning about. You say he's *dating* someone?"

"I only *think* so. He's not giving me any details. Didn't he look fine when you stayed with him after the door was broken?"

"Yes," Mrs. O'Malley said as she sat on her computer chair and powered on the monitor. "It isn't fair that men keep getting better and better looking with age."

"What do you mean? You look very pretty with your hair cut that way and with your new glasses and trim figure."

Mrs. O'Malley laughed lightly. *"Trim."*

"You know that you and Aunty Q have lost weight. You both look great! I'm jealous. I sit behind these stacks of records all day, and my butt is morphing into a built-in seat cushion."

"Oh, Darla! No! You look good, too," she said, laughing once. "Now that we've gotten the complementary part of our conversation over with, I think we should talk about paying a visit to Kris' mom. I don't want to wait. Can you go over there with me this afternoon? I'll call her and make sure she can spare the time. Maybe about one o'clock? Can you get away today?"

"Hang on." She covered the phone for a moment. "We're all set. Jack thinks that's a good idea, too. Do you want to call Daya, or should I do it?"

"I will. I'll only call you again if she isn't able to visit this afternoon. Tell Jack hello. Oh, and Mack said to say hello to you, and he hopes you two got more sleep than we did."

Mrs. O'Malley disconnected the call, and a second later hit the speed-dial button for the Dehlvis. "Daya? Hello! I hear you have some big news and excitement going on at your house. Yes. Yes. Oh, I'm extremely happy they all said yes to the adoption. When are you going to see the boy again? And is it now a definite thing that you'll adopt him? Oh, I understand. Still, I'm sure it will work out. My heart is simply *bursting* thinking about what a loving thing it is that you're doing for Kris and now for the new boy. And as always, Dev and Bijay. Yes, we sure do. He is? Well, I know Kris is excited, too. Um, Daya, are you going to be home later today? Darla and I would love to visit you for a while this afternoon. How about at one? Oh, good. Okay. We'll see you then. Should I bring some bakery from Miss Allison's shop? You haven't? You haven't tried it yet? Oh, I know you love to bake yourself, but sometimes it's nice to let someone else fix a treat. Okay. I'll stop over there first. We'll see you at one. Great. Bye-bye now."

"Funny how I rarely need to hear more than your end of a conversation to know what's being said," said Mr. O'Malley as he restocked the shopping bag supply.

She grinned at him.

"I'll call Darla to tell her we're on for one o'clock."

Mack stood straighter. "But you just told her that you wouldn't call unless you *weren't* going over to see Kris' mom this afternoon."

"Oh. I did? Well, she'll be expecting my call, anyway."

Mack laughed, shaking his head and petting Haiku, who was taking up most of that section of the countertop with his very long, fluffy body.

"Hey!" Mrs. O'Malley said, her hands on her hips. "You were going to see about having today turn into a sunny day. What happened to that promise?"

"I'm running behind in my errands. Maybe by the time you leave here after lunch, the sky will clear up."

She smiled at him again, grabbing the phone. "Darla? Okay. I'll be ready at about twelve-thirty. I know, but I told Daya we'd stop by Miss Allison's and get some pastries to go with our tea or coffee. Great. See you then."

"Thirty minutes early? How long does it take to get a few doughnuts?" Mack asked, counting the cash register's start-of-day money.

"We'll have to visit Allison, too, silly."

"Twenty-nine, well, thirty-two, of course, thirty-three and fifty-eight cents. Done." He wrote the figure on a strip of register tape and put it through the slot below the cash drawer.

Doris, the cat shelter volunteer, stepped into the bookshop, closed her umbrella, and leaned it against the coat rack to drip onto the plastic mat below. "Pink! I love it! What a refreshing color for your front door, Mavis. I was passing by and had to come in to see it better."

Mrs. O'Malley told her a short version of the break-in story.

"That's terrible! Are you okay? Were you hurt? Did they hurt the cats?" Doris asked, her voice concerned as she asked these and other questions. She backed to the sofa and sat down.

Mack said, "The cats are both fine. The door was the only damage. He was very, very careful when he was mistreating the books."

"Well, then he's nothing like the hooligans who broke into the hardware shop last year. Those fellows took pains to wreck as much of the place as they possibly could."

"Honestly, Doris, it was a miracle that we were here to catch them. We hardly ever work late. I think it was about the latest we've ever stayed working here. I don't know if it was a coincidence he broke in right as we were leaving, or if he'd been watching for us to go," said Mrs. O'Malley as she had a flashback to two nights before.

Mack grinned, which was a strange reaction to what his wife had said. "And now we're wallowing in woefulness, aren't we, Mave?"

Mrs. O'Malley snickered.

Doris raised an eyebrow at both of them.

Mrs. O'Malley explained. "I promised Mack that I'd write a poem called 'Wallowing in Woefulness' after going through that ordeal. I'm thinking about trying creative writing. I want to be artistic, like the rest of my family."

Doris wiped raindrops from her glasses with the hem of her red-striped sleeveless blouse. "I think the one and only poem I wrote was in the ninth grade. We were supposed to write a haiku. It went ... 'My shoelace untied / As I ran to the bathroom / My trip was cut short.'"

Mack winked at Doris. "What? That was it? No other poems since?"

"No. That, my friends, was the extent of my poetic expression for this lifetime. Well, speaking of poetry, I popped in to see how your new poetically named foster cat is doing. Where *is* Haiku?"

All three of them looked around.

"He was right here a minute ago. Haiku? Where are you?" Mrs. O'Malley spotted a long, fluffy brown tail behind the mini refrigerator. "There he is. I should have looked there first."

She pointed, and Mack lifted the cat into a hug.

"Gosh, I forgot how big he is," exclaimed Doris. She put her glasses back on her nose. "You are one enormous kitty, my furry friend. How's your new diet going?"

Mr. and Mrs. O'Malley met each other's eyes, both silently making an "uh-oh" expression.

"Ah. Well, never mind. There's been a lot going on here. We'll just let your next home and family worry about that diet, right Haiku? You can get all comfortable and get to know some people, and before you know it, you'll be adopted and loved forever." She headed for her umbrella. "I'm going to the pawn shop to check on Sylvia."

"Who's Sylvia?" asked Mack, releasing Haiku.

Doris leaned on the end of her umbrella. "She's a gorgeous cat with very unusual markings. Another foster, of course. You should pop over some time to see her. She's all white, but her tail is pure black, then there's a space, then a black dot. When she raises her tail, it forms a perfect exclamation point."

Mack covered Haiku's ears before he asked, "How come *we* didn't get the cat with built-in punctuation? After all, *we're* the fostering site that's filled with commas, periods, semicolons, and all that. Hardly seems fair."

"Well, I did give you this beauty named Haiku, didn't I? He's poetically perfect for your shop. But, if you'd like, go over and adopt Sylvia, why don't you? You can afford to hire another permanent shop cat, can't you?" Doris waggled her eyebrows at him.

Mrs. O'Malley looked hopefully at her husband, but he shook his head. It was the kind of head shake, however, that might mean "yes" after they'd gone to look at the cat, so Mrs. O'Malley decided right then and there that they shouldn't take a chance.

Doris shrugged, raising her umbrella. "Ah, well. It was worth a shot. You'd better hurry if you want to see that cat. She probably won't be available for adoption for very long.

Some English professor, librarian, or author will surely swoop in and grab her up. Ta-ta, folks!"

When they were alone again, Mrs. O'Malley sat on her chair and let Buglit climb onto her lap. She should have been working on the addresses and other paperwork for the books that had sold on the internet, but she couldn't make herself concentrate. She was tired from lack of sleep and sick with worry about too many things. A phone call from a man in New York who wanted to purchase a book they had listed online—a history of maple syrup production in Maine—roused her into action again.

"I know it's raining, and that I'll be gone for the afternoon, but don't we need a plan of attack regarding the books in the storage unit?" she asked after hanging up.

Mack rubbed his chin with his palm. "I say we let things cool down for a while. I should call the police station or walk there. We don't even know if the man who broke in here is roaming around free or not. I'm assuming Matt has been interviewed by now. His story might go a long way to preventing that crook from being released."

Mrs. O'Malley looked as gloomy as the weather outside. She pulled her chair closer to the computer and got to work at last, the cat still on her lap. "Call them, I guess. It's too rainy to walk there. All this is making me depressed. Why have there been hardly any customers lately, anyway?"

"A lot of the students are getting ready for final exams at the college. You know this is always a slow time of the year for us. At least we're still selling books online. And, after we sort through the books from the auction, we'll have a lot of interesting, fresh stock to sell in the shop and on the internet. Cheer up."

He turned off the radio station's slow orchestral music and put on a Cajun CD. "What you need is a good dose of crocodiles and crawfish, bayous and levees. There. Isn't that better?" Mack asked. His elbows flapped and his neck bobbed to the accordion and harmonica music.

"You know, while you're doing that crazy hopping around is precisely the minute a whole busload of old ladies is going to come walking in here."

"Let's hope!" he said, gyrating some more.

She burst out laughing, sending Buglit to the floor and Haiku racing along the hallway.

Just then three elderly ladies in yellow raincoats and hats came into the bookshop, happily surprised to be met with quite the party going on during such a wet, dreary day.

Allison was rolling out dough in her kitchen behind the sales and display counter of her tea shop, Miss Allison's Pastries of the Past. All around the main room were dozens of bakery-themed antiques, fiberglass animals, and other vintage items that had been advertisements for food in decades past. Since Mrs. O'Malley had last been in the shop, Allison had added a framed poster of Regular and Aussie, the two cats she'd adopted from the O'Malleys' bookshop the year before. Another new item was an enormous metal antique gorilla who was holding a flour sack and a spatula. On a pedestal below his feet, neon green and red letters spelled out, "You'll flip for Sally Jean's Flapjacks."

When Darla spotted the gorilla, she put a hand to her chest and said, "Holy bananas, Allison! Wherever do you *find* these things?"

Allison emerged from the kitchen, wiping her hands on her long apron before lifting it from around her neck. She was wearing one of her many vintage outfits. This one was a white jogging shorts ensemble from the 1970s, complete with a sweatband on her forehead. Two wrist sweatbands in white and blue terrycloth were pushed far up on her forearms to avoid contact with any food or ingredients.

"And where did you get those vintage Nikes?" Darla asked, walking closer. "Those aren't a replica. Those are actually from the seventies!"

"I spend too much time on eBay and Etsy," Allison answered. "You like them? Swoosh!"

"I envy you your sense of style. I tend to put on whatever's clean, or that doesn't have too much baby vomit on it."

"Oh ... baby vomit," Allison said dreamily. "That sounds *adorable.*"

All three ladies laughed as they walked to the display cases together. Allison stepped behind it to wash her hands at a porcelain sink that had a bronze hippopotamus head for a faucet.

"Speaking of babies, when are you and Todd getting hitched?" Darla asked as she browsed the cases of delicious-looking pastries, breads, doughnuts, muffins, and fudge.

"Soon. Maybe at Christmastime. There's no big rush since we're getting married in my parent's house. We don't need to book a venue that way. Just a few close friends and family. We'll say our vows, have some pastries and coffee, and then leave on some fab honeymoon."

Mrs. O'Malley's eyes widened. "I had you pegged as a lady who longed for a big wedding, Allison."

Allison slipped on a pair of plastic gloves. "I can almost guarantee it *will* be rather large. My parents have many social circles because of the charities they're involved with. My dad is on several boards, and mom has eight million relatives. However, I'm determined to keep this a very *small* large wedding."

Mrs. O'Malley slowly studied the offerings in the display case. "I'll have to get in here more often, even if it's only to keep up with your ever-growing menagerie. I'm a little glad that your cousin Roger no longer has his bakery close to our bookstore. It makes it easier to stick to my diet. When I walk to the post office, I always force myself to studiously ignore your inviting teacup-themed decorations as I pass by your door."

Allison took a closer look at Mrs. O'Malley from head to toe. "I *thought* there was something different when I saw you at the picnic. You look significantly slimmer, Mrs. O. I'd better not tell Roger you said you don't miss his shop. He's been hinting that he wants to come here and work for me. He's not handling retirement well."

"I thought his new dog, Noodle, would be keeping him busy. And his new photography hobby," Mrs. O'Malley said, glad that the subject had moved away from her diet since she was preparing to buy several fattening treats.

"Noodle P. Toobsox is now very handsome and well-fed, and there are a thousand photos of him on Facebook, but Roger still talks about coming in here at least one or two days per week. He wants to start making pasties."

Mrs. O'Malley looked confused. "I thought you were getting over your mixed-up way of speaking, Allison. Don't you mean 'pastries'?"

"Nope. Pasties. Roger, Marilyn, and Noodle vacationed in the Upper Peninsula of Michigan for a week, and apparently, they survived solely on pasties, giant cinnamon rolls, coffee, and jerky."

Mrs. O'Malley still looked confused. "I have no idea what you're trying to say they ate."

Allison laughed as she grabbed a cardboard box. "Pasties are these hearty meals made of ground meat or meats, diced potatoes, carrots, rutabaga, and onions baked inside a pie crust. Each pasty is so large that you need two hands or a plate and fork to eat them. He got very attached to them up north, and he thinks my shop could sell as many as he could make. I'm not sure this would be the right kind of restaurant for them, though. I don't sell any sort of meat or sandwiches."

"Now I want one, though," frowned Darla.

"You can buy them online. I ordered two dozen so I'd have some to share with Roger. I'll save one aside for you, Darla. You, too, Mavis."

"Oh, that would be very sweet of you. Say, did you hear about the new antique shop going into the building the carpeting store vacated? This town can use one. We haven't had one since Donna's closed."

"If so, it won't be as good as your sister's shop. I've been there three times already to look for gifts and anything that might fit in with my menagerie here. See the chef's hat on Featherlite Flour's parakeet?" She pointed to the sign-holding plaster bird near the front door. "I got that there. Fits him ferpectly. Oops. I mean perfectly."

Mrs. O'Malley nodded. "Quainty's place gets better by the day. Folks for miles around are telling each other about her selection. I think she'll do well with it for a long, long time."

Darla pointed out her selections in the display case as the two other ladies chatted, and Allison boxed them using squares of wax paper. A group of college kids poured into the shop and stood behind Darla and Mrs. O'Malley. The women finished their order, paid, said goodbye, and left for their meeting with Mrs. Dehlvi.

"Come in, come in. Hang your umbrellas on this rack. You are very welcome! I have tea made—hot and cold—and some coffee for you in particular, Mrs. O."

"Thank you, Daya," said Mrs. O'Malley as she and Darla walked from the front door to the living room. Darla handed Mrs. Dehlvi the box of pastries.

108

A moment later, a zooming silver blur raced out of Kris' bedroom, took a detour over the sofa, and bounded into the middle of the living room where it finally came into focus.

"Stomper! Oh, hello! Come here and let me hug you, Stompykins. Awww. I missed you, too. Look, Darla. He remembers me. Yes, Stomper. I am *very* happy to see you, too!" said Mrs. O'Malley, hugging her old friend, a former bookshop foster cat.

Mrs. Dehlvi smiled, watching Stomper rub his forehead under Mrs. O'Malley's chin. "That cat is a funny cat. We are good companions all through the day. We have our routine. He and I like to read the same books, and we like to garden together. He always stays near, right where I am weeding and planting and such. He is a very good cat for me—for all us. Thank you again for bringing us together, Mrs. O."

Mrs. O'Malley nuzzled the cat's forehead once more. She then put him on the floor where he wound around and around all three ladies' legs until they'd sat at the table in the dining room.

"How does he get along with Pip?" Mrs. O'Malley asked.

Mrs. Dehlvi smiled. "They are coming along, coming along. Every day I see some new proof that they are indeed coming along nicely. Pip is a very funny cat, also. Stomper likes to be my cat and Kris', while Pip mostly plays and sleeps with the two younger boys. We all get along fine."

On cue, Pip stretched and yawned, standing in his cat bed near Mr. Dehlvi's recliner.

"That one black spot over his eye is adorable," said Darla, bending to pet the cat. "I don't think I've ever seen such a marking on a cat."

Pip squinted at the ladies, pleased to have gotten what he was sure must be compliments.

A bright red and blue tablecloth had been laid out on the dining table, and freshly cut flowers of five different types sat at the center in a peach-colored ceramic vase of an unusual design. It almost looked like the miniature of a building you might see in a touristy part of Florida.

"Oh, Daya—that is ... I *love* that vase," exclaimed Mrs. O'Malley as she took a seat.

Mrs. Dehlvi smiled proudly. "I never use this one, but today is a special occasion, yes? I took it out of the back of my corner cabinet for our tea and talk. It is by Ettore Sottsass, and that is all I know—other than I love it. It was a gift from my father many years ago. My father would give me too many things if I allowed him."

Tea and coffee were poured after bakery was set out on a pink tray. As soon as the women had settled in to talk, yellow rays of light streamed through breaks in the clouds.

"Such a lovely day now you have come," said Mrs. Dehlvi, smiling at her company. "I do not often have ladies to tea, you know. Most of my friends are working ladies. Too busy. This is a *very* pleasant day for me."

Darla and Mrs. O'Malley looked at each other with apprehension.

"Daya," began Mrs. O'Malley, a note of warning in her voice. "We wish we were here to chat with you about the coming adoption and how beautiful the weather turned out today. But ... we're not. I'm afraid we have some startling news. It's about Kris."

Mrs. Dehlvi raised a hand to cover her mouth, her eyes going back and forth between Darla and Mrs. O'Malley. "Has the hospital called you and not here?" she asked quickly. "Has the school called? Is he unable to see again?"

"No, Daya," Mrs. O'Malley said, smoothing the tablecloth where her cup had wrinkled it. She looked at the woman reassuringly, despite dreading what she and Darla were there to say. "It's news of a different sort."

Darla sighed and lowered her cup onto its flowery saucer with a slight clink. "I'm the one who has the news about Kris. I don't know that what I have to tell you will really matter at this stage of Kris' life, but I thought that you and Mr. Dehlvi and Kris should know something. Mavis and I talked, and we decided to tell you first. You can tell your husband, and together you can talk to Kris."

After Mrs. Dehlvi took an unsteady sip of tea, she held the cup in both hands, looking at the reddish-brown liquid instead of at the ladies. "I feel like a little child now. Afraid. Afraid to hear what it is you have to say."

Mrs. O'Malley patted her arm. "Please don't be. This may amount to nothing at all in the end."

Darla told as much of the story as she could remember about the incidents that had happened many years ago, and then about what she had seen at the library the day before. Mrs. O'Malley and Mrs. Dehlvi never interrupted until almost the end.

"Show her the print of that article, Darla. See? These were Kris' parents. They're also the couple Darla saw who wanted to buy Ricki's baby," Mrs. O'Malley said, pointing to the pixelated faces smiling up from the creased paper.

Mrs. Dehlvi was very quiet. After a few moments, she pushed her chair back and went into the kitchen. She returned to the dining room with a small white pot of coffee and refilled Mrs. O'Malley's cup before carrying it again to the kitchen.

Darla and Mrs. O'Malley waited, but Mrs. Dehlvi didn't come back to the dining room for several moments. Darla folded the print and put it into the pocket of her yellow slacks. She shrugged at her aunt, wondering what they should do next.

Mrs. Dehlvi finally appeared at the edge of the dining room again. She leaned against the wall for support, looking weak and miserable. "I will tell Falak. Thank you, ladies. I need to think for a while about what you have told to me."

Darla and Mrs. O'Malley carried their cups, saucers, and plates into the kitchen, passing a very somber Mrs. Dehlvi.

She was uncharacteristically quiet as she stared only at the floor. Mrs. O'Malley tried to hug her goodbye, but the woman blocked her with half-raised arms.

"No. Please. I will cry as soon as you leave. Please ... do not make me cry before you go."

Darla wasn't going to let things end with that statement. She pulled Mrs. Dehlvi by the hand over to the sofa where she then sat with her. Mrs. O'Malley followed, sitting in the paisley recliner. Stomper stood near the television, his silver spotted tail nearly straight up, concerned but quiet.

"We need to talk a little longer, okay, Daya?" Darla still held the woman's hand. "We aren't going to leave you while you're this upset. I didn't tell you this to make you cry or to hurt you and your family. I think it's important that you know that there may be relatives of Kris' out there who don't even know he exists. If Ricki *did* sell her baby, and if that baby is Kris, there could be all sorts of consequences. What if the family *does* know about him? Or, what if the police have been searching for Ricki's baby? What if there's a genetic condition in that family? I couldn't keep this to myself, right? And, honestly, it would explain a lot. Why else would a young couple, after they passed away, have no living relatives who could have taken in Kris to raise him? And another thing ... what if it *wasn't* an illegal adoption all those years ago? What if the state knows about it and that's why they didn't seek close relatives when Kris needed someone to care for him? See? I told you what I know so you can find answers to these very critical questions. Don't tell me that you haven't wondered about some of these strange things before."

Mrs. Dehlvi nodded, tears in her eyes. "But he is *ours* now. *I* am his mother. Falak is his father. Dev and Bijay are his little brothers who love him. Dontae is coming soon, and he will be another brother to our Kris." She blinked a few times. "I do *not* want to lose him."

112

Mrs. O'Malley had a sudden thought. She rocked forward too quickly in her chair, and her purse slid to the floor. "Daya—what if you waited to try to find out more? It won't be too many years before he's eighteen. And, if Darla hadn't seen that photo in the newspaper, no one would have been the wiser, anyway."

Mrs. Dehlvi raised her eyes to look at the two ladies, her dark eyes damp, yet her expression growing stronger. "This is a karmic situation. You, Darla, were meant to see it, just as you were meant to go to the meeting with Ricki so long ago. You are the connecting line between us all. You are a chosen guide. To ignore this and to go on as if nothing had happened would be to deny some future beneficial event its own happening. I am sad, yes, but I will not be sad for much longer. Sitting here and listening to my heart, I believe that this has come about for a *good* reason."

Darla stood, retrieved Mrs. O'Malley's fallen purse, and gave it to her before saying to the still-seated Mrs. Dehlvi, "That is a very remarkable way of looking at things. I envy you your ability to make a tough thing seem ... fortuitous. I'm now a connecting line. I can see that we're *all* connecting lines to our friends and family. It's an interesting philosophy, and I'm going to look at it that way, too. How about you, Aunty Mavis?"

Mrs. O'Malley wiped her eyes with a tissue she took from her pants pocket. She blew her nose before struggling to get out of the large chair. She found that she couldn't answer, imagining too many unhappy endings to the story.

On the drive back to the bookshop and record store, Darla said, "I forgot to ask—do you know anything more about the man who broke into your place?"

"Yes. I totally forgot to tell you. Mack called the police this morning and found out that the man has never had so much as a parking ticket. The officer wouldn't give us any details, but he did say that we can sue for damages. He'll be sentenced for burglary. Even though he doesn't have a record, there could still be jail time on top of fines. Right now, he's out on bail, which is not good news. His sentence will depend on if there are what are called 'aggravating factors,' like if we can prove he threw a baseball at Kris that temporarily blinded him." She looked at her hands. "I just wish I knew what he was after. What was in those two boxes of books that he wanted to buy from Kris?"

"And why was it worth risking his freedom?" Darla asked, steering her pickup truck onto Main Street. She parked in front of the bank. "But books, though. Why? I don't mean to belittle books in general, but they aren't all that easily sold for fast money. It's not like there were *diamonds* in those boxes."

"We think there may be something hidden in the bindings. Or, maybe there were only books on *top* in those boxes. It could be that the man got to the auction site at the crack of dawn, found whatever it was that got him excited, and stuck them under some books figuring that that would be a good way to legitimately buy whatever it is he wanted. They could always later say that he bought so-and-so at auction and produce a receipt."

Darla raised an eyebrow. "Huh. I kinda doubt that. I mean—think about it. Don't folks who buy books at auction usually rummage through the boxes before they bid? How could they prevent other people from digging through the books? Also, didn't Matt re-box all the books?"

"Oh. Yeah." She crossed her arms. "Heck."

Darla laughed. "I love your face right now. You look cute when you're puzzled, Aunty Mavis."

Mrs. O'Malley opened the door on her side of the truck. "In that case, I have a feeling I'm going to look mighty cute all summer long."

Chapter Ten

"Should we take at least some of the books out of the storage unit? I don't think the criminal will try anything funny again. Do you?" asked Mrs. O'Malley the next morning.

She had been standing in front of one of the display windows, enjoying the sunlight before opening time. Buglit leaped onto the ledge beside her and squinted a greeting, and Haiku stretched out on top of the displayed books in a window a few feet away, enjoying the sun, too.

"This is the kids' last day of school, so I thought I'd work here today clearing out some of the books that are in the storeroom before Kris and I haul in more boxes. Should we bring them here, or sort through them in the storage unit?"

"I think you should bring them to the shop. I don't like the idea of you two out at the storage facility all day. It makes me nervous."

Mack turned on the stereo and the overhead lights. "Unlock the door, please." He thought for a moment. "I suppose we *ought* to go through them here, where there are plenty of people around. I doubt seriously, though, that that goon had any friends in on the caper."

Mrs. O'Malley smiled at the words "goon" and "caper." She patted Buglit's head before stepping to the door. While twisting the lock, she asked, "Do you suppose Kris has been told about Ricki by now?"

"Hmm," was all Mack replied.

"Hello, folks," said Mrs. O'Malley's brother, Danny. He held the door for a smiling, pretty, middle-aged lady. She was carrying a bag of cat food.

"Danny! I didn't know you were stopping by this morning. Feels like we hardly see you anymore. Hello, Lucille. Mack, do you remember Darla's mom? We met her at the picnic."

"Sure. Hi. Are you having a good visit with Darla, Jack, and the baby?" Mr. O'Malley asked before he stepped into the bathroom to put away some rolls of toilet paper he'd taken from home.

Lucille nodded. "And Dan."

"Well, of course," said Mrs. O'Malley. "You two are grandparents together now, aren't you?"

"And so forth," said Danny, winking at his sister.

Mrs. O'Malley slightly gasped, but then thought that she must have misunderstood.

Mack stepped back into the main room and tried to change the subject. "So, have you heard the jukebox yet, Lucille?"

"We danced to it last night," answered Danny. "Luce spent the night at Darla and Jack's. Lila Pearl and Patrick thought our moves were hilarious."

"That baby! L.P. loves to rock 'n roll. When one song ends, she pats the side of the jukebox, asking it to play another. I suppose she thinks she's performing magic," said Lucille, shifting the bag of cat food in her arms. "Mack, here is some food for the felines. Where would you like it?"

"Right here in my hands, thank you," said Mack as he took it from her. "Here's Buglit, leaping up to thank you."

"Hello! Buglit, is it? That is one adorable name."

"She lives here in the bookshop full time. The other cat, Haiku, is one that we foster. Haiku? Want to come over and say hello and thank you for this nice—no? Okay. He raised his head for a second when I called, but then plopped it back down again."

"We saw him in the windows when we were coming in. He's a big'un," said Lucille. She threaded her arm through Danny's and stood near the counter, smiling.

Mrs. O'Malley couldn't resist asking as she sat on the arm of the sofa, "Are you two ...?"

Danny shrugged.

116

"We're seeing how it goes," said Lucille.

"Yeah. What she said," Danny said as he kissed his ex-wife on her temple.

Mrs. O'Malley was visibly affected by the nearness of such romantic displays. She was about to ask another question when Mack nearly shouted, "Did you hear about our break-in the other night?"

"Yes. Just terrible! I can't imagine there's much crime in town. I suppose it made the papers," Lucille said as Danny put an arm around her waist and slid his thumb through one of her belt loops.

That movement sent a rush of color to Mrs. O'Malley's cheeks.

Mack saw her reaction and said, again a little too loudly, "No. Not that I saw, anyway. If we get to the bottom of the story, then it might be worthy of newsprint."

Lucille could see that Danny's intimate touching was making Mrs. O'Malley uncomfortable, so she moved away under the guise of visiting with Haiku at the windows.

"What if someone wants to buy the gardening book this cat is snoozing on, Mavis?"

"I think they're out of luck until after the sun has shifted," Mack answered for his still red-faced wife.

"What do you mean by 'the bottom of the story'?" Danny asked. "What have I missed?"

Lucille attempted to lift Haiku, but he wasn't cooperating at all and she let him spread out on top of the books again.

"Well, what *do* you know?" asked Mack.

"Only that someone smashed your door to pieces and that's why you're now sporting that new rose-tinted entranceway. That's what Jack told me last night."

Mr. and Mrs. O'Malley filled them in on the rest of the details.

"What—if you don't mind me sounding rude—what would a criminal want with a couple of boxes of vintage reading material?" Danny asked.

Mack said, "Mavis and I didn't get through all the boxes that evening. A lot of the ones Matt packed at the auction are still unopened out in the storage unit."

"Let me know if you need a guard when you're going out there to work, and I'll join you. Or, are you toting them back to the shop still boxed up?"

Mack tugged an earlobe. "We were talking about that earlier. I suppose bringing them here where there are a lot of folks milling around would be wiser."

"Sounds good. I can still go with you to load them into the van whenever you'd like."

"I was going to ask Kris to go with me tomorrow, but we can go now if you have the time. Or, do you two have plans?"

Danny shook his head. "We had breakfast at that unusual tea shop. I'm free now. Luce is heading home later today. I can drop her back at Jack's, then she can pack and take off. I'll come back here later this morning." He put an arm around Lucille again. "Well, I'll take this young lady over to Jack's to pick up her belongings, then I'll drive back here."

"Thanks for the kibble, Lucille," said Mrs. O'Malley, standing from the arm of the sofa. "I hope we'll see you again soon. This must be quite a drive for you. Don't you live in Ohio?"

"I'm retired now. I taught my last math and science classes last week. First thing I did when I got home was to do a load of laundry and pack for this trip. Now I'm free to concentrate on my glassmaking. I've been creating pieces for years and years, but only in my spare time. I'm thinking of renting a small space in a downtown somewhere. I might like to open a shop. I'm not tied to Dayton now, so I guess I can move anywhere I'd like."

"Well ... retired? You're so *young,*" said Mrs. O'Malley.

"I've put in my years—believe me! I loved teaching, but I want to do something else with my time." She paused, tugging on Danny's arm. "We'll go now so Dan can get back here to you, Mack. It was nice to see you both again. I love your bookstore! I'll have to browse to my heart's content the next time I'm in town. Have a wonderful day. Goodbye!"

When they were alone again, Mrs. O'Malley said, "Oh, Kris will be disappointed to miss going through the books." She sucked in a breath. "Wait—does he remember anything about the auction? Maybe he doesn't."

"Don't worry. There will still be plenty left to sort through tomorrow. I'll use Danny's help to get about a third of the boxes brought over. You and I can go through what will be here today and actually clean, price, and shelve them instead of simply pulling them out of their boxes."

She hesitated. "I'm not sure we'll be pricing and shelving all them as they come out of their boxes. What I *do* recall from the other night is that a lot of the books are nicer than average. I'll list those for sale online. I guess I can stack the better volumes behind the counter like we do with other big groups that need to be listed that way. I don't want to drag this out, either. While you're gone, I'll make more open space at this side of the room and shove the sofa closer to the bathroom. How about running to the sandwich shop before you go?"

"What would you like?"

"Um, egg salad on a crescent roll. And a small fruit salad, please. And a yogurt. Strawberry. And what did you think about that *romance* those two have going on?"

Mack hugged her against his side, smiling to himself. "I wondered when you were going to bring that up. All this talk about books and boxes and moving heavy furniture—I *knew* it wouldn't last long. You're like some sort of Jane Austen character."

She put her cheek on his shoulder. "I never in a million years would have thought that Danny and Lucille would get together again. I like the look of them together."

"It doesn't sound like they *are* together. She came for a visit. They probably had some twinges of nostalgia, that's all," he said, letting her go as the Mary twins pushed into the shop.

"We caught you, you love birds," said the younger Mary, grinning. She placed a flowery fabric bag full of paperbacks onto the sofa. "Rascals! Who needs romance novels? Just come into the bookshop."

"Mary! Don't tease," said the other Mary, putting her own bag of books next to Elephant Gerald.

Mack winked at them and peered into their book bags. "Any baked goods in there?"

"Mack!" exclaimed his wife. "I swear, you're having more doughnut withdrawal symptoms than *I* am."

He shrugged as he went toward the door to get their lunches. "Mine is a low-grade doughnut fever. I'll survive. Or I might not."

"Have your legs turned to jelly?" the older Mary teased.

"No, but I *am* feeling a little crumby."

While Mack and Danny were at the storage unit, Quaintance rushed into the bookshop.

"Mavis! Mavis!" she said, more excited than Mrs. O'Malley had ever seen her. She threw her purse onto the sofa and did a dance with plenty of arm movements. Finally standing still, she said, "Guess what! Guess!"

"You saw an alien at the Piggly Wiggly," guessed Mrs. O'Malley.

Her sister picked up her white purse only to slap it down again. "No! And *where* is there a Piggly Wiggly anywhere in this whole state? Guess again. A serious guess this time."

"Hmm. Did L.P. say 'Gramma'?"

"Oh, I wish! No!" She shook her head. "Guess again."

"You've found out that our brother and his ex-wife are having a fling."

"Oh, ha! Don't be silly," retorted Mrs. Cumber, clearly unaware of that situation. "Guess again."

Mrs. O'Malley reluctantly decided to let the Danny and Lucille story wait until later. "Well, since you're nearly jumping out of your skin with glee, I'm going to guess that you won a trip for two to beautiful Bora Bora."

Mrs. Cumber put her hands on her hips and complained, "You're not even trying."

Mrs. O'Malley nodded hello to a young couple wearing college t-shirts who had come in.

"Do you give up already?" Mrs. Cumber asked her sister.

"I couldn't possibly guess, Quainty. What?"

"Well, remember how I was going to have my own art exhibition in Lamarr, but then the gallery gave my date away to some big-shot from Chicago?"

"I do. That was sure a real disappointment, Quainty," Mrs. O'Malley said.

Mrs. Cumber did a triple hop in place before she finally said, "The gallery manager called me this morning. My show is back on again! I have a new date!"

"No!"

"I do!" Mrs. Cumber insisted. "In about a month. Eeeee!"

"Really? That's wonderful, Quainty! I'm not surprised. You should have had another chance right away."

Buglit leaped onto the countertop to hear what her lady friends were excited about. She rubbed a cheek against Elephant Gerald's uplifted trunk, satisfying a sudden itch.

"Mr. Grant-Jones said that some well-known art collector who had expected to come to my show called the gallery to ask when my alternate date was going to be, to be able to meet me and purchase an original painting. He saw a few examples of my works on the internet back when my show was first announced. Can you even *imagine* such a thing? A collector is interested in my artworks!"

Mrs. O'Malley hugged her sister tightly, jumping up and down right along with her.

"Mavis! It just occurred to me ... now I have to do it all over again! Oh, gosh."

"Do what again?" Mrs. O'Malley asked, releasing herself from the hug.

"When my show got canceled, I randomly put all my artworks back into my painting room. Then Elwood and I decided to move some of them so they wouldn't all be stuffed in that one room now that we finally moved our bed downstairs. That means I have to pick out my favorites for the show all over again. Ay-yi-yi!"

Mrs. O'Malley reached for her mug of coffee. "If you ask me, it should be easier this time. Since they're divided into two rooms, you can sort through them faster. Want me to help you some evening? Or, do you want to make the decisions on your own?"

Mrs. Cumber paused. "I think ... I wonder if Mr. Bookstore would do the helping—or the both of you. He was the one who saw value in my artworks when no one else ever had. I feel like I should have had him help do the picking-out the first time, but I was too shy to ask. Would you ask him for me? Please? I'll even make a banana cake for the occasion."

"You ought to know by now that you don't have to be shy with Mack."

Quaintance sat on the red sofa. Haiku jumped onto her lap, surprising her. "Well, hello there, big fella. Oh, Mavis! He is gorgeous! Ain't you a gorgeous kitty? Yes! Oh, look at his thick, tree-trunky whiskers stretch way out when I scratch under his chin. Say … where's this one's collar? Are you keeping him?"

Mrs. O'Malley sat, too. "No. He scratched it off almost immediately. You name the night, and we'll come over. How about if we bring Kris, too?"

Her sister nodded and smiled, still petting the cat. "I'm … I don't know how to say it. I was over the moon happy about that show. Then when it was canceled, I said to myself, 'I knew it. Not good enough, you old fool.' I was a little relieved not to have to go somewhere fancy and pretend that I was a real artist and eat cheese in cubes and all that. I've been enjoying my new shop so much that I almost didn't think about getting another chance. Or, I guess I didn't *let* myself think. Now, though … I swear, Mavis—I'm a little bit scared."

The young couple stepped back into the front room, each holding two books. "We wondered if you have a wedding-planning section," asked the attractive young woman with dark blonde hair. She then grinned and held out her left hand, showing the ladies a slender band with a small diamond solitaire.

Quaintance took the young lady's hand to examine the ring. "When did you two get engaged? That is a lovely ring. Is it vintage?"

"It is," she answered, letting Mrs. Cumber examine it longer. "And … just a few minutes ago, near a bookcase full of Nietzsche and Kierkegaard."

Both ladies rose to congratulate the young couple with handshakes.

"But why here?" asked Mrs. O'Malley. She felt sorry for Haiku, who had been unceremoniously dumped onto the floor, and bent to pick him up again.

The young man put his arm around his fiancé and said, "We met in the philosophy stacks about this time last year. I wanted a book on Schopenhauer, and Sarah already had one tucked under an arm. Neither one of us really likes Schopenhauer now, but we think it's great that he brought us together."

"We've both recently graduated," Sarah said, hugging the young man's arm, her hair falling behind her back as she looked up at him. "Now I feel like we're ready to take on anything."

They tried to pay for their philosophy books, but Mrs. O'Malley gave them to the couple as an engagement present, along with two softcovers about weddings and one wedding-march sheet music book.

"Aww ... sweet," said Mrs. Cumber. She grabbed a tissue from the box near Elephant Gerald and wiped her eyes. I am *such* a sucker for romance."

Mrs. O'Malley grabbed a tissue and wiped her eyes and nose, too. "We sure do have that in common. Mack thinks I'm a crazy lady when it comes to lovey-dovey displays in person. You know, he even today accused me of being a Jane Austen character."

Quaintance wiped her nose again, then stuffed the tissue up one of her red-checkered shirt sleeves, looking confused. "He did? What made him say that?"

Mrs. O'Malley took a long drink from her mug. She glanced around as much of the bookshop as she could see, making sure they couldn't be overheard. "I had a visit today from Danny."

"Oh. That's nice. He probably visits you more often than he does us. We're quite a long drive away for a casual drop-in. So, is there anything new since we saw him at the party?"

Mrs. O'Malley coughed lightly. "Yeah. I'd say so."

"Well?"

She leaned forward. "Lucille was here, too."

"Okay. Why are we whispering?" whispered Quaintance, one eyebrow raised.

"They were in here together. As in ... *together* together. Like, he had his lips on her face and his thumb through her belt loop."

Mrs. Cumber flopped onto the sofa cushions, landing with a noticeable bounce. "What? That's not true, Sissy. Are you sure it was Lucy? I mean, do you know who she *is?*"

"Of course I know her! Good golly, Quainty, we talked for like a half hour at the picnic."

Quaintance sat straighter and fixed her mussed hair. "I don't think you're seeing things clearly. You must have only *thought* that they were being romantic. They broke up years and years ago. Besides, she's way over in Ohio. And I thought she was teaching. I thought she was involved with an air-traffic controller. Are you sure?"

"I know what I saw. I know what the two of them said. She's retired from teaching, there was no mention of a boyfriend, and she almost seemed interested in moving to Anders Lake. And I *did* see them touching romantically. Why is it hard to believe? They were *married,* after all. I think they're sweet together."

Mrs. Cumber shook her head.

"What?" asked her sister.

"Theirs was not a marriage made in heaven."

"Everyone changes. Everyone grows up through the years. Danny, apparently, never had any other women in his life. I was starting to think that he would stay single forever. Well, now I think he was still in love with Lucille. Maybe no one else would do."

Quaintance shook her head again. "I don't think she'll move here, Mavis. She might have baby fever over little L.P. and wants to play grandma, but I can't see her falling back into Danny's arms. Lucy looks like a young woman still, and Danny looks his age. Oh, he's a good-looking older fella, I'll say that, but I can't believe she'd leave all her teacher friends, her house, her familiar surroundings, and glass studio friends for Anders Lake."

"Well, it's silly to speculate."

Mrs. Cumber shrugged. "She broke his heart. Or, he broke hers. I only know some of the story of their divorce, and that was the little I heard from Darla when she lived with us. Danny didn't talk about his personal life to me. Well, as you say—everyone changes and grows up. Lucille is very mature now and has her head on straight. I hope she's sure of her feelings before giving Dan too much hope."

"I like her. I do."

"I never said I *didn't*," Quaintance said defensively. "I probably even *love* her. She's been a part of the family for decades, in one way or another. I'll go so far as to say that she was likely the lesser of the guilty parties in their marriage break-up. I wish … maybe I wish they wouldn't go back toward each other. I wonder if they're both lonely. It's hard to be single when you're older. I hope they aren't reaching back in time simply because they were once in love and comfortable together."

Mrs. O'Malley inhaled and bit her lip. "I don't think so. Lucille has had serious relationships in between, from what Darla has said."

Mrs. Cumber shrugged. "No use talking about it. It'll be how it'll be. I probably shouldn't discourage them, even if my opinion is ever asked for. They're not kids, after all. I'm worried that Dan might get hurt again. Disappointed again." She looked through the windows. "Oh, and here's the van pulling up. I'm going to visit a while with Darla, but then I need to get back home to my antique shop. Elwood is an enthusiastic clerk, but he'd rather talk than sell."

"I'd rather talk than sell, too," Mrs. O'Malley said, elbowing her sister. "Especially with you. You're my favorite sister, you know."

Mrs. Cumber laughed.

126

Mack stepped inside and tossed his set of keys on the countertop. Danny came in behind Mack.

Mrs. O'Malley looked at the two men who stood together, almost looking like brothers themselves. "I wish things had been different. I wish we could have all been together in the same part of the world, knowing each other all along."

"We know each other now, though," said Mrs. Cumber. "I'm going to be satisfied. I'll fall apart if I let myself think about us being young together, too."

Mrs. O'Malley cleared her throat of some emotion. "So. Did you men look through any of the books while you were there at the storage unit?"

"Nope. We loaded about thirty or forty boxes and headed back here."

Danny shook Mack's hand. "Well, I'm heading back to my studio. I'm working on a cedar chest for a couple of newlyweds. She wants to keep her wedding dress in it, and some of the linens she inherited from her great-grandmother. That's what she asked for from the groom instead of a fancy honeymoon."

"Oh, that is such a lovely idea," said Mrs. Cumber. "But I hope they did have at least *some* honeymoon together. I remember mine still." She smiled broadly, evidently remembering a happy time with Elwood.

"That reminds me, Mack!" exclaimed Mrs. O'Malley. "While you were gone, the sweetest thing happened right here in our bookshop."

"Did Allison drop off some doughnuts?" he asked hopefully.

She rolled her eyes and huffed. "Even sweeter than baked goods. You and I are apparently responsible for two young people getting together. They met in our philosophy section last year, and today—while you were gone—they got engaged in that same section. Can you believe it?"

Danny looked around. "Are they still here?"

127

"No. He gave her a ring right here in our very own bookstore."

"We should advertise a singles night," said Mack. "And then put up a sign stating that every engaged couple gets to adopt a shelter cat after the wedding."

"What if they're allergic?" Mrs. O'Malley asked, smiling.

"To dating?" He shook his head. "Then they shouldn't come to our new singles night."

Mrs. Cumber laughed. "We would have had such fun together if we'd been couples together all these years."

Danny nudged Quaintance. "You and Elwood were so much fun when you were younger." He tilted his head back to laugh. "I can still see Waldo running around the yard, squealing in panic, with that chicken chasing him onto the porch, the both of them zooming ninety miles an hour right through the house and out through the back door!"

Mack got a drink of water as he asked, "Who's Waldo?"

"He was the neighbor's pig. A state fair breed champion American Yorkshire. The Robertsons brought him over one afternoon when a bunch of us young folks were gathered at our place before heading over to the lake to swim," said Danny. He grinned before he went on, "Waldo had been pestering Dad's chickens, and one of the hens had had enough. Everyone's question number one: why was Waldo over there? And number two: how did he not destroy half the house? He ran through the front screen door and out to the back door he rammed open."

"Quainty!" laughed her sister, her hand over her mouth. "Oh, no! Really?"

"We have stories," she said with an impish grin.

"But, wait. I want to hear about your honeymoon, since we were on that subject."

Mrs. Cumber gazed into the distance, collecting her memories. "We went to Lambton Shores in Ontario for a few days. I wanted to say that we'd had an exotic, foreign holiday, but Canada was all we could squeeze out of our limited pocketbooks. It was fun, though. We drove in Elwood's old Nash Rambler station wagon. We camped using a leaky tent that Uncle High Score had bought at some auction or another. It was *fun.*"

Mrs. O'Malley smiled, but then sighed and said, "Now that you and Danny are both here, I ... I want to share a poem with you that I wrote."

Mack, Danny, and Quaintance looked at each other, puzzled.

"You wrote a poem?" asked Mack.

She took a folded sheet of paper from under the monitor. "I did." She raised her eyebrows at her husband. "Remember? You gave me that challenge."

"Oh, yeah," Mack said, crossing his arms, smiling. "What was that title again?"

"Wallowing in Woefulness."

Danny and Quaintance glanced at each other, all humor leaving their faces. Mrs. O'Malley saw their reaction. She nearly reassured them that her poem wasn't a sad one, but, in thinking about what she'd written, she decided maybe it was.

"Read it to us, please," said her sister, sitting on the sofa. She patted the cushion next to her, and Danny took a seat. Mack leaned against the reference bookcase.

Mrs. O'Malley glanced around the main room of the shop, making sure that no customers were nearby to hear her as she started to read.

"Wallowing in Woefulness

Life without my sister, my brother, too
was ... as it was.
They were unknown, unmissed
My only-child childhood happy
busy and loved

129

Green leaves touched my window
and that maple seemed to be enough of a family tree for me.
I could sit high inside of it,
my back against its trunk
and see as far as I wanted to see
nestled with the bark supporting me
thinking of family as my adopted folks and theirs
not dreaming of others that would share my same blood
thicker than sap
that ran in blue rivers beneath my comfortable skin

But then my world flipped.
I found brother and sister, niece
deceased parents
heard stories, met a history I did not know
as its leaves brushed against my soul.
Smiling by day
happy to be retrieved into arms and branches
hugged closely
but wallowing in woefulness in secret by night
missing a beautiful past I couldn't even dream about

In quiet darkness, I mourn
Mourn all that had spun on without me for decades
on a farm not so far from me
not so very far at all.
And I cry out this repeated thought:
My spirit should have tried to find them.
Why did I never try at all?"

She folded the page in half, then in half again. The room was silent except for the stereo's classical music and the faint sounds of the air conditioner.

Mack moved to his wife. He took the paper from her fingers. "Nothing woeful here, my dear. That, I must say, was just about perfect." He winked at her, and she blinked back at him, pleased but embarrassed.

Danny and Mrs. Cumber sat silently. After a moment, Danny put a hand over Quaintance's and gripped it tightly. They seemed unable to lift their eyes.

Mrs. O'Malley, seeing their reaction, said, "Oh, *no.* Oh, Danny and Quainty. I'm terribly *sorry!* I shouldn't have blurted it out like that. I don't know why I shared it, now. Oh, dear! I wasn't thinking of your feelings at *all."*

Quaintance shook her head and looked into her sister's eyes. Her face was red, and her eyes were moist. "It was beautiful, Sissy! I think it was especially meaningful to me because I've only known my own point of view. I hadn't thought how you must have felt when we came into your life like we did. *I* was overwhelmed, but I thought you were fine. I spent my life knowing about you. Missing you. Terribly. And Danny missed you—maybe even more than I did. What I just heard you say was very touching. It let me see things as you must have felt them, and still do. That's why I'm sad. We should have talked more about our feelings." She paused, waiting for her brother to look at her.

Danny did at last, but he merely nodded and looked away again. He wiped a hand across his stubbly chin.

Mrs. Cumber stood up. "I knew you were gone. It was *our* fault for not looking harder for *you.* There'll never be a way to make it up to you. Never. I'm so, *so* sorry about this, Mavis."

Mrs. O'Malley sobbed. After a few seconds, she said, "We didn't find each other only to blame each other ... for anything. The generation that separated us wouldn't want us to stand here feeling guilt and regret. That generation did not separate us for any shameful reason. I understand. I don't blame anyone for *anything.* I didn't mean to make it sound like I'm angry. I'm not. I'm ... mournful. Or, I should say that I used to be. Maybe writing it on paper let me make my peace with missing out on a life with a brother and sister and our father and grandfather on the farm. If I had stayed there with you, it would have been a burden on the family. I had a wonderful childhood, and it and everything afterward led me to Mack, my friends, my life now." She stepped closer to the sofa to take Danny's hand. Smiling into his eyes, she continued, "Now I feel that I have it all. Everyone and everything. From this moment on we're going to do nothing but celebrate."

"Well said," said Mack.

A young man in a business suit came into the shop then, carrying a box of books. "I heard that you take books in trade. Will you look at these?"

Mr. O'Malley stepped forward to wait on the customer. Mrs. O'Malley and Quaintance sat again with Danny on the big red sofa. Seeing them settling in, Buglit leaped onto the back cushions, and Haiku jumped onto Danny's lap.

"We're okay," said Quaintance as she scratched Haiku's neck. "The Kinonen kids are quite all right."

"'Kids.' Ha!" Danny said, breaking his silence.

Mrs. O'Malley was about to come up with some philosophical statement about how you're only as young as you feel when the Mary twins pushed into the shop past Mack, there again since they'd had to cut their earlier browsing short.

"Hiya, kids," one of the elderly Marys said, waving as she and her also-gray-haired friend Mary passed them to head to the far end of the main room.

"See?" laughed Quaintance. "Perspective is important."

The three siblings all stood as Mrs. O'Malley said, "Dan, did you hear your sister has a new exhibition date scheduled?"

Danny's eyes widened in surprise. He said to Quaintance, "I'm your agent! How come I'm the last one to know when, of all things, you go off and get yourself a show somewhere?"

132

She smiled. "Not just somewhere, brother. The *same* somewhere as before. The gallery called and asked me to take a new date."

"Oh, terrific! That is amazingly great, Quainty! When?"

"In about a month."

He exhaled as if he'd been holding his breath for a long time hoping that would happen for his sister. "I am so happy, Sis! I still get a cut even though I had nothing to do with this show, right?"

"Um, noooo."

"Scrooge," complained Danny.

All three of them laughed.

"Okay. I need to think about getting back to my own projects," said Danny. "Mavis, I know you two need to go through the auction books. Let me help Mack get them into the shop, and then I'll take off. Quainty, are you heading back to your Barntiques?" He surreptitiously slid the poem off the countertop and put it into the back pocket of his jeans.

Mrs. O'Malley saw the move, but she didn't say anything about it. Her face was slightly pink with emotion as she briefly hugged Quaintance, saying, "She is. I'll let you go. Thanks for visiting, and I am very, very happy about your new show."

Danny walked Quaintance outside after they'd said goodbye to Mack. Mrs. O'Malley watched through the window as her brother and sister spoke to each other for a couple of minutes.

"Thirty-five dollars in trade, Mavis," Mack said.

She nodded but wasn't paying attention to what he'd said. She was trying to figure out what was being discussed outside under the small tree near the van.

Mr. O'Malley looked from his wife to the couple his wife was staring at, saying softly, "I like your poem, Mavis. Keep

133

writing. I think it's great you found a way to say what you've been feeling."

She pulled her attention back to her husband and nodded. "How much in trade?"

"Thirty-five."

"Thirty-five. I'll let the man know. You go ahead and bring in the books."

As soon as Mack stepped out of the bookshop, Quaintance and Danny stopped talking and separated. Mack then swung open the side doors of the old, blue cargo van, and he got busy with the task of hauling boxes into the shop.

Chapter Eleven

On the evening of the last day of school, Mr. and Mrs. Dehlvi announced that Dev and Bijay were going to a friend's house to spend the night. Kris was surprised, because usually when there was going to be a sleepover, the boys talked about it for days in advance. They seemed as surprised as Kris did when their mother made the announcement. Once they'd all eaten together, the boys hastily packed their overnight bags and were then picked up by Mrs. Goodman and her two sons.

As soon as Mrs. Dehlvi closed the front door, she asked Kris to shut off the television. Mr. Dehlvi sat in his recliner in his night clothes and robe, holding a cup of hot tea. He motioned for Kris to sit on the sofa next to Stomper.

Mrs. Dehlvi sat on the other side of the cat. She seemed sad and nervous, making Kris' stomach tighten into a hard knot.

"Little Kris—I mean *Kris,*" she started, but couldn't think of how to continue. She petted Stomper's silvery fur, and he shifted so she could pet his stomach. He purred against her leg as if he understood her worries. Pip went to sleep in the corner of the dining room on a floor pillow that already had a lot of his white fur on it.

"Your mother and I have had some news," Mr. Dehlvi said, taking a sip of tea and swallowing it loudly. His eyes softened as he put his cup on the end table and leaned forward. "We now intend to tell you what it is, but your mother and I are reluctant to do so."

Kris looked back and forth between them. "Am I going to be blind again?" he asked, breathing a little harder.

"No, no, no, Kris. Nothing like that," said his mother, shaking her head for emphasis. "No. This is not us saying anything like that to you. All right?"

Kris nodded, still anxious.

Mrs. Dehlvi found she didn't have the energy to speak. Eventually, she pulled her loose, dark hair off her neck to one side, trying to cool herself. She finally looked to Mr. Dehlvi for help.

"I think that we will start with Darla," he said.

"Darla?" asked Kris, his eyes widening. "Is *she* okay? Is it the baby? Oh, Mom!"

Mr. Dehlvi spoke the answer. "They are all fine. Yes. Quite so. But Darla held a key that we did not know anyone possessed. Let me start again." His father leaned back in his chair and pulled a lever, lifting the footrest into place with a snap. "You and your friend Katrina were standing at the theater door, yes? Wanting in for a photo of your parents?"

Kris nodded, confused. He hadn't told them.

Mrs. Dehlvi, more relaxed since her husband had started the conversation, took up the story, feeling that she could tell it best since she had heard it directly from Darla. Her Indian accent was heavier than usual, a sign to Kris that she was feeling emotional. "She took you to the newspaper, and then to the library. There she helped you to find the article about the accident, and that article included photos of your mama and daddy, as they had looked when they were younger people."

Kris nodded again. The worried look left his face. He thought the story couldn't possibly be a terrible one if it was only about an accident that had happened years before.

"She printed out a copy of the article for you, but she also asked for a second copy for herself."

"Really? I didn't see her do that. Oh, yeah. I think Kat and I were looking at the case of new arrivals when she was at the librarians' desk. Why in the heck would she want a copy?"

Mrs. Dehlvi took a tissue from a box on the end table. She gripped it with both hands for a moment before wiping her nose. "When she left you, she went quickly to talk to her aunt—your Mrs. O. They talked together. Both of these ladies visited me this afternoon. I then spoke to your father in his office, and now here we are, sharing this news with you."

Kris felt more confused than ever. "News? *What* news? I mean, it was strange of Darla to want a copy of the accident story, but I don't know what you're trying to tell me. How could anything about my first mom and dad be news?"

Mrs. Dehlvi wiped her eyes and sniffed softly. "She thinks, little Kris, that your mama and daddy were not your real parents. A lady named Ricki that Darla worked with as a waitress a long time ago might be your real birth mother. This is what Darla thinks."

Kris sprang from the sofa. He hit his knee on the coffee table and cried out, which caused Stomper and Pip to run from the room in fright. Holding his knee, he swiveled back and forth from his father to his mother, his face incredulous. "Why would Darla say that? What? No! That can't freakin' possibly be true. *What?* Darla would have told me right there in the library. What are you *saying?*"

"She needed a moment to think. The memories of her time with this girl Ricki were unclear to her at first, but she is quite sure now of the details that she told to me."

Mr. Dehlvi popped the lever on his chair again, this time sending the footrest down. He left his chair and sat on the sofa, pulling Kris with him.

To Kris, it felt like the world had switched into slow motion. He could smell the woodsy odor of his father's soap, and feel the cushions under him, holding him as if he were afloat. His knee pounded with pain. He focused on the steady rhythm of his own breathing, and it reminded him of a song his first mother sang to him at night when he was very young.

Mr. Dehlvi said, "Darla thinks that a girl she worked with when she was a waitress was pregnant with you. Darla went with her—Ricki—to meet your parents at a restaurant. Apparently, they convinced this girl to go home with them so she could give birth there. They were arranging to raise this girl's baby in exchange for money."

Still feeling as though none of what he was hearing was real, Kris tried to stand again. His father held his arm, keeping him seated. "Listen. Listen. All is fine. All will be well."

Kris pulled away and pounded his legs with his fists. He squeezed his eyes tightly shut. Every inch of him resisted this news. In an instant, his slow-motion world slammed into a faster gear. "Mom ... Dad ... no," he said, referring to his other set of parents. "I was *yours. No!*"

Mrs. Dehlvi stopped his hands from pounding his legs. "Oh, Kris. We don't know if this is true or not. Darla never saw Ricki again, and anything could have happened. She told me that the one thing she does know for sure is that the couple who had talked with Ricki about her baby was the same couple in the photos of the accident. However, there could have been any outcome after that meeting."

Mr. Dehlvi cleared his throat. "Your mother is crying because this could mean that you may not belong to us, Kris. There may be another mother and father for you somewhere. A father who never knew he had a baby boy. That is not fair for him. You may have siblings or half-siblings. Grandparents and cousins and aunts and uncles. Or, perhaps ... perhaps the father *did* know. He may be missing you and looking for you even now."

In the light of early morning, Kris remembered every word, every glance from the night before as he sat staring through his open window. He wished that his little brothers were there in the house. He wished Stomper or Pip had been

138

on the bed when he woke up. He grabbed a pillow and hugged it tightly, aching for something to hold. His world had been spun upside down again, and he hated it. His temples throbbed with a dull headache.

A thousand questions swirled in his brain as he padded along the hallway to the bathroom. Who was he? Where is Ricki now, if anywhere? Who is her baby's father? Did his parents really buy him? Did he have brothers and sisters out in the world somewhere? Or, was he the same person as he'd always believed he was—the real son of parents who had been killed years before?

Sitting alone at the dining room table with a bowl of cereal, he tried to calm himself down. His legs shook as if they had a mind of their own, and his sore knee kept hitting a table leg. One second what he'd been told didn't matter, and the next second it *did* matter. He wanted to get out of the house. School was over for the summer, but he had the bookshop to run to.

Kris took a quick shower and got dressed. When he emerged from the bathroom, his parents were sitting at the table with cups of tea. They were still in their night clothes. It was strange to see them in the light of day dressed that way, and with their hair uncombed. They didn't look rested.

"Come come," said Mrs. Dehlvi, motioning for him to sit with them.

Kris shook his head, wanting to run as fast as his legs would carry him. His heart pounded in his chest. He looked at the front door and back to his mother.

"Yes. Please."

Stomper rubbed his head against the boy's leg, then reached for a hug. Kris fought with himself for a moment before lifting Stomper into his arms. Kris stood against the wall, not sitting at the table, but also not leaving. He looked at the Dehlvis, took in a long breath, and let his eyes roam the dining and living rooms of his home. He scratched his cat's tabby-patterned neck. "I decided: when I'm eighteen I'll find out."

"Too many people know already," his father said sadly, looking at his tea.

"I don't care. I'll ask them to keep quiet for now. They will if I ask them to," Kris said, letting Stomper go to have his breakfast in the kitchen. "Nothing should mess up our bringing Dontae here. I thought about that in the shower. If there's any problem, you might not get to adopt Dontae. He needs us. We need to have him, too. Please. *Please* let me make this decision. I'll be eighteen before you know it. I'll be an adult then, and in the meantime, no one can take me away from you. *Please,* Mom and Dad!"

Mr. Dehlvi looked over at his son's urging, pleading eyes. Kris raked his fingers through his dark blonde bangs, lifting them off his sweating forehead.

Mrs. Dehlvi reached for Kris with both arms while she still sat, and Kris did finally walk to her. She hugged his waist, her robed arms holding him tightly, keeping him there. "We love you more than you will ever know. I do not want to do something that you have asked us not to, but we are honorable people. If we cannot adopt a boy because we were not aware of this situation, then the world is not the fair place I have always lived in. No. There could be no way that Dontae would be barred from us. Not over this, at least. We did nothing wrong. And the state will not take *you* from us, either, Kris."

Mr. Dehlvi said, "We will do this: we will tell the police what Darla has said. If they know of a missing child fitting your age, then so be it. We will go from there. It will likely take genetic testing to prove that you are someone else's child, but I think if there is no missing boy fitting your age in this area, then there will be no testing. And when you are eighteen, as you said, you may decide if you would like to find this Ricki on your own."

140

Mrs. Dehlvi felt Kris shaking, but couldn't think how to calm him down. She only looked at her husband, and he only looked at his wife.

"I will go to the police station alone today," said Mr. Dehlvi, standing. He nodded to his son, looking determined. "Kris, I know you want to be getting to your first day of summer at the bookshop, so off you go. Daya, we will have some prayers and breakfast. I'll meditate for the rest of the morning, and then I will go to make this report."

Kris felt his mother hesitate, but then she did slowly lower her arm as if balancing a newborn fawn, waiting to see if he would stand or fall.

"Kris! You're here already," called Mack from across the parking lot. Kris was sitting on the back steps, waiting for the O'Malleys to arrive.

"And Matt and Katrina, too," exclaimed Mrs. O'Malley as she walked around an SUV carrying a ceramic travel mug of coffee and her purse. "Your first day of summer vacation and you kids all got up early to come here?"

"We all know about Ricki now," said Katrina, walking to meet Mrs. O'Malley halfway to the door. She linked her arm through the woman's. "I'm glad Kris came over to get us this morning. I wondered why Darla was acting super extra strange at the library, and now I know."

They all looked at each other for a moment, all feeling the same way.

"Kris said his dad is going to talk to the police today," Matt said as Mack unlocked the back door. The group moved inside, and the door closed behind them. The soft scent of used books was familiar and welcome. Buglit mewed her morning greetings, excited to see more people come in through the back door than she had expected.

141

As Mack turned on the lights and air conditioner, Kris said, "Yeah. I wish he wouldn't do that. I asked my folks not to do *anything* about this. I worry that they won't be able to adopt the new kid. Dad said that he'll ask if there's a missing person's report on a boy my age. If there isn't, he'll let it drop. I can always do some investigating on my own when I hit eighteen. If I want to."

"Why would there be a missing person's report?" asked Mrs. O'Malley as she put down her coffee and purse. "If Ricki *sold* your folks a baby, you wouldn't be reported as *missing.*"

"There's a father out there. He might be looking for his baby."

"That's assuming he knew he'd fathered a child." Mrs. O'Malley sighed. "Layers upon layers. But don't you want to know for your own peace of mind? You must have questions. And ... you might have brothers or sisters and other relatives. Are you sure you want to put this off for years?"

"I have brothers and a sister in my mind. Right? I've got Dev and Bijay, and Matt and Kat. If there are others hanging around somewhere, I'll find out about them later. If I choose to. I can't know how I'll feel in three years."

"Three years? Aren't you only fourteen, Kris?" asked Mack, switching on the stereo.

"I'll be fifteen this fall."

"Me, too!" said Katrina and Matt at the same time.

"That seems impossible," Mrs. O'Malley said, shaking her head at the mysteries of flying time.

When all the lights were on, after the cats had been fed and watered, after the litter boxes were cleaned, and the first customers of the day had come inside to shop, Kris stood in front of the stacks of books from the auctions that had been taken from their boxes. "This doesn't seem like all of them. I thought we had the van full."

"There are a ton of boxes left in the storage unit," said Mack. "We took these out of their boxes yesterday and looked carefully through them, but only to see if any might be ones that the thief may have been crazy about. I need to sort them all again into books I can price and shelve based upon my own knowledge, and ones I'll have the missus look up on rare book sites on the internet. If she sees any that are worth more than average, she can list those ones for sale online; otherwise, she'll price them for our shelves."

Kris sat on the arm of the sofa petting Haiku, who was stretched out drowsily along a back cushion. The boy whispered to Mr. O'Malley, "Well, *did* you find anything super rare and valuable in this first group?"

Mack shook his head.

Matt stood with his hand on the door. "Come on, Kat. Let Kris get to work. We'll head to the lake after we stop by home for our lake-going stuff. I'll walk Browser, too."

Katrina looked at Kris, then back to her brother. "Um … you know … I was going to help Mrs. O wrap books for mailing. You go on ahead, though."

Mrs. O'Malley resisted her first instinct to tell Katrina to go with Matt. Something in the way the girl had spoken made her think that Katrina was hopeful that she could stay in the shop. "Well, that would be very nice, young lady. I can always use another pair of helpful hands."

Matt glowered at his sister. "I thought we talked about pairs of shoes. Don't you want to try some others on?"

"No. These are cute and comfy. And smart. And just my size," she said indignantly.

"Oh, do you need to shop for new shoes, dear?" asked Mrs. O'Malley, slightly confused.

Katrina pointedly shook her head at her brother, her blue eyes flashing a warning that he should stop talking in code about Kris. "You go swimming. I'll meet you at the lake later."

Mrs. O'Malley looked at Kat's pink sandals. "Oh, those *are* very nice, Katrina. But if you had planned to shoe shop today, that's fine."

"Matt's confused," she said, glaring at her brother. "I might not want to wear these forever, but I love them now."

Matt shrugged. "Well, bye, everybody."

"Bye!" they each called in return.

Mrs. O'Malley and Katrina walked around to the computer.

"Grab a pencil, Kris, and we'll start pricing these," Mack said, lifting a heavy black leather Bible from the top of one stack.

Kris stepped to Elephant Gerald and took a sharpened pencil from its vase back. "So, you're sticking around here for a while today?"

"I thought I'd help Mrs. O with the internet sales," Katrina answered, her face reddening.

"Oh. That's nice. It balances things out in here."

She faced Mrs. O'Malley so Kris couldn't see how happy she was that he wasn't upset to have her in "his" bookshop.

Mrs. O'Malley had already warmed up the computer for the day. She sat on her chair and Katrina looked over the woman's shoulder. "First off, Katrina, I make a list from the emails of all the books sold since the last time I mailed out a group. See? I copy the notifications' title to this document, go back to the email and copy the author, then add the inventory number. Each of those numbers has a little code in it to let me know what color the book's spine is, and if it has a dustjacket or not, or if it's a softcover or hardcover. And the number at the end is a size code. I repeat this back and forth over and over until I have what I call a 'findy list.' I print it out and use it to locate all our sales that will later be wrapped and mailed."

Katrina watched her copy and paste and copy and paste for a few moments before asking, "Why don't you use an Excel file? If you can download a sold-listings report from each site you sell through, you can copy the columns containing your book title and author and the description codes, which also will have their own column. You can then create a findy list document in no time at all."

Mack, Kris, and Mrs. O'Malley all looked at her in surprise.

"What?" Katrina asked.

"I don't know how to do any of that," Mrs. O'Malley admitted. She got up from the chair and had Katrina take her seat. "You show me what you're talking about. Please."

As Katrina did just that, Mrs. O'Malley said, "Mack, why didn't we hire this girl years ago? Think of all the time and trouble she could have saved me every day!"

Katrina's cheeks reddened again; she felt embarrassed but pleased. A couple of minutes later, she said, "There! Done. Print this out, and you're all set to search for the books that have sold."

As the printer was warming up, Mrs. O'Malley said, "How about if I show you how I've been dealing with customer addresses and receipts?"

"Sure. This last semester we studied a *ton* of things that might help save bunches of time." She paused to examine the computer's icons. "I see that you've already got the program installed that I learned about. I'll show you how to use it for bookselling and inventory. If … if you'd like me to, that is."

"Well, my dear, that would be fan-tastic!" She looked at her husband. "Macky, I'm getting more modernized by the minute over here!"

"I can hear that. Thanks, Kat," he called, not looking up from the stack he was sorting.

Kris sat on the arm of the sofa again, smiling at Katrina. Having her there made the bookshop seem even more fun. He turned his attention back to Mr. O'Malley and the job at hand, writing the price and code in each book as he was given it before separating the books into new stacks—one for each room in which they would be shelved.

Katrina printed out two copies of the findy list, and she and Mrs. O'Malley searched the rooms and shelves to find all fifteen books they would need to wrap. Kris and Mack continued to get a lot of the common books priced and in stacks for shelving. The rest were being put behind the counter for Mrs. O'Malley to later research on the internet.

Customers came and went, books were mailed to their new owners, lunches were eaten, and jokes were told. Kris let himself mostly forget how upset he had been the night before and that morning. Buglit gave Haiku a bath in what was his favorite sunshiny spot in one of the display windows.

"Still nothing in this group, Mavis," Mack said as he and Kris were nearly through them all. "I mean, there are some really *good* books, and some great ones on Michigan waterfalls and Western Chinese history, but nothing that would be worth committing a crime over."

"Are you one hundred percent sure?" Mrs. O'Malley asked him.

"Unless I'm totally off my game, I'm very sure."

She eyed the stack of flattened boxes. "Well, maybe you'll find some rarities when you look through the next group."

When all the first large group of books from the auction had been priced or set aside, Katrina said to Kris, "I can help shelve them, too. That way you and Mack can go pick up another load from storage right away."

"Don't you want to get to the lake, Katrina?" asked Mrs. O'Malley.

Katrina's lips parted in surprise. "The lake? Oh, yeah. The lake. I forgot. Matt's long gone from there by now, I'm sure."

"I'll put these flattened boxes in the basement. After that I'll be ready to go when you are, Kris," said Mack. "Thank you, Kat. You're a big help."

She rubbed her nose to secretly smile behind her hand. She glanced at Kris for his approval, too. He didn't disappoint.

"Just don't take over my whole job, Kat," Kris said, pretending to scowl.

She looked over her shoulder and twitched her freckled nose at him.

After Mack and Kris had left, Katrina took each of Kris' book piles from the back side of the sofa and shelved them carefully. She wasn't familiar with all the sections in the shop, so she had to ask a lot of questions. When she was nearly done, she took a break for a cup of water.

After Mrs. O'Malley closed the cash register after ringing up a sale of books about penguins to a boy and his mother, Katrina said, "Mrs. O? I've noticed that when you get a book with a dustjacket ready to mail you put the jacket into a clear, protective sleeve thing. Why don't you put expensive dustjacketed books into those sleeves before they go out on the shelves?"

The woman slid her hands into the pockets of her slacks. "Well, I guess because it would take too much time. They look a zillion times better in the sleeves, don't they? They make the colors pop. We have a lot of the sleeves on hand since we buy them in bulk, but every time I think about putting one on each jacket, I nearly break out in hives. It would take too long. I'd never get my other work done."

"But wouldn't it mean more sales? I know if *I* saw a book in a sleeve, I'd be way more likely to put down my money than if it didn't have one. I know if I see something colorful and shiny, I want it."

Mrs. O'Malley sat on her computer chair. She pushed up her glasses and sighed. "I agree. Well, maybe I can select a few each day—some of the more expensive books that are in the cases to start with."

"Orrrrrr," said Katrina, stretching that word out dramatically, "you could have *me* do that."

"Oh, sweetie pie. You are young, energetic, and on your summer break. You need to go out in the sun and wind, ride your bike, play with your dog, eat ice cream, and read funny and heartbreaking books. You should *not* be stuck in a stuffy bookshop with two ancient old-timers and a lot of book dust."

Katrina, a look of resolve on her face, pulled her blonde hair into a ponytail, and secured it with a rubber band she found in Elephant Gerald's back. "I'll go and get some of the rare books from the cases to start with. Besides being prettier, by putting them in sleeves, they can't get damaged from handling. Any dustjacketed books out on the open shelves will stay protected, too."

Half an hour later, the O'Malley's van hovered in the street for a moment. Kris jumped out of the passenger side and shut his door again. Mack then drove off without him.

"Where's Mack going?" asked Mrs. O'Malley to Kris when he came into the shop.

"There weren't any close parking spots on this side of the street. He's going to drive around a few blocks and try parking again." He took his cup and filled it with water from the sink. "Hey, Kat. I didn't think you'd still be here. What's up?"

"I'm putting new sleeves on the dustjackets. I finished shelving."

He swallowed his water while looking at her over the rim of the cup. "I don't know ... I think you'd better cut this out, Kat! You're making me look lazy!" he teased. "I hope this is a one-day thing for you. I doubt the O'Malleys would let me keep hanging around if they get the idea that they can have you, instead."

"I don't think you should hog them," she said, teasing back.

"If you let them see how smart you are, they won't want *me* in here apprenticing. It might be fun to have you stay, but I can't take that chance."

Katrina resisted smiling. "I think, then, that maybe they *should* replace you with me. Yes, that would be for the best, now that I've had a little time to consider the matter."

"You go off and find your own booksellers."

"But I like *these* booksellers."

"Yeah, but I found them *first*. They've been *my* cool bookselling friends for like ... forever!"

"Hog!"

"Thief!"

"Stingy!"

Mrs. O'Malley laughed as she went to the storage room.

Kris was still smiling as he pushed open the door to see if Mack was coming. A parking spot had just become available. "Here he comes."

The next batch of boxes was soon in place behind the big red sofa. Buglit took a few leaps and bounds until she'd made it to the top of the tallest stack. From there, she meowed very loudly, her mouth wide open in joy at staking a prime claim at the peak of the book mountain.

"Look! She didn't even need to put hiking boots on to get up there. Shall we get you a little flag with a kitty face on it?" Kris asked, petting the calico.

Buglit didn't know he was teasing about the flag. "Rrrowl!" she said, thinking it was a very good idea.

Katrina slid the dustjacket of a 1940s children's illustrated novel into a plastic sleeve as she said, "Mrs. O'Malley?"

"Yes?"

"I've been thinking."

"About what?" she asked, sliding on her chair closer to the girl.

"From helping you to find the internet sales today, I know that you shelve the online-listed books right in with everything else."

"Uh-huh. That way our in-store customers can easily look at those books, too. When they sell in the shop, I remove them from the internet."

"Wouldn't the online books be easier to find if you made them stand out on the shelves somehow?" Katrina asked, taping the folded edge of the sleeve onto the paper backing.

"Well, yes. What do you have in mind?"

Katrina wrapped the newly-sleeved jacket around its book, admiring how shiny and attractive it looked and how much brighter the colors of the three bears in the woods seemed. "I think you should be able to see the online books from across the room. How about ... hmm ... maybe ... oh, how about if you put flags in them."

At the word "flag," Buglit spun around to face Katrina.

"Ohmygosh! She understood what you said, Kat," laughed Kris.

Mrs. O'Malley smiled, her eyes bright with interest in Katrina's idea. "A flag?"

Kat put the children's book on a stack with other sleeved books. "Yep. You can cut colored paper strips and have a variety of them ready at the computer." She paused to think some more. "At the end of your description code, put another number or letter that also tells you the color of the flag for that book. Put it in the middle of the book, leaving a couple of inches of the flag showing at the top. If anyone in the shop buys a flagged book, ink it with a rubber stamp that has your store's hours and name so they can use it as a bookmark. Oh! I had another idea! Inside the rear of the internet-listed books, put a sticky note with the book's title, author, and online inventory number on it. When you sell one in the shop, you don't have to go to the computer or jot down the info right then. Just peel off the note and remove the book from the internet after the customer leaves. But pencil in the price, too, so dishonest people can't switch prices on you."

"Are you quite sure you haven't been working in a bookshop in another town, Katrina, dear?" asked Mrs. O'Malley. "Every one of your ideas has been such a big help. Isn't she wonderful, Mack and Kris? Wonderful! I feel like writing a letter to your mother to tell her how smart and clever you are. Oh, but I suppose she must know. She's lived with you your whole life!"

Katrina and Kris glanced at each other and giggled.

Mr. O'Malley thought he saw a familiar face looking through the shop's window. He immediately went from smiling to shook up, as if thunder had crashed loudly on a sunny day.

"What?" asked Mrs. O'Malley.

Mack looked at the man for a few seconds more as he walked along the sidewalk, visible through most of the windows as he went.

"Oh, nothing, as it turns out. I thought it was the man who broke in here. The one we think hit you with a baseball, Kris. But don't worry, Mavis—it wasn't him. I guess I've got that guy on my mind constantly, now."

Mrs. O'Malley glanced away. "We need to be on our guard, don't we? I had let myself stop worrying. Isn't there anything we can do to keep our shop and everybody safe?"

Mack looked around the main room and down the hallway, making sure no one could hear their conversation. "I have a restraining order in place. I don't think there's anything else we can try. I just wish I knew what books he's after." He lifted Buglit from her perch on top of the tallest box stack. "If you can stay longer today, Kris, I think we need to move faster. We should try to get all the way through the books today. I'll leave you and Mavis to sort through these while I go and get the last load out of storage. Let's power through them all today and have our answers. I think we'll

151

all rest a lot easier if we know the deal on that group of books. Okay?"

"I can stay as long as you'd like," said Kris, eager to help.

"I only want you to stay here until I get the last group. Mrs. O and I can finish sorting them ourselves through the evening. No use keeping you here very late."

"I don't mind. I'm not looking forward to going home. I know Dad went to the police today. Since he didn't come in here to tell me the news, I think it must be bad. I wanna put off hearing what he found out, at least until I've helped you with the next group of boxes."

"We'll see, dear," said Mrs. O'Malley, her eyes sympathetic. "Mack, you can go. But be *careful.*"

"Kris—it's only two o'clock. Maybe your dad hasn't even made it to the police station yet. Or, it could be that he wanted to talk to your mother about what he found out before they talk to you together tonight."

Kris brushed dust from the front of his shirt. He grimaced. "That's not making me feel any better."

Mr. O'Malley poured himself some juice, drank it down, and checked his pants pockets for his keys and cell phone. He quickly kissed his wife. "I'm leaving. Call me if you need anything. Remember that Jack is right next door, and Danny isn't far away."

Mrs. O'Malley nodded. "We're okay. I'm going to look in the storage room for some colored cardstock. I think we bought a boxful at an auction a few years ago. By the time you get back, Katrina will have thought of fifteen more great ideas for the business. I'd better do what I can to keep up with her."

Katrina grinned and snuck a look at Kris to see how he'd reacted to that statement. He winked at her, Mack-like, his closed lips curving slightly upward before both kids went back to work on their projects.

Nearly an hour later, when Kris was alone in the main room near the science fiction paperbacks, the front door opened a few inches. A man placed an envelope on the countertop inside the door. He made sure it had been seen before ducking out again.

"Kat—look," Kris said, pointing.

Katrina had returned from carrying a stack of sleeved books to the rare book room to replace them in their showcases and on shelves. "You mean this?" she asked, picking up the plain white envelope. It had nothing written on the outside.

They heard the sound of a paper-cutter coming from the storage room.

"Mrs. O!" Kris called.

An older lady stepped out of the children's book room. "Yes?"

"Oh, I meant the other Mrs. O, Mrs. Oleson." He walked a few paces to meet her near the entrance to the room of mystery novels. "How are you today?"

"Fine, Kris. I'm suffering from my allergies, but I see an allergist tomorrow, and I hope he'll get them sorted out. Next week my granddaughter Aemelia is staying with Wade and me for four whole days! We'll have to bring her shopping here. I'm getting a few teen novels today to have books on hand to give her when she comes. She's such a voracious reader that I hope at least one of these will be new to her." She smiled, seeming to really see him at last. "How are you? I still can't get used to your new voice. And you're so *tall*, now. How are your little brothers and your parents doing?"

Kris wanted to get to Mrs. O'Malley to show her the envelope, but he did take a few moments to talk to the woman about the other Dehlvis.

"Well, you tell them hello for me. I'll check out now with these books," Mrs. Oleson said at last.

"Mrs. O," Kris said slightly more urgently than he intended as he opened the storage room door. "Mrs. Oleson is ready to leave." When the shop owner stepped into the hallway and closed the door behind her, Kris added in a whisper, "Some man put this on the counter." He handed her the envelope before they reached the cash register, then went back to work.

Mrs. O'Malley held the envelope, looking at it in confusion. She flipped it over, checking to see if it had writing on its back. She gave it to Katrina to hold while she rang up the sale.

"I'm sorry we're messy in here, Marge. We bought a full vanload at a couple of auctions on Saturday. Everything should be organized in a day or two. I hope."

"Messy? Oh, you mean the stacks. I used to work at The White Elephant, a clothing consignment shop. Now *that* was messy. Hangers all over, bell-bottoms and pencil skirts, stripes mingling with polka dots. Yish! This is a paradise of organization compared to that shop." She took the bag Mrs. O'Malley handed her, smiled, and said goodbye.

"Ooooh," said Katrina, her eyes widening as the woman left. "A clothing consignment shop. When I'm old enough, I want to work at one of those. Think of the vintage dresses and tops, the disco pants, old Levis, and acid-washed sweaters. Wowsers!"

Kris made a face.

"What?" she said defensively.

"Why work with clothes when you could work with books?"

"Well, maybe I'll do both." She thought for a few seconds, then raised a finger in the air. "Katrina's Togs 'n Tomes."

Mrs. O'Malley offered, "Or, how about Kat's Pants and Pages?"

"Or ...." Kris broke off, embarrassed that he wasn't able to think up another name. "Or maybe we should find out what's in that envelope."

Mrs. O'Malley grinned. She took it back from Katrina and tore it open. She sat on her chair and unfolded a handwritten page. She read it to herself, finishing it as Mack pulled to the curb in the van.

"What is it, Mrs. O'Malley?" asked Katrina.

The woman sat limply, her face pale. She took off her glasses and put them beside the computer. Her mouth was slack as if she'd had a shock.

Mr. O'Malley backed into the bookshop with a large cardboard box in his arms that looked heavy. He made it to the sofa and dropped the box onto the center cushion. "Whew! That's a big one." He loudly exhaled and took out his white handkerchief to wipe the sweat from his face. "Kris. Did you find anything special in this group while I was gone?" He hadn't noticed that his wife was sitting as still as a statue.

Kris raised his eyebrows. "Um, Mr. O? Mack? I think something's wrong with Mrs. O."

Katrina said, "Some man put an envelope on the counter. Kris said that's all he did. He reached in and put it down. Mrs. O just read it, and now ...."

As Kat was talking, Matt pushed into the shop. He had on swimming trunks, a t-shirt, and flip-flops, and a striped towel was around his neck. He looked miffed.

"Hey, Kat! What happened to you? I ended up having to spend the whole day trying to talk to other random girls on the beach. Why didn't you ever show up?"

Katrina pointed at Mrs. O'Malley. "Not a good time, Matty."

Matt hung his towel on the coat rack and looked at their faces, getting a slight chill. "Uh, do you need me to do anything?"

Mr. O'Malley stuffed his handkerchief into his back pocket. "What happened? Mavis? *Say* something."

She snapped out of her shock and looked at him. "Macky ... oh my *gosh,* oh my *gosh!*"

Mr. O'Malley took the letter from his wife as Katrina gave Mrs. O'Malley a cup of water.

Kris picked up Haiku and placed him next to the cash register. The boy rested on his elbows as he scratched the cat's neck and chin.

The woman drank in sips as Mack read the letter. Halfway through, he leaned his hip against the countertop, giving Kris the impression that he needed some support because the letter contained shocking news.

The longer Mr. O'Malley took to read the letter without saying anything, the more questions Kris had. He saw that Matt and Katrina were anxious to know what it was all about, too. Kris looked at his hands, noticing they were covered in loose fur. He'd been absentmindedly petting Haiku so long and hard that he had enough loose brown fur to stuff a small pillow. He wiped up the fur and tossed it into the trash. "Sorry," he whispered into the cat's ear when he returned to his place near Mack.

"What's going *on?*" asked Matt impatiently after Mack had lowered the letter. "Did somebody die?"

"Matt!" scolded his sister. She threw a wad of scrap paper at his chest.

"Well?" asked Kris softly. *"Did* someone die?"

Mr. O'Malley pulled out his wrinkled and damp handkerchief and wiped his neck and face again. He took off his plaid shirt while holding the letter, but still looked overheated in only his t-shirt. He lowered himself onto the sofa cushion to the left of the box he'd put there a few minutes before. "I'll read it out loud to you kids. That's the best way of explaining what it says."

Mrs. O'Malley said, "Mack!" from her chair, not even looking at anyone. She just wanted to call to him, knowing that by that point he must have read what she had.

"I know, Mave. Hang on. Let me read this out loud so the kids can understand why we're acting this way. I can move this box. Come over here and sit by me."

Before Mack could make a move to get up, Kris and Matt hurriedly lifted the heavy box from the sofa to the floor. Buglit jumped on top of this new perch as Katrina helped a very shook-up Mrs. O'Malley from her chair to sit next to Mack. The three kids then stood apprehensively in a row facing them.

Mr. O'Malley finished his water, put the cup on the floor at his feet, and took a deep breath. "Here's what it says.

"'Bookstore people and kids: I won't bother you again or break in again, because there's no point now. It's been long enough that you must know what you have from the auction that's so valuable.

'I went early to the auction to look through the books. When I found one, then two, then six, then nearly two dozen of the rarities, I nearly had a heart attack! What a find! I wanted them so badly, but I knew I couldn't afford to bid much, and certainly *nowhere* near what I was sure they would bring if other knowledgeable book collectors saw them. I gathered them all together into two boxes and waited, standing where I could see them before the sale started. When people started to gather, I stood right in front of them where I could block other bidders from seeing what was underneath the worn magazines I'd put on top of those fantastic books. When that kid bid on the whole, entire group of books, I panicked. I tried to buy the boxes from the skinnier kid, but he wouldn't be bought or bribed. That gave me a fever. It boiled up in me. I was furious! I wanted those books!

'I found a baseball in one of the auction's boxes of toys, and in a rage I went to the road and I threw that ball as hard as I could at the skinny kid. I only meant to take my anger out on him—I didn't think I'd actually hit him! I waited around to get my chance at the books I wanted, so I know that an ambulance came. I overheard that I'd blinded that boy. I panicked again, but I stayed. I tried to get them away from the other, big kid, but he was suspicious and I couldn't fool him. I almost hurt him, too. I almost did something to that kid right there in front of everyone!

'I knew I should have gone home and forgotten about them, but I needed and wanted those books! I almost went into the bookshop one time to casually find out if the books had been priced and were for sale, but I saw the bigger kid looking at me and got too scared. It wasn't too likely that you would have put them out at a cheap price. One look at them and you'd know how special they are. Eventually, I went back to look in the windows at night. I saw them all piled in the middle of the floor. I broke in. I was dumb about it. This all went really badly! Everything is awful now. I'll probably go to jail for a long time since I'm admitting to you that I also hit that kid with a ball. I don't care. I deserve it.

'I hope you get a lot of money for those auction books—and you will. I figure they're worth close to a half million dollars. I didn't know the true value of what I was looking at while I was at the auction. I had a good idea, though. I took photos and did research at home later, kicking myself that I'd messed up so badly. I didn't get the books, and I didn't just come to you to tell you what you had. You must know yourselves, by now.

'Tell those boys I'm sorry, too. – Charles'"

The three kids stared at each other in amazement, then they looked at the O'Malleys.

"Is that for *real*, Mack?" asked Kris. He lowered himself to the floor, facing the sofa. Buglit stepped from the top of the box to his lap. She rubbed his chin with her forehead.

Mr. O'Malley leaned forward and handed him the letter.

Kris scanned it before asking, "So, the guy who wrote the letter ... was the same one who hit me? I wish I could remember anything helpful about that day, but I don't. There he was, poking his head through the door right there, and I didn't even recognize him."

Katrina bit lightly at the edge of her thumbnail. Her eyes were distant as she asked, nearly whispering with incredulity, "A half a million *dollars?*" Her voice got louder. "That's coo-coo crazypants! You three said you haven't found anything at all worth a bunch of money, let alone two boxes full of whatever he's talking about. Mr. O, you're a book dealer with a ton of knowledge, right? How can there be anything you missed? Or have you? Have you gone through them all?"

Mack got out his damp handkerchief again to wipe his face. "I'm trying to remember. Hmm. I don't think we have gone through them all. We got tired on that first night and were heading home when I heard the sound of breaking glass. Let me think." He put away his wilted handkerchief. "No. There were still full boxes when we were leaving, and … now I'm not sure if we even had them all out of the van, then. No—we sure didn't. And then, while I was waiting for the repairman to get here, I re-boxed everything we had taken out. So, it *is* possible that the same two boxes that this letter refers to are in the load I just now drove here to unload."

"You're not thinking clearly, Mack," said Mrs. O'Malley. "We *didn't* bring anywhere near all them in from the van that first day. Now that they've been in the storage unit, the two groups from the auctions could have been mixed up. Maybe we only *think* we've seen all the books from the auction the boys went to."

Mack thought for a moment. "I remember that on Sunday I had Matt helping me to bring the books inside. He brought boxes in that he took from the double doors at the side of the van. I took boxes out of the back. The books that Matt got out were the ones I loaded in at the auction I went to. The ones in the rear were from the other auction. The two groups *are* mixed up!"

Kris stood from the floor as quickly as he could without actually flinging the cat across the room. "Let's get the rest of them in here!"

"Now!" said Matt.

"Oh, holy wowsers!" said Katrina, hugging her brother's side and jumping up and down.

"It's a joke," said Mrs. O'Malley somberly. "Don't get excited. This is another shot of meanness from that miscreant book thief."

"Do you think so, Mavis?" asked Mack. "I'm *not* so sure. I've seen collectors go crazy before. I've seen large men take books from the hands of children at book sales. I've seen women punch men in the stomachs or hit them on their heads with atlases. I've been to rummage sales that look more like a running-with-the-bulls event. This has the ring of truth to it."

"But ... but ... oh, for gosh sakes!" she unexpectedly shouted. Her eyes were wide and excited again. "Go and get those books out of the van, you men! Who *knows* what's true anymore? But we have to find out, right?"

Mr. O'Malley stood and pointed dramatically to the street. "To the boxes, boys! We'll have the mysterious cardboard containers inside in no time, Mavis."

And they did. Soon the boxes were inside the bookshop in haphazard stacks around the main room.

"Matt and Katrina, I hate to keep you here any longer," Mrs. O'Malley said after she'd opened the top flaps on a box. "Run on home now. Kris can stay for a while if he wants to help us look through the books. Kris, why don't you call home to let them know you have a special project here this afternoon? I know you're usually home by this time. I don't want them to worry about you, especially since there have been all those other things going on at home."

Kris nodded and walked outside with Katrina and Matt to say goodbye.

"Good luck when you get home today. I don't even know what that means, though," said Katrina. "Is it a good thing if you have a living bio-mom and dad, or is it a bad thing? I think the Dehlvis are the best, so I don't want you to have to leave them." She turned her head and the wind blew some of her blonde hair out of her eyes. "How do you feel?"

"I feel like it isn't a good sign that my dad didn't stop by the shop after he went to the police station today. That has me all super worried. But, like you said, there are a lot of ways to look at this. I feel ... mixed up. And," he added, stepping closer to his friends to make sure he wouldn't be overheard even though no one was around them, "I'm freaked out about the rare book thing, too. Are you guys okay to walk home? Are you scared? You can ask Jack and Darla for a ride if you're mom's not home yet. Even Mack can do it."

Katrina eyed her brother. "Where's your towel?"

"Inside, still."

"Go and get it and call Mom."

"I will," Matt agreed, pushing the shop's door open again.

Katrina hugged Kris, letting him go after only two seconds. He grabbed her and hugged her back as her arms were dropping.

"Thanks for being such a good friend, Kat," he said softly into her ear. "Both of you. You and Matt are like a sister and brother to me. I'm glad you stayed here all day today. It helped me forget about my first parents and that Ricki person. I was depressed out of my head this morning. Just ... thanks."

As he let her go, she couldn't have been less happy if he had said that he hated her.

She surreptitiously wiped a tear from her cheek as Matt joined them again, his towel around his neck. He said, "She'll be here in a minute. No use taking up your book-sorting time outside, Kris. We'll stay right here. If I spot the auction dude, I'll knock on a window to get your attention. I'm sure that letter honestly meant that he's done messing with all of us, but it's better to be safe than sorry."

Kris let out a long, slow breath and walked into the shop again to call home.

"What's the matter?" Matt asked, noticing Katrina's frown. He snapped a maple leaf from a low branch.

"He said that you and I were like his sister and brother," she grumped. "Crap."

Matt laughed.

"Shut up. Wait until you're moping around because some hot girl you want to date says she likes you like a brother."

He stopped laughing, as if he had someone in mind. "Oh. Yeah, that would suck. But still, Katty-Kat, it *was* kinda nice of him to say that."

She shrugged. "I give up. I guess I'll move on and crush on another one of your friends."

Matt looked up the street for their mother's car. "Steve likes you."

"No thanks."

"Picky."

"Am not. He's terrible."

Matt grinned. "I like him, though."

"He doesn't flirt with you, then argue with you in the same five seconds."

"No. I'm lucky that way."

Katrina watched Kris and the O'Malleys through the shop window. She shrugged again. "I can't help it. But I'll try. I'll spin my love dial over to 'like' and be glad to take whatever the heck he wants to give me."

"You talk like you're ancient and the years are just speeding by." He glanced up. "Oh, look—here's Mom."

The girl reluctantly climbed into the front seat as Matt got into the back.

"Hi, kids. Kat, I had no idea you were going to be in the bookshop all day," said Mrs. Karlsson as the kids buckled up.

"I was helping Mrs. O'Malley. I can see why Kris loves working there."

"Well, that's very nice, but I worry about you. What about that man who hurt Kris? You have to be careful now, you know."

"Not anymore," said Matt. He slapped his hand over his mouth when he realized he may have said too much.

"Oh, is he in jail now?" asked Mrs. Karlsson as she drove around a corner.

Katrina answered for him, "He will be. He turned himself in today, it looks like."

"Well, good! So," she said, lowering her visor, "do you two want to hear about my big, exciting day in the world of automotive sales?"

Katrina listened to her mother and brother talk on the ride home, but she didn't hear them. All she could think about was the mysterious letter to the O'Malleys and what could be in the boxes of books that might be worth a wagonload of money.

Chapter Twelve

"Well, that's everything," said Mrs. O'Malley. They had carefully examined each of the books from the last group, looking for author signatures, for money between their pages—any unusual thing at all.

Mack flattened the last box after cutting through its tape. "I may be blind or not worth my salt as a dealer, but I did *not* see a single book in this group, either, that could be valued at more than a few hundred dollars. Not that that's anything to sneeze at, of course. I don't know what could have been worth these crimes and headaches we've been through. Literally, right Kris?"

Kris drew his eyebrows together, looking over the stacks of unboxed books that were here, there, and everywhere. He stepped closer to four stacks of books on the far edge of the countertop. "These are very, very old, Mack. Are you sure they aren't worth more than you think?"

"They *are* extra nice. Late seventeen-hundreds books in what were once attractive bindings. I'll have Mavis look them up online, but they aren't anything superb. Leather-bound English county histories and topography. Some religious titles. Poetry. Travels in Italy and France. Things like that."

"But *look* at them. The group equals about what would fit in two average-size boxes, right?" Kris asked, putting a hand on top of one of the stacks.

Mrs. O'Malley lifted Buglit from the sofa and walked to where Kris stood. "He's right, Mack. And they're the only books that seem to have the potential to be worth a lot."

Mr. O'Malley brushed leather flakes and dust from his hands onto his pants before joining them. "Hmm. Well, the bindings are interesting. The gilding on the page edges is still bright on them all." Mack picked up one of the books and examined the spine and the page edges. "If there was anything bound into the boards, we couldn't know unless we took them apart, that would mean that Charles—the letter-writer—would have had to do the same thing at the auction. Since he didn't rip them apart, that's not the answer." Mack put that book back on its stack and picked up another. "The leather on these needs to be treated with a consolidant before this red rot gets worse. I know *that,* anyway."

"We've been at it for hours, and here it is already after six o'clock," said Mrs. O'Malley as she let Buglit hop out of her arms to the floor. "Mack, I think we should box these eighteenth-century books. Maybe lock them in the storage room overnight."

"You don't want to take them home with us?" asked Mr. O'Malley.

She shook her head, yawning. "Kris, can we give you a ride home?"

He yawned, too. "Naw. I'll jog. I'll be home before you're even closed for the night. Jogging will wake me up a little. I know there's some reason Dad never came here today. Some reason that he never called." He combed his fingers through his dark blonde bangs and yawned again. "Probably gonna be another long talk when I get home."

Mrs. O'Malley frowned. "Oh, Kris! I hate that there's been so much disruption in your life lately. I almost hate to send you home. I want to hang onto you here for a while longer."

Looking at the floor between them, Kris sighed. "I gotta go."

Minutes later, when Kris reached the last corner and could see his house, he was surprised that Tatyana was standing in front of his mailbox, leaning against a Neighborhood Watch sign. She was in torn jean shorts and a pink t-shirt that didn't fit well.

"Taty! Hi," Kris called. He stopped jogging and walked the last several steps to the end of his driveway.

She looked at her outfit. "These are not what I wanted to wear to say goodbye, but except for what I'm going to wear tomorrow, my nice clothes are packed already. We're leaving for the airport at five in the morning."

She took one of his hands in hers, her dark eyes shyly staring at their joined fingers.

Bijay opened the screen door. "Krissy! We are eating in three minutes and twenty-two seconds, Mom says. We've been waiting for you."

"Okay. I'll be right in, Bij," Kris called back. The door closed, but Bijay watched his brother through the screen.

"I'll let you go. I just wanted to say … farewell." Her very large, dark eyes met his warmly. "I will write you my first letter now." She inhaled deeply as she found her words. "Dear Kris, how are you? I am fine. The flight was very, very long, but I have traveled these skies before and knew how long I would be looking at the tops of clouds. I listened to music and read most of the way, and I thought about you and my life in America. I'm back in my homeland, and maybe I will stay here this time with those I love and who love me. Or maybe I'll return in the fall when classes begin. Dear Kris, please write when you have time, now that this letter carries my address. Dear Kris, please don't think about me very much. I … I suppose that our time is over now. I will sing a song for you when I am by myself, a song about rain. I'll remember holding your hand in the rain and singing with you on your front porch. Dear Kris, you were the first boy I ever loved. Dear Kris, goodbye, my friend."

Kris shook with sorrow, surprised at himself. He flung his arms around her neck and hugged her tightly. She kept her arms stiffly at her sides at first, but then raised them to hold him more gently than he held her.

"My parents say goodbye, too," she said, barely above a whisper, more emotion in her voice than there had been a moment before. "They like you. My mother resisted a trip

166

back to Botswana because she didn't want to hurt our friendship, but I sat with her and told her that I was not meant for you. Not really. I know you'll find her, whoever she will be, and she will be blessed."

Kris stepped back, wiped his eyes with his hands, and looked for several long seconds at Tatyana, making a memory. "Have a wonderful trip. And ..."

"And goodbye."

Bijay called through the screen, "Krissy!"

Tatyana grasped Kris' hands and squeezed them once more. "The last time I kissed you was the last time ever. Take care of yourself and your brothers. All three of them, when the new one comes. You are a *fabulous* big brother, you know."

She sighed and let go of his hands, then crossed the street to her house. Kris walked toward his porch steps, emotions pounding in his heart. For that moment, he almost felt as if he *had* loved her—at least in a way—and now she was leaving. Probably forever.

Bijay reached to the lever on the door to unlatch it. Holding the door open for his brother, he exclaimed, "Krissy, I haven't seen you in a whole day!"

"I *know!* You spent the night away, and then I was gone. I missed you and Dev." He smiled tearfully at Bijay as he stood inside near the door. He could smell the spices from the kitchen. He heard the television, the sink water running, sizzling from the stovetop, and a car with a muffler problem driving by.

He waved to everyone as he went through the house to his bedroom. He changed into clean pajamas since the clothes he had worn all day were very dirty, dusty, and smudged with old leather smears. He used the toilet, washed his face and hands, and walked out to the living room.

The TV was off, and the Indian music softly drifting from the speakers in the hallway could easily be heard.

"Come come come, Kris. Take your seat. We have prayed already but will wait for you if you would like to say words, too," his mother said from her spot at the dining room table.

Kris stood holding onto the back of the sofa. His legs felt unsteady. His eyes wanted to close as exhaustion hit him like waves crashing on the shore. "I'm ... I have to go to bed now."

His world blackened. He felt himself falling. He didn't care.

The next morning, he was still weary. He couldn't remember what had happened the previous night after he had changed before dinner.

Kris left his room, went to the bathroom, and walked into his parents' bedroom. The clock on the wall read six-forty. He watched his mother and father sleep for a moment before crawling between them.

"Are you in pain?" his mother whispered. "Do you need anything?"

He didn't respond except to shake his head. Mr. Dehlvi had barely moved since the moment Kris got into bed, and he was already snoring again.

"I will tell you what I think," she said softly. "You were not ready to go back to school when you did, and you were not ready for a full day at the bookstore and running around. Just rest today. Eat plenty, and drink water. If you still do not feel well, back to the doctor we will go. Okay?"

Kris nodded, his eyes already closed. His mother separated the layers of blanket and sheet. She kept the sheet over herself but flipped the thin blue blanket over her son.

Three hours later, Kris opened his eyes to see a bedroom not his own, but familiar. He didn't hear anything except a distant lawnmower purring and birds chirping. His mother, passing by the open door, saw that he was awake at last. She came in and closed the door behind her. Her dark eyes were concerned.

"How are you feeling?" she asked, not liking the dark circles that were still under his eyes. They had faded, but not enough.

"Sad, I think." He frowned and blew a puff of air through his nose.

She smoothed a pillowcase with one hand, watching herself do it until she felt able to look at her son again. "Your daddy did not go to the police."

His eyes opened wider. "Why?"

"After you had gone to the bookshop yesterday, he and I spoke together. It is a big tribulation for us as your parents, but it is a bigger tribulation for you. Your father and I talked for a long, long time. We have decided that your will should be the final word. You are not a little boy, after all, even though I still call you my little Kris. If you do not want to find out anything until you are eighteen, well ... that is how it shall be."

Kris slowly sat up. He swung his legs to sit next to her, his bare feet not quite touching the floor. "I'll get dressed. I should mow today. I should have done it a couple of days ago, really."

"Your father wants to do it. He was waiting until you had awoken."

"I should do more of the chores around here."

"You do plenty. You can mow when you are fully healed from your concussion. Your doctor had ordered you not to do strenuous things. Have you been careful about that, Kris?"

He hadn't remembered that a doctor or anyone had said such a thing. In fact, he didn't remember much about being in the hospital at all. "Yes. No. I don't know. From now on I'll be careful, Mom."

"It is a mother's right to worry. Your father—he worries, too, in his silent way."

Kris looked at his toes. "Dev is exactly like Dad in a lot of ways. Bij is more like you. I might not be related to either you or Dad from birth, but I think I inherited worry genes from both of you."

"Dev is an old soul, yes," she said. "When he was first learning to speak in sentences, he said the most amazing things. Bijay is almost his opposite, enjoying childhood in nearly every way. His heart is pure and full of love. That will serve his new brother well, I am sure."

In the shower, Kris relaxed for the first time in a long time, and he felt like he could think about the Ricki situation from other angles, something he couldn't do while he was fearful.

When the warm water was running out, he finished rinsing and left the shower. Drying off, more worries and what-ifs came into his head.

He wrapped himself in a large, white towel and walked into his own bedroom. As he dressed, he could hear that another lawnmower had joined the neighborhood chorus. A car playing loud rock music drove by. The sun was shining, the breeze was blowing, leaves were shaking in that breeze, kids were playing somewhere, and life was going on.

He found his parents in the back yard. Mr. Dehlvi was reading a magazine, sitting on a green metal chair with his back against the outdoor table. Mrs. Dehlvi was kneeling in one of the gardens, planting a row of flower seedlings. Stomper was on his side near her, snoozing.

"The boys are at Donnie's house until this afternoon," said his mother from the flowerbed. She stopped pushing soft, brown dirt around a stem and leaned back, her knees still on the cushion she used for gardening. She shook a strand of hair out of her face and smiled. "Do you want some lunch or breakfast? I made vegetable soup yesterday, and some chapathi. I can warm the soup in a few minutes. Or, I could make you scrambled eggs."

Kris shook his head. In a few minutes, he was back outside carrying a bowl of corn flakes, a spoon, and a napkin. He pulled a chair near his father at the table that sat at the center of a decorative spiral of dark red bricks. Birds called to each other in the trees overhead. His father continued to read while his mother dug with a spade and planted, pouring water from a sprinkling can after each seedling was in place.

Kris swallowed a spoonful of cereal. "I should call the bookshop."

"I have already. I left a message on their answering machine when I got up hours ago," his mother said. She stood, removed her soiled gloves, and walked to the table to sit with them. "You look much more rested today. The circles under your eyes are nearly gone. You were still recovering from your accident when you did too much. Do as your mama says to you, Kris. Be a lazy boy today."

Mr. Dehlvi turned his chair around to join the conversation. He took off his glasses and placed them on top of his closed ancient history magazine at the center of the table.

Kris looked at the tabletop. "But I need to get to the bookshop today. Super big stuff is happening. They got a letter from the man who hit me with the baseball! And what he said in that letter was *huge."*

"Your mother wants you to rest. I think you should listen to her. Your eyes still look sleepy."

"I know, Dad, but ..."

"How about this?" Mrs. Dehlvi said. "Rest on the sofa for two whole hours. No reading with those tired eyes. Listen to music or the television. After that, you may go."

"Did your mother tell you that we agreed to let things be as they are now until you are eighteen?" asked Mr. Dehlvi.

171

"Yes, but ... *wait,*" Kris said urgently, determination in his voice and eyes. He pushed his bowl to the side. "Wait."

His mother and father waited. Mrs. Dehlvi rested her elbows on the table, something she rarely did. The breezes played gently in her hair, a phone rang in a house beyond the backyard fence and was answered, and still they waited.

"I have to say ...." he said at last. "I think I've changed my mind. I think I *do* want to talk to the police. Today."

Mr. Dehlvi shook his head, not looking up. "No. I won't let you go. Not today. Rest today. Think some more."

Kris reached for his bowl and ate in silence, quickly finishing his cereal.

"I feel fine now. I must have slept for like sixteen hours. I've been thinking and thinking, and even dreaming about this thing. How I might actually be some whole, different kid than who I think I am, in a way. It isn't fair to that other couple—if they exist as my birth parents—to keep this a secret, even though I wouldn't have known about them, like *ever,* if Darla hadn't seen their photo. But now I *do* know about Ricki. Now I *do* have to do something about her. I should tell maybe the same social services lady who put me with you guys—Miss Valentine. I guess if I talk to someone, it doesn't have to be the police, right?"

"It is a matter for the police, Kris, if anyone is told," said his father. "If this woman wanted to put her baby up for adoption, that was her right. However, to take money for the baby was not legal. They all should have done things properly. I think it sounds as though Ricki not only wanted to have her baby adopted, but to make a large amount of money for carrying the child. If this was true, then your adoption could not have been legal. Perhaps it came to light when your parents passed away, and that may be why the state workers did not contact any of your family members. If the arrangements were made without a paper trail, the state would not have been able to find your biological family, and they would likely not have pressed the family of the people you thought were your parents to take you in when you needed a home." He made a fist but didn't pound the table with it. "Such a mess."

Mrs. Dehlvi put her hand on her husband's wrist. "Falak, why couldn't we do as Kris suggests? We could start with social services."

Kris clicked his spoon on the edge of his cereal bowl. "But why would they have needed to do it? They were young people. Mom and Dad weren't sick. Why didn't they have their own baby? If they *did* buy Ricki's, I mean. And if they were going to adopt a kid, why not do it the real way?"

"There are many medical reasons why a couple would not be able to have their own baby," Mr. Dehlvi said. He made a motion with his hand signaling it was a topic for another time. He answered his wife's question next. "I think we could start with Miss Valentine, dear. Her office may have all the answers we seek. It will ultimately be a matter for the police, but we can perhaps start with a softer approach. And Kris … I have heard that adopting a newborn can take a long time. Years and years. There are many, many older children waiting for good homes, and adopting an older child is a faster process. But if your mom and dad had their heart set on a baby, they may have felt that going through the proper steps for a newborn meant too long of a wait. Whenever there is impatience," he said, holding up one finger the way he did when he said something philosophical, "there is trouble that will follow."

"All of our questions may never be answered," said Mrs. Dehlvi. "If you feel ready to find some of your answers, we can start today. Because in two days we will be bringing Dontae home."

"Two days? That soon?" Kris asked, astonished. "I thought you had home study to finish and stuff like that."

Mrs. Dehlvi shook her head. "We are through with everything. They are preparing some paperwork on their end, and Dontae will see a doctor today or tomorrow. Then we can go to the foster home to make him ours."

Kris took in a deep breath. He listened to the sounds of the neighborhood and thought some more. "Later this summer, then. Once Dontae is settled in, *then* I'll do stuff about my stuff."

"You say 'stuff' far too much, Kris," said his father.

Kris shrugged. "I try not to."

"I think you speak very well, except for saying 'stuff,'" defended his mother. "But don't slouch so, dear. Indian children are taught not to slouch."

"He is not an Indian child, Daya."

"He is my child. I am Indian. He should not slouch. That is all that I am saying," argued Mrs. Dehlvi.

Mr. Dehlvi smiled. He put his glasses back on his face. "Okay, Kris. Do not slouch when you are saying 'stuff,' and all will be well."

"You should begin to practice yoga every day."

"He's fine, Daya. He is fit and slender and strong."

"He can join the other boys. Would you like to practice yoga, Kris?" his mother asked. "I have an extra mat in the closet."

Kris shrugged again. His mother had been getting increasingly strict with him over the past couple of months, and both of his parents wanted him to join in on more of the family's traditions. It made him feel more and more like a Dehlvi and less like an adopted son.

"See? He is fine, dear. Stop picking on him so."

"I? This boy is one of my three favorite sons! Why would I 'pick' on him, as you say?"

"Well, leave him be, Daya."

Kris stood from the table, smiling. He went to stand between his parents. Sobering even as he listened to them

174

gently argue, he said, "I don't know *what* I'd do if I had to leave you."

The adults both stopped speaking. Mrs. Dehlvi hugged Kris around the waist from where she sat.

"As we have told you—that will not happen," Mr. Dehlvi assured.

Kris exhaled slowly, and said, "We'll wait a while to talk to anyone about this. That's what I've decided. Let's get comfortable with Dontae before we worry about my stuff—I mean my ... situation." He yawned. "Tatyana is gone. I meant to get up to say goodbye again. I think she said they were leaving at five this morning. I'll probably never see her again. Ever." He walked around to the other side of the table for his bowl.

"You were too young to be serious," his father declared, smoothing the crease in his magazine. "You should play the field. Find five or ten girls to date this summer."

"Falak!"

"Five, then. Maybe not ten. Ten would be too hard to manage."

"Falak!" Mrs. Dehlvi scolded again.

Kris wasn't cheered by their teasing this time.

"What is it, Kris?" asked his mother. "What is wrong?"

"I feel pretty terrible about Taty."

"Why? You were not nice to her?" his father asked. "I know that I always saw that you were very kind to that girl. Or, are you feeling sad that she is gone? I don't think that is it, Kris. I don't think your heart was deeply touched by her. I could tell. She was a hand to hold. I don't think she was lodged deeply within your heart. I would not tease you if I thought you were losing a great love."

Kris sat again even though he had intended to go back inside. "I think ... what might be bothering me is that I didn't know until last night when we said goodbye that ... I think she loved me. Like, for real. I didn't expect to feel so sorry."

175

His father tilted his head. "There comes a kind of sorrow when you love someone more than they love you. You cannot change their feelings, and it hurts you. But then there is a kind of sorrow that comes when you see that someone loves you much more than you do them. And you cannot change your own feelings, try as you might. When affections are not equal, or nearly so, it is a hard thing."

"Which way around was it for you, Dad?"

"I have only ever loved your mother. So." He said this with finality, but then winked at Kris, indicating that there was likely more that could have been revealed.

Chapter Thirteen

Earlier that same day, not long after opening the bookshop, Mr. and Mrs. O'Malley heard the sounds of shoes slapping on the sidewalk before the bookshop door was forcefully pushed open.

"Well?" asked Matt and Katrina in unison, both panting and sweaty.

"Did you kids run the whole way here?" asked Mack as he adjusted the air conditioner.

"What did you find after we left? What was so rare and valuable?" Katrina asked breathlessly. But then she clapped both hands over her mouth, realizing she shouldn't have asked about the books in case unseen customers could overhear her.

Matt rolled his eyes. "Geez, Kat."

"That's all right. No one else is in here," Mack said, moving the white metal stepladder back to its usual spot near the gardening books. He folded his arms as he returned to the front of the room. "And we didn't find a thing worth a fortune, even after carefully examining them over and over again. There was no cash or rare documents stuffed inside. No signatures. No diamond-studded bindings."

"I wonder if we're being hoaxed by that baseball-thrower. Charles. What if he simply wanted to drive us crazy?" Mrs. O'Malley asked as she dropped onto her computer chair. Buglit immediately jumped onto her lap.

Katrina took a few steps and looked down the hallway.

"He isn't coming in today," said Mrs. O'Malley, understanding Katrina's glance. "When Kris got home last evening, he fainted. They brought him to bed. When his mom left a message this morning, she said he had been up, but only long enough to fall asleep again in their bed. She said she thinks he overdid it. He tried to do too much too soon."

"Fainted? I can't picture Kris fainting." Katrina said, a crease of worry between her eyes. She pulled nervously at her braid, playing with the elastic band. "I should go over there and check on him."

"Leave the kid alone, Kat," said her brother as he gave her a dark look. "Besides, he'll probably sleep all day."

Katrina bit at a hangnail on her thumb. Dropping that hand, she asked, "He really *fainted?*"

Matt ignored her and asked the O'Malleys, "There aren't any more books left in the storage unit?"

"No. Not a one," said Mr. O'Malley.

Katrina said, "The books must be *here.* We've just gotta figure this puzzle out."

"And quickly," said Mrs. O'Malley.

"Why?" asked Matt, sitting on the sofa to re-tie his sneakers. "I mean, what's the rush if the books are all here?"

"We can't trust that Charles hasn't told other people. What if he wasn't lying about the books being worth a fortune? It's a game of time. If he tells someone who's not imprisoned or jailed or whatever, *they* could come after the books. We don't know which books are the valuable ones, or why. But if we solve the puzzle first, we can sell the books, have the money, and be rid of what a thief would be coming here to steal. We need to beat the crooked clock."

"Sounds like the title of a Hardy Boys' mystery," said Matt. "The Case of the Crooked Clock."

"Are you going to call in some other book expert?" Katrina asked. She sat on the plush chair near the door. Haiku was reclining against her legs, getting a good-morning pet from the girl.

"That's not a bad idea," said Mrs. O'Malley. "Mack? What do you think?"

He yawned. "I think I'm tired. I didn't sleep well again last night."

178

"Well? What about that man who looked at our Poe booklet last year?"

Mr. O'Malley lowered himself onto the red sofa. He yawned again. "No. Let me think for a while longer."

Matt stood. "Come on, Kat. I'm heading over to Steve's house. They put a new basketball hoop on the side of their garage."

"Oh, joy," she said sarcastically. She hefted Haiku onto her lap, and he pressed his forehead to hers. "I like this cat. Don't you like this cat, Matty? He's bigger than Browser!"

"Let's go. You spent the whole day in here yesterday."

"You go on. I hate playing basketball," Katrina said, still petting the cat.

"Well, that's okay. Steve said you can watch us shoot baskets and get us drinks. Play cheerleader—that kind of stuff."

"Uh-oh," said Mrs. O'Malley.

"Oh, no! He *didn't*," said Mr. O'Malley. Then he laughed. "I think you need to leave before Haiku lets your sister stand up from that chair."

Matt mentally replayed what he'd just said. "Hey! *I* didn't say that. *Steve* said it."

"You should run now," advised Mrs. O'Malley.

Matt looked at each of their faces, Katrina's darkening one last. His eyebrows went up. "Bye!" he shouted as he pushed out of the shop.

Katrina giggled, her face against Haiku's neck. She looked up. "Matt thinks I should like Steve as much as he supposedly likes me. That right there is one of the reasons I may go without a date to the prom next year. My only prospect is a caveman of some sort."

"He might change," Mrs. O'Malley said. "Maybe he'll grow on you one of these days."

"No. Honestly, Mrs. O—no and never."

"Well, Miss Katrina," said Mrs. O'Malley, trying to lighten the girl's mood, "would you like to help me again today?"

"I would. But I need to run an errand first. I'll be back after lunch if that's okay," she said as she lowered the giant cat to the floor.

"We'd love to have you whenever you can be here with us."

"Is Kris still asleep?" asked Mr. Dehlvi that late afternoon as he came through the front door after a trip to the college library.

His wife nodded. She leaned against the kitchen doorway, feeling tired herself. "I should probably wake him now. He needs to eat. That bowl of cereal was not nearly enough since he is still healing from his injury."

She stepped into the living room and stood at the back of the sofa. "Kris?" She brushed his too-long bangs from his forehead.

He didn't say anything or open his eyes.

"I don't like how long he's been sleeping," said Mr. Dehlvi.

"The hospital doctor said it might take a couple of weeks for him to get back to his usual self, remember? I think he went back to school too soon—back to the bookshop too soon. I did not want him to miss the very end of his school year and tests, but now I think I should have kept him home."

"Kris?" said Mr. Dehlvi firmly as he shook his son's blanket-covered toes.

Stomper jumped up beside his boy. Sitting near the pillow, he pawed at Kris' face.

"I'm up, I'm up," Kris said groggily, yawning and stretching his legs. Stomper jumped to the floor again. "What time is it? I should get to the bookshop."

"Not today. It's nearly their closing time. Eat a small bite and stay awake now or you will not be able to sleep all night tonight," said his father.

"Is it really late? Where are the kids?" Kris asked as he sat up.

"In the back yard," his mother said, folding the blanket. "They have been playing board games so you could sleep. Dinner will be ready in an hour. Eat a snack now. You slept for five hours this time."

Kris yawned widely and reached down to pet Stomper. After stepping from the bathroom, he asked, "Any of that fruity rice pudding left?"

His mother stepped into the kitchen for a moment. When she returned, she handed him a spoon and small dish. "I had some ready for you."

"Thanks. I'll eat it outside with Dev and Bij. I feel bad that they had to be quiet all day."

Mr. Dehlvi clicked on the television as he kicked back in his recliner. He opened his newspaper as he said, "Not *that* quiet. You were soundly asleep."

"They did try to be considerate of you," Mrs. Dehlvi said. "But I heard evidence that sinking battleships is hard to do without *some* enthusiasm and sound effects."

Kris took his rice pudding through the back door and put it on the table beside the Candyland game board. He noisily pulled one of the metal chairs across the patio bricks to sit between his brothers. He adjusted the large umbrella over the table to put all three of them in its shade.

Bijay slid his game piece on the board before he hopped up to hug Kris. He smelled of sunlight and fresh air.

"Are you staying awake now?" Bijay asked, his large, dark eyes hopeful.

"Yep."

"Don't get hit by a baseball again," warned Dev.

"Your turn," reminded Bijay, antsy to continue their game.

"I won't," Kris said after he swallowed a spoonful of rice pudding. "I didn't want to the *first* time, you know."

"Your turn."

"I *know,* Bij." Dev finally took his turn.

"How come you're eating that?" Bijay asked, swinging his legs under his chair.

"Mom thinks I'm starving or something."

"*I'm* starving. Think I could have a bite?" the boy asked hopefully.

Kris shared a spoonful, but then ate the rest slowly, savoring the delicious flavors. He forced any thoughts of the bookshop and the exciting book mystery to float away into the trees for the day. He knew he'd go to see the O'Malleys in the morning. Right then he only wanted to sit in the back yard with his little brothers and watch them play a game and listen to them laugh and tease each other.

Kris had no trouble staying awake through dinner and an evening of reading in his room. At nine o'clock, he went to his open window and leaned through it to feel the cool air on his face and neck. Darkness still hadn't fully come, but it was close. One by one, streetlights flickered and stayed on, and several lights shone in windows up and down his street. Two teenage boys with a soccer ball kicked it between them as they walked home. A few fireflies sent signals to each other, and frogs sang from puddles and back yards all over the neighborhood.

He then looked at Tatyana's large house. It was dark. It made Kris think of death, somehow. The other houses felt alive as they prepared for the evening, but Tatyana's was empty—a thing waiting for occupants that might never return.

He left his room to say goodnight to his parents, saying he felt well but wanted to keep reading until he fell asleep. The younger boys were in bed already and had come to his room to say goodnight a half hour before.

"I'm glad you stayed home today. You were overtired," his mother said as she stood to pour herself another glass of nimbu pani.

He walked to her, stretching his arms and back. "I do feel much stronger. I think you were right. I needed to take today off to sleep. I hated to miss going to the bookshop, but I'll go tomorrow." He stood with her in the kitchen to have some of the lemon drink, too. "Mom, I feel like I haven't had a good chance to really talk with you in a while about anything other than Dontae and Ricki. Something else super major is going on."

She switched on the soft light over the stove before reaching into the freezer for a few ice cubes. She paused, the ice still in her hand. "Is it about the man who hurt you?"

"Sort of. Yes. Well, yes and no."

She dropped the ice into her drink before handing Kris the pitcher. "What yes and what no?"

"The man who threw the ball at me—and who broke into the bookshop—wrote a letter to the O'Malleys."

"A letter? That is very old fashioned of him. I would not think that a criminal like that would write a letter of apology. Or, was it not an apology? Did he make threats, instead?"

"He explained why he did what he did. He admitted hurting me, and he said he won't hurt me again. He got all crazy and threw the ball at me when I wouldn't sell him some rare books he freaked out about."

"Don't say 'freaked out,' Kris. I don't like that."

Kris laughed. "You get stricter with me every day."

Mrs. Dehlvi inhaled. Her eyebrows went up slightly. "Do I? Perhaps I do." She took a sip. Holding her glass in both hands, she admitted, "I may be starting to 'freak out' a little myself as we get closer to bringing a new boy home. I am sorry. But not much. You should not say 'stuff' and 'freak out' and things like this." She smiled. "Maybe I am thinking of you more and more as my own blood child. I am strict like this with Dev and with little Bijay. I am not, though, even half as stern as my mother." She raised her eyes to the ceiling dramatically. "Hoo! She was tough!"

Kris laughed, but then went back to his story. "Anyway," he said, "the man said he saw books at the auction that he claims are worth a fortune. After Matt bid on every single book, he wanted to buy some from us. Apparently, I said no, that he should go to the bookshop in a couple of days to buy them from Mr. O'Malley. That's why he broke into the shop. He knows something that we still don't—that about two boxes full of books are worth a *fortune.*"

"What do you mean when you say that you still don't know? I do not understand."

"Well, we've been through every single book from both of the auctions. None of them stand out as being worth more than a few hundred dollars. It's a mystery. Either this dude is faking us out, or we're all too stupid to see what we have right in front of us."

"Don't say 'dude,' either. Unless you are speaking about a cowboy. Then you may say 'dude.'"

He smiled. "I think I'm probably gonna keep on saying all these words you don't like."

She took another sip, her eyes half closed. "Hmm." She sighed. "So, is it possible that you and the O'Malleys are being 'faked out'?"

Kris shrugged. "I hate that I had to miss whatever's going on at the shop for a whole day. We need to get to the bottom of this before that man starts to talk to people about what he's positive the O'Malleys have. Other bad men or women might go after them even though that gentleman will be behind bars."

She snorted lightly. "Oh, Kris—go ahead and say 'dude' if you want to."

He grinned. "You noticed me trying not to say that, huh?"

She patted his arm once, smiling. "I'm glad we can stand together and laugh." Picking up her glass again, she walked with him into his bedroom. "Be careful, please. If you are tired tomorrow, promise me you will call so I may drive you home for a rest."

"I do promise that, Mom."

"Good boy. Now go open your book and read until you fall to sleep. If you are not awake by your usual time for bookshop-going, I will tap on your door."

"Thanks. Goodnight."

"Are you cool enough in here?"

"I'll put on my fan if I get hot."

"Do you want to have more to drink while you read?"

"Nope. I'm fine."

She hovered in the doorway. The world outside Kris' window was dark at last. "I worry. I have visions of a baseball flying through that window, coming to strike you."

Kris sat on his bed and pushed the sheet and light blanket to the footboard with his feet. He was in his gray summer pajama shorts and top. He looked very young to her one moment, and all grown up the next.

"Just think, Mom. In a couple of days, you'll have four boys to worry about."

"Arey! Oh, dear! That's right! Tomorrow we'll have to buy another bed. Will you have enough room?"

Kris looked around. There would be room, but not much. He nodded. "Plenty."

"When you come home from the bookshop tomorrow, your father and I will have the new bed here," she pointed, "and a new dresser there."

"And I can share my books and everything else. Don't look so concerned, Mom. I'm bummed I won't get to help you and Dad get the furniture bought and moved in. I kind of want to stay with you all day, but I'm super jumpy to find out if the O'Malleys have found out what that—that dude was after."

"Don't fuss about furniture. We will not need help. We will also buy a new dresser for your brothers' room. They are so grown up, and each needs their own. I wish this house had more closet room. Ah, well, well. It is more of a worry that we have only one bathroom for so many boys and two adults."

"Speaking of furniture, Mom, what about this idea? How about if Dontae takes my bed for the first night? I can sleep on the couch. Then we can all take him shopping the next day to pick out his own bed and dresser."

She tucked a strand of hair behind her ear and looked around the bedroom as if trying to keep a memory of it before new furniture would be added. "That, little Kris, is a very nice plan." She smiled at him before closing the door.

Chapter Fourteen

"Aunty Mavis! I have a new poem," Darla said through the front door the next morning, a Saturday. Her voice was a little muffled, but it was clear and loud when Mack unlocked the door and held it open wide.

"You do?" asked Mrs. O'Malley as she put her purse down.

"I wrote it last night to take my mind off your predicament. It calmed my nerves to concentrate on finding the right words and on calling images onto my page."

Mack flipped the open sign around. "Did your dad tell you about Mavis' poem?"

Darla's eyes lit up. "No, he did not. *You* never told me, either, Aunty Mavis. I had no idea. May I read it? Please?"

Mrs. O'Malley hesitated. Then she sat on her computer chair and pushed the power button on the computer tower. "It isn't a cheerful thing to share, Dar."

"I'm glad."

"What?"

"You're such a sweet, upbeat person that I should think your poetry would *have* to be at least a little bit of the opposite. What's the use of writing anything if it's only going to reflect what we all see from you, day in and day out? I'd be more excited to read a heartbreaking poem from you than one that's charming and funny."

Mrs. O'Malley blinked, absorbing what Darla was saying.

Buglit, excited to have her people in the bookshop again after the long night and morning, leaped to the chair and mewed hello.

"It's great, I'll admit," said Mack as he rested on the arm of the sofa. "I gave her a challenge to try to write a poem with a particular title, and she sure did do just that."

187

Mrs. O'Malley picked up the cat to hide her embarrassment.

"So, Aunty Mavis—do I get to read your poem?"

"I guess so," she said, lowering the cat a little. "But I can't read it out loud again. I did that for Mack, Danny, and Quainty, but I can't do it again."

"I get that," Darla said. "There are poems of mine that I've only read to Jack. Some I've only read to the baby. A few that my mom has heard, but no one else."

Mrs. O'Malley lowered the cat to her lap. "Really? Well ... how come *I* didn't get to hear those poems?"

"For the same reason that you probably won't show your poem to Kris. Different poems are for different audiences, and some are for only your very own self, which is absolutely fine."

"Speaking of poems, are you going to read us your new one?" asked Mack.

"Oh—yes." She pulled an ATM receipt from one back pocket, put it back, and then took a larger sheet of paper from the other. "Okay. Ready?"

Mr. and Mrs. O'Malley both nodded. Mrs. O'Malley pulled her chair closer to Darla, who stood near the mini refrigerator holding her handwritten page.

"It's hard to tell my legs from stones
sitting in this stream that barely moves.
Brown, clear water sliding over me
seeks a warmth I cannot give.
I have wandered through a cloud of green
dragging with me memories
of a long-lost world of childhood I once knew.

Bubbles break this shattering surface slowly
telling stories as they do
Their voices match my recollections
of friends I'd lost so long ago.

I listen carefully as they bloom
fluttering like wrens whispering in my ears.
But what they tell me I don't want to know:
that I'm not the same as I once was

Old neighbors say I was a sweet young girl
visiting upon their front porch steps
A grandma wonders if I became a writer
like I swore I would back then
My first true friend asks if I ride horses
like the ones we used to talk to
through the leaning fences of the farmyards
while our bikes waited by the road.
A teacher calls to me to ask me
if I played a concert for a king
Another voice asks if I paint word murals now
or, did I train my voice to sing

And I break down, there in the stream
More bubbles swirling up like dreams.
I stand to find my legs, at last
are less like stones and more like trees.
We won't be what those old voices expected.
We won't be what childhood promised.
Life since then has changed us, changed us
and now I move like my true, older self
along a rough and unexpected footpath"

Darla finished reading as Kris pushed into the shop. He
was startled that no one said anything to him when he
arrived. He wondered if something terrible had happened
that he didn't know about.

"Is everything okay?" he asked.

Mack stood, forcing a smile. "Yep. Hiya, kiddo. Are you
all rested now and ready to rock and roll?"

"I think so." He looked from face to face. "Why is
everybody acting weird?"

Mrs. O'Malley stood and reached for a tissue from the box next to Elephant Gerald. "Darla finished reading us her new poem right before you came."

"Oh," Kris said softly, unsure what to say next. He went past Mr. O'Malley and Darla to put his lunch away in the refrigerator. "I wish I hadn't missed it."

Darla pushed Kris' bangs from his forehead like a mother would. "It wasn't one of my funny ones. You probably wouldn't have liked it."

"Why? You like my poems that aren't funny."

"That is true," Darla said. She pressed her lips together and exhaled through her nose. "I'll type it up later and bring you a copy. Okay?"

Kris nodded as he lifted Buglit into a hug.

Darla said, "Did you hear that Mrs. O'Malley has also started writing poetry?"

Kris scratched Bug's neck as his eyes widened in surprise. "You, Mrs. O? That is super cool. Is it all about books? Or, wait! *I* know. It's about finding your brother and sister. I think that's probably what you wrote about."

Mrs. O'Malley shared a look with Darla and Mack. "Amazing! You're absolutely right. That *is* what I wrote about."

Darla asked, "Kris! How did you ever guess?"

Lowering the cat to the floor, he said, "I wrote one of my first real poems about my brothers."

Darla had a flash of memory of watching and listening to Kris' touching poem last year, and she squeezed his arm softly, feeling even more emotional than she had before.

"We sure missed you yesterday," said Mack, standing to switch on the lamps and overhead lights.

"What happened with the auction group? I can't believe I slept the whole day! I could hardly fall asleep last night. It was partly 'cause I wasn't all that tired, I guess, but mostly because I kept running over and over in my mind pictures of the books, trying to figure out which ones could be extra valuable."

"Nothing. You didn't miss a thing," Mrs. O'Malley said. "We were so busy yesterday that we couldn't get back to dealing with our mystery. Yesterday was the annual campus visitation event. There were loads of people all over the downtown like there usually are on that day. I was glad Katrina came back to help us in the afternoon. She directed customers to book sections, told them where we mark our prices in the books, and generally kept us sane."

Kris grimaced.

"What?" she asked.

He didn't answer for a moment. There was no way to put his feelings into words that didn't sound like he was a little kid whining about his people being stolen away by someone new. He pretended he was making a face for a different reason. "I'm just sorry I wasn't here to help, too."

"Well, folks—I need to get over to the record shop," Darla said. "L.P. is having a fierce, bad morning. Teething is no fun, apparently."

"Oh, dear," Mrs. O'Malley said. "I wish I was an old-timey granny with home remedies to share. What did your mom and Jack's mom say?"

"You know, I haven't even asked them for suggestions. Guess I'd better get on that. Okay, folks. Have a less-hectic day today, and I hope you find your answers. And if you do find your answers, get me over here at once to tell me the news!" She waved before pushing through the door.

Kris sat on the sofa, thinking. "Mack? Matt boxed the books after I left in the ambulance, right?"

Mack nodded.

"So, he would have taken them out of the boxes they were in at the auction, then packed them more securely and put them all lying flat like we always do, right? Did you tell us to do that on that morning? Did he repack everything?"

"Yep. Each of the books was packed lying flat. Matt was there for a long time before I got back to him, so he'd finished the job on his own."

Kris blew out a long, hard breath and stomped his feet on the area rug. "Dang."

"Why the 'dang'?"

"I guess I was hoping that if my memory *did* ever come back from that day that I could picture the advertising or writing on the two boxes the man was standing in front of. The ones he wanted to buy from me. But, if Matt re-boxed all the books, that memory wouldn't help, anyway."

"No. No, it wouldn't. And all of the books are out of boxes now, anyway."

Suddenly, Mrs. O'Malley gasped. "Macky! What were we thinking? Oh, dear and heck!" She slapped a hand to her forehead, her eyes widening. "We put a lot of those books from the auctions out for sale already."

Mack didn't react.

"Oh, gah!" Kris said, jumping up in one swift move.

"I don't see any problem," Mr. O'Malley said calmly, leaning his shoulder against a bookcase. "I priced and we shelved only the commonest of those books, Mavis. The others that looked to be worth more went behind the counter. Almost a hundred percent of them are still there since we've been busy with customers."

"Well, are you sure the ones out on the shelves for sale already are not the books mentioned in the letter?"

A family came into the shop just then, so Mack answered only with a firm nod before saying hello to the group.

"Do you have dinosaur books for children that cover the newer theories of their anatomy?" the father asked. "Ben has a summer project to do for the Scouts. Oh, and we need books on origami for Emma. Nathan needs a reference book on water systems, and I want to look over your Egyptian history."

"And I want to read some science fiction and fantasy this summer," added the mother. "Last night I finished a novel by Ray Bradbury. Do you have anything of his in stock? Or, are there other writers you'd recommend?"

Kris swung into action, happy to be back in the shop. He led the family members to different sections around the main room and into the other rooms. He spent several minutes in the children's book room checking the publication dates on the dinosaur books, and made sure they weren't too difficult for Ben by having him read a paragraph of each.

When the family had checked out, and after a few other customers had come and gone, Kris and the O'Malleys were alone again.

"Should we look at those really old books again?" asked Kris after he'd taken a drink of water.

"I think we should," said Mr. O'Malley. "Or, rather, *I* will. I'll do it in the storage room, though. No use taking them out of there again, especially during business hours. You can help the missus to fix up the place. There were so many people in to browse and buy yesterday that the shelves are somewhat messy."

"But the lighting is too dim in there, Mack," Mrs. O'Malley said. "Put in a brighter light bulb if we have one."

"We don't, but that's all right. I can see just fine in dim light. I'm part cat in that way. I'll bring my reference books in there. You've already looked them up online and didn't find that they were worth a stellar amount, but maybe there are some hints in my detailed reference works."

"Remember to look for diamonds sewn into the spines," she said.

"There aren't any diamonds. You *know* that."

"Still, there has to be *something* we're missing."

"Unless there isn't."

"But the letter said—"

"That Charles person could be lying. You've said as much a hundred times, yourself."

"I don't know, Mack. I feel like it wasn't a lie. Or it was. Gah! I'm waffling again. What if the books we're looking for *were* stolen from the storage unit at some point? What if they're not here? What if someone snatched them at the auction while Matt was taking care of Kris after he'd been hit with that ball? What if Matt wasn't keeping an eye on the whole, big group while he was packing?"

"Then Charles wouldn't have bothered to break in here, still wanting them."

She grumped, seeing his point.

"Don't grump. I *will* keep looking them over, and if I can't find the answer to the mystery with those very old books, we'll start studying the others. You've only barely begun to look those up on the internet. Whenever you're not handling sales, use the whole rest of the day to work on these stacks, Mave. Kris is here. He can take care of helping customers and everything that doesn't involve the cash register. If Katrina comes in later, she can handle everything involved with the internet sales. Okay?"

She nodded.

Mack glanced up. "Hey, Kris. You never said. What did your dad find out at the police station?"

"He didn't go."

The O'Malley's glanced at each other, surprised.

Kris stepped closer to them and put his back against the counter. He stared straight ahead at the reference books. "I'm going to social services later this summer to tell them what Darla said. We'll go from there. We want Dontae to feel settled first. Mom and Dad are sure that the Ricki thing would in no way be a problem with this adoption, so it shouldn't matter if we wait a little while. That gives me some time to think it through, too. Dad had said that he didn't mind if I waited until I was eighteen, but I feel … obligated to talk to someone about it sooner rather than later."

"I wish I had a solid opinion on this, kiddo, but I find that I don't," Mack said, crossing his arms.

Kris turned around and played with the pens and pencils in Elephant Gerald's vase back. His mind switched to the letter from Charles. "What else could be so valuable about a book if it isn't the book itself, and it isn't something hidden in the bindings? The books aren't signed, printed on rare old dollar bills, or anything. I'm stumped."

"We'll figure it out," Mack said. He chose six rare-book reference volumes from the cases behind the counter. "I'll be in the storage room, Mavis. Yell if you need me."

Mrs. O'Malley filled a watering can and walked to the far end of the main room to the hanging plants. She said, "Kris, I don't think I told you my sister's big news. Did I?"

Kris thought for a moment. There were so many big stories floating around that he wasn't sure if he'd heard news of the Cumbers or not. "I don't think so. What?"

"Remember how she was supposed to have a solo art show in Lamarr at that gallery before it was unfairly taken from her?" She saw that he'd nodded, so she went on, "Well, the gallery owner called and said that she has a new date for a show next month. Can you believe it?"

Kris was relieved that the news wasn't bad. "I hope they don't take it away from her *again.*"

Mrs. O'Malley finished tending to the last plant after pulling off some dead leaves. "She wants all three of us—you, me and Mack—to help her choose which paintings to include in the show. After the last one got canceled, she put everything back in her upstairs rooms all out of order."

"I miss the Cumbers' farm. I miss the way it looked last year. When we were there for their shop's grand opening party, it didn't feel the same anymore. Seemed like even Billy the rooster looked different than he did before the whole place got fixed up and painted and rearranged."

"Every thing and every one changes, Kris. Look at you, for example. You're much taller this year, and your voice is deeper. You aren't shy and sad like you used to be. You have some fuzz on your face, even. The Cumbers have things exactly the way they want them now. They have their bedroom on the main floor so they don't have to go up and down constantly, the barn was cleaned and made sturdy again, and the chickens have a new yard and house. I think their farm looks wonderful now." She paused after emptying the watering can in the bathroom sink and putting the can at the bottom of that room's closet. "But I know what you mean. The way it looked last year was ... homier. The way it is now is better and safer, though."

"I guess." He remembered when he had first looked through Quaintance's paintings the year before in the upstairs of the Cumbers' home. "Going through Mrs. C's art sounds like fun. Nobody else paints like she does, that's for sure! When are we going?"

"I don't know when she wants us. I'll have to ask."

Kris thought about the unusual painting of the boy hanging in the rare book room that Mrs. Cumber had given them. The professor at the college had called her style "outsider art," meaning that she'd taught herself and that her paintings are somewhat primitive.

Kris sat at the computer. "Mrs. O? Can I use the internet for a few minutes before you start listing books for sale?"

She was surprised, but said yes. "I'll decide which of these books I want to list first while you do your research."

"Thanks."

She hadn't questioned him as to what he wanted to look up, so it was shocking to her when she glanced at the screen a few minutes later.

"This is what Dontae has," he said. "See these hands?" He pointed. "And these faces? There are a ton of different ectodermal dysplasia types. I know about Dontae's hands and feet, scars on his lips, and missing teeth. He doesn't sweat much. He's had some surgeries on his eyes, too."

Mrs. O'Malley stood straighter. "Oh, that poor *boy*," slipped out before she could stop herself from saying such a thing.

Kris kept silent, still scrolling through search-result photos. He then clicked away from the images to medical articles. He read parts of the ones that weren't too technical for him to understand. "I meant to do this before."

"Maybe you shouldn't have done it at all, Kris." She put a hand on his shoulder, trying to think of the right thing to say. "Dontae will have his *own* face, his *own* hands and feet. Every single person is unique, even if they share a medical condition or diagnosis. You'll get to know him, and you won't even notice these things after a little while. I'm sure of it."

He swallowed, embarrassed. "Mrs. O, I mostly wanted to learn about ED to know how to be a better roommate. He'll be sharing my room, and I wondered if there was anything special I needed to know to keep him from overheating or getting hurt."

"Your mom and dad will know what to do for him as far as all that is concerned, Kris. Your job will be to make sure he feels like a part of your family as soon as possible. It sounds like that little boy has had a hard life."

"Yeah. It makes me feel like I've been overreacting to my own troubles."

She put an armful of books next to the cash register before turning to Kris. "You haven't." She looked at him to make sure he knew she'd meant that. "It's good that Dontae will be rooming with you. He'll see how well you're doing after being adopted, and it will make him see that fitting into a new family is perfectly possible."

Kris glanced back at the computer screen. The article he'd been scanning included a photo of a boy with claw-shaped hands. He clicked the X at the top of the screen, which returned it to the screensaver of a green field dotted with wildflowers. Suddenly, today felt like the last page of a chapter in his life.

The afternoon went by quickly. Katrina never came into the shop, but she did call to say she had a full day of piano practicing, babysitting, and grocery shopping to do. Her mother had to work late, so Katrina was going to make dinner. She said she would visit Kris in the evening after they ate.

"I don't think I'll be here at all tomorrow," Kris said as he was getting ready to walk home that afternoon.

Mr. O'Malley had long before given up his study of the eighteenth-century books in the storage room. They were locked for another night. He offered Haiku and Buglit each a few fish-shaped treats, and as he watched them crunch and chew, he said, "No? Oh, that's right. You're getting a new brother tomorrow."

Kris stared through the door. "I feel ... like I'm not ready for this to happen. There's everything that's going on with the auction books, and with this thing that Darla remembered about my first parents. I still worry that my sight will blank out again. Sometimes I'm woozy and tired. I almost wish Dontae wasn't coming to our house until all this excitement is over with."

The O'Malleys glanced at each other.

Kris sighed. "But then I think that maybe this is the way my life is now. There's always going to be this thing or another thing going on. If I ask my folks to wait, that's not fair to Dontae. I remember how relieved I was to be fostered

198

by the Dehlvis over two years ago. What if Dev and Bijay had said to wait because they had too much going on?"

Mrs. O'Malley then pulled Kris to the sofa and sat him down. "I think you're also worried about taking on the duties of a big brother to a boy with some physical challenges."

"I was the new kid once. I *want* to help him."

"I know, I know. But you shouldn't worry that Dontae will be your new *job*. Just be a brother to him. Be his friend. Your mom and dad will take care of the rest."

Hours later, after the Dehlvis had eaten and the dishes were washed and put away, and while Mrs. Dehlvi had gotten out her vintage blue-and-white-checked *Joy of Cooking* book to start work on baking a chocolate cake for Dontae's arrival, someone knocked on their front door.

"Commmpany!" shouted Bijay. He had been at the bookcase near the dining table looking through his coloring books, planning to create a picture for Dontae.

Mr. Dehlvi lowered the volume on the television and reached for the footrest handle of his recliner, but Kris told his father that he would answer the door.

It was Katrina, and she was holding a box wrapped in blue gift paper tied with a wide yellow ribbon.

Kris held the door open for her, surprised that she'd brought a present for someone.

"Hello, Mrs. D," she said, smiling shyly, standing where she could see into both the kitchen and living room.

"Come in, come in, Katrina. Please, take a seat on the sofa."

"I can't stay. I wanted to bring this over for Kris and his brothers. Here, Bijay," she said to the boy who was jumping up and down, his eyes on the package.

Kris and Mrs. Dehlvi followed Katrina and Bijay into the living room.

"Where's Dev?" asked Mr. Dehlvi, leaning forward in his chair to watch the package getting unwrapped.

"Devvy!" called Bijay. A few seconds later, his older brother was out of the bathroom, watching the unwrapping, too.

"There's one for each of you," explained Katrina.

Inside were four navy blue t-shirts of various sizes, each one with white lettering that said, "The Fabulous Dehlvi Boys."

Bijay quickly found the smallest one. He took off his red shirt and pulled the new one over his head and his arms through the sleeves. "It fits!"

"It does indeed, Bijy-bij," said a smiling Mr. Dehlvi.

"What does it say? The big word, I mean," Bijay asked.

"Fabulous," his mother told him. "That means you are all very, very terrific."

Dev lifted out the second largest t-shirt, and Kris took the largest for himself. Kris held it against his chest, showing that his shirt would fit him, too.

"We're like a rock band now," said Dev, trying on his shirt. He then made air guitar and dance moves before flopping back onto the sofa.

"Thanks, Kat," said Kris as he neatly folded his shirt. He laughed at Dev and Bijay, who were both pretending to be guitarists. "We'll wear them tomorrow. Dontae, too."

"Won't you sit for a while, Katrina?" asked Mr. Dehlvi.

The girl seemed to consider it but then shook her head. She said, "Um, Kris? Can I talk to you for a minute?"

"Thank you, Katrina!" called Bijay.

"Thank you," said Dev, winding down his stage act.

"Yes. Thank you for your kind thought and gifts. Please come again, any time," Mrs. Dehlvi said before stepping back into the kitchen.

Kris opened the front door and walked outside onto the porch with Katrina. He sat on the cushioned bench there and indicated that she should sit, too.

She stayed standing. "I wanted to say that I'll be thinking about you tomorrow. This is a big deal. I don't know how I would feel if my mom brought someone new into the house and wanted us to be a brother and sister to them. And ... you've finally got used to having a new family, and now you're getting another brother. Now there's Dontae and so many other things happening at the same time. I thought and thought about what I could do, and I finally came up with the t-shirt idea. Kind of lame, I guess, but—"

He shook his head and said earnestly, "No! Are you kidding? They're perfect!"

She blushed, staring at the white-painted floorboards. She began inching backward toward the steps. "I should go." She nervously pulled her blonde hair from her neck and over the front of her shoulder.

"I want you to stay," Kris said softly, a different tone in his voice.

Katrina stopped backing away. She glanced up. She couldn't read his expression, but he almost looked lonesome for her. Her heart leaped.

"Okay," she answered, not moving.

Kris pulled her by the hand until she was sitting beside him. "I should buy you a t-shirt, too. 'Fabulous Katrina' sounds about right."

"Don't."

"Why not?" he asked. He could feel her arm against his.

She could feel his arm against hers. "I'm not fabulous. *You* are. Your whole family is."

He was breathing harder. He looked at her profile, at her long eyelashes, her soft, peach-pink lips. "Kat, I—"

"I have to go," she insisted, popping upright. The warning from her brother about waiting to tell Kris her feelings for him replayed in her mind. "Good luck tomorrow. Bye!"

She was out of sight before Kris could think what to say back to her. He sat until he could breathe normally again, then went back inside where his father said, "Get ready. I'm taking you and your brothers to the mall for haircuts."

"You are?"

"Haircuts!" yelled Bijay, who was starting to have the bad habit of announcing everything.

"Your mother decided for us. Let us go before the barbershop closes for the night."

Kris ran his fingers through his long bangs. "I don't really need—"

"Yes yes yes," his mother called from the kitchen. She appeared in the doorway, shaking her finger, her eyes determined. "I don't want shaggy boys going to get their brother tomorrow. Go!"

Kris sighed. Bijay cheered. Dev rolled his eyes. An hour later, all three boys and Mr. Dehlvi had fresh haircuts.

Chapter Fifteen

The Dehlvis ate breakfast at a pancake restaurant the next morning. By ten o'clock they had finished eating and were relaxing at their booth table, talking and laughing. Kris sensed that his parents were nervous, despite acting jolly.

Mr. Dehlvi had put on a suit that morning, but his wife asked him to change into brown slacks and a tan polo shirt. She then tried on three different dresses before settling on a pair of light green pants and a flowing pink top. The boys all wore shorts and their new t-shirts.

"More hot tea?" offered their waitress.

"No, thank you. We are quite finished with our delicious meal," Mr. Dehlvi replied.

She smiled and tore off the check, leaving it on the table. Mr. Dehlvi took out his wallet and picked up the bill. After a few moments, he realized he couldn't see the numbers.

"They are on your head, Falak," Mrs. Dehlvi said, pointing.

"Oh." He lowered his glasses over his eyes. "Better."

The boys and Mr. and Mrs. Dehlvi laughed, and this time Kris sensed that his family was truly relaxed.

"Well," said Kris, "are we ready?"

Mr. Dehlvi looked at his wristwatch. "It is time. Boys? Does anyone need to use?"

"Me!" said Bijay, raising his hand as if he were in school.

"I'll go, too," said Kris.

"I should, also," said Mrs. Dehlvi. She was at an open end of the booth and left first.

Kris took Bijay by the hand, and the boy skipped happily past the tables and other breakfast-eaters. Kris let his brother use the men's room first, and as he waited outside the door, Dev stepped behind him in the hallway that was decorated with vintage tablecloths and aprons.

203

"I'm going to burst!" Dev said, his eyes wide.

"Well, then you go next."

"I don't mean that way, Kris. I mean that I can't stop being full of nervousness."

"I've been meaning to talk to you guys about Dontae. I'll do it in the car in a minute."

Dev shrugged and slid his hands into his jean shorts pockets. "Talk to us? What about?"

"Wait until we're all in the back seat together."

They heard a whoosh and sink water running. Bijay emerged. "All done!"

"Great. Okay, Dev—you go next."

When they were all loaded into the car, buckled in and pulling onto the street, Kris said to his brothers, "Yesterday I read up on ectodermal dysplasia a little bit and looked at photos. Mom and Dad know what Dontae looks like, but we don't. I think that you guys should know that—"

"Kris. Stop talking now, please," said Mrs. Dehlvi.

"But I was going to tell them what he looks like."

"You have no idea what you're talking about. I know you mean well, but don't say any more."

"Why, Mom?" asked Dev, leaning forward.

"Why, Mommy?" echoed Bijay.

"Because Kris does not know what he thinks he knows," Mr. Dehlvi said as he steered the car onto the highway ramp. "Looking at pictures of other people with this condition means nothing. Everyone is different. I wish you had talked to me first, Kris."

"But shouldn't they know what Dontae might look like?" complained Kris, hotly embarrassed.

Mr. Dehlvi glanced in his rear-view mirror, meeting Kris' eyes before looking back at the road ahead. "I have told you that his fingers are fused together in groups. He has had cleft lip and palate surgery. He has three toes on each foot. He has some missing teeth. He cannot sweat enough to keep himself cool. He has a big heart and a lot of determination to do whatever he sets his mind to doing."

Kris felt even more embarrassed.

"I didn't mean to say ..." Kris tried to explain.

"I did not tell Dontae what you boys look like," said his father.

Mrs. Dehlvi turned, looking at her sons in the back seat. "Kris, we arranged to take you in before we had met you, just as we arranged to take Dontae in before we met him. I gave birth to Dev and Bijay and became their mother without seeing them first. What is on the outside should not matter. We don't mean to make you embarrassed. I know—*we* know that you meant well. This is a happy day. You are about to meet and bring home your new brother, who will love you in no time at all. Soon you will see only his heart, and he will see only yours."

Kris felt as if his face were on fire. He should have listened to Mrs. O'Malley when she told him almost the same thing when he was looking at photos on the internet. He eyed Dev.

His brother merely sighed and announced, "I think I'm hungry again."

"Not possible," said Kris, smiling at last.

Dev shrugged. "I feel a rumble in my stomach. I thought maybe it was hunger."

"That is nerves," said his mother. "We all have them this morning."

"Not Dad," said Bijay.

"That is not true, Bij. I feel that way, too." He pulled off at the next exit, slowing to a stop at the end and signaling a left turn. "This is a big day for us all."

Kris eyed the interior of their car, a four-door sedan. "Where will Dontae sit?"

"Up front with us," said his mother.

"Shall we say, Daya?" asked Mr. Dehlvi, driving onto a street at the north end of town, past the campus.

"Say what?" asked Dev. He looked at his brothers to see if they knew something that he didn't.

Kris and Bijay shrugged.

"You can tell them, Falak," Mrs. Dehlvi replied, nodding at him.

"We will be shopping today for a new or used SUV or van. That was going to be a little surprise for you all. How do you like that news?" their father asked, looking for the boys' reaction in the mirror.

"What?"

"We *are?*"

"Yipee!"

"Are we keeping this car, too?" asked Kris, his voice still a bit rough with emotion. He had a particular reason for asking.

"I don't know. We have not decided fully. Probably we will trade in this one, and I will use your mother's small car when I return to work in the fall. Or, we'll keep all three to be prepared for next year." He turned his head to wink at Kris.

Kris would be able to drive in just over a year. The news that there might be an extra vehicle in the driveway made his heart soar. He forgot that he had been terribly embarrassed a short time before.

In another minute, Mr. Dehlvi pulled into the driveway of a small home on a street of similar houses.

The sun was bright and warm, and a breeze swept in and around a willow tree in the front yard. A red swing set was in the side yard, and next to it was a covered plastic sandbox shaped like a turtle. Kris saw white curtains part in a downstairs window. Within that part, he saw a boy's face smiling at them as the family piled out of the car.

Kris' heart was pounding with anxiety, but Bijay performed a jumpy dance as soon as he'd left the back seat.

The door to the house swung open, and a woman stepped out. She was someone that Kris recognized. It was his own former social worker, Miss Valentine, a younger woman with long black hair and a very tanned, pleasant face.

"Hello, Dehlvi family," she called. "And Kris! Hello again. Do you remember me?"

The Dehlvis and Miss Valentine met on the front lawn near the steps of the house. Kris nodded in reply, but he couldn't make himself say anything. Miss Valentine was who he had thought he should talk to later in the summer about Ricki. He never imagined he'd see her before then.

Behind Miss Valentine, in the doorway, stood Dontae, smiling but obviously bashful. He had on an orange shirt and black jean shorts, short white socks, and black leather shoes. A heavyset, older woman using a cane stood farther inside in the shadows. Dontae turned back to her and hugged her, hiding his face.

"Won't you come on out, Dontae?" the social worker coaxed. "This is your new family. You know Mr. and Mrs. Dehlvi already. And these fellas are your new brothers. Kris is the oldest, then Dev and Bijay. I know the boys from a couple of years ago. They are very nice, Dontae. Want to come out and say hello? Sure, you do. There. That's a good boy."

Kris shook the boy's hand first, followed by a suddenly-shy Bijay. Dev waved hello from a few feet away. He was trying not to look at Dontae's hands with their fused fingers.

Mrs. Dehlvi bent to hug Dontae, and when she stood, he stayed in her arms, his face hiding from everyone.

Kris was surprised that this boy who he had never met was already very attached to his mother.

"I have a few more papers for you to sign if you'd like to step inside. Kids, you can play out here for a few minutes. This won't take long."

Dontae made a sound of protest, clinging to his new mother tighter.

Bijay walked around to see Dontae's face. He patted the boy's arm. "Dontae, do you want to show me your karate moves?"

Mrs. Dehlvi put the boy down, and at first, he stood still, eyeing everyone to see if they were going to accept the way he looked. Dontae, seeming to have decided that these boys were probably not going to tease him, nodded. With Bijay right behind him, he ran around and around them all before stopping, bowing, and kicking out and chopping.

Bijay was impressed, and the two of them spent the next few minutes chopping at the air and kicking the turtle sandbox lid while the adults went into the house.

A dog barked from somewhere behind the house. Dev sat on the steps below the front door, apparently listening to the conversation taking place behind him in the house. He moved out of the way when his parents and Miss Valentine came to the door again.

"Here we are, boys. I have your bags ready, Dontae," the social worker said cheerfully, holding the door as the Dehlvis walked down the steps. "I think you're all set to go home with your new family."

Kris took the two cloth suitcases from Miss Valentine. Her lilac perfume was the same as it had been when she'd taken him from the house he'd lived in before he moved in with the Dehlvis, and memories from that day washed over him.

"Are you okay?" she asked. The lines between her eyes deepened in concern. "Kris? Is everything all right? You look upset."

"I'm good. I ... was remembering when you took me away last time."

She nodded and sighed. "I remember that, too. Did I ever apologize to you for placing you there? We were short-staffed at that time, and in desperate need of placement homes for fosters then. I am really very sorry you had such a bad experience."

"It's okay. I'm doing good now. Honestly." He stepped slightly nearer to whisper, making sure she could see in his eyes that he was sincere, "I mean it, Miss Valentine. With all my heart. These are the *best* people you could have put me with."

Her lips quivered. "Oh, Kris. I'm *so* heartened to hear that. And how lovely that they're taking in Dontae now, too. Let me know if you have any questions or concerns at any time. Do you want my card? Your mom and dad have one, but I can give you one, too."

He relaxed, thinking quickly. Surely, he could tell her about Ricki now, instead of waiting until the end of the summer. She was right there in front of him, smiling at him. He took a breath in, almost ready to tell her at least a short version of the Ricki story, but he merely shook his head, instead. "I'll get your number from Mom if I need it, and … um … there *is* something, actually." He paused. "I might want to talk to you at some point in the future. Not about Dontae or the Dehlvis, though."

Miss Valentine tried to read his face for clues as to what he might be talking about, but gave up and said, barely above a whisper, "You know you can talk to me about anything. Say yes to me right now if there is a problem." Her face sobered. "I mean it."

Kris shook his head emphatically, meeting her eyes directly. "Nothing is wrong. I'll talk to you after things settle down. Thanks, Miss Valentine. Thanks for Dontae, too."

Satisfied that he was sincere, she said, louder, "You're already a young man. I can't believe the transformation in your height and voice." She swallowed. "I know things could have gone differently for you. I guess they did, at first. But now I feel I can count you as one of the highlights of my career." She watched as he put the suitcases into the trunk of the car.

"Dontae!" Dev said when he saw what was in the trunk once Kris had opened it. "I forgot! We have a present for you."

He reached around Kris to grab the small gift box tied with a yellow bow. Mrs. Dehlvi had rewrapped it the night before since Katrina's box was too big for just one shirt.

Dontae had retreated to the safety of the front of the house, suddenly too afraid to get in the car. Kris saw through the door window that there were other children inside. The older woman with a cane came into view again. She opened the door to say a few words to Dontae. The boy climbed the stairs to hug her one last time before he went out again.

The social worker took Dontae's hand, and he hugged her hips, looking back toward the house. She bent and whispered to him. Dontae nodded and allowed her to lead him to the wrapped present Dev held out.

"Our friend Katrina had these shirts made for us. Want to open it now and put it on? It's like the ones we're wearing."

Kris closed the trunk and stepped closer to his parents, watching as Dontae opened the package, forgetting to be shy.

Dontae held the shirt as Miss Valentine picked up the box and wrapping from the ground. She and Dontae smiled at each other.

"What does it say?" he asked Miss Valentine.

She read it aloud, pointing to each word as she said it.

He held it above his head, showing off the print. "It fits!" he declared as if he had put it on already.

"It does, buddy! Look at that. You are going to look great in this cool shirt they brought for you. Want to put it on?" Miss Valentine asked.

Dontae nodded happily, eyeing the other boys as if for permission.

Kris noticed that his parents were standing silently together, arm in arm at the edge of the driveway.

"We're going car-shopping!" announced Bijay to the boy in the front seat. "I've never been car-shopping before, have you, Dontae?"

"No," he answered. "But I like this car. I wonder why you need another one. It has a lot of great features and styling."

Mrs. Dehlvi giggled. "Did you hear that in a commercial?"

"I *like* commercials. I like this car, too."

Bijay had taken the center position in the rear. He leaned forward as far as his safety belt would allow him to lie with his head on the back of the front seat, trying to be as near as possible to his new brother.

Noticing this, Dontae turned around to touch Bijay's hair, curious if it felt the same as his own since it was almost the same color, but of a different texture.

Bijay didn't react, seeming to understand. After the boy turned back around, Bijay reached over the seat to feel Dontae's curly black hair in return.

Dontae asked, "Is it touchably soft?"

"Yep," said Bijay. "Cool! I like how it goes in wiggles. My hair is non-wiggly. Want to feel my head again?"

"Wait until we are out of the car, Bij," Mr. Dehlvi warned. "I do not want to get into an accident. Then the police officer will ask 'how did this happen, sir?' and I will have to say that my boys were feeling each other's hair while I was driving fifty-seven miles per hour on the highway."

Everyone laughed, and Mrs. Dehlvi put her arm around Dontae's shoulders and gave him an affectionate pat on his arm.

Kris relaxed in his seat, no longer anxious, the way he had been all morning. He had memories of being made to feel very comfortable by the Dehlvis when he was afraid in the beginning. It was like watching that happen all over again from a different point of view.

Barely another minute passed before they were on an exit to one of the busiest streets at the north side of Anders Lake. A few seconds later, they were pulling into a car dealership.

There wasn't a cloud in the sky, and bright sunlight glinted off every part of every car on display and the glass-walled building. Mr. Dehlvi found a place to park, and all six of them got out.

"Want to see my feet?" asked Dontae.

Bijay's eyes lit up. "Yeah!"

Mrs. Dehlvi shook her head. "The pavement here is too hot. You two little ones will go with Kris into the air-conditioned building to wait for us. There will be potties in there, and Kris will get you a cup of water or buy you both a drink from the machines." She reached into her purse and pulled out several one-dollar bills. "Here, Kris. This should be enough for all of you. You may go too, Dev, or you may stay with us."

Dev wanted to look at the cars, so Kris, Dontae, and Bijay went together into the dealership's waiting area. A familiar woman in a dark blue skirt suit and with dark blonde hair in a soft knot at the back of her head met them when they first sat down.

"May I help you?" She stopped walking, surprised. "Kris? Well, Kris! Are you here looking for Katrina?"

Kris stood as soon as he and the boys had sat down. "Mrs. Karlsson! I didn't know we were at your workplace. My folks are looking for a bigger vehicle now that there are six of us in the family. They're outside with Dev. This is my new little brother, Dontae."

Mrs. Karlsson stepped closer to the younger boys and stuck out her hand to Dontae. When she first saw his fused fingers, she almost retracted her hand. She caught herself. Shaking his hand firmly and smiling, she said, "Very nice to

212

meet you, Dontae. Have you gotten all settled in at your new home?"

Dontae took his hand from hers and motioned for her to bend to his level. "I think you're very nice," he whispered. He gave her a tight hug around her neck, something she wasn't expecting.

"You're a little *charmer,* aren't you?" she laughed, standing straighter.

"We haven't been home with Dontae yet," said Kris. This was our first stop after we picked him up.

"Really? Well, we're happy you've come. Is anyone helping your mom and dad? Should I go out and check?"

"I don't know. They'd be glad to see you, though. I don't think Mom and Dad know you work here, either."

She nodded. "Kat's in my office for the afternoon. You boys go back there if you'd like. She'll be *so* glad to see you. It's the third door along the hallway, on the right. I drove her to her piano lesson down the street earlier, and she'll wait until my shift is over to go home with me in a few hours. She's curled up on the floor on pillows, reading."

Mrs. Karlsson waved at the boys as she went through the side door.

Kris stood, unable to decide what to do next. To stall, he walked a few paces to the drinks machine that stood beside a suspended television and a magazine rack. "Who wants what?"

"Juuuuuuice!" said Bijay. "One that's apple or peach or red."

Dontae sat, swinging his legs, his eyes looking at the grey-patterned area rug.

"Okay. Juuuuice it is. How about for you, D?" Kris asked.

Dontae shrugged, still not looking up.

"Get apple. That's always good," said Bijay. He then pulled Dontae over to the machine. "Pick."

Kris said, "Don't be shy about having Mom and Dad get you stuff, okay? I was the same way when they first fostered and then adopted me. I always wished I had my own money. I couldn't get used to them buying me things."

Dontae's eyes flew open. "What?"

Kris paused, thinking. "Didn't you know? I was adopted by the Dehlvis, too."

Dontae shook his head slowly. He then pointed at the lettering on Kris' t-shirt.

"Sure, I'm a Dehlvi, and now you're one, too. We four kids are the Fabulous Dehlvi Boys, just like it says. You know what? After you pick out a drink, we'll take it and say hello to the nice girl who got us these shirts. Okay? Her name is Kat, and that lady you hugged is her mom. So, come on. Pick out a drink."

He pointed to a red juice box. "A-four. Thank you, Kris."

Kris went to the water dispenser and got himself a cup of water. He drank it down quickly and threw his cup away before leading Bijay and Dontae to Mrs. Karlsson's office.

"Kris!" Katrina said from the floor of her mother's office. "What in the heck are you doing here?" She stood, glancing at the page number in her paperback to memorize it. "And wowsers! Is this Dontae? Hello!"

Dontae hung behind in the doorway, his arm through Bijay's.

"Yep. This is our fabulous new brother," Kris said, smiling. "Weird how I ended up seeing you today. Mom and Dad are here shopping for a bigger car. We just came from the home where he's been staying. Dontae? Want to say hello and thank you to Kat for our shirts, buddy?"

"Thank you," he said softly.

"Thank you," echoed Bijay, softly, too.

Dontae stepped forward and slightly bowed. Kris wondered if that was something he'd been practicing in his karate classes.

214

Bijay, seeing this, offered Katrina a bow, too.

"You're welcome, boys." She shared a look with Kris, indicating that she, too, was charmed by the little boys. "I'm usually never here, but now that I'm taking piano lessons twice per week, getting a ride from Mom means that I get to sit around in the air conditioning on poofy pillows on a regular basis. Saturday is my usual lesson day, but my teacher had to shift me to today since her son was playing in a concert in Lamarr." She looked at her fingers and wiggled them. "I'm going to take lessons at our school, instead, starting this fall. If I still like playing by then, that is. Come on in, guys. Everybody grab a pillow."

Bijay grinned and flopped onto a purple one as Dontae perched solemnly on a blue pillow, holding his juice box with care. Kris sat on an office chair watching Katrina cross her long, slender legs as she claimed the largest pillow again.

"How's it going?" she asked him.

"Good."

"I'm hungry, though," complained Bijay. "Where are we eating lunch?"

Kris put an elbow on Mrs. Karlsson's desk. "Well, I don't know. I can't believe all those pancakes wore off already, Bij. I'm still kind of full."

"We should have chicken," said Dontae after taking a sip of juice. "The commercials say it's 'clucka-lucka good!'"

"Yeah! Chicken," agreed Bijay. He bent to let Dontae pat his hair.

"Sounds like these two are ready to eat," Katrina said, wondering about the exchange of hair-patting going on next to her.

Kris asked, "What are you reading?"

"A mystery. Well, I think I know who did it, but I guess you could still call it a mystery."

"I just got done with a book-themed fantasy by ... Cornelia ... um ..."

"Funke?"

"Yeah! That's it. I meant to check if the O'Malleys have the next book in the series, but in all the excitement of these past days, I forgot."

"They *did* have it, but now I do. And the next book, too. I'll lend them to you."

"Super! So, did you like them?" he asked, rolling his chair closer.

They discussed the first book in the series while Dontae and Bijay took off their shoes and socks to show each other their feet.

"*Here* you are," said Mrs. Dehlvi as she stepped into the office. "Would you like to look at the cars? We need your opinion. Hello, Katrina. Your mother surprised us in the used car section. How nice that we had a friendly face here to help us. Don't the boys look handsome in your presents? That was very thoughtful. I will have them write to you to thank you more properly."

Katrina stood, and the three boys stood, too. Kris pushed Mrs. Karlsson's chair back under the edge of the desk.

"Oh, there's no need for that, Mrs. Dehlvi. Honest," the girl said.

"Bijay and Dontae—what are your shoes and socks doing on the floor? And why is one sock missing?" their mother scolded, her hands on her hips.

Katrina lifted a few pillows until they found the missing sock.

"We were looking at our toes and stuff," said Dontae.

"Oh, ho! Kris, we have another 'stuff' sayer in the family. Now I have *two* of you running around. Before you know it, *I'll* be saying it."

Bijay protested, "I say 'stuff,' too. Don't forget about me."

"Well, for now, I want you both to tuck your feet into your socks and shoes and come with me. We have car-choosing to do. Come come come, you boys. Katrina, will you come along, as well?"

Outside, two, then three, then four SUVs were examined inside and out. Then two were decided against, and then one more was eliminated.

"Is everyone too hungry to take it for a test drive now? Should we find a lunch first?" asked Mr. Dehlvi as he stood outside the open door of the nearly-new silver-toned SUV, his arm resting on its edge.

"I can hold it for you until tomorrow if you'd like to think about your choices some more," offered Mrs. Karlsson. "And there are three other auto dealers right on this street. Don't feel rushed."

Bijay climbed into the SUV and took a seat in the row farthest to the rear. Dev scrambled in, too. Kris got in behind the front passenger seat, and Dontae stepped in, sitting in the back next to Bijay.

"I think we will give it a test now," laughed Mr. Dehlvi.

"This one has even *more* features and styling," said Dontae.

Katrina poked her head in through the side door to softly say to Kris, "Nice haircut, by the way." She raised her eyebrows twice and smiled, adding another layer to the compliment.

Kris had no idea how to react, but it didn't matter. Kat had skipped off toward the dealership building in a flash.

After a lunch of fried chicken, mashed potatoes, and coleslaw almost two hours later, Bijay finally stopped sneaking looks at Dontae. He'd been fascinated by the way his new brother ate without very much difficulty at all, despite having fewer fingers to work with. He couldn't use a knife but had no trouble holding a glass, a fork, or drumsticks.

Mrs. Dehlvi finally asked Bijay to pay less attention to other people and more attention to his own food.

Dontae said to her, "I would be looking at someone like me, too. He can't help it. Bijay and everyone can ask me anything. I've done it before."

"Done what before?" asked Dev after wiping his mouth with a napkin.

"Answered lots and lots of questions. I sometimes don't know what to say, but mostly I do. I know I've had a lot of operations, like on my eyes, mouth, a foot, and stuff like that." He played with his straw. "I know I was born different. I don't sweat very well. But I think I'm done having operations now—except on my mouth—so Miss Valentine said I can forget what I had done and look forward to things only getting better."

Mrs. Dehlvi, who was sitting beside him, placed a hand on Dontae's arm for a second. "Oh, we may have questions, but mostly they will be things like 'do you want ice cream or cake for dessert?'"

Dontae's eyes widened. "That's easy! Both!"

Everyone laughed.

"But not now. I'm soooooo full!" he added, sliding down in his seat for emphasis.

"Oh, I'm soooooo full, too!" claimed Bijay, sliding a little, too. He knew better than to actually slide to the floor under the table, but he was tempted. He waited to see if Dontae did. He didn't.

"Now that we have a bigger car—an SUV—we can plan a summertime trip somewhere if you would like," said Mr. Dehlvi. "Maybe go to an amusement park, or to a campground. A museum would be interesting. Or, we could go to see the world's largest ball of paint. I have taken the summer off, so there is no reason to stay home every day until it's time for school again."

Kris panicked. How could he pack and leave for a trip when being away from the bookshop for only one day made him anxious? He fought with himself for a few seconds before asking his father, "Um, would I have to go, too?"

Mr. Dehlvi took in a long, slow breath, crossed his arms, and then uncrossed one to draw Kris' attention to what it said on his shirt. Then he let his breath out and looked at Dontae. When he darkly met Kris' eyes again, he could tell that his point had been made and understood. There were four Dehlvi brothers in the family, not three. "I think that we should step outside to have a talk, Kris," he whispered, leaning close.

Kris' face reddened. He shook his head. "We don't need to. I'm sorry I said that." To Dontae, he explained, "I work during the summer at a used bookshop. There's been a ton of big, exciting stuff going on lately, and I'm anxious to find out what I'm missing while I've been gone. I didn't mean that I don't want to go with you and Dev and Bijay on a trip. I'm just all curious about what I'm missing at the bookshop. Okay?"

Dontae seemed puzzled. "Okay." He looked around the table, then shrugged. "Can *I* get a job in your bookshop?"

Kris smiled, relieved to have been forgiven. "Do you like to read? The shop I work in has books of all kinds."

"I like to *hear,* so far. I don't know many of the words in books." He sighed. "I probably can't work in your shop, then."

"Maybe someday, though. I'll help you with your reading over the summer. What types of stories do you like to hear?"

Dontae thought.

Bijay said, "Anything with animals in it. That's what *I* like."

Dev said, "Anything with magic."

Dontae's eyes brightened. "How about we hear a book about a magic animal?"

Kris felt his father relax beside him. A small lump in his throat that he hadn't been able to swallow was melting away while the boys talked about books and characters. He was still too embarrassed to look in his father's direction.

On the drive home, Kris had time to think clearly about how he should be acting and feeling as the oldest brother to three boys. He'd always seen Dev and Bijay as the established sons of his adopted parents. They didn't need him, really. They had each other. If he joined in on games and trips out, he was welcome, but not necessary. He wasn't sure why he felt that way, but he did. Now that Dontae was a part of the family, things seemed much different. He wasn't sure how he fit in, or what role he'd play as the oldest brother and second newest. There was no real reason *not* to take part in things that the three of them would be doing; it just hadn't occurred to him before that things would change very much. Kris felt his bookshop job, and time with Matt, Katrina, and Steve, melting away from him.

When everyone had arrived at the Dehlvi house at last, and when the front yard seemed to be full of Dehlvis, Kris held back his urge to run inside to phone the O'Malleys for news. He had to be a part of the family, he knew, and they had to come first.

The Hawns, friends of the Dehlvis who lived two houses away, crossed the street. Mr. Hawn called a greeting. "Hello! This must be Dontae. How are you? We heard that you were coming to live on our street, and now, here you are." He and his wife both shook the boy's hand.

Then Bijay shook Dontae's hand, pumping it high and low. Both boys grinned at their own silliness.

"We are doing well, thank you," Mrs. Dehlvi said, reaching back into the car for her purse and some paperwork. She shut the door and stepped close to the Hawns. "This is Mr. and Mrs. Hawn, Dontae. They have a swimming pool that our boys use, and they have a great, big dog—a Saint Bernard—that they call Roland."

"Hi," Dontae said shyly, linking an arm through Bijay's. "I don't know anyone named Roland. Is that usually a dog name or a people name?"

"I named our dog after my wife's father. They almost look alike. Especially their eyes," said Mr. Hawn, who then laughed airily with his lips together as he pushed up his glasses.

Kris stared at Mr. Hawn. He hadn't realized until then that his neighbor had grown a mustache and beard.

"We'd love for you to come swimming, too, Dontae. Any time you're hot, you get permission and come over. If that's all right with your new mom and dad, of course," added Mrs. Hawn.

"That sounds *very* nice, thank you. Dontae has some trouble keeping his body cool. It would be a good way for him to be comfortable on hot days. That is most kind of you, thank you," said Mrs. Dehlvi, her voice more emotional than usual.

Kris thought that his mom looked like a weight had been lifted from her shoulders that involved more than only how to keep Dontae from overheating. He then had a thought. "Dontae, did I hear that you have a cooling vest to wear?"

He nodded and pointed to the trunk of the car. "It's in my red suitcase. Yep. I only need it when I'm running around or when it's hot. I haven't even worn it yet this year. I do my karate inside, and I played in the school gym during recess on warm days this spring."

"Well, we'll leave you to settle in and get unpacked," said Mrs. Hawn. "We wanted to say hello. Remember, boys—when we're home, and when you have permission, you may use our pool. Our own kids are grown and gone, so there it sits, waiting for little swimmers."

The Hawns left for home as Mrs. Dehlvi walked to Kris. "I know you are curious about the O'Malleys. Go call them now. We'll get Dontae's things inside and put them in your bedroom."

He paused, watching as Mr. Dehlvi unlocked the front door to hold it open as the other boys went inside talking a mile a minute.

"Are you sure?"

"Yes. We will likely order take-out later. We have the chocolate cake to eat for dessert. This is a good time, before the O'Malleys go home for the evening."

Inside, he sat in his parents' bedroom with the door closed to make his call. It was quiet, and he knew his own bedroom was being occupied as clean sheets were put on the bed, and Dontae's luggage was unpacked.

"Mack? It's Kris. It was a good day, yes. And guess who I saw today? Mrs. Karlsson and Katrina at a car dealership. We're getting a used SUV so we won't be all squashed. Kat was in her mom's office after her piano lesson. No, we didn't know. Silver. Dontae's here now. Fine. I think so. I don't know. Maybe. I've got a different life now, all of a sudden, it feels like. He's doing okay, I think. Bijay is super excited to have him. They're already good buddies. I know he's right in the middle of them, age-wise, but he seems more like Bijay's age for some reason. I'm not tired. No. I think I'm all better. How are you guys? Any news on the mystery? Uh-huh. She did? Funny cat! I can picture that. Did you find out anything more? I guess I'm glad, though. I'd hate to be off and away when you find out. I'll call in the morning one way or the other. I'll see how it goes, and if we have plans—hey! I just remembered. We *do* have big plans. At least for part of the day. We need to pick up the new SUV after Dad talks to the bank and his insurance company; then we're going furniture shopping for a new bed for Dontae, and a new dresser for him, and one for either Dev or Bij. We're going to be sharing a room for now. I might get the basement, eventually. Okay. If I can, I'll stop in tomorrow; otherwise, I'll call sometime during the day. Call my dad's cell phone if you have big news, and that's whenever it happens. I do, too. Okay. Bye!"

He hung up, replaced the phone on the charger, and opened the door to the hallway. He saw that no one was in the bathroom, so he stepped in and closed the door behind him. After using the toilet, he looked in the mirror as he washed up. He saw a few spots of acne before realizing the faint dark circles that had been under his eyes since the baseball hit him had almost vanished.

After leaving the restroom, he went into his bedroom. Mrs. Dehlvi was tucking a clean blue-striped top sheet around the bottom edge of the mattress.

"Any big news, Kris?" she asked, looking up.

Kris shook his head.

Dontae appeared in the doorway. "This one?"

Kris smiled. "This is your room, D. I'll sleep on the sofa for tonight."

Dontae looked alarmed. "Do you *have* to?"

"Do I have to what?" asked Kris, confused.

"Sleep somewhere else."

"This bed is too small for both of us. You'll be okay. I'll be right out in the living room." Kris put his arm on the boy's shoulders.

Dontae frowned. "I think this is a pretty big bed."

"Would you like Kris to stay in here with you?" Mrs. Dehlvi asked.

Dontae looked at the bed. "I think we'd fit."

Kris didn't ask him if he would be scared or lonely. Instead of arguing about it, he would simply wait until Dontae was asleep before fixing up the sofa for himself. "I always sleep on the passenger side of the bed. Do you want the driver's side? If you don't, that's okay. I can switch things for one night."

Dontae shook.

"What? What's wrong, Dontae?" Kris asked, frowning.

"I thought ... I thought we were going to be in this room together *forever*, not just one night. Am I moving somewhere else tomorrow? I thought this was where I was going to live now." He sobbed, surprising Mrs. Dehlvi and Kris.

Mrs. Dehlvi left the end of the bed and went to hug her little boy. She eyed Kris, and in that look, he understood that she realized that nothing about this was automatically going to go smoothly.

"Why would you think that?" She patted his back tenderly. "No no *no!* You are staying with us from now until you leave us as a man. I don't know why you got scared, but believe me, Dontae, you are *staying*." She then *shh-shh-shh*'ed and said a few comforting words.

He pulled away and wiped his eyes with his arm, frowning and sucking in breaths. "Really? Then why did Kris say for *one night* he would switch sides of the bed?"

"Ohhhh," said Kris, understanding. "Didn't Mom and Dad tell you what we're doing tomorrow?"

Dontae sniffed and shook his head. "What?"

Mrs. Dehlvi sat, saying, "Why, you are going shopping for your very own bed. It will go right in this same room with Kris' bed. This one is too little for two big boys like you. You may choose whatever new bed you like in the stores, and your own dresser, too. They can match, or they can be different. And Bijay or Dev will get a new dresser. They should each have their own now. And—this I did not tell Kris yet—Kris will be getting a new bookcase. See how his books are piled against that wall? Such a *shame* for nice books to be piled as they are. We're getting Kris a tall, new bookcase."

Both Kris and Dontae's eyes were wide with happiness.

"Really?" they both asked.

Their mother nodded. "Now, let us finish making the bed. Your daddy will take measurements in both bedrooms to know what will fit." She lifted the comforter from the back of Kris' desk chair and spread it over the bed, smoothing it at the four corners and tucking it in at the bottom edge. "Pillows go next, in their new cases. Good. Hand me that extra one I bought yesterday, Kris. Dontae? Do you want one pillow or two?"

He shrugged. "This one is pluffy. One is enough." He took two breaths, happy but still emotional after crying. "How ... how will I pay you?"

Kris knew that feeling. He continued to have it for a long time after the Dehlvis adopted him. He thought about saying this to Dontae but felt shy about answering for his mother.

"Tusk! Do you think we would do all this if we weren't happy to do so? All this is needed, and ... you will pay us with your smiles and contentment. You cannot take money and possessions with you when you leave the world, but you can take with you all manner of goodness, happiness, and love."

As soon as the bed had been made up, Stomper trotted into the room from the hallway. He bounded to the top of the comforter, crowing his arrival with a hearty "Mrrrrrow!" He had expected to find Kris and maybe another member of his usual household, but instead saw Dontae. His whiskers stood straight out from his face. The cat then looked to Kris for an answer.

"Dontae, this is one of our cats. His name is Stomper. Or Stomps. Or Stompy, Stompinator, Fuzzer, Fuzzmonster, and a few other names that we call him all the time. There's another cat here, too, named Pip." He picked up the tabby and sat with him on the edge of the bed. "Stomps, this is Dontae, your new human brother."

Dontae stepped back a few paces, almost into the hallway. He shook his head, his eyes fearful.

225

"He doesn't bite or scratch. Want to pet him?" Kris asked.

"This is a funny, cute cat. There is no need to be afraid," added his mother. She sat next to Kris and gave Stomper a scratch under his chin. Stomper lifted his head and closed his eyes.

Dontae shook his head again.

"Okay. That's okay if you don't want to pet them now. But don't be afraid. Pip and Stomps are sweet. They'll be here whenever you feel like saying hello," Kris said. He put the cat onto the bed. Stomper settled in for a nap after circling a few times. He winked at Dontae, who then went to find Bijay and Dev's bedroom.

"Biiiiijay!" they all heard him call.

Kris went to the wall where his new bookcase would stand if he got one. "You don't have to buy me anything, Mom. I won't mind. You're spending a lot of money right now. I don't need a bookcase."

She stood, sighing. "Kris, I will not have you going back to your old self now that Dontae is here to influence you. I have been meaning to get you a proper case for your books for a long time. Since we are all going shopping tomorrow, that is the perfect day."

Kris looked away. "Can I pick out a bookcase from anywhere? Does it have to be from a new furniture store? If it's about the same price or cheaper, could I get an antique or a vintage one?"

"We have to think about delivery. A new store will have a van or truck."

"Oh, yeah. Well, if Mr. O'Malley will pick it up in his van, can I get a used bookcase? An antique one?"

Mrs. Dehlvi yawned a very long yawn, covered by the back of her hand. "That would be fine. Ask Mr. O first before you go looking, though. I suppose some antique shops deliver, so that is a possibility, too." She yawned again. "I do not know why I am very tired today. It must be all the excitement."

Kris yawned, too, and Stomper yawned and shifted positions.

She laughed lightly. "We are contagious, it seems. Now. Big brother Kris. Do we need to sit back down on your bed for a talk?"

Kris shut his door, his cheeks feeling hot. He put his back against the wall, slouching. "I feel like I've said and done a lot of wrong things today. Is that what you want to talk about?"

She sat again, patting the comforter beside her. "Come come come. That is not it at all."

Kris did sit, but he didn't know what she could mean.

"I saw you speaking to Miss Valentine."

"Oh."

His mother swallowed. "I know you did not talk long enough to get out your story of Ricki, is that right?"

"No, I didn't. I didn't even hint about it. I only told her that I want to talk to her later this summer. I said that it wasn't about Dontae, and it wasn't about you and Dad. I don't know why I said anything this soon. I think seeing her and remembering how cool she was about getting me with this family made me want to spill my guts, at least a little bit."

"Don't say 'spill your guts,' Kris. Ish!"

He playfully leaned his shoulder against hers.

"As to the things you feel you have said and done wrongfully today, I have forgotten them if they were there. We are all going to say and do things that maybe we shouldn't. And he will feel the same way in return. He will worry that he isn't doing things the right way, isn't saying the right things. We are all going through this change of our family together. Even the cats. Is that not correct, Sir Stomper?"

227

Stomper opened one eye after hearing his name but immediately closed it again.

"I think Dontae and Stomper will like each other before too long," said Kris. "Okay. I guess I feel better now. Oh, and I called the bookshop. They've been too busy to deal with the auction books at all. That's what they said, anyway. I halfway think they're waiting for me to get back there. I told them I'd probably be away again tomorrow." He paused, wondering if he should say more. "Mom?"

"Hmm?"

"I … I feel torn between being with the family and being at the bookshop. I'd be okay with going to the shop less if there wasn't so much going on there right now. I don't want D to feel like I'm dissing him. That's why I told him a little bit about why I'm antsy about the bookshop."

"Don't say 'dissing,' dear. I don't know what that means, but I don't think I like that word, either."

Kris leaned into her shoulder again, laughing. "Oh, Mom, you do *too* know what it means. But I'll try not to say that and 'spill your guts,' and 'stuff,' and 'dudes,' and—"

Mrs. Dehlvi stood, raised her arms, and shook her hands in the air. "Arey!" she cried, pretending to be horrified at so many objectionable words at once. Then she giggled and lowered her arms to hug Kris.

"I am sure that Dontae did not even notice," she assured him, walking to the door and opening it. She yawned again. "Come to the living room, and we'll talk about what to have for dinner. As I predicted earlier, I am too tired to prepare anything tonight."

Mr. Dehlvi appeared in the doorway. "Here are Dontae's suitcases. No use unpacking much tonight. He will have his own dresser tomorrow if it is delivered that soon."

Dontae chose what they had for dinner, a pie from his favorite pizza parlor, Mega Giant Lotsa Toppings. An hour later, the chocolate cake was brought out for dessert. After that, Mrs. Dehlvi changed for the night. Wearing a flowing cherry blossom patterned robe, she sat on her usual end of the sofa, nearest Mr. Dehlvi, who was in his recliner. The younger boys colored in coloring books while Mr. Dehlvi caught up on the news on TV. Dontae had some trouble holding a crayon, but he seemed happy to be relaxing after the long, busy day.

Kris sat watching the news, but he wasn't paying attention to what was being said or shown. He was worried about his mother and how tired she'd seemed over the past few days.

"Mom? Do you want some tea or anything?" asked Kris.

Dev glanced up as if he'd meant to ask her that when she came back into the room.

"Maybe some water with a slice of lemon, thank you." She leaned forward to examine the coloring projects. "We should get a few more coloring books tomorrow. I think those must be nearly entirely filled, hey?"

Bijay flipped through his dinosaur book. "Three dinos left. Dontae has about ten birds. Dev has a bunch of lizards, I think. I was going to take over that one after my dinos are done."

Kris went into the kitchen while Dontae climbed onto his father's lap. Bijay silently climbed up, too, to sit on the other side of Mr. Dehlvi.

Mrs. Dehlvi took the offered glass from Kris, placed it on the end table, and switched off the brass floor lamp that stood between the table and the recliner. The light outside was pinkish blue, and the flowers in their flowerbeds were bowing their heads, sleeping already. Dev, also wanting to cuddle, got up to sit next to his mother.

Mr. Dehlvi switched channels to an old movie set in England during the 1940s that Kris didn't recognize, and then he lowered the volume. Kris sat on the floor with his back against the sofa, feeling very content as the black and white images transported him to another place and time.

An hour later, Kris went into the bathroom to wash and to get into his pajamas. The three younger boys had gone to their bedrooms long before. When Kris went into the bedroom for his pillow and the spare blanket, he heard muffled sobs.

"Dontae? Are you okay, buddy?" Kris asked.

"Mrs. ... I want Mrs.," Dontae said quietly, sadly.

"I'll get her," Kris said, starting to leave the bedroom.

"No. Not her. I want my *other* Mrs."

Kris wondered if he should ask his mother to come into the room. If Dontae didn't want this mother, then would seeing her upset him more?

Kris walked to the bedroom window open to the night air. "D? Come over here look through the window. Come on. The moon is shining tonight."

Dontae wriggled until he was out of bed. They both looked out at the trees, yards, and houses.

"This is what your new neighborhood looks like at night. Look over there. That's where the Hawns live. Mrs. LeDuke's house is the one with the circular sidewalk. And the Allens are down from her house, the one with the little trees out front? You should see all the fantastic things they have in their garage. Oh, and if you look the other way, you'll see houses of other people we know. Everyone around you is very nice, Dontae. There's no reason to be scared now that you're with us. There are a lot of kids who live in these houses, too. You'll get to know them, and you'll always have friends to play with."

Dontae pointed. "Is that a tree swing?"

"Yep. The Youngs live there. They have a cat named Princess and grandkids that visit all the time. Human grandkids, I mean. Not cats. And the Allens have grandkids that visit them, and so do the Hawns. Other houses have kids about your age who live there full time, and some houses have older kids about my age."

"I don't know if I wanta do stuff with kids other than you and Dev and Bijay. They might laugh at me and push me down."

Kris wondered if that had happened before. "You're tough. You'll get back up. I used to be picked on a lot in school. Things change if you let things change. It took me a while to figure that out."

"I'm different. You're normal. I'm … different."

Kris walked Dontae back to bed. "There's no such thing as 'normal,' D. We all have stuff about us that makes us different from other people. I used to be so sure that no one would want to be my friend that I didn't try. I avoided other kids. I was sad and scared for a long time, and mad that nobody pulled me aside and said that they thought I was cool and wanted to be my friend. I didn't realize that that's not how it works. You have to *be* a friend to *have* a friend. Okay? I had to relax. I had to talk to kids and smile. It wasn't easy, but eventually, I did. And if some of the kids I talked to didn't want to talk back, well, I moved on. See how quickly Bij and Dev got to liking you? I'm sure that will happen with a lot of other boys and girls, too. Give them a chance."

"Okay."

"And as far as the whole 'change' thing goes, I'll tell you what our dad told me a long time ago when I couldn't let go of sad feelings about my first mom and dad, and even about the last family who fostered me, right before I came here to live. Dad said that everyone walks a road in this life. You shouldn't carry the scenery you pass with you as you go, dragging it along. Let the rocks and hills stay behind you as you walk toward tomorrow. Don't forget the lessons and the memories, but keep going without looking back in fear."

Dontae stretched out, and Kris covered him with the sheet and comforter. While he waited to hear Dontae breathing evenly, Kris sat on his desk chair by the window, looking out at his neighborhood again, his mind churning with too many worries, realizations, and happy thoughts. He stayed until he was tired enough to go to sleep on the sofa, leaving the whole bed for his new brother.

Kris woke up later than usual, forgetting at first that he'd gone to sleep on the sofa. The house seemed very quiet, as if everyone else was still asleep. He went to the bathroom and returned to the living room, looking through the large window to the back yard at the bright, sunny day. He folded the blanket and carried it into his bedroom, along with his pillow.

After putting the blanket and pillow on his chair, Kris felt free to look closer at Dontae in the soft morning light that filtered into the room through his summery curtains. Dontae's face was not what he was expecting after looking at photos and reading articles on ectodermal dysplasia. There were tiny scars on his upper lip and above it, but those were the only evidence that he'd had surgeries on his mouth. His long eyelashes rested on his face softly, and his eyes, also, left no sign of being treated. Kris looked closely at Dontae's hands for the first time. He could see how the fingers were fused together—two on one hand and three on the other. He thought of the photos he'd seen online of other children and adults with ectodermal dysplasia. Each was different from the others, and he was sure that—like his mother had said—each had family and friends who never saw past the beauty of their loved one's heart.

Kris looked at his clock. 8:42. He yawned and stretched, accidentally bumping his end table and rousing Dontae.

The young boy scanned the ceiling, looked at the walls and furniture, and then at Kris. He asked, sitting up, "This is our bedroom?"

"Yep. Remember everything about yesterday?"

Dontae nodded. "I need the potty."

"Remember where it is?"

He didn't move or say anything.

"Want me to show you where?"

The boy shook his head, got out of bed, and left the bedroom. When he entered the room again, he asked, "What town is this?"

"Anders Lake. Same as before. Your last house was in another part of the city, past the college."

"Oh." He scratched his back.

"Bijay might be up. Want to go see?"

"I guess. Bye!"

Kris washed, brushed his teeth, and got dressed. When he came out of his room, he heard cartoon sounds from the TV and water running in the kitchen sink. It almost felt like an average day, even though it wasn't.

"Do you still think you would like an antique or used bookcase?" his mother asked, rinsing out a tea kettle.

"Yeah. When are we going out? Are we getting the new SUV first?"

"We are. We'll then drive back here and switch to the new car so we'll have more room when we shop for furniture and clothing and coloring books and some other things Dontae should have that I did not see among his belongings. We will go as soon as every one of the Dehlvis is ready. We have a lot to do."

That evening, Kris sat at the patio table in the back yard holding a hot chocolate. His three brothers were already in their beds, and his mother was snoozing on the sofa while his father sat settled into his recliner and with Pip curled on his lap, reading a book on the immigrant experience in America.

Kris enjoyed being alone for the first time that day. He put his feet on the chair next to his and watched fireflies strobe along the back fence and bushes. Stomper appeared at the glass door behind him, patting and pawing to be let out. Kris slid open the door, then closed it behind the cat.

"So, Stomps—what do you think of the new family member? Think he'll warm up to you and Pip eventually?"

Stomper's tail rose straight up, and he squinted at his boy, but he didn't offer an answer. He strode with typical cat confidence in the darkness to sniff for messages in the breeze, walking respectfully along the edges of the garden to leave Mrs. Dehlvi's flowers undisturbed. Crickets sang in their strange, syncopated way, and a distant loon let the world know that there was sadness somewhere, but also hope.

Chapter Sixteen

The next morning, Kris walked to the bookshop with Dontae at his side.

"Are you sure you don't need to bring along your cooling vest, D?"

"Nope. I don't usually wear it unless I'm running around outside when it's warm, or sitting around when it's hot."

"How do your new shoes feel? Are your feet getting sore?"

Dontae looked at his white sneakers as he walked. "They're *great*. I've never had ones like this before. I've always had hard shoes. Except for my karate shoes."

"Hard?"

"Like, black ones or brown ones that are stiff and hard. I've never had soft shoes that are for walking around outside."

Kris wondered then if maybe his parents should have been given a guide as to what sort of shoes Dontae was supposed to be wearing. Were they given instructions about anything?

Going to a shoe store yesterday had been something Kris had been worried about, but Dontae had no self-consciousness about his feet, even with the store worker who had helped to find a pair that fit. Kris had been worried about shopping for clothes for Dontae, too. He kept asking his parents if they were getting fabric that would make him overheat, or clothes that he would have a hard time buttoning or zipping. Then he remembered that he was supposed to concentrate on being a brother and not a father, and he eventually let himself relax and enjoy a day out with his family.

"These shoes make me feel bouncy. Wanna bounce, Kris?" Dontae asked.

"Uh, okay." He followed Dontae's lead, skipping along the sidewalk for half a block.

When they arrived at the bookshop, Mr. O'Malley was unlocking the door, and the mailman was handing over that day's selection of letters and bills.

Mack grinned at the boys, holding open the door for them. "Hey, missus! Guess who? Make that guess who, times two!"

After a few seconds of silence, Mrs. O'Malley could be heard rushing along the hallway to the front room, calling, "I'm coming! Is it Kris?"

She rounded the front counter and fairly skidded to a halt. "Kris! We haven't seen you in days! And this boy with you. Is this Dontae?"

Dontae, startled by the woman's enthusiasm, partially hid behind Kris, who stood near the coat rack.

"This is my new little brother," said Kris as he moved aside to gently push the boy in front of him. "Dontae, these are the people I was telling you about, Mack and Mrs. O."

"More cats," said Dontae, pointing to Haiku and Buglit who were giving themselves baths on the back of the sofa.

"He isn't so sure about cats, I guess," explained Kris. Kris bent and pointed to the cats. "These kitties are also very sweet, D. They don't bite or scratch, either."

Haiku paused in mid-lick to look over at Dontae as if he were insulted that such a thing would even be considered a possibility.

Kris said, "If you're going to work here, you're going to have to like cats, D. This bookshop takes care of kitties for the cat shelter. People get to know the cats while they browse, and, after they apply to adopt, they can take them home to be their own, forever and ever. That's how I got Stomper. He used to live right here with Mack and Mrs. O'Malley."

Dontae seemed to be considering what Kris had said. "So, this is like a foster home? For cats, though?"

Kris nodded.

Dontae's eyes took in the front room from one end to the other before he whispered to Kris, "Where do they potty?"

Kris led Dontae by his hand into the cats' room at the end of the hallway. "See? The kitties have everything right here in this room. Food, water, litter box, and a tower to climb if they want to take a nap in private."

Back in the front room, Dontae looked around again.

"Do you want a drink of juice? Or, would you like to use the bathroom? It's right there behind that white door," Mack said, trying to guess what the boy was thinking.

"I thought there was a big exciting thing going on here. That's what Kris said. He said he couldn't stop thinking about all the big stuff going on here at the bookshop. But," he shrugged, "it doesn't look all that exciting to me."

Kris and the O'Malley's glanced at each other, and all three laughed. Kris patted his brother on his back and pointed at the sofa, indicating that he should sit down. Dontae did, but he chose a cushion at the far end, away from Buglit and Haiku.

"It *is* exciting, once you know what's going on," Mrs. O'Malley said. She sat next to the boy and thought about how to tell him about the auction and the books.

"I already told him all about the auction and the mystery of the books yesterday," Kris said, picking up Buglit. He sat on the last empty cushion and let the cat settle on his lap. "He said he can't figure out the answer to our mystery, either. I was hoping a fresh, young mind might figure it out for us."

Dontae stared at Buglit. "So, that cat is a foster boy?"

"Nope," Mrs. O'Malley said. She smiled and took Bug from Kris. "This is my own forever kitty. Buglit used to be fostered here, but after we'd gone through a few adventures together, I couldn't let anyone else adopt her. Haiku, the

237

other kitty, *is* a foster cat. Isn't he huge? Look at his long, fluffy tail."

"Why isn't Haiku staying here forever, too? Don't you love him as much as Buglit?"

Everyone was silent for several seconds.

"Oh, that *question!*" sighed Mrs. O'Malley, raising her eyes to the ceiling for help. She let Buglit go, and the cat walked over to the computer chair.

"We can't keep them all," said Mr. O'Malley. He took a bottle of orange juice from the mini refrigerator and poured some into a cup. Handing it to Dontae, he added, "If we'd kept all the cats we've fostered from the start, then it wouldn't have been very long before we'd have run out of room. We've had dozens of cats adopted from here, and that wouldn't have happened if we weren't letting other people take them home all along."

"That's what Mrs. Stornburger said. Only about little kids. She said almost the same thing when I asked if I could keep living with her."

"I didn't meet her," Kris said, leaning forward to look at Dontae. "Was she that lady with the cane who stayed in the house?"

Dontae nodded. Then he frowned. "She probably misses me."

"Oh, I'm sure she *does,*" said Mrs. O'Malley. She put an arm around the boy's shoulders and pulled him against her side. "I'm sure you miss her, too. But you know what? Even though I love and miss each and every kitty who's been in our shop over the years, I get a happy feeling about them mixed in with each twinge of missing them. I know they all have very nice, loving homes now. Just like you do. Just like you'll always have a family to love you, and who you'll love back. It's almost magical when things work out that way. It makes me believe *anything* is possible."

Haiku walked to the end of the sofa, behind and above Dontae's head. He then stepped down to sit next to the boy.

Dontae cautiously pulled out of Mrs. O'Malley's hug. Looking at Mack for encouragement, Dontae held out his fingers for the cat to sniff.

An hour later, Kris walked Dontae home along a slightly different route than they had gone on the way to the bookshop. Dontae carried a paper bag that contained three storybooks the O'Malley's had given him to keep.

"See all these big, old houses? They belong to fraternities—brotherhood groups of students who go to the college. Oh, and here's one of my least favorite things," Kris said, pointing ahead to a large bush.

"A crack in the sidewalk?" asked Dontae.

"No. A lilac bush when it doesn't have flowers anymore."

"Lilacs. Those are purple things. They smell strange, don't they?"

"Strange? They're my favorite scent when they're in flower."

"I don't know. They're purple, but they don't smell purple, so *that's* weird. Nothing grapey about them, or blueberry-ish, or *any* other purple smell."

"Huh," Kris said, considering the argument. "Well, I like lilacs. Only not after they're done blooming for the year."

"I touched Haiku a little."

"I saw that. Good. Now we'll have to try Stomper and Pip. They're really *very* nice."

Dontae and Kris stepped off the sidewalk to get out of the way of two ladies who were jogging by them. "Why don't you have any dogs, though?"

"We just don't. I *know* a few dogs," Kris said, hoping that was close enough. "My friends Katrina and Matt have a little terrier named Browser. And my friends Jack and Darla have Patrick, who is a medium-sized mixed-breed dog. The Hawns

239

have a Saint Bernard named Roland, remember? There are other dogs up and down the neighborhood streets, too. I don't think we'll ever have one, ourselves, though. We're more of a cat family."

"Oh. I just wondered. Mrs. Stornburger has a dog named Fritz. He knows tricks like jumping rope and pulling stuff off the kitchen counter. Cats in commercials look like they don't care *what* brand of food you buy. Dogs, though, get really excited to gobble whatever brand they're doing a commercial for."

Kris grinned, "I think you're right, D."

They turned to walk the last block before home. "Do you think Dev likes me?" Dontae asked.

Kris' eyebrows went up. He hurriedly replayed in his mind how Dev had been acting these last few days. "I think he does. I honestly do. He's more serious than Bijay. He was the older brother before I came along, and he feels more responsible, I think. But I know him, and I can tell that he's happy that we have you in the house with us."

"I think I need lotion," Dontae said, changing the subject unexpectedly. "My hands are dry." He held one out to show Kris. "I don't know if there's any lotion in with my stuff I brought from Mrs. Stornburger's house."

"If you don't have some, we'll get it for you. Or, maybe Mom has one you can use."

Just then Kris noticed Mr. Hawn standing on the Dehlvis' front porch, leaning against the railing as if he were waiting for them to get home. Kris' stomach knotted. He pulled Dontae by his free hand, making him almost run the last half-block.

"What?" Kris asked breathlessly, certain that there was a problem.

"Your dad took your mom to a doctor," Mr. Hawn said, descending the porch steps before walking toward the boys. "Your brothers are at our house. I tried calling the bookshop a few minutes ago, but you had already left. Come on over. We'll talk there."

After Kris had left the bookshop with Dontae, Mrs. O'Malley went into the bathroom and closed the door. Something about her talk with the two boys had touched a nerve or triggered a memory that really wasn't a memory. She wasn't sure why, or what the real reason was, but she had to lean against the sink for a few minutes alone to quietly cry in private.

When it seemed like her time in the room had been too long, Mack rapped lightly on the door. "Mave? Everything okay?"

She grabbed some toilet paper and blew her nose. She ran cool water over her hands and wet a washcloth for her overheated face. Breathing deeply, she opened the door at last, trying to wear a blank, pleasant expression.

Mack saw only the pain in her eyes.

"Want to talk about it?" he asked, pulling her toward her chair. Buglit was asleep on it, her tail curled around her body until the tip covered her nose. Mack lifted Bug, motioned for Mrs. O'Malley to sit, and he handed her the cat.

"I don't think so, Mack. I … I don't know what upset me like that. Only, maybe … I sometimes feel guilty that we foster cats and not children."

"We've talked about this in the past, and after each conversation, we feel settled in our hearts about the choices we've made. I know we're always going to feel this way—at least a little—but we had our good reasons for choosing felines. We live in an apartment that can only hold the two of us. We barely make ends meet. We work here all day, seven days a week. We're far from ideal foster parents."

"I know. But I still get that old urge."

"We helped Kris along, didn't we? I feel like he's … well, you know how I feel about him. It's like *we* adopted him, too."

Mrs. O'Malley took a bracing breath and nodded.

Danny pushed open the front door.

Mr. O'Malley held out his hand for a shake. "Danny—how are you doing? Back from Ohio, I see. *That* was a whirlwind trip."

"It was. But it was long enough to do what I'd set out to do." He put his elbows on the counter to peer around the cash register. "Maisie? Don't you even say 'hello' to me anymore?"

"We've had an emotional morning," Mack said. "Kris brought his newly-adopted brother into the shop for a first visit. It seems to have brought up some feelings."

Danny, still leaning across the counter, said to his sister, "I have some juicy news if you want it. I'm pretty sure it'll cheer you up."

She sniffled, hugging Buglit to her chest. "As if I'm just some old gossip!"

"Well, okay, then. I wouldn't want to insult you further by telling you all about my trip to see Lucille. I'll go next door and talk to Jack and Darla, instead." He winked at her, waiting for a reaction.

She suppressed a smile before saying, "Shut up about going anywhere. Spill!"

He stood straighter, grinning. "You're sure now? I don't want to wreck your melancholy mood or anything."

"I think you already did," Mack said, realigning a shelf of messy science fiction books.

Mrs. O'Malley put Buglit down and pulled her chair closer to her brother. Her eyes expectant, she asked, "What's this about Lucille?"

Danny ran his fingers through his gray bangs and slid a hand into his jeans pocket. His handsome, slightly bristly face gave away no hint of what he was about to say.

"Danny?" she prompted, growing frustrated at his extended silence.

He finally said, "She's going to be moving here to town. We're going to open a business together, just like you, Quainty, and Darla have businesses."

"You are? Doing what? Are you two *together* again?" she asked, standing to walk to his side.

"Hey, great!" said Mack, stopping his work.

Danny said, "She's always wanted to have a permanent space to sell her glassworks. She had been making pieces in a studio where she rents space for many years, and you know I rent a room at the back of the lumber yard that I call my studio, but it isn't, really. We want to find a place to rent or buy together. We'd work in one part of the building and sell in another. I have commission work now like I did out west, but I don't have a reputation here yet. The jobs I've been getting are nothing like the high-end ones I'm used to, and the money I'm taking in here is hardly anything, comparatively. I would hate to move away from everyone again, so I feel like the answer is to try to up my exposure by going full-on retail. I'll have my woodworking and carving, and Lucy will have art glass. When I'm available, I can handle the paperwork and deal with clients. When she's between projects, she can do those things. And, if it goes well enough, we can hire someone, and then devote all the time we want to our projects."

Mrs. O'Malley was slightly disappointed.

"What?" asked Danny, sitting on the arm of the sofa.

A pair of teenage girls came into the shop then, asking for romance novels.

Mrs. O'Malley pointed to the section as she said to her brother, "I don't know, Dan. I was promised juicy details. I *am* happy for you that you're going to have a studio together, but you didn't exactly put any spring in my orange pigtails with that bit of news."

Danny eyed her mostly gray hair, looking for pigtails that weren't there.

Mack grinned. "It's an obscure reference to Pippi Longstocking. Never mind." He put an arm around his wife's back. "She probably thought you were going to talk about love and romance, destinies, and hearts and flowers."

Danny looked confused. "Didn't I say all that?"

Mack shook his head. "Nope."

"Well, it was implied."

Mrs. O'Malley perked up again, her blue eyes shining behind her glasses. "It was? Well, then—great! But, I need details."

Mack squeezed his wife's arm before going into the bathroom for paper towels and spray window cleaner.

Danny wiggled his eyebrows. "There's been an awful lot of kissing lately. There. Is that enough detail?"

Mrs. O'Malley's mouth hung open in surprise. "Really? So, then … you're officially a couple now? Not just business partners?"

"We don't want to mess things up with deciding what it is that we're doing. We're old people having some fun. Well, *I'm* old, anyway. She still looks like she could pass for thirty on most days. We'll see how it goes. If we don't kill each other by working together day after day, then I guess we'll go from there." He paused, and his voice dropped to barely above a whisper. "I've never stopped … I-I've never stopped …"

Mack sprayed the door and wiped it vigorously, not watching his wife's reaction.

That afternoon, Kris sat alone on his bed, his back against his pillows. He was holding a paperback book about early space travel in one hand, but he wasn't reading it, and he hadn't absorbed a word of it during the past twenty

244

minutes as he stared through the window. He was glad that he asked to keep his bed near the outside wall. Dontae was happy that he was closer to the bathroom and wouldn't have to walk around another bed in the middle of the night.

A *baby*. His mother was going to have another baby. There would be five kids in the family. Five! He'd never lived in a house where there was a baby.

Dev appeared in the bedroom doorway. Kris couldn't tell how he was feeling from studying his expression.

"Can I come in?"

"Yep."

Dev closed the door behind him, blocking out the sounds of Bijay and Dontae playing on the floor with their trucks and their mother using the blender.

"Are we supposed to be happy about this, or not happy about this," Dev wondered aloud. He walked around the beds to sit facing the window. His dark brown eyes looked worried.

"Dev, I swear if you don't stop going around with worry in your eyes, you're going to get stuck like that! You're a little kid! Cut it out! Of course we're happy about it. We're going to have another little brother or sister!"

"Think it could be a girl?"

"I'd say there's a fifty-fifty shot, yeah." Kris looked to the ceiling. "Geez. A girl. I hadn't thought about that possibility. She'll have to be tough to survive with four boys in her house. It might not be a she. It could be another boy."

"Mom and Dad seem too old to start with another baby."

"Gosh, Dev—they're only in their mid-thirties. Some people don't *start* having kids until they're even older than that."

Dev took in a long, deep breath. Without looking at Kris again, he asked, "Tell me how you really feel. Either way."

Kris paused, his mind trying to sort out what he had been thinking before Dev came into the room, and how he honestly felt now. "I ... have no idea. Dev, I've got about eight million things to think about right now. I've got stuff going on that you don't know about, okay. Stuff from my way-long-ago past. And then there's that mystery about the auction books. I'm semi-worried I might lose my eyesight again, or that I've got a medical problem from getting hit by the baseball. There's Dontae, who is not a problem, but he *is* a new person in the family. Taty left, and maybe she's never coming back. I want to be at the bookshop but feel like I can't go off and leave you boys for whole days this summer. There's the time I spend thinking about girls in general. I wonder if I should shave. I worry about acne. There's a new baby coming, and it's cool and unexpected, but there's going to be big changes, and ..."

"Okay!" cried Dev. "I guess I'm glad I don't have your set of problems." He glanced at Kris. "I was worried about Mom, and not just today while they were at the doctor's office. I've secretly been worried for a while. She's been so tired."

"It wasn't much of a secret, Dev."

"Even though I know it was only because she is going to have a baby, I still can't stop being worried. I think you're right when you said I'm going to be stuck this way." He was silent for a full minute. "Kris? What did you mean? What were you talking about when you said something's going on that's got to do with your long-ago past?"

"I don't want to keep any secrets from you. I *will* tell you about it, but not tonight. Okay?"

Dev raised one eyebrow at his brother, but he did nod in agreement. Kris smiled, thinking again that Dev looked like a young version of their father.

Kris leaned sideways into his propped-up pillows. "Let's do this. Let's make a deal. I promise to quit worrying so much about all my stuff if you promise to quit being worried about all your stuff and everyone else's stuff. It's summer. There's no school. Remember? Think of all the fun, sun, games, new brother, more noise, running around, playing with all your old toys again now that you have someone new to play them with. Think about a trip somewhere with Mom and Dad. Think about no homework."

"But are we happy?"

"Don't keep *asking* that. Just *be* happy. Stop worrying. Dontae is going to pick up on your fears. You don't want him to keep asking me what he already asked me earlier today: 'Does Dev like me?'"

"Did he actually say that?"

Kris nodded.

Dev stood. "I *do* like him. I'm sorry he had to ask you that. What should I do now?"

"That's up to you. I don't think you need a plan. Drag a board game out of the heap in your closet and get Bij and D to play for a while until dinner. Be a kid. Mom is going to want you to relax about the baby, about her, about Dontae, about your life in general. You being a worry-wart isn't going to make her pregnancy easier."

"Gah! Don't say that word!" Dev covered his ears dramatically.

"What word?"

"The 'p' word. Gross!"

"What did you call it when she was going to have Bijay?"

"I was like two and a half years old when he came along. I had no idea what was going on with Mom's stomach when it was getting bigger and bigger. All of a sudden this crying little milk-barfer came into my house from out of nowhere. Now, though, I know what's coming." He went to the door and opened it, then glanced back at Kris. *"Yikes."*

"Go play a game. If you pick a good one, I'll play, too."

"Yeah?" He finally seemed happier. "You will?" He then called into the living room, "Who wants to play a board game with me and Kris?"

"I do!" answered Bijay.

"I do!" echoed Dontae.

Kris walked into the hallway. "Give me a minute or two, guys. I need to call the bookshop first."

He used the phone in his parents' bedroom. From there, he could hear his father using a power drill in the front yard.

"Mack? We're okay. I'm sure. Um, can you put the phone where it's between your head and Mrs. O's head? I'll wait. Ready? Mom went to the doctor's office today because she's been tired for days and days, and today she almost fainted. Dad said that he'd had enough, and there was no arguing. When they got home, we found out that she's going to have a baby. Ha! I know! Did you both hear that? Yep. I don't know. I don't think she knows a date yet. Weird, right? Right after we got Dontae. I guess you never know what to expect. Okay. I'm going to play with the boys now. Dev's picking out a game. I'll see you tomorrow morning. I will. I will. Me, too. Bye!"

When he stepped back into the hallway, he could see his mother in the kitchen, shaking water from a head of lettuce into the sink. He looked at her stomach. Even though she was wearing fairly snug slacks, he couldn't see anything different about her waist.

When she noticed him, she smiled beautifully. Joyfully.

His whole world lit up, and his heart nearly burst with happiness. She made him believe in that one moment that everything *was* going to be just fine.

Chapter Seventeen

"Dontae has a new bed," Kris said the next morning in the bookshop. He was in the middle of telling the O'Malley's about his last few days. "It has a headboard that is supposed to look like an old-time sailing ship. His dresser looks like four vintage suitcases stacked on top of each other, all in a different color. The straps are painted on, and the pulls look like suitcase handles. I'm glad *that* dresser went into my room. Dev picked out a dresser that looks like one a grandma from the old country would want. It's this cloudy, dusty blue with yellow stars painted on the front of the drawers." He made a disapproving face.

"Well, it sounds very *nice* to me," said Mrs. O'Malley. "I probably have a lot in common with grandmas from old countries, though."

Mack laughed.

Mrs. O'Malley threw a paperclip at him.

Kris smiled, saying, "I'm going to have a bookcase in my room, too. I didn't get one when we went to the new furniture stores. I want an older one, from like a thrift shop or an antique mall or someplace." He turned to Mack, who was recovering from his bout of hilarity. "Mr. O? I was hoping that if I found a bookcase I like that you'll put it in your van and bring it to my house. Will you? If I find one I want, I mean."

Mack swallowed his last bit of coffee for the morning. "Nope." He shook his head for emphasis.

"Mack!" chided his wife. "You most certainly *will.*"

"That's okay, Mrs. O," Kris said, his hands out, indicating that he didn't want them to argue about it. "I only have permission to get a case from a used furniture store if I find a way to get it home. I'll make sure wherever I buy it from has delivery."

Mr. O'Malley raised his eyebrows. "I'll do you one better, kiddo. I'll *make* you a bookcase with my own two hands."

Kris' eyes slid to the bookcases that were against the walls of the front room of the bookshop. He remembered Mack had said he'd made them himself many years ago. They were sturdy and strong, but plain.

"You will?" Kris asked, trying to sound pleased. "Do you have time? And gee—you will? That would be, um, fantastic! I could have an O'Malley Original in my room."

Mrs. O'Malley argued, "Kris is right. You have no time for that unless you come back here after dinner in the evenings and make it in the basement. Is that what you had in mind?"

"It's not like it would take fifty hours, you know. I could knock one out in two—maybe three hours—easy. I have all those boards downstairs in the corner behind the exercise bike going to waste." He drummed his fingers on the countertop. "Although if you want it stained and not bare wood, the layers of stains *would* take quite a while. Or, if you'd prefer, I could paint it in the color of your choice."

Kris hesitated, looking back and forth between the two O'Malleys.

"Back up, back up," said Mrs. O'Malley loudly, shaking her head. "Mack, he wants an *old* bookcase. Making him a *new* one is doing the opposite of that."

They both looked at Kris, who merely shrugged, not wanting to hurt Mr. O'Malley's feelings.

"How about this, then," said Mack, tapping a pencil on his open palm. "How about we head to the Cumbers' antique barn this afternoon? The van is empty, and I'm all set to haul a bookcase if you find one that you like. If you don't find a case there, we can go out to Millers' Mall. Sound good?"

Kris frowned. "I don't want it to seem like I wouldn't like your homemade case, Mr. O."

Mack winked. "I rescind the offer."

"I don't have any bookcase-buying money. Today I was only going to ask you about using your van."

"I'll tell you what. Call your folks and ask if I can take you to the Cumbers' and Millers' sometime this afternoon. If you find one you like, I'll buy it and get the money from your parents later. Okay?"

"Aren't you too busy here, though?"

"This kid likes to worry about minor details too much, Mavis. He'll have an ulcer before he's sixteen."

"I'll call home," said Kris, thinking that Mack was probably right about an ulcer.

Four hours later, after things had slowed at the bookshop, Mack and Kris left for Yolandaville, heading for Aunty Q's Odd Art and Barntiques. Arriving at the Cumbers', Mack pulled into the newly-paved drive and parked in a spot near a young maple tree, facing a long row of white-flowered bushes. Three other vehicles were in the lot, too. A rooster crowed in the distance.

"Billy!" said a suddenly-excited Kris, hopping out of his side of the van. He ran to the chicken house as fast as his long legs would take him.

Kris scanned the scurry of chickens in their fenced-in yard, but his friend the rooster was nowhere to be found. "Billlll-y!" he called.

"Err-err-err-err-errrr!"

"That came from the Barntiques, I think," called Mack. He'd taken off his plaid shirt and left it behind in the van. He then tucked a loose corner of his t-shirt into his tan slacks as he walked the path to the shop.

Almost before Mack had finished his statement, out from the open doorway of the barn charged a large, fluttering rooster.

"There you are, Billy!" said Kris, opening his arms and kneeling on the lawn.

They were still hugging when Mrs. Cumber appeared in the doorway. Her hair was bright pink again, and she was wearing a pink sweatshirt and blue jeans. She paused to smile at the vision of Kris and Billy having a reunion.

"Howdy, young fella! Howdy, Mr. Bookstore! How are you all doing today?" she asked, smiling broadly.

Mack arrived at the entrance to the shop. "Good, thanks. Looks like you have a few other customers today. Do you have any bookcases for sale, Quainty? Kris is looking to fill out his bedroom with a case for all his old books."

Mrs. Cumber wiped away a little moisture from her eyes. "Seeing that boy hug my rooster like that, and seeing you come here to me, gave me a memory of the first time we were together, back before I knew Mavis and I were sisters. Wasn't that a day? Wasn't that a summer? I can't thank Providence enough, though I surely do try."

Mack smiled warmly at her and watched as Kris and Billy walked toward them.

"My sissy told me just now on the phone how you're a new brother again, and how you're gonna be a new brother one more time next year. Whew and gosh! What a blessing! Ain't we all blessed, hereabouts? Yes. I told Elwood, and he thought I was fooling about the baby coming. He almost can't believe it!" She hugged Kris, pulling him into the barn. "You're taller than I am, you big thing, you!"

Kris paused, realizing, as he'd done before, that Mrs. Cumber had more of a country accent and used funnier expressions when she was at home. "Your hair is all pink again," was all Kris could think to say.

"Didn't you hear?" she asked, pulling back in surprise.

"About what?"

"I got a date for a new art show in Lamarr next month. I got a new date, can you imagine? Me?"

252

"I did hear, Mrs. C. That is so *great!* Mrs. O said that you want us all to come out to help you pick paintings for the show."

"I do, I do. We need to think about doing that soon. The gallery is antsy to get me and my works to them to plan the display order and talk prices." She looked over to Mack. "How about this Sunday, Mr. Bookstore? I'm only open until four o'clock on Sundays. Can you come out that evening?"

"Sounds fine. I'll tell Mavis."

"Well, there they are, in the flesh," said Elwood Cumber, coming through the door. Billy bawked and quickly got out of his way.

A middle-aged woman dressed all in white put an amber glass candy dish on the counter, saying she wasn't done shopping yet. A man on the other side of the barn was examining a tramp-art box, and another customer, a young woman, was sitting on several antique chairs one after the other, testing them for comfort or size.

"Hello. Haven't seen you in quite a while, Elwood. This place been keeping you busy?" asked Mack, shaking the man's hand.

"Oh, yes. I can't even *tell* you how busy." He pushed up his square, black glasses. "We thought we'd have a leisurely retirement business, this, but we never have a dull day. And now we have Quainty's art show to get ready for, too. I think I was more retired before we retired, Mack."

"That's how it happens. The bookshop that I have now was supposed to be a casual thing. Something interesting to do after my Army career. Well, then along came Mavis, and she decided no—we were going to take it seriously and make a real go of it. So."

"So," agreed Elwood. He then noticed that his rooster was in the shop and said, "Billy? Are you in here bothering the customers again? I thought we had us a talk last week. You agreed you were going to take care of your chicken ladies and lay off the human ladies. And now here you are again, browsing the aisles like we'd never had a talk at all."

Kris laughed as he started to look around at the shop's offerings. Billy followed him, making occasional comments about what Elwood had said, but then Elwood scooped up the bird and carried him outside.

The barn was much fuller than it had been during the grand opening party in April. There were more antiques of nearly every kind, and a new row of metal shelves had been added to the far end of the barn. On it were quilts and other soft goods, canning jars, recipe books, kitchen utensils, mixing bowls, and other homemaking items that would have been in a house many, many years ago.

Most of the bookcases he looked at were full of small antiques, tools, or books. Only a few were empty and for sale. He rounded a corner and saw a seven-foot-tall case that was not only empty but outrageously ornate and interesting. The dark wood had unusual carved patterns on both sides that were very intricate. The front had no carving, but it did have tiny inset diamonds of mirrors in the center of each shelf face. Kris didn't have to look at any other bookcases or at any other antique shops. He wanted this case.

He searched high and low, back and front, and on each of the shelves for a price tag, but didn't find one. His stomach tightened. That wasn't a good sign. No tag probably meant the Cumbers were keeping it for the shop and it wasn't for sale, or that it had already been sold. He wondered if he should even ask about it.

Kris wandered through the displays of antiques and vintage car parts, old farm tools and horse equipment until he reached the Cumbers and Mack, who were still visiting. No other customers were in sight.

"So, fella. Find anything you'd like?" asked Mr. Cumber. He had a hand on an antique world globe.

Kris swallowed, looking to Mack for help in answering, even though the man couldn't possibly know why. "Um ... I don't know."

"I bet *I* know," said Mrs. Cumber, grinning. "He found our treasure in the back. You found it, didn't you?"

Kris imagined huge dollar signs sparkling in front of his eyes now that she was calling the bookcase a "treasure." His father had given him a spending limit, and he was sure it wouldn't be enough to buy it.

"A treasure, huh? Let's go look," Mack said to Kris, waving one hand in the direction the boy had come from.

Kris hunched his shoulders, embarrassed and wishing he could disappear. It wasn't going to be his. I couldn't be, and it was humiliating to show them what he liked but couldn't afford. With a sigh, he finally led the three adults to the back of the barn and pointed silently to the bookcase.

Mack whistled.

"Ain't it pretty?" asked Mrs. Cumber.

"Do you like it, Kris?" asked Elwood. He then winked at Mr. O'Malley.

"Is this what I think it is?" asked Mack, stepping from side to side, examining the bookcase closely.

"It is," said Mrs. Cumber in delight. "He brought it yesterday through the back door."

Kris looked puzzled. "Who? What?"

"This is one of Danny Kinonen's pieces," said Mack. "Mrs. O's brother. See his initials on the back at the bottom? I've seen others that he made with mirrored diamonds as decorations in his shop, but this one is *spectacular*. He *really* outdid himself. That must be old wood, too. No? Well, he did a great job staining new wood, then. And the carving is *amazing.*" He said softly to the Cumbers, "I suppose Mavis has told you that Danny and Lucille are going to open a shop together in Anders Lake."

"Silly ideas," scoffed Mrs. Cumber, her hands shooing away the topic. "If they break up again, then what?"

"Oh, I don't know, Quainty. We fall more in love every day we work this place together, don't we?" asked a romantic-eyed Elwood. He elbowed her, and she laughed.

"Anyway, I'll be happy for them," she said soberly. "I will. It'll be nice to feel sure that Danny is staying around permanently. If it takes Lucy coming here to do it, then okay." She seemed to shift into a different mood before saying, "Now, back to the task at hand. Kris, do you think you'd like to have this fine thing back at your house?"

Kris breathed in and out. "How much does it cost?" he squeaked.

"Well, now. Hmm. It's kinda priceless, ain't it?" She rubbed her chin with the top of her fingers, looking at the bookcase. "El, what do you think?"

"I'd say just about ... oh ... free. Yep. I'd say that'd be just about right."

Mack rapped his knuckles on a nearby dresser and shouted, "Sold!" as if taking the final bid on an auction lot.

"Wait!" insisted Kris, confused. He looked from one cheerful face to the next. His mouth opened in surprise and his eyes widened. "Free? I can't—"

"Can you help me load it into my van, Elwood?" asked Mack, walking toward the main entrance. He took his keys out of his pocket and bounced them on his palms.

Mr. and Mrs. Cumber followed Mack through the shop.

Kris trotted after them once he'd snapped out of his shock. "Wait! Mack! He didn't mean it!"

"Come on over here, pumpkin," said Mrs. Cumber. She pointed to a white painted bench near a worn-out roll-top desk and a burgundy Victorian settee. "I'm going to let you in on a secret." She sat on an oversized pickle jug. "You've been set up, my boy."

He scowled in confusion. "What?"

"This was *all* a set-up. Hoo-ee!" she laughed, folding her hands on her lap in delight. "Danny brought that bookcase in last night so you could discover it here."

"I don't understand. At all," Kris said, leaning forward. He brushed his bangs aside and exhaled slowly. "Say that again, please."

"Your mama told my sissy that you wanted to go shopping for a bookcase and asked if Mr. Bookstore would do the hauling if you found one you liked. Well, Mavis talked to Danny, and then Danny, Mack, and me and Elwood all set a trap-trick for you. Danny brought his favorite bookcase here to us yesterday. So, then, whenever you got around to asking Mack for help, he would suggest that he take you here to shop. And once you were here, we were sure as shootin' you'd go wild for Danny's creation."

"But … Mack tried to talk me into letting *him* make me a bookcase."

Mrs. Cumber put a lock of her pink hair behind an ear and tugged on that ear's lobe. "He did? Well, that wasn't part of the plan at all. I'll have to find out why he threw that monkey wrench into the plot." She paused. After a moment, her eyes lit up. "Wait! I'll bet it was one of those … diversionary tactics. Did my sissy then talk him out of it right away?"

"Uh, yeah. I think so."

"Well, then, I'd say that that—my fine young friend—was a red herring. It only makes our trick all the richer. Ha!"

Kris heard the van drive up and park outside at the far end of the barn. It was happening! The bookcase was actually going to be loaded into Mack's van and delivered to his house. And into his bedroom! He couldn't help himself. He slapped his hands over his mouth to keep from excitedly yelping like a little kid.

Mrs. Cumber chuckled again, her eyes crinkling at the edges.

"But why, Mrs. C?" asked Kris. "Why would Mr. Kinonen give me a bookcase that he worked tons and tons of hours on? Did Mack buy it from him?"

Mrs. Cumber stood from the pickle jar with some difficulty, and Kris followed her back through the barn until they reached the rear entrance, which was big enough to drive a car through.

"Your Kris wants to know the true poop. I thought he should hear it from you, Mr. Bookstore."

Mack stepped backward out of the rear of the van. He adjusted a few old blankets on the floor of the vehicle that he kept in there in case a load needed extra padding. He winked, then he and Elwood walked to the bookcase.

"I'll grab the top half," said Mack. "Ready? Okay. Up!" They lugged it around a tall metal rack of vintage aprons and frilly bed jackets, out to the lawn, and into the van, its open shelves facing up. "There. If I take it easy on the drive, it should ride fine."

"But Mack," protested Kris as he walked out to the rear of the van to stare in at the case. "You can't just *take* it."

"I'm not, kiddo. *You* are."

Mr. O'Malley swung the van doors shut with argument-ending bangs and said goodbye to the Cumbers. Billy darted and clucked his complaints that he hadn't had a hug goodbye. Kris vaguely waved to them all as he jostled and bumped along in the van over the lawn, away from the barn, and onto the paved drive.

When they turned onto the road at the end of the driveway, Mack finally began to offer an explanation. "We all think the world of you, you realize. I'd do anything for you. Mavis would do anything for you. So would Jack and Darla, the Marys, Matt and Katrina, your family, and just about everyone who knows you even a little bit. You never ask for a thing. Let us do this for you."

Kris unbuckled his seatbelt. Kneeling, he admired what was now his. The road was uneven, causing him to hold the back of the seat tightly, practically hugging it. He tried to protest again, but there was a lump in his throat so large that air barely passed over it, in or out.

"Matt! You have got to come over to my house! Right now! Don't ask questions. No, I'm not hurt. I don't mean like it's that kind of an emergency. It's a good kind of a thing. I can't wait for you to see what's going into my bedroom. No, it's not a pinball machine. Don't guess—just come over. Okay. See you in a bit. Bye!"

Kris hung up and ran back outside to watch as his dad and Mack carefully unloaded the bookcase.

Soon it was standing upright on the sidewalk. The Dehlvis ooh'ed and ahh'ed over it. Bijay and Dontae ran their fingers into the grooves.

Dev stood next to Kris, shaking his head and smiling in admiration. "Arey!" Dev said, using one of his mother's expressions of disbelief. "Is this really yours, Kris?"

"Yep."

"I hope it stays in the house after you leave for college or whatever," he said, "and I hope I get to take over your bedroom."

"I was thinking about moving to the basement, eventually, but now I think I'll live in my bedroom for the next forty years."

"It is *lovely,*" exclaimed Mrs. Dehlvi. She placed her arm through Kris', still admiring the bookcase. "This is a lovely, lovely gift. I don't know how I will thank everyone who gave it to you."

"I'll do the thanking," Kris said.

"It is a mother's place. You will thank them, of course, and I will also thank them for this honor." She put her hands over her face. "If there had been a crown placed on your head, I could not be more ..."

Kris wasn't sure if she was extra emotional because of the bookcase or because she was expecting.

"Here. We are coming now," announced Mr. Dehlvi.

Kris walked onto the front porch to be ready to hold open the screen door. Just then he heard two car doors slam shut and a car drive away. Kat and Matt ran onto the porch steps. They examined Kris' gift, smiling and shaking their heads in amazement.

"What's the story?" asked Matt as he came behind Mack and Mr. Dehlvi.

Kris waited until after the men had carried the case through the doorway. "Danny Kinonen—Darla's dad—made this himself. And the O'Malleys' and Danny and everyone gave it to me. Can you believe it?"

"Yes," said Katrina firmly. She didn't go on to explain her reasons.

The Dehlvis, Karlssons, Pip, and Stomper followed the men the short way along the hallway and into Kris and Dontae's bedroom, which was the first door on the left. After some maneuvering, the case was finally set upright and in place against the far wall, near the bedroom's single window.

Kris, Katrina, Matt, and Mrs. Dehlvi sat together in a row on the edge of Kris' bed. Another row of onlookers sat on Dontae's bed, and Mack and Mr. Dehlvi stood with their arms crossed, admiring the bookcase again now that it was in its place.

"This is spectacular, Kris," said his father as he examined the case more closely. "It should be in a palace. Now your mother will say that we need all new furniture in this room, and new carpeting, and new wallpaper, and some fine art for the walls. You wait and see."

260

"But I just got my bed and dresser," complained Dontae. "I don't want to go shopping again."

"Me, neither," said Dev. He held Pip for a moment, but the cat squirmed away to sniff and investigate the new piece of furniture.

Bijay bounced on the mattress. "But shouldn't *our* room have a shelf thingy like this one?"

"Oh, geez," said Kris quietly to Matt, not anticipating that sort of a problem.

"Never never mind, Bijy-bij. You have a much bigger closet in your room. Now things are more equal, hey?" Mrs. Dehlvi countered, standing. She went to Bijay and kissed him on the top of his head.

A minute later, the only ones left in the bedroom were Kris, Matt, Katrina, and Mack. Matt stood. He walked from one side of the bookcase to the other, and then back again three more times. "Kris? Did you notice that?"

"What?"

He went back to stand at the side of the case nearest the window. "When you move, the images of the carvings look different. It depends on where you are. This little part right here looks like a man climbing a mountain when you look right straight at it, but when you go towards the front, it looks like he's going into a cave. Come here and see what I mean."

Kris, Katrina, and soon Mack, all followed Matt's directions. They saw that other areas had differing images, too, depending on where you stood to view them.

Mr. O'Malley whistled. "I don't know about you kids, but I just got even more impressed with Danny's carving abilities. I knew he'd been getting big money and major clients before he moved here, but I had no idea *how* fantastic his talent is. Kris, this is a *true* work of art you have here."

Kris plopped back on his bed, grinning and overwhelmed. But his excitement quickly wore off, replaced with a feeling close to guilt. "I shouldn't have this!"

Mack glowered at him. "Oh, stop it already. Danny gave this to you because he thinks you deserve it. We *all* think you deserve it. You'll have it in your own home one day, and it'll be full of the books you love the most." Mack ran his hands along the shelf boards. "Want to put your books on it now?"

Kris bit his lower lip. "Mack?"

"Yeah," he answered, not looking away from the bookcase.

"Mack, this is reminding me of … I don't know."

Matt asked, "What? A past life you lived in the Gobi desert as a wandering woodcarver?"

Katrina lightly punched her brother on his arm.

"No," Kris said soberly, standing again. "I feel like … this seems super familiar. Isn't there something else that looks like one thing straight on, but totally different from the side? Paintings? Books?"

Mack exhaled slowly, thinking. "Yes, uh-huh. There are paintings that change appearance from side to side to front, and there are sculptures, too. Lots of things have been created that way on purpose." He paused and the color drained from his face.

"Mack?"

"Here, Mr. O. Have a chair," said Matt, pulling the desk chair around for Mack.

The man sank onto it, his eyes seeming almost hollow.

"Mr. O?" asked Kris and Katrina together.

Kris wondered if he should run to tell his parents that there was a medical problem. "Do you need help, Mack? Water? An ambulance?"

Mack finally said, "Remember how I promised to immediately tell you kids if I discovered the truth behind the auction books and why they were supposed to be worth a lot of money—at least according to Charles the crook?"

"Yeaaaaah," said Kat, stepping back to lean against the windowsill. "Are you saying that you figured it out now, all of a sudden?"

The color quickly bloomed back into Mr. O'Malley's face, and he stood as if he'd been sitting on a spring. "Come on. Get into the van and let's get back to the bookshop. Kris, tell your folks we're going. *Now.*"

In the van, all four of them squeezed into the front and only seat rather illegally and uncomfortably.

"I'm not even going to ask," said Matt. "I'm going to wait until we get to the shop."

"Well, *I* am," said Katrina, who was crammed between the boys and had one of her legs on top of one of Kris'. "I can't wait. *What?*"

"I can't say yet. It's only a theory right now. I need to take another look at those eighteenth-century books. Thanks to Matt and Kris, I'm positive that all will be clear to us in a matter of minutes."

Soon the kids were rushing into the front room, looking around for Mrs. O'Malley. She was shelving books in the rare book room.

"Hello, kids! I didn't expect to see you back here today. I'm glad, though. I was dying to hear how the trip to Quainty and Elwood's went."

As soon as he saw her, despite his excitement about the rare books, all Kris could think of to do was to hug her. "I *love* it. I can't believe you and Mack and Danny did that for me. And the Cumbers."

She hugged him in return. Letting him go, she said, "Tell me *everything*. Were you surprised? Oh, I *wish* I could have been there to see your face!"

"I was super shocked, *that's* for sure. I've been feeling overwhelmed with problems, you know. And it felt like there was going to be no end in sight to all kinds of changes and troubles. The bookcase, and what Mack and Mrs. C, said to me today, well .... I'll never, ever forget it."

Mrs. O'Malley wiped away her tears, nodding.

"But now we have a bigger thing going on," interrupted Matt from the entrance to the hallway.

Katrina had been in the room with Kris and Mrs. O'Malley, and she was wiping tears from her eyes, too. "Oh, *Matty.*"

"What? It *is* a bigger thing! Mack figured it out!"

"Mack figured what out?" asked Mrs. O'Malley as she put her tissue back into her pocket.

Matt glanced up and down the hallway, looking for customers. "About the you-know-whats. The *auction* books," he whispered, his eyes widening.

Chapter Eighteen

Mrs. O'Malley cleared her throat, trying to get her voice to return after crying. "Where *is* Mack?" She hadn't seen him come in with the three kids.

"He must be in the storage room," Matt said.

"I'm right here," Mack called, passing in the hallway. "Let's look at these in brighter light. Follow me, gang."

"It's nearly closing time. Should I lock the doors?" asked his wife.

"Is anyone in here?" he asked, putting a few of the old, flaky leather-bound books on the front counter.

Mrs. O'Malley had Kris look through the rooms to make sure they were alone as she locked the door and flipped over the open sign.

"All clear," Kris reported, stepping into the main room. He then pulled a pencil from Elephant Gerald's back to click it nervously on the countertop. "Mack? Did you really figure it out? For real?"

"Bring a lamp over here, Katrina," Mr. O'Malley said, pointing. That one, from the table near the wall. Okay, now plug it in and put it right here. Thanks. Well, if Matt and Kris accidentally helped me to figure out the truth about the mysterious auction books, then I am about to reveal all." He pulled the lamp closer to the stack of books. "Ready?"

No one replied. They were all leaning in, holding their breath.

Mack took the top book down from the stack. He put it next to the small candlestick lamp and gently slid the pages at a particular angle.

Everyone—even Mack, who was already half-expecting the revelation—gasped. Buglit leaped to the computer chair, and Haiku rubbed Matt's legs.

The pages, once angled, revealed stunning, intricate artwork that used the book's page edges as a canvas. The painting was in swirls and spirals, with tiny cats, dogs, goats, pigs, cows, ladies' faces, flowers, and many other items hidden in those swirls.

"Oh, Mack! Look at *that!* How … how did we not think to look for this before?" asked Mrs. O'Malley, incredulous.

"Whoa!" said Matt. He looked at Kris, who looked back and forth at Mr. and Mrs. O'Malley.

"Are they all like that?" asked Katrina, eyeing the other books in the stack. "I mean, you can't see the painting if you don't flex the pages, right?"

"They're all gilt-edged, including the several others still in the storage room, so maybe they are," Mack said. "Gilding was used to hide the paintings. Don't let the cats up here. I'll check these few other volumes and go back to the storage room for the rest. Ready for book number two, everyone?"

They nodded, and Katrina changed places with Matt to stand next to Kris. He grabbed her hand, and she could feel that he was trembling, waiting to see the next book's page edges.

The others in the stack *all* had similar paintings.

Mack retrieved the rest of the books in question in groups of three and four at a time, and—sure enough—*they* were all painted, too.

"You told me about this sort of thing once, maybe last year," Kris said, still holding Katrina's hand. He changed from merely gripping her hand to interlacing his fingers with hers. "It's called fore-edge painting, right? The artist put the book in a vise at an angle and then painted a scene at the edge of the pages. After it dried, they put gold over the very edges of the pages when they were in their closed position. That way, it was like a secret. The book merely looked like it had gold edges—like a lot of books did then. When the book was open at an angle, ta-da! Art!"

Mrs. O'Malley, remembering something she had read about fore-edge paintings, said, "Wait, wait, wait! You only tried it one way. Flip this book over and fan the pages again."

"Most were painted on one side, Mavis. But let's find out."

Sure enough, all were painted twice—one scene when the book was angled in one direction, and another scene when angled the other way. They were all paintings that had those unusual swirling patterns.

"Oh, Mack!" exclaimed Mrs. O'Malley as if a lottery ticket had just been scratched off to reveal a huge prize.

Mr. O'Malley swallowed. "I don't know how to say how extraordinarily rare this find is. And the paintings are totally out of this world. Look at this style ... and detail. I've never seen work like this, even in the museums I visited in Europe when I was in the military."

"Wowsers! Oh ... wowsers!" said Katrina, voicing everyone's thoughts. "Both edges are painted. Is this group worth a lot of money? Is that what that thief knew, and we didn't know, until now?"

"I'm certain of it," Mack answered, leaning away from the books to absorb what he'd seen. "I guess I never expected to find such things in my lifetime. That house—mansion, really—may have once had some fantastic antiques within its walls. What I saw for sale at the auction didn't seem like anything special. Merely a general mishmash of the contents of a household and barn that had been in storage for a long time. The furniture was older, but average. I saw no paintings, sculpture, or anything that would have led me to think that I should have paid a lot more attention to the books. On the other hand, I was rushed. Kris and Matt, did you see anything special about the household items?"

Kris said, "I still don't have my memory back."

"Oh, that's right. Matt?"

"I don't know. I was mostly concentrating on the hot dogs and books and Kris getting hit on the head. And the creep that bothered us. Stuff like that."

"We'll have to get these into a safe deposit box in the morning, Mack," said Mrs. O'Malley, shaking. "This reminds me of last year when we had Quainty's Edgar Allan Poe book."

Kris let go of Katrina's hand to turn around to put his back was against the edge of the counter. "This isn't the same at all. We had major big questions last time." He looked at Katrina, who then turned to lean against the countertop, too. "This time, with these books, it's absolutely real."

"What are we going to do with the books tonight, Mack?" asked Mrs. O'Malley.

Matt suggested they call a security guard company. His cheeks were a splotchy red from excitement.

"I don't think they work like that," said Mack. "I guess we'll act like nothing is different. Just close the shop the rest of the way, feed the cats, and go home. Charles hasn't done anything in all this time—well, since he broke in—and it doesn't appear as though he told anyone else we have ultra-rare and valuable books in here."

Mr. O'Malley and Kris each carried the books down the hallway to the storage room, taking a few trips to complete the task with care. Mack then locked the door, jangling his key ring as if it helped him to think.

"I don't know, dear. Are you sure about this?" Mrs. O'Malley asked. She was hugging Buglit, who acted as if she'd had enough of hugging already.

Mr. O'Malley sat. "I know you. You're going to give me no rest or peace all night. To ease your worried mind and to save me a long night of your fretting and moping, I'm going to sack out on this sofa. You take the van and go home or go over to Danny's for the night. I honestly don't think it's at all necessary, but I think you and the kids will feel more at ease if you know I'm right here."

His wife hesitated but then gratefully nodded. "I'll go to Dan's. Will you be okay here? There's a blanket in the storage room, on the top shelf of the white case. There's a throw pillow on the big chair in the kid's book room. Want me to make up the sofa for the night before I go? And let me get you a sandwich from the deli."

He shook his head. "You go home now." He looked at the kids. "Will you all walk home, or do you want to squeeze in the van again with Mavis?"

"I'll walk," said Kris.

"Me, too," said Katrina.

Matt nodded. "I feel like I need a walk."

Mack switched off the lamps and overhead lights, but then he stopped walking and slapped his hand to his forehead. *"Holy bananas!"*

"Ohmygosh!" said Katrina, stomping her feet.

"Gah!" cried Mrs. O'Malley, dropping the cat, who ran down the hallway and away from the excitement.

"This is so ... *wow!"* shouted Matt, his fists balled at his sides and his face reddening again.

Kris rushed to Mrs. O'Malley and hugged her tightly. Soon everyone was hugging everyone else and whooping, stomping, and laughing.

After a full minute of this, Matt asked, "But how will you sell them? How do you make the books turn into money?"

Mack thought for a moment before asking Mrs. O'Malley, "Should we contact Rawl's and Bristol's? And maybe a west coast auction house?"

"You don't think we should list them online ourselves? Try eBay, or list them at a set price on the usual rare bookselling sites?" his wife asked.

He shook his head. "I don't, no. For one thing, an auction house will hold them, protect them, insure them, advertise them to the right potential buyers, and do some things we're not even aware of that are necessary for a high-priced sale. Probably they'll offer a guarantee of authenticity. *I* could do that, of course, but what would my own guarantee mean to potential buyers? Plus, the auction company's experts will do the heavy research, or already have a lot of knowledge that I don't." He looked at his hands. "This group of items is beyond my scope of experience. It's not just because I've never handled a fore-edge-painted book before, but because these paintings are so unusual for their time. They're dark and sensuous, swirling and spiral, and almost religious, too. And there's one, remember, that has a spiraling scene from a prison or dungeon. Another is of wine and fruit that's also a landscape if you adjust your eyes slightly. I don't think I've ever seen photos of book art that looks like this. There *is* a slight chance that we have modern paintings done on eighteenth-century books. If so, these are worth a whole lot less than ones done near to the date that the books were published. There's *a ton* involved in getting to the truth of the artist and the truth of their monetary value. I'm in over my head."

She frowned. "Being able to know when you need help is smart, too. But I think you're sure that these were painted close to their publication time." She sighed and sat on her computer chair. "Okay. I'll agree to your plan. How about if I stay for a while and have dinner here with you. We can order a pizza."

"Celebratory Chinese?"

"Victorious double cheese gets my vote. With extra sauce. And a side order of *oh holy cow!*"

"Is that on the menu?" he laughed.

"It keeps hitting me in waves. Like, one second I'm okay. We're talking sense and making plans, and then *pow!* I'm half falling over in shock."

Matt nodded. "Me, too. Now I know why Kris gets so jazzed to come to your shop. You never know what's going to happen or what's going to walk in through the door in a grocery sack."

"Mostly romance paperbacks, you realize," Mack said.

"Well, ever since we went to that auction it's like we've been in the middle of the plot of a mystery book," Matt said. He wiped sweat from his forehead with his t-shirt sleeve.

Katrina walked to hug Mrs. O'Malley goodbye. "Okay. Matt and I are leaving. You enjoy your dinner, and we'll probably see you tomorrow. We might be going over to Dad's tomorrow, though. If he remembers to call, that is." She pulled her hair off her shoulders. "I sure envy Kris his happy home. Three brothers and happily-married parents."

"Kat!" said Kris, his voice cracking. "Oh, geez! I forgot to tell you guys something huge!"

She looked doubtful. "I was right here, remember? I was the one standing beside you when the big discovery was made."

"No! Something *else* major," he insisted. "I can't believe I forgot to tell you guys. First, it was the bookcase, then it was rushing over here, and then Mack discovered the secret to the books."

Matt and Kris looked at each other, both wondering what could possibly be considered major news compared to the fore-edge paintings.

"Is it about Ricki?" asked Katrina.

"Something about Dontae?" asked Matt. He sat on the arm of the sofa.

"No, no, *no*. It's about my *mom.*"

"Is she okay? I remember you saying that she was sleepy lately, and you were getting a little worried. Is she sick?" asked Katrina, moving back to stand near Kris.

Kris smiled so broadly that his rarely-seen dimple showed. "She's not sick. She's going to have another *baby!* Can you believe it? We just got Dontae, and now—"

"No *way!*" said Matt, who looked at the O'Malleys for confirmation.

"Kris! Really?" Katrina asked, hugging him briefly. Holding onto one of his hands, she said, "I'm fabulously relieved that she's not sick or anything like that. But wowsers! A baby! That will make ... *five* of you. You're going to need a bigger house."

"And a *bus,*" added Matt. He brushed his dark-blonde bangs out of his eyes, looking comparatively more shaggy-haired since Kris had gotten a shorter haircut.

"Good thing the SUV we got has a bench seat in the very back." Kris blew out a long, slow breath. "Wonder if it's going to be another boy."

"Your mom should *totally* have a girl this time," said Katrina, finally letting go of Kris' hand.

There was a knock at the door. It was a teenage girl with short brown hair and a sweet, apple-cheeked face. She knocked again when no one moved toward the door.

"That's Josie," said Katrina. "I wonder what she wants."

"Should I let her in?" asked Kris, looking at Mack.

"Yes. Sure. Why not?" Mack said, nodding.

Kris held open the door as the girl walked in. She looked sheepishly around the room, noticing that the lights were off. "Oh, you're already closed. I won't come in, then. I want to talk to Kris for a min."

"I'm leaving for home now," Kris said. "Want to walk with me?"

"I'd *love* to." She grinned as if she'd been given a wonderful compliment. She quickly waved to the others in the room and said, "Okay ... well ... bye, everyone. Nice to see you, Kat and Matt."

When she and Kris were outside, Josie twirled around before walking backward, talking him to talk excitedly.

Katrina's nostrils flared as she put her fists on her hips.

"Ohhhh, boy," said Matt. He stood and led his sister through the door by her elbow. "Let's go before you pop a gasket."

Mack stood to lock the door again. Not wanting to turn back around after doing so, he adjusted the welcome mat.

"And *what*, I ask you, was *that* girl doing with our little *Kris?*" demanded Mrs. O'Malley, her fists on her hips, too.

Mack knew his wife's outburst would be coming. Finding nothing else to do, he bravely faced her. "He's not little. Obviously. And he's not a bad-looking fellow. Naturally, there are going to be girls who might want to—"

"Not again! We went through this last year, right up to last month. I'm not against him liking girls. I just don't think he has to do it already. He's a *boy*. He should *wait*. And that girl is clearly not the right one for our little Kris. She was far too perky. And besides, she's not … she's not …"

"Katrina Karlsson," Mack finished, winking at her.

She plopped onto her chair again, sulking. "No."

"Must you always be doing some sort of matchmaking? There are Danny and Lucille to think about if you need to think about romantic possibilities. And then there's us, of course."

She stopped sulking. "There *is* us. And I shouldn't meddle, I know. But, Kris—"

"Will be fifteen at the end of the summer. Next year he'll be driving, taking girls out to do whatever kids these days do that qualify as dating."

"But Katrina likes him. I can tell. It isn't fair that she has to watch him hang around with yet *another* girl."

Mack sighed, long and loudly. "How about that pizza, Mave? Don't forget we're celebrating. Right?"

"I know. And that is so great what you discovered." She tried to smile, but her lips went another direction entirely. "Poor Kat."

"Maybe you're misreading that situation. She's what? About fourteen or fifteen, too? She might not even be interested in boys yet."

"I can tell. She has a crush on Kris. She did last year, too, from what I could see when they were together. Poor Kat!"

"Stop saying that, Mavis! It's not as if they're of a marriageable age and time is running out to start a family. Dating around is a good idea while they're still kids. Gives you an idea of what you like and don't like in another person."

She shoved her glasses further up her nose. She pushed a button, and the cash register printed the day's receipts. "Now, about that pizza: how's Chinese sound?"

"Better than pizza, thanks."

"Curry chicken?" she asked, getting the phone book.

"Yeah. And extra rice. And some veggies. Pork eggrolls. Mushrooms in sauce. Sweet and sour chicken. And whatever you want, of course."

"Piglet."

"Oh, and dumplings. And noodles. I may want to eat again while I'm sitting here by myself late at night. Get some extras to take with you to Danny's."

"I forgot to call him. I'll do that first. Maybe he'll want to eat here with us," she said, hitting a speed-dial button on the phone.

After Mr. and Mrs. O'Malley and Danny had eaten their take-out dinner at the table in the children's book room, and after the leftovers were divided between them, Danny finally asked why the two of them were splitting up.

"*Splitting up?*" asked his sister.

"Didn't you say you wanted to spend the night with me? And isn't Mack sleeping here on the sofa?" he asked, pointing in the direction of Mack's future bed out in the front room.

"It's just for tonight," said Mack. He caught his wife's eye. "Mavis, do you want to tell him now, or when you're back at his apartment?"

She yawned, feeling overly full. "Danny, we'll talk later. I need a mental break for a while. Dinner was nice, but I still don't feel like talking about it yet."

"Fine by me, as long as divorce isn't a topic of discussion. You two sure do make a great couple. I hate to think that you're breaking up."

"He's kidding, right?" asked Mack, aiming a thumb in Danny's direction.

"I think so. Nobody could be *that* dumb," joked Mrs. O'Malley.

"Aw, you guys are cute together. I'm glad I came for dinner to smooth things over so you two don't give up on your marriage."

"You're in a goofy mood tonight, Danny. Did the moo shu do that to you?" asked Mrs. O'Malley.

"I started the morning with a song in my heart, and I can't stop feeling as light as air." He reached for a fortune cookie. "By the way, did Kris get my bookcase yet?"

Mack took a cookie, too, noisily extracting it from the plastic wrapper. He winked at his wife and said, "Boy, did he ever! You should have seen the look on his face when we told him he was taking it home, and for *free*. It really meant a lot to Kris." He snapped open his cookie and pulled out the fortune. "Just as I suspected: 'You will meet with great wealth and happiness.'"

"I'm glad you told me he wanted a bookcase. I made that over the winter—carving on it when I didn't have commissioned work—but I didn't want to sell it. I think I was waiting until I found it exactly the right home." He broke his cookie in half and removed the fortune. "Hmm. 'You and an old love will be a new love once more.' Well. That's a *good* one, don't you think?" Danny asked, smiling at the little white slip of paper.

"You made that up," accused his sister playfully. "Let me see it."

"No. It's my fortune, and I don't want you to jinx it," he said, holding it above his head to keep her from grabbing it.

"That goes for me, too, Mavis," said Mack as he tucked his fortune into his shirt pocket.

"I think both of you made those up, and now you don't want me to see what giant fibbers you are. That's what *I* think." She reached for the last cookie. "Mine says, 'Your husband and brother are wonderful, but they do not always tell the truth. And they are especially big fibbers after a large, delicious meal.'"

"You know, I think she made that one up. Don't you, Mack?" asked Danny.

"I do. Our fortunes are word-for-word what we said, but I'm pretty sure your sister invented hers. Ah, well. It's been quite a day. We'll forgive her this time."

She smiled and then sighed. "Well, I'm ready to go. I'll grab my purse and say goodnight to Haiku and Bug." She stood, unexpectedly sobbing.

"Mavis! What is it, for goodness sake?" asked Danny, standing. He looked at Mack for an answer, too.

"It's been a wildly emotional day. Mavis, do you want to talk here, or do you still want to wait to tell Dan when you're over at his place?"

"I don't know why I'm *crying,*" she said between sniffles. "Everything is fine, and I'm so happy about today, but it … it all hit me again."

"You go on with Dan, Mavis. I'll see you tomorrow morning. When you get back here, I'll dash home, wash and

276

change, and grab a bite to eat. Then I'll run my errands as planned."

Danny's face grew concerned. "Neither one of you has told me exactly—or even vaguely—what prompted this separation for the night. Is that criminal on the loose again? Have you been threatened? Are you in trouble? What can I do to help?"

Mack shook his head. He cleared the table and pushed in his chair. "No, no. We've finally figured out the real and spectacular answer to our auction books mystery. Now we're spooking ourselves into thinking that I need to guard the books here overnight. Wait until you *see* what's so fantastic about them!"

"What?" Danny asked, putting his bag of leftovers back onto the table. "And why is this the first I'm hearing anything? I've been here for like an *hour.*"

"I didn't want to talk about it until I'd relaxed for a while back at your place," Mrs. O'Malley said, walking toward the door to the hallway. She seemed weary after her short burst of tears. "But since you wheedled that much out of us … Mack—you might as well tell him the rest. I'm going to feed Bug and Haiku and put away the day's register receipt. And fix up the sofa."

"Wheedled? When was there any wheedling?"

"Oh, you know it's hard to keep a secret around you," Mack joked.

"Well, if you're done picking on me—yes. Please. Tell me what you know. I'm still betting that there was something sewn inside the spines or the covers."

Mrs. O'Malley grabbed the cat food and water bowls and took them into the bathroom to wash them. While carrying the clean, full bowls back to the cats' room, she heard Danny whoop and holler. She was grinning as she closed the cats-only room door again.

When she walked back to fold the cash register receipt, Mack was still showing off two of the fore-edge paintings to an astonished Danny.

"Maisie!" Danny said, his eyes wide with amazement. "These are wild! How did we never notice the paintings before? I swear I examined a couple of these books closely at one point."

"And I looked them over, up, down, inside, and out. Admittedly, I was doing it in the dim light of the storage room, but still. I guess if you aren't specifically fanning the pages out at just the right angle, the images stay hidden, or your mind thinks you're simply seeing the gold-painted edges. Each page has such a tiny amount of the overall image that you can't possibly tell that it's part of a whole."

"Hey—" Mrs. O'Malley said, putting her hands on her hips again. "Didn't you say that better light wasn't necessary in the storage room? Didn't you *swear* that you have eyes like a cat?" she scolded.

Mack shrugged. "Um … meow?"

Kris decided not to say anything about the fore-edge paintings on the old books to anyone, including his parents, until the O'Malleys specifically told him that it was okay to do so.

"Who was that girl you were talking to on our porch?" Kris' mother asked as the two of them set the table for dinner.

"Her name is Josie. She's in the high school band. I think she plays the flute. She wondered if I wanted to try out for the color guard since she's a drum major during the band's marching season."

"What is the color guard?"

"It's a bunch of mostly girls who twirl flags and batons and stuff in front of or behind the band. Their practice for the summer starts next week. Band camp is at the end of July, at the college. Josie wants me to join since only girls are members so far this year. They usually have a few boys who do fancy sword twirling. I told her I'd think about it, but I don't want to do that."

Mrs. Dehlvi eyed him. "Is that all she wanted?"

Kris looked away. "No. She asked me if I wanted to go to a movie tonight."

"Oh?"

"I told her I'd think about it."

"Is that also a thing you do not want to do?"

He shrugged slightly. "I'd like to, I guess. She's a fun person. But I said I'd ask you and Dad first before calling her. Are we doing a family thing tonight?"

"No. You may go. See an appropriate film, please. I don't like a lot of what gets shown at the cinema."

"Okay. Is it all right if I call her now? That way she has time to get ready. Girls like time to get ready."

"Yes, we do. Go ahead now." Mrs. Dehlvi smiled to herself once Kris had left to use the phone in her bedroom, glad that he was able to move on to another girl after having guilty feelings about Tatyana.

"Steve? It's Kat. Want to go to a movie tonight? With me, I mean. Just you and me, not Matt. Okay. There's one starting at seven-thirty that I want to see. No. I'll meet you there. Okay. I'll see you in a while. Bye."

"Did I hear what I think I heard?" asked Matt, stepping inside the front door after walking Browser.

"I'm going to a movie with Steve. No biggy."

"But I thought you hated him," her twin protested, hanging up the leash.

She flipped her hair defensively. "You know I don't go around *hating* people. Sheesh!"

Matt went to the refrigerator and pulled out a pitcher of iced tea. "This is because of Josie, right? You think she's after Kris and you're going to show him that you don't care."

"That makes me sound ... jealous."

"Well?"

She reached for the dog and kissed the black spot on his forehead. He licked her cheek in return. Browser was still panting after his walk in the heat outside, so she put him where he could lap noisily at his bowl of water near the pantry door.

"Mom? Is it okay if I go to a movie tonight?" she called.

"Which one are you seeing?" Mrs. Karlsson asked from the laundry room.

"Some animated dinosaur thing that also has live action parts and a teen romance. It's a treasure-hunt story that ends with a cross-country chase of cavemen on pterodactyls."

"You're making that up," Mrs. Karlsson said, stepping into the hall with a pair of jeans over her arm.

"Honestly, I'm not." She laughed. "The promos make it look good. I guess I'll find out if you let me go."

"Okay. You and your brother be careful, though. It might already be dark by the time it lets out."

"I'm not going with Matt. I'm going with Steve."

There were a few moments of silence. Mrs. Karlsson stood motionless, the pair of jeans still hanging from her arm. "Oh. Well, then, maybe Matt could go, too, but with another girl. That way, when you argue with Steve, you won't be stuck walking home alone."

"Moooo-oom. Why would I have an argument? *I'm* the one who asked *him* out."

"You did?"

Katrina nodded.

"Because you *always* end up having a fight with Steve," Matt said. He took a sip of his iced tea.

Katrina sighed. "Well, don't worry. This time I'll be nice. And I won't talk about any sore subjects. I swear."

"Take my cell phone in case you need a ride. Buy your ticket and snacks yourself. Steve shouldn't have to pay for both of you since the night probably won't end well. Plus, you asked him out, not the other way around." Mrs. Karlsson added, "Kat—what were you thinking? *Steve?*"

Mrs. O'Malley hugged Mack goodbye at their door before stepping onto the sidewalk with Danny. "I'll call you before I leave for home in the morning. Sleep tight. Don't let the book bugs bite."

Mack grinned and winked at her, giving her the response she needed to feel better about leaving him behind for the night.

Outside, she said to her brother, "Oh, Dan. I didn't tell Jack and Darla our news, even though I promised faithfully to call them over. I didn't tell Quainty and Elwood, either. I suppose tomorrow is soon enough. Or *should* I call them all tonight? What do you think, Dan?"

"Hey, Kris! Hey, Katrina!" Danny called loudly, waving to the line of people waiting for tickets outside of the movie theater across the street.

Mrs. O'Malley swung around to look. "Kris and Katrina? Where?"

"Right there in line. See? Kris is with that brown-haired girl, and Kat is with some redheaded boy. At least I think that's who they're with. It's hard to tell from here."

As Danny was pointing out the kids to his sister, Kris waved back. Katrina didn't react. She hadn't heard Danny because she was already having a heated argument with Steve.

"I think you should wait until tomorrow to talk to everyone. That gives you a night off from thinking and worrying about those books," Danny said, walking toward his truck. He then noticed his sister was still near the bookshop, staring at the line outside the theater.

"Mavis? Are you coming?"

She reluctantly followed her brother, her purse in one hand and some of their leftover dinner in a bag in the other. "I wonder if Kris knows that Kat is a few people in line ahead of him."

"Probably. Or not. Okay, here we are."

She opened the passenger door distractedly. "I wonder if they're going to see the same movie."

"Probably. Or not."

A sparrow landed on a tree branch beside her and chirped. She frowned at its cheerfulness.

"Are you getting in?" Danny asked, already seated behind the wheel. "Mavis?"

"Oh, all *right,*" she huffed. "You are so bossy!"

Chapter Nineteen

Kris heard Dontae get out of bed early the next morning, but he was too sleepy to move before the sun had decided to rise. In the dim light, he looked at his bookcase. It was too large for the room. Kris has a feeling that he was inside a fantasy novel where everything was as ornate as his bookcase, and that if he shifted his focus to the magnificent carving on the side of the case, he might fall forward into that world.

Kris woke up again an hour later to unusual sounds coming from outside. He sat, stretched, and stepped to his window. Stomper had been sleeping on Kris' bed ever since Dontae had left the bedroom, and when his boy stood, he slowly pushed into a sitting position to give himself a morning bath.

On the front lawn, Dontae and Dev were either wrestling or learning a strange form of synchronized dance. It slowly dawned on him that Dontae was showing him how to do karate moves.

"Where *is* everybody?" asked Bijay as he padded into Kris' room.

"Come and look," said Kris.

"What are they doing? We haven't even had breakfast yet."

"I think that's karate. See how Dontae is kicking? Now Dev is trying to do it."

Bijay was grinning, but as he turned to look at Kris, his face quickly melted into an expression of disappointment. "Nobody came and got me."

"I think they were both up early this morning and didn't want to wake you up." Kris scruffled Bijay's already-messy hair. "Put on some clothes, and we'll go outside and watch them. Okay?"

Bijay rubbed an eye, still frowning. "Okay."

A few minutes later, Kris passed the entrance to the kitchen with Bijay. He said, "We're going out to watch the karate demonstration before eating. I'll bring all three of them back inside after a few minutes."

Mrs. Dehlvi didn't answer, but she did nod.

"You okay? Mom?" Kris asked.

Bijay ran to her and hugged her legs. She was still wearing her long, silken robe. "Mommy?" he said worriedly.

"I have what is called 'morning sickness' now. The baby causes me to feel like I'm sailing on a boat sometimes. Yish. Please do not have such a sad face, Bij. I know from carrying you in my tummy, and from carrying Dev, that this sickness in the morning does not last much longer. Maybe another month."

Kris made a face. "Really? A month?"

"Yes. But it will go by quick quick quick." She looked at Bijay and smiled as brightly as she could manage. "And early next year you will be a big brother at last. This time to a new little boy or girl."

Bijay took in a breath. "If it's a girl, will I be a sister?"

She laughed. "No. She will be *your* sister. You will still be a brother."

"Oh." Shifting his attention in a flash, he asked Kris, "What about karate?"

"Which reminds me," said Mr. Dehlvi as he walked behind them from the hallway. He was dressed for the day in brown knee-length shorts and a short-sleeved shirt. "Miss Valentine had said that we should enroll Dontae in karate classes again. And later this summer we will need to enroll him in his elementary school."

Mrs. Dehlvi went to sit at the table with a cup of tea. "We should transfer Dontae's medical records to Dev and Bijay's pediatrician."

"Does he need a specialist? Did Miss Valentine say?"

She swallowed some tea. "No. We will make any doctor he sees aware of the ectodermal dysplasia. There would be no such a specialist here in a small city. ED is very rare, hey? He has had many surgeries, but I think that he is done with all that, other than implants that will come later when his mouth is bigger and his jaws have stopped growing. We need to find a dentist right away. Maybe Dontae may have implants now, and new ones when he is fully grown. We have the report from the doctor he saw very recently. He sent us a note with some helpful tips, Kris, if you would like to see it. It says that we will always have to take care to keep him cool and to help him with certain tasks—like using a knife and some delicate work with his hands until he has better coordination. He does very, very well already, but we should keep working with him."

Mr. Dehlvi stepped to the front door. He opened it, and he, Kris, and Bijay went out onto the porch.

Mr. Dehlvi picked up the newspaper. "What goes on here this morning?" he asked Dev and Dontae.

"Lessons," answered Dontae. "Look! Dev learned a move already. He's a good student."

Dev bowed and slowly stretched. When he finished, he stood as usual again and smiled, looking pleased.

"He didn't do anything," complained Bijay.

"He stretched. That comes first," said Dontae. "There's a lot more to it. I only taught him the first thing so far. I usually wear my karate shoes, not sneakers. I don't think you're supposed to wear regular shoes."

Mr. Dehlvi unfolded the newspaper to glance at the front-page headlines. "Thursday already. Our summer is flying by." He looked at Dontae and asked, "Where did you last take karate classes? Here in town?"

Dontae didn't answer.

"Maybe he doesn't remember," suggested Kris, taking a seat on the top step.

"I remember," said Dontae softly. "But I don't want to go back to that place."

Bijay walked toward them and said, "Me, neither."

"Me, neither," said Dev.

"I don't want to go back there, either," said Kris.

Their father laughed and dropped the paper to his side. "Such solidarity is admirable in brothers, but why, exactly, do my four boys want to avoid this place that three of you have never even heard of?"

Dontae linked an arm through Dev's and kicked at a little clump of grass. "I liked going there at first. But then I kept being told to toughen up once these new boys started taking lessons with me." He looked at Mr. Dehlvi. "I *am* tough. I just like people to be fair. I don't think some people should pick on you because you were born with hands and a face and feet and things that are different. Do you?"

Mr. Dehlvi shook his head. "Come in for breakfast. I'll tell you a story from my own, unfair childhood. It will come after prayers. It will be our lesson for the day."

At a few minutes after eight o'clock that morning, Mrs. O'Malley used her key to let herself into the bookshop. Only a few businesses were open at that time of the day, so Danny had been able to glide smoothly along the empty parking spots out front before stopping to drop her off.

"Mack?" she called, locking the door behind her.

"I'm over here. Groaning," Mr. O'Malley said before actually groaning. "My back is *killing* me."

She walked around the counter and found him on the floor. He had taken off the sofa cushions and put them there, where there was more privacy.

"I tried sleeping in the storage room, but there wasn't a good way to lay out the cushions. I don't think I got to sleep

286

until three in the morning. And those cats!" he said, sitting at last with a great effort. "They were so excited to have overnight company that they wouldn't leave me alone. Kneading, purring, rubbing, discussing politics, mewing … arg!"

"They love you very much, Mack," she said, smiling and petting Buglit.

"Arg," he groaned again, holding his back and stretching it awkwardly.

"I brought you some coffee. Get up. I'll put the cushions back on the sofa. Just sit on it for a while and drink before heading home for a shower and some food. When you get back, we'll go over to the bank."

"Coffee? Yes. Standing up? Doubtful."

Mrs. O'Malley leaned down to kiss Mack tenderly on his forehead, one of the few spots on his body that didn't seem to be in pain. "My watchdog hero."

A full two minutes later, he had managed to pull himself upright using the shelves of the counter. Sitting again on the reassembled sofa, he said, "I think we were silly to be worried last night. After all, before we figured out about the books, they'd been sitting here unattended."

She shivered. "I'm glad you did it, though. I would have been scared and panicky all night. As it was, I slept like a baby over at Danny's. In the evening, we watched an old slapstick comedy and ate another round of Chinese, then some cheese popcorn an hour later. I took a long soak in the tub after Dan went to bed. When I drifted off, I felt comforted by your tender-loving presence here at the bookshop."

Mack scowled, his mouth full of lukewarm coffee.

An hour and a half later, Mack let himself into the bookshop again, changed and fed, but wracked with back pain and a headache.

"Oh, dear! Do you want some aspirin?" Mrs. O'Malley asked from where she was working on the computer.

He shook his head. "I took a couple of them at home."

"I'm going to call Jack to carry the books over to the bank."

He shook his head again. "I need to rent a secure box first."

"Don't say exactly what we've got, okay?" she said anxiously.

"The bank workers won't ask, and I won't tell. They'll only want to know what size box I want, and they'll tell me that I can't put anything illegal or dangerous in there."

"Oh."

"Plus, I need to photograph the books first. Or, you do. You're always the one who takes shots of books when we get requests by phone or internet. We have about a half hour until our opening time. I'll get the books out a few at a time. Where do you want to set up?"

"Hmm. I guess in the kids' book room, on that table. I'll bring the floor lamp over, and that should be enough light. In the meantime, start thinking about which auction house will be getting the photos."

He paused.

"What?" she asked. "In too much pain to think?"

Mack twisted his back a little, testing. "I'm doing better. No, I was just thinking: if these do actually sell for big bucks, what happens when we finally have the money from their sale? Do we officially retire?"

She pressed her lips together, glancing around the front room. Images of her customer friends came through the door, waving and laughing, talking to them a moment before going to their favorite shelves to browse. "I ... hadn't planned that far ahead."

"I'm not ready," he said definitively.

"I feel close to ready, but no—I'm not ready, either. We'll put the money in a savings account for a while. Then, when we *are* ready, it'll be there." She frowned, watching in her mind as images of her friends waved goodbye and vanished.

"I'd hug you, Mavis, but I honestly can't. Ouch."

She smiled tearfully and reached for a tissue.

By ten minutes past ten o'clock, photos had been snapped and the rare books put away again in the O'Malleys' storage room. Mack unlocked the front door and flipped over the open sign. "I think we'll need the air conditioner on today," he said. "It's supposed to be in the mid-eighties this afternoon."

"I wonder where Kris is?"

"Nearly here. I see him crossing the street now."

"He can go with you to the bank. In case you need help walking." She gave him a cheesy grin before sobering. "Sorry I didn't finish taking the photos in time to go over there with you before opening time."

"I'll tell you what, Mavis—taking Kris along as a crutch doesn't sound like a bad idea. That was sure no fun time I had on the floor last night. And those cats! Every time I almost drifted off, one of them either purred in my ear or decided I needed a deep-tissue massage."

She laughed, pointing a scolding finger at Haiku, who couldn't have possibly looked more innocent as he sat on the back of the sofa, his long, fluffy tail wrapped around his feet.

"Sorry I'm late," Kris said. "We were having a long talk over breakfast. I couldn't get into the bathroom to take a shower for like a half an hour because each one of the boys had to go potty first and wash up."

"You're just in time," Mack said as he went through their usual routine to open for the day. "I had Mavis take photos of the books before we opened. She finished about three minutes ago. Geez, Kris. It sounds having only one bathroom is a royal pain. How is that going to be when you boys are back in school and your dad is back at work?"

"I hadn't thought of that. We had a system before Dontae came along. Mom would wake us up at different times, with Dad going first, me next, then Dev, then Bij. I guess we'll do that again but push it back fifteen minutes to fit in Dontae."

Mrs. O'Malley looked doubtful.

"I'm heading to the bank to reserve a safe deposit box. You want to join me or stay here?" Mack asked.

"I'll go with."

When they returned, Kris saw through the windows that Katrina and Matt were sitting on the sofa talking to Mrs. O'Malley. Katrina had just finished saying that she'd had nearly the worst night out possible with Steve.

When Kris saw Kat and Matt, his face reddened. He pushed open the door, and he and Mack went into the shop.

"What'd you think of that awful movie last night?" she asked.

"Oh, were you there, too?"

She sighed. "You know I was. I went with Steve. He asks me out all the time. I finally gave in. It's nice to be wanted."

Kris shrugged, his face growing even redder. "I was there with Josie. She's in the band. She wants me to try out for the color guard so we can be together more."

"Oh. Nice. Yeah … Steve and I will probably be dating a lot over the summer. He's practically one of the family already since he's been Matt's friend for years. Mom *really* adores him."

Kris tried not to miss a beat. "Josie is super pretty, don't you think?" He looked to Mrs. O'Malley before adding, "She's very … bouncy, as Dontae would say."

"I think bouncy and perky can be awfully irritating after the first day of hanging out with someone," Katrina said. "Don't you think so, Mrs. O?"

"I love perky," Kris countered. "Perky people are happy. They make you happy just to be around them. Don't you think so, Mrs. O?"

Katrina cut in, "Well, I think Steve is great because he's the exact opposite. He's very deep and serious."

Kris balked. "Steve is about as deep and serious as a shallow mud puddle."

The girl crossed her arms, scowling.

Kris felt like he was winning. "Mrs. O, don't you think someone who's happy and outgoing makes for a better person to date than a mud puddle?"

"I am staying out of this conversation entirely," she said, raising her hands in the air and then making a downward movement with them. "But I will say this: I've never heard a worse bunch of *hooey* before in my whole life."

Matt choked on his own laughter.

"Shut up, Matty!" his sister ordered.

"Now, now, kids. Let's change the topic," Mack said. "I've been to the bank. We can fill the safe deposit box anytime we're ready. Kris, you carry one box of books and Matt, you take the other over there. My back is k-i-double-l killing me from sleeping on the floor while a yowling pack of feral cats climbed all over me the whole night long."

Kris snickered. Katrina snickered. Mrs. O'Malley laughed, and Matt smiled at his sister, relieved that the tirade was over.

"Steve is awful," Kat finally admitted, still slightly giggling. "Oh, my gosh, he is the *worst.*"

"Josie and I are going out again on Saturday," Kris said. "We're going to Lamarr with her parents and sister. They have tickets for a play. *Our Town.* Her uncle is starring in one of the lead roles."

Matt looked sympathetically at his sister. She turned away so no one could see her reaction.

"I *love* that play," said Mrs. O'Malley a bit too loudly. "My mother read it aloud to me one summer when I was about nine or ten years old. We would sit outside under the oak tree on lounge chairs when she had free time from cooking and housework. I remember getting such a spooky, melancholy feeling from the story and the way she read it. I read it again a few years ago, but I didn't feel the same way as I did when Mom read it to me."

While she spoke, Katrina had time to compose herself, still turned away from the others. She flipped her hair over her shoulders and cleared her throat. "While they're at the bank, want me to put some dustjackets in sleeves for you, Mrs. O?"

"Sure, sweetie. I'll go pull some rare books off the shelves that have nice jackets. Thank you."

Kris saw the remains of a tear on the bottom of Katrina's cheek that she hadn't wiped away. He suddenly felt terrible. It never occurred to him that Katrina might like him in a non-brotherly way. He had started having different feelings for her since the day they had walked to the theater and library together, but he never thought that she might return those feelings. She'd pulled away from him the evening she'd delivered her t-shirts gift. Had she really wanted to stay sitting with him on the porch, but was too shy? The weight of his promise to Josie felt like a hundred thousand pounds crushing his chest.

Matt, noticing the way Kris was looking, and the way his sister was acting, had a sudden idea. "Rats!" he shouted.

"What?" asked Kris, his voice shaking even on that single syllable.

"We have to read that play *Our Town* this summer, and *Romeo and Juliet*, too. I wish *I* could go with Josie to see it on the stage. Do you think she'd let me switch with you? I know her a little bit, too, and she's never looked at me like I was a toad or anything. Are you super stoked to go on Saturday?"

Mrs. O'Malley appreciated what Matt was attempting but thought it would be very rude if he invited himself along, especially on a family outing. "Matt, maybe you can get tickets for you and Katrina and your mom if you'd really like to see it. Josie invited Kris, not you. You were right here yesterday when she came by, so ..."

Matt stood up. He didn't know what to do, so he headed for the storage room. "Is it still locked?"

Mack, who had been trying to stretch his kinks out for the past couple of minutes, said, "Yep. Hang on." He tugged at Kris' sleeve as he walked by, silently asking him to follow.

When the three men had left for the bank, Mrs. O'Malley placed a short stack of rare books on the counter near the display window. She then took hold of Katrina's hand and squeezed it. She whispered, "I'm sure Kris can see how you feel now. It's enough."

She sobbed and covered her face with her bent arm. "He *doesn't* know. He *doesn't* care. And ... *I* don't care."

"Oh, Katrina. Being a teenager is difficult anyway, and there are all these hard-to-understand emotions piled on top of your heart. Listen to me. You have your whole life ahead of you. If you get this beat up at fourteen, you'll never make it to twenty-five without a nervous breakdown. Just relax and enjoy your summer. Forget about feelings if you can, other than friendship. Kris is a great friend to you and your brother, isn't he? So ... let that be the fun, wonderful thing that it is." She sighed, watching Katrina lower her arm to shake her head. "I know you're going to go on pining, but I do wish you would hear what I'm saying. Do you still have a crush on the boy you had a crush on two years ago?"

She took an unsteady breath. "No."

"How about the boy you had a crush on before that?"

"No."

"See? Maybe if you relax and can be happy with the way things are right now, it might lead to a relationship that's very much better on down the line. Can you at least try?"

Katrina reached for a tissue and blew her nose, then took in two long, deep breaths. "I'll try." She then hugged Mrs. O'Malley, cooling her face on the woman's cotton blouse.

Mrs. O'Malley stepped back to say, "Here. Put a dustjacket sleeve on the dragon book for me and let me see what it looks like when it's all pretty and shiny. I'll bet that golden dragon will pop right out at our eyeballs."

Katrina smiled but didn't move. "I will. In a minute."

"Hello, beautiful ladies," said Mr. Johnson as he came into the bookshop. His accent was uniquely his own. "How are you doing this fine, sunshiny ta-day?"

Mrs. O'Malley cleared her throat and said, "Fine, fine. How are you? How are things at the Helping Hands Center?"

"Good'n all, good'n all, Mrs." He put both hands into his jeans pockets. "Say, do you have any books of sheet music? You know, piano-scratchers? I'm tired of the ones I have in my bench. I'm playing often, and my repertar is gettin' dull."

"We sure do. See that lamp on the wall, there? Just to the left of it is our music section. The taller shelf contains sheet music books, and the shelf below it has single songs in the plastic tubs. Each single song is a dollar, and the books are all individually priced inside the back cover."

"Very nice, Mrs. I'll go'n see." He nodded once in thanks and blinked at Katrina.

Mrs. O'Malley asked, "How's Judy Towd? I have *got* to get over to your place to visit with her one of these days."

"She's a might fragile, but she likes her new wheeled chair. She says it's comfy, and she can wheel it real fine on her own. We sit together for every meal, her'n me. Once in a while, she'll sing along as I play. Feels like we're young again."

Mrs. O'Malley nodded. "Never too late for love, is it?"

Mr. Johnson pulled the tub of sheet music from the shelf and put it on the end table. He smiled. "Ha! Don't tell *her* that, but I guess that's how I do feel."

"You mean to tell me that you haven't told her yet? What are you waiting for? Your ninetieth birthday?"

He shrugged, looking at the tub. "I'll get 'round to it. We're not going anyplace."

Katrina gasped and then laughed. She whispered, "Oh, holy wowsers! That's going to be me and Kris. We'll be old, and I'll be in a wheelchair, and we still won't have said anything."

Mrs. O'Malley grinned and elbowed the girl, teasing, "Well, I'll remember to prod him along a little when you're both about thirty-five, just to make sure that doesn't happen."

"And now that that job is done," said Mack when he and the boys had returned from the bank, "I need to call the police."

"You think so?" asked Mrs. O'Malley.

"I do. We should tell them the real reason for this whole break-in and for hitting poor Kris on the head, especially since they've taken this case seriously."

She nodded.

Katrina kept her head bowed over her dustjacket project, deciding and changing her mind a dozen times about what the next words out of her mouth should be to Kris. Part of her was disappointed that Josie had snagged him so soon after Tatyana had left. The other part of her was angry that she hadn't made it clear to him that she liked him romantically, all because Matt had warned her to leave Kris alone in that way until they were older. And yet another part was hearing Mrs. O'Malley's words of advice. In the end, Katrina decided that the woman was right. She looked up and saw that Kris was neatening the shelves of science fiction. Matt was near him, reading the rear cover of a paperback.

"Hey, Kris," Katrina finally said. "How is your mom feeling?"

He was startled to hear her voice in his ears instead of only in his mind. He'd been replaying what she'd said before he went to the bank. "Uh—she has stomach pains. Morning sickness."

"Bad?"

"I don't think so. She's not stuck in bed with pain or throwing up or anything. She said she'll likely have at least some sickness for another month. That seems like forever to me."

"She must be getting fairly far along, then, if that's what the doctor told her," Mrs. O'Malley said, heading for the restroom. "A month will go by fast," she added, closing the door.

"A month? Yewww. But it'll be worth it, though. She'll have a new baby," Matt said, surprising everyone. He noticed their reactions and said, "What? *I* like babies. I mean, I don't want one this *year,* but *I* like babies."

Kris caught Katrina's eye. She quickly glanced away, so he walked past Mack, who was searching for the non-emergency number for the police station. Kris moved the computer chair aside and leaned against the countertop, facing her. He took a deep breath and whispered, "Hi."

"Hi," she said as quietly as he had.

Mack dialed the phone and began talking.

Kris reached for Katrina's hand and held it loosely. She let him, but couldn't meet his eyes. She instead looked at their hands, her heart pounding.

"Friends?" he asked, holding her hand tighter.

"Yep," she said, sniffing once and blushing.

He let go and walked away again.

Mrs. O'Malley had missed the whole thing.

Half an hour later, Mr. O'Malley was back from his meeting at the police station. He had given an officer the letter from Charles and a copy of one of the photos of the fore-edge paintings. "He's in custody. I don't yet know for how long," he reported to Mrs. O'Malley and the kids.

"What do we do now?" asked Matt. He had been waiting in the shop to hear if Mack had learned anything new.

Kris said, "I'm going to run home to eat in a while. Kat, Matt—are you staying here today?"

Katrina put a handful of unused dustjacket sleeves and the tape dispenser under the countertop. "My week is messed up, and I'm on a different schedule with my piano teacher. I have a lesson this afternoon. Mom is coming home to take me to lunch. She'll drop me off before she goes back to work. It's a short walk from my teacher's place to the car dealership, so I'll spend the rest of the day with Mom."

"I'm probably going to find Steve. Maybe we'll go swimming. It's supposed to be hot today," Matt said. "Unless you need me," he said to Mack.

Mr. O'Malley shook his head. "I think I'll research rare book auction houses and email some of the photos Mavis took earlier. I noticed each of the books in that group had a tiny label inside the rear cover. Each label has a drawing of a stylized lion on it, and a number. Kris, I can use you today, but Kat and Matt—we'll see you tomorrow if you come by."

"Okay," said Kris with a wave to them all, "I'll see you when I see you. Bye." He stared directly at Katrina. When she finally met his eyes, he held her gaze a for a moment before looking away shyly, smiling as brightly as she had.

Chapter Twenty

Kris sat with his mother outside at the patio table. They ate flatbread and chicken curry left over from the night before. The younger boys were near the garden setting up a plastic racetrack that Dev and Bijay hadn't played with in over a year.

Mrs. Dehlvi pulled hair out of her eyes as a sudden breeze shifted the tilt of the large umbrella at the center of the table. "Your father is at the home store. He's thinking of putting in a second bathroom. Perhaps in the basement."

"I wonder, Mom, if a bigger house—"

"That is my wonder, too, Kris. That is my wonder, too. A second toilet, at least, is needed right away. I must run run run so so often with the new baby in my stomach. Yee!"

"There'll be seven of us next year. When you bought this place, weren't there just the two of you?"

She nodded, swallowing a bite of bread. "Seems like only yesterday, but now I have four big boys."

"Did Dad have this job waiting for him before you moved to town?"

"Yes. That is why we moved to this country. This was our first home after a short stay in a tiny apartment near campus that cost us much too much money."

They ate in silence for a while. Kris swallowed some ice water, thinking that he really wasn't very hungry. He still had butterflies in his stomach every time he thought about Katrina. When he thought about Josie, he felt regretful. He did like Josie, but she wasn't ... Katrina.

"Dontae loves a combination of peanut butter and jelly on soft, white bread. I have had it, of course, but find it to be very sweet. I do not know why that is all he will say that he wants for lunch," Mrs. Dehlvi said, watching her young sons. They had left the track to play a leapfrog game. Stomper and

Pip lounged on the warm bricks of the patio at a safe distance from the jumping boys.

"Do his teeth or mouth bother him, do you think?" Kris asked. "I know you said Dontae will need implants eventually, but I wonder if he also needs some kind of treatment right now."

Mrs. Dehlvi raised one eyebrow and turned her attention to the yard. "Come to me, Dontae. Please."

Dontae made one last leap, landing hard on his hands.

Mrs. Dehlvi winced. "Oh, his hands! Arey!" she whispered.

"What?" asked Dontae as he stood in front of her. He wiped his fingers on his shorts, getting off some of the dirt.

"Does your mouth—or do your teeth—hurt you? Your mama wants to know."

He made the same unsure expression he made every time she referred to herself as his mama, mother, or mom. "No. I'm okay. I had operations, but that was a long time ago. I don't remember much about them now. I wish I had more teeth, but I can chew most stuff. My feet hurt, but not as much this year as they did last year." He looked down. "I like these shoes. They're soft."

Kris said, "He told me that he's never had sneakers before. He's only had hard-topped leather shoes like the ones he was wearing before, other than his karate shoes."

"Oh?" she said, looking at Dontae in surprise.

Dontae nodded as the other two boys walked onto the bricks of the patio behind him. Bijay lifted Pip, petting his neck and scratching him under the chin.

"But your mouth—it does not hurt you at all?" she asked Dontae again.

"No, Mrs.," he answered earnestly.

Mrs. Dehlvi pushed her plate back and angled her chair away from the table. "Kris, I want you to do this, please," she said, holding Dontae at her side as she sat. "Please tell our

Dontae that he most certainly may call me 'mama' or 'mom.' We had a long wait with you before you said it," she breathed in and out before continuing, "and I don't think my heart can take another long wait with this boy."

Kris sighed. He looked at Dev, who seemed very interested in the conversation. "Dev, I think *you* should tell Dontae that. You're the one who finally convinced me to say it to Mom and Dad. Remember?"

Dev shifted. He linked his arm through Bijay's even though he was still holding Pip. "Dontae, we think you should say it now ... if you want to. Kris said he didn't say "mom" for a long time because he was worried about us hearing him say it. Like he was hording in."

"Horning," Kris corrected.

"Like he was horning in, taking a spot in our family that ... what did you say then?"

Kris took over, saying to Dontae, "I told Dev that I felt like I was intruding. Like I didn't have the right to say 'mom' and 'dad' when I wasn't their real son. He told me that he *wanted* me in the family, and Bijay wanted me in the family. He said that there was no difference between us. We were all the same as each other, and we should all call each other brothers, and we should all call Mom and Dad 'Mom' and 'Dad.' That would make it feel like we were a real family who wanted each other."

A single tear ran down Dontae's cheek. "I never have before."

"Never have what, D?" asked Kris, leaning toward him and taking his hand.

"Said that before."

Kris looked at his mother, surprised. He didn't know Dontae's background. Not much of it. Maybe his parents knew more.

"Want to try it?" coaxed Bijay.

"We *want* you to," said Dev earnestly.

Dontae, feeling shy, turned to hide his face against Mrs. Dehlvi's shoulder. He then turned his face slightly toward the boys, and after a few moments of shallow breathing, finally said, "Mom."

Mrs. Dehlvi pulled the boy onto her lap and rested her cheek against the top of his head, rocking him and whispering lilting words in a language that may have been Hindi, or one that is only used when mothers speak softly to their child's heart.

Kris went back to the bookshop after lunch, hating to leave his brothers. As he walked, he thought that he should limit his days in the bookshop to two or three per week. His parents would probably be glad. He felt, though, like he was choosing between families. He often had an image of himself standing on the edge of two pages, balancing on two separate worlds. Especially in the summer, when he was at the bookshop nearly every day, intensely involved with the O'Malleys' lives. He often felt split in two, torn like the page of a book, incomplete if he only read one half or the other.

As he rounded the corner onto Main Street, he nearly ran into Darla as she was coming out of the pharmacy. Darla was carrying L.P., her purse, and a cloth shopping bag, looking as though she could use an extra pair of helping hands.

"Hi, kid! How's it going? Amazing, spectacular, out-of-this-world news about the books! Aunty Mavis told me about it a little while ago when I brought her and Mack some sandwiches."

"I know! But wow—scary, too. Who knew the O'Malleys had those kinds of things in their storage room for all that time? And to think Mack hadn't seen the paintings—and probably wouldn't have realized it for a long time—if it hadn't been for your dad's carvings."

L.P. twisted around to see Kris, one of her very best friends.

Darla handed L.P. to Kris so she would stop begging and reaching for him. "My dad's carvings? I ... huh?"

Kris told her about the bookcase as they walked.

Darla was astounded to hear the rest of the story. "Good thing Matt noticed! It was a good thing they sparked a memory for you, and good that Mack picked up on what you meant and realized it might be the key to the whole *mystery.*" She took the baby back into her arms when they got to the record shop.

"I'm going to get to carry a baby around all the time, soon," said Kris, smiling at L.P.

Darla stopped walking, her face frozen in shock. "You're going to *what?*"

"My mom. She's having another baby. Didn't Mrs. O tell you that?"

Darla shook her head, smiling. "She is? Another baby? Wow. More news Aunty Mavis didn't tell me. That's some major ... and right after you all adopted Dontae, too. Didn't she know she was expecting when she and your dad were making adoption arrangements?"

Kris brushed a wasp from his shirt and made sure it had flown far away from L.P. "She told me that she'd had some suspicions, but she was too busy to take her symptoms seriously. I don't know what those symptoms are. I only noticed that she was tired way more than usual. When she about fainted, Dad took her into the doctor's. That's how they found out that it's a baby that's been making her all worn out."

Darla watched Kris shake L.P.'s hand goodbye. "You're going to be a big brother to a baby this time. You've never been in a house with a newborn. They're ... well, a big change."

"I've been warned. Dev said they're noisy."

"How does he remember?"

Kris shrugged, then laughed once. "Must have made a big impression on him. He called Bijay a "little milk-barfer.""

Darla laughed as she gently bounced L.P. "Kris? I've been to your house. I was there with Aunty Mavis to visit your mom. That house … how are you all fitting in it?"

"I was talking to my mom about that over lunch. Dad's gonna try to put in a new toilet in the basement. I'm not sure what their plans are. I'd sure hate to move, though. We all really like our neighbors."

Darla nodded. "Well, I've got to get this one changed, as you can tell. I usually leave her with Jack if I need to run an errand, but he was on the phone with an internet customer. Lila Pearl did a little bit of business of her own when we were in the check-out line."

"Bye, L.P. I'll see you later."

"Um … I was thinking. If you can, stop by the shop later today."

Kris raised an eyebrow. *"Your* shop, you mean?"

She nodded. "I have a plan that I want to talk to you about."

He shrugged. "Okay. I'll come over in a while."

She pushed through the door into her record shop. Kris watched Darla carry L.P. along one of the long aisles toward the small bathroom at the far end.

He went across the alley and into the bookshop, relieved to be in air conditioning. "I didn't realize how hot I was. Feels good!" he said, standing in the stream of cool air.

"Enjoy your lunch?" asked Mrs. O'Malley. She was gathering a stack of old Life magazines that had slid from their bottom shelf on the far end of the room.

"Yeah, but may I use your phone real quick? I need to call my mom."

"Sure," she said on her way into the rare book room.

Kris dialed his home number. "Mom? I just got here. Oh, I stopped to talk to Darla for a little while. Yeah. I told her your news. She's very happy for you. Yep. Anyway, the reason I called is because I got hot on the way here. I heard the kids say that they were going to see if Dontae can shoot hoopies this afternoon. It's too hot for D to do that sort of thing. Why? I know, but—Okay. I know. Fourteen, almost fifteen. All right. Bye."

He put the phone on the charger. He looked wilted.

"Is everything okay at home?" Mrs. O'Malley asked.

Mr. O'Malley emerged from the hallway. "Hiya, Kris."

"I kinda got yelled at a little bit, that's all."

"Why?" asked Mrs. O'Malley.

"I called to warn Mom that it was too hot for Dontae to play basketball today. She asked me how old I am, and did I remember that I'm not forty-five with a mortgage."

"I understand how you *both* feel," said Mack. "You want to be a responsible big brother, but your parents want you to relax and be a kid for a while longer." He crossed his arms. "I don't see a solution. You're going to have this problem for years to come. And I can guess that she sees even more concern and hovering from you coming along the pike now that another family member is on the way." Mack patted Kris' back as he passed him to sit at the computer. "I think it's tenderhearted of you, but I can see your mom's point."

"Not helping, actually," said Mrs. O'Malley dryly.

Mack turned on the computer monitor. "I could tell you to relax and let your folks be the parents, but you aren't actually going to listen to me. The only thing I can say that might be of value is this: don't get upset if your mom and dad get exasperated with you over these things. That will only add to the stress. Maybe try this—keep your mouth shut if at all possible. You can still have those feelings of wanting to offer advice or direction, but don't act on them. If there's some real emergency or imminent danger, then yes—do or say something. How does that grab you for an idea?"

Kris thought about it. "Oh, I guess that would work. I'll try it. Thanks, Mack."

Just then Allison came into the shop, followed by a woman who looked very much like her, only with shorter hair and a slightly thinner nose. Allison was wearing a 1950s summer party dress, blue with white polka dots, and a halter top with ties that went around her neck, under her hair. She had on red sandals and bright red lipstick. The other woman wore white slacks and a sleeveless purple blouse and carried a large brown cloth case.

"Allison!" cried Mrs. O'Malley. "I'm so glad to see you."

"Meerrrowl!!!" said the case or its contents.

The woman in slacks placed the case on the floor, unzipped one side, and Regular emerged. He shook himself, blinked twice, and mewed loudly again.

"Reggie! Is that you, kitty?" asked Kris, right on top of Mrs. O'Malley, who had asked almost the same thing.

The black and white cat with golden eyes took a few seconds to realize he was back in the bookshop. When he did, he was thrilled. Regular pounced onto the sofa cushions one by one, hopped onto the back cushions, leaped to the floor, scampered in a circle, ran down the hallway and into each room, and back out again. He then hopped onto Mack's lap before stepping onto the countertop where he caught his breath and squinted at Mrs. O'Malley. "Merrewl!"

Upon hearing a familiar voice, Buglit left a windowsill where she'd been napping and ran to the sofa. She sat looking at her old friend, then stared at Mrs. O'Malley, her eyes full of questions as her tail swished happily.

"He's here for a visit, Miss Bug," answered Allison with a lilt in her voice. "I've been saying for a long time that Reg should pay a call on the bookshop, and today is finally the day. Todd's got this semester off from teaching. He's minding the shop while I get to spend the day with my sister." She motioned to the other woman. "This is Stephanie. Steph, this is Mack O'Malley, Mavis O'Malley, and their fine assistant, Kris."

Buglit invited Regular to sit with her, and he did. Bug sniffed and sniffed her old friend, making sure he was the same cat she remembered.

"We're happy to meet you, Stephanie. Do you live here in town?" asked Mrs. O'Malley.

Stephanie moved the cat's case out of the way behind the sofa. "I do. I have one of the homes on the east side of the lake."

Kris could picture those houses. He saw them every time he swam. Massive, expensive-looking, and each with a large amount of land around it and a boat launch.

"Your sister told us last year about your inheritance, and that you both were involved with charities and special projects. That's a wonderful way to spend a life," Mrs. O'Malley said, sitting to pet Regular when Buglit would allow it.

"I came in for another very particular reason, Mavis," Allison said, putting an arm around her sister. "Steph needs a cat."

"I don't *need* a cat, Allie. I *want* one."

"You need one. You just don't know it yet. I had no idea that I needed Reggie and Aussie, but I sure do."

"How are the two of them getting along together? I remember Aussie was a real handful," Mrs. O'Malley asked.

Kris looked puzzled. "I don't remember a cat named Aussie."

Mrs. O'Malley told him, "She was out as fast as she was in. Miss Allison took Reg and Aussie home the same day."

Allison said, smiling, "Aussie is still awesome, and she and Reggie get along beautifully—when they aren't tearing through the house like little maniacs, knocking everything off the shelves or playing discordant duets on my baby grand."

"You're not doing a great job of talking me into a cat, Sis," said Stephanie.

"Steph is the funny one in the family, can you tell?" Allison asked, bumping her hip against her sister's.

"I might get a dog, instead. Or a teacup pig. I hear that ferrets are interesting, too," Stephanie said, all the while watching Regular and Buglit together.

"Where is the cat you're fostering now?" Allison asked, ignoring her sister. She looked around the room.

Kris looked, too, and found Haiku's tail swishing at the edge of the mini refrigerator, the rest of his body hidden. "There's Haiku. Want me to fish him out?"

"Haiku? Like, the poem?" asked Allison, delighted.

"Yes," said Mack. "We very nearly got Sylvia, who is over at the pawn shop. Sylvia, apparently, looks like a walking exclamation point when she holds her tail aloft. We didn't get a cat with built-in punctuation, but we did get a poem."

"There he is," said Mrs. O'Malley when she saw the cat in Kris' arms.

Kris carried Haiku to Allison and Stephanie. "He's still a little shy, but he likes to chase stuff. When I wad up a piece of paper into a ball and throw it, he'll bat it around forever. He's very quiet unless he gets some catnip, and then he makes the weirdest *rowel-rowel* sounds."

"Get a load of the cat salesman over here," laughed Stephanie, petting Haiku's long, luxurious fur.

Kris countered, "I'm not pushing. I *love* having Ku here. But I know that the O'Malleys would want him to get adopted so they can bring another cat here from the shelter so *that* kitty doesn't mostly have to live in a cage."

Stephanie sighed. "An even more convincing paragraph, kid." She took Haiku from Kris and hugged him to her chest. Her eyes closed with pleasure. "Where do I sign?"

Mrs. O'Malley grinned. "At the shelter. When you're finished there, come on back for your very own rescued cat."

Buglit sat up. She looked at Haiku and seemed to have a feeling come over her as if she knew that Haiku had found his forever human companion. She mewed, and Haiku pushed away from Stephanie to land on the sofa cushion next to Bug and Regular. Buglit started washing Haiku's forehead in what seemed to be a farewell bath.

"I almost forgot," said Kris an hour later. He had been shelving a lot of the recently priced and flagged, internet-listed books from the auction.

"What?" asked Mack from in front of the computer. He was doing research on auction houses, and more research on fore-edge painted books.

"I told Darla that I'd run over there to talk to her about something today. Is it okay if I go now?"

Mack looked away from the screen to say, "Sure. Oh, and tell Jack that I want to pay his dad for the use of his storage unit if he'll let me."

"Okay. I'll probably be back soon. Darla didn't say what she wanted to talk about. I think I know, though."

Mr. O'Malley only said, "Hmm," and returned his attention to the screen.

"Leaving, Kris?" asked Mrs. O'Malley as she walked from the hall to the front room.

"Only for a while. Darla wants to talk to me about something."

After he'd gone, Mrs. O'Malley stood with her hands on her hips. "Did he say what Darla wanted to talk to him about?"

Mack yawned. "No."

She pushed a lock of hair behind her ear. "I wonder why *I* wasn't invited."

Mack didn't answer as he moved and clicked the mouse.

She took a sip of her coffee as a wisp of worry trickled down her spine.

"I'll tell Dad what Mack said, but I know he won't take any payment," Jack said while searching through his many displays of older record albums for one by John Coltrane that wasn't where he'd put it.

"Kris? Come on back here to the office, okay?" called Darla. Kris couldn't see her, but he could tell where her voice had come from.

"The baby's upstairs in her crib, asleep," Darla said once Kris had come through the office door. "Want a drink? I bought a case of this pineapple-orange concoction. It's actually really good."

"Sure. Thanks."

She pointed to a padded stool near some electronics equipment that Jack used to fix record players for customers. "Sit." She handed him a chilled bottle and sat on another tall stool. "I've been thinking and thinking about the situation with your bio-parents."

"Oh?"

"You sound surprised."

"It's just that ... I haven't. Not lately. There's so much else going on, like us getting Dontae, the book thief and book mystery, my mom's pregnancy, and a bunch of other stuff. Oh, and the gift I got, of course. Your dad's bookcase. Man, oh *man!*"

She smiled, twisting open a drink for herself and taking a swallow. "Sounds like you love it."

"Beyond that. It is the coolest thing I could ever imagine *seeing,* let alone *having.*"

They both heard a noise, and Darla pointed to the baby monitor. "She's moving around. She'll go back to sleep in a minute."

"So, you wanted to talk to me about my first parents?" Kris prompted.

Darla cleared her throat and released her brown hair from a ponytail holder. "That thing was giving me a headache." She took another drink. "Kris, I think that I'd like to try to find Ricki."

Kris inhaled. He hadn't been expecting that. He thought Darla was going to say that she'd remembered some new details from long ago, or that she had advice for him if he went to talk to someone at social services. "Why?" he asked, not understanding.

"If she'll talk to me, maybe then we'll know if she is your mother, if she kept that baby, or if she put him or her up for adoption with another couple."

Kris drank almost the whole bottle of juice in one go. "I told Mom and Dad that I'd put off dealing with this until later in the summer."

"I'm sure I won't be able to track her down right away. If I *can* track her down."

"So, you'd use the computer ... the internet to find her?"

"No. I only remember her first name. I thought I'd drive over to the town where I was a waitress and ask around. See if anyone remembers her and knows where she lives now. Or, at least if they remember last name."

"Oh. I guess that would be okay. If you want to, I mean. It's a lot of trouble for a maybe."

"It would put my mind at ease."

He drank the rest of his juice, then held the empty bottle loosely. He remembered a favor he'd wanted to ask her. "Darla?"

She took his empty bottle and put it in a bin with other empties. "What, kid?"

"I don't know where your dad does his work. Could you take me there so I can say thanks in person?"

She looked pleased. "I'd love to. Let's tell Jack we're going. He can clip on the baby monitor while he works."

Ten minutes later, Darla and Kris arrived at the rear entrance of a building owned by the Anders Lake lumber yard. The sound of electric saws and the smell of sawdust filled the sun-soaked air. The plain wooden door was open, and they walked in without knocking.

"Dad? We came by for a visit. Are you too busy to talk right now?"

"Darla! No, no. Come on in. Who's with you?"

Darla pulled Kris into the room.

"Kris! Hello! You've never been here before, have you?" Danny removed his thick leather gloves to pat the boy on his back. "Come on in and take a look around. I've got several projects going at once. Here's a cedar chest that I've nearly finished. Over there's an oval dining table with a grooved pedestal and drop leaves. And these are miniature versions of a bookcase, chair, and desk that I'm making for a dollhouse. Don't tell Darla, but they might be for Lila Pearl." He grinned at his daughter.

Kris admired the large pieces for a few moments before lifting the tiny bookcase. As he put it down again, he saw that there were minuscule books on the dollhouse desk. He finally said, "I came to tell you ..."

Danny switched off a bright bare light bulb that hung over his tool-strewn worktable as he sat on a low bench. He brushed sawdust from his hairy forearms onto the rough, shaving-covered wooden floor. "I see."

Kris cleared his throat and tried to speak again. "I really, really want to say thanks for ...." His throat constricted, and he felt like he could barely breathe.

"I think he's very emotional about your gift, Dad," Darla said, trying to help.

Kris blew out a long, shaky breath. He tugged at the end of his blue jean shorts, not looking up. "It isn't only the bookcase that means so much." He collected his thoughts. "I … other than books, I haven't wanted things of my own since my folks passed away. People and cats, yes, but not things. I don't like feeling the weight of them. It's like they're burdens. I had toys and video games and a bike and all that usual stuff when I was a little kid, but once I lost Mom and Dad—my *first* mom and dad—I haven't liked owning more than what's really needed. I don't ever intend to leave the Dehlvis, but I guess in my heart, in some small way, I've never felt fully settled. I have what I need like clothes and a backpack and a desk to do my homework on and a lamp to see by at night. Anything else—other than books—kind of made me upset."

"And then I gave you a giant bookcase."

Kris swallowed, finally looking at Danny. "You did. And I know Mack and Mrs. O were involved, and the Cumbers, too. It was like all of you were saying, 'Here. Take something permanent that you can look at when you drift off to sleep and that'll be there when you first wake up. There are reasons to stay. So stay.' I woke up this morning and there it stood, holding *everything,* in a way, sitting in a house with me and my family. It's all carved, and excellent, and real. And you gave it to *me,* like I mean enough to be … worthy of it."

Danny sniffled. He looked at his calloused hands, then at Darla, and then through the open door. "Good God, kid! If that wasn't the greatest thank-you speech ever made, my name's not Kinonen."

"I think I've decided who to contact first, Mavis," Mack declared as Kris was pushing into the shop again that afternoon.

"You have? Oh, but don't settle right away. Write or call other auction houses, too. Hello, Kris. That must have been some talk with Darla. You were gone most of the hour," Mrs. O'Malley said from one of the display windows. She had changed out a display of books on flowers and gardening for books that made good, light beach reading.

Kris sat on the arm of the sofa, his hands on his knees. He glanced around to see if they were alone. The Mary twins were at the far end of the shop, and a woman was in the history section, so he only said, "She might look for Ricki. And we walked over to see your brother for a while."

"I thought this might be about Ricki," Mrs. O'Malley said quietly. She stepped beside him and handed him Buglit to hold. "And you went to Danny's? That was nice."

Kris looked at her from where he sat, saying more with his eyes than his words had.

"You look tired," said Mack, removing his glasses. "Why don't you head on home now? I'm going to be on the phone for what will probably be a long time with Bristol's—if I can get someone on the line—and then maybe Pacific Book Auctions or Bonhams. I'll let you know how it goes tomorrow. Looks like it will take forever to get the books to auction no matter which company we sell through. We can't count on getting a big check any time before the next twelve months. I've uploaded the photos from the cell phone. They're all ready to email if I get any interest."

"You will," said Kris. He put Bug onto the floor and looked around for Haiku. "Ku? You here, kitty?"

"He's still here," said Mrs. O'Malley. "Stephanie will go to the shelter tomorrow to fill out the paperwork and apply to adopt him. They'll likely let her take him home right away."

Haiku's head appeared around the corner of the backing board of the front display window. Kris called him again, and he stood, arching his back and rubbing his cheek on the board. After the third time Kris called him, the cat bounded to the floor and slowly walked to the boy's outstretched hand.

"We're gonna miss you, Ku, but you'll love your new house and person. You might even convince her to get a second kitty to wash your head for you."

Haiku squinted into Kris' eyes, hopped to the back of the sofa and down onto the cushions to get into position for a stomach rub.

"I meant to ask, are we for sure going to the Cumbers' on Sunday?"

Mrs. O'Malley looked at Mack as if she had almost forgotten about that plan. "Uh … yes. I think so. Had we decided on a time? I don't remember."

"Let me think," said Mack, trying to remember.

"Mrs. C told us when we were at Barntiques that any time after they close at four would be fine," Kris said, smiling at the purring cat.

"It's a good thing one of us was paying attention," said Mack, putting his glasses back on.

"So, it's a definite plan, then?" Kris asked. "I just need to tell Mom and Dad what I'm doing. I'll be gone with Josie to that play the night before, so maybe I won't come over here on Sunday. Can you swing by my house to pick me up for the Cumbers'?"

"Sure," answered Mack. "We'll see you then."

The woman looking at history books stepped to the counter. She put three books next to the cash register and said to Mrs. O'Malley, "I can't resist these books! *Look* at how beautiful their dustjackets are."

Mrs. O'Malley smiled and said, "We have a new helper now, Joyce. Katrina is putting these clear sleeves on the books for us, and I agree—they look extra attractive with that extra sheen."

Hearing that the books from the country auction wouldn't sell for a long time and that the O'Malleys wouldn't be getting paid for them for a long time, made Kris cheer up. He'd been worrying that more change was coming on the near horizon. If the O'Malleys had a lot of money, maybe they would want to close their bookshop and retire, leaving him without his home-away-from-home. Knowing that they wouldn't be getting paid for a long time gave him some hope that the shop would be open for at least one more year.

Kris left the bookstore as the Mary twins brought their paperback selections to the register.

Chapter Twenty-one

The next morning was Friday. The O'Malleys were at their shop two hours before opening time. Mack had wanted to sleep one more night before making a final decision about which auction house he should call or email about the rare books. They decided to do their calling early in the day before customers were in the shop.

"So ... you're sure this time? Bristol's?" Mrs. O'Malley asked, sitting on the sofa with her mug of coffee.

Haiku stretched his full, long length in front of the door, gazing through it at sparrows hopping from branch to branch in the sidewalk tree, his head cocking and his ears twitching. Buglit was lounging near Elephant Gerald. She seemed to be questioning the accuracy of her internal clock since her people were already in the store.

"It's ringing," Mack said, the phone to his ear as he sat at the computer. "Yes, hello. My name is Michael O'Malley. I recently acquired a collection of twenty-two books from the eighteenth century. The books are on a wide variety of topics and are worth a nice amount each, but there is—hello? Hello? Yes. I'm here. I'm sorry. I didn't realize I was speaking to an answering machine. Did you hear any of that? Yes." Mack took a quick sip of his coffee. "Like I was saying, the books all have these fantastic fore-edge paintings that I believe are contemporary to their publication dates. Eighteenth. I'm certain. I've been a used and rare book dealer for several decades. At auction. Very recently. They're in a safe deposit box. Anyway, what brings these to a higher level, and why I thought your house might be interested in them, is that every one of them has a two-way fore-edge painting. I do know what that means. Safe deposit box. I did. Well, my wife did. I can send you the photos if you'd like. What's unusual about them is that the artist or artists were painting in a way that seems eccentric for the eighteenth century. Or the twenty-first century, for that matter. They're almost indescribable. No, not modern. I do think they were done at or near the time of publication. Why? The colors. The details. You or your experts would decide for sure, of course. Do you feel like you'd be interested in putting them in a rare book auction? After you examine them, I mean."

Mrs. O'Malley's mind tried to fill in the other side of the conversation as Mack went on. She wished she had thought to have him push the speaker button.

Mack gave his details to the representative and asked where to email the photos.

"Well?" Mrs. O'Malley asked after Mack had hung up the phone.

"He's interested. I honestly couldn't tell you *how* interested, but I feel encouraged. I did get a short warning, though, that if we have them sell the books, we would have to wait quite a while. They have no openings in their calendar for nearly eight months for books, even extraordinary ones. He said that, if we'd like, the house could try to find a private buyer and arrange a sale that way. It would possibly take less time, but we may not get as much money."

"What about a commission?"

"He didn't talk about it, but I think if we sell through a major auction house, the *buyer* pays all or most of the commission."

She stood holding her coffee. "Want me to email the photos now?"

He nodded. "As soon as you're done, I'm going to call Bonhams. If they aren't interested, I'll call one or two other auction houses. I like all the ones I selected yesterday based on my research. Whichever one agrees to sell them for us first is the one we'll go with. Okay?"

She smiled.

An hour later, Mrs. O'Malley had sent the photos she'd taken of the rare books to three auction houses. The fourth house did not want to listen to what Mack had to say. They were too booked up for a full year.

"Now, what?" she asked, facing Mack, who was filling the cash register with the change he'd gotten a few minutes before at the bank.

"Now, we wait. It might take a few weeks to hear back from anyone. I read that four to six weeks is typical. You make contact, send in your details, and wait."

"Hmm," she said. "Did you leave the door unlocked when you came in?"

"No. Are we ready to open? It isn't our usual time."

"I'm ready. I'm going to run to Allison's to get some doughnuts to celebrate. I've been fairly strict with my diet, but today feels like a doughnut day."

"It felt like that when you visited Daya, too," he teased.

"Yeah, but this time I'll let you in on the action. Want a frosted raspberry danish?"

"Oh, geez. I have to choose *one* flavor after living in a dessert desert for ages? I can't. Just get me something you think I'd like. Good thing I brought extra coffee in the thermos today."

A few minutes after she left, the phone rang.

"Hello? Oh, yes. This is Mr. O'Malley. Uh-huh. It was an estate that had been vacant for a very long time. I don't remember now, but I think for about ten or fifteen years. Things had been in storage for that long. I will say, though, that it appeared that the better items from what seemed to me to be a true mansion were missing. There were no fine pieces of furniture, no paintings, no other such things that a house of that grandness probably once held. I suspect that the auctioneer or some other seller of the contents ten to fifteen years ago didn't even look through the books. They were put into storage right on the property with the general, less-valuable household items, and those are what were sold recently."

A group of three college-age men entered the shop. Mack waved, and they nodded.

Mack walked around the shop with the phone to his ear as he switched on more of the lights in the main room, hallway, and in each of the smaller rooms, all the while continuing to listen to and answer questions.

"You do? You've seen it before? London? I was thinking of researching the labels, but I hadn't gotten around to it yet. We have an open bookshop, and ... yes. So, you're familiar with the earlier collection that they were a part of in the 'fifties? Wow. Right. I do. Anders Lake. It's not close to Lamarr, but it's not too far. I think I'd prefer not to do that. I think I'd rather ship one of the books to your own office in New York, instead. You will? Okay. I'll look for your instructions soon. Oh, and will there be insurance attached to the shipping label? Thank you. Very good. Yes. You, too."

He sat on the padded computer chair again, remembering the way he'd felt a year before when the Edgar Allan Poe booklet was found at the Cumbers'. This felt different. This time he had no doubt that the fore-edge paintings were what they appeared to be. He'd finally found books worth enough so that—when they sold—he and Mrs. O'Malley could retire. He sighed. Was this what he'd been trying to do since he'd opened the shop? Was he only trying to make enough money selling books so he could *quit* selling books?

The radio news ended, and an orchestral piece by Felix Mendelssohn began, familiar and distracting.

"We'll take these," said one of the young men that Mack had forgotten was in the shop.

"Whew!" said Mack after standing at the cash register. "These are some heavy-duty classics you've picked out. *Moby*

Dick, Ulysses, and *Gravity's Rainbow.* Just a little light summer reading, guys?"

"We're going to put them in a box, jumble them up, and have Jason's girlfriend reach in without looking to choose who gets which book. We do this every year. These three were next on our list, so I'm glad you had them," the tallest young man said.

"They are hard, but very enjoyable, too. I don't have *Ulysses* tackled yet, myself."

Mrs. O'Malley returned carrying two bags from Allison's bakery.

"Now, doughnuts," Mack said as the customers were leaving, reaching for one of the small, white bags, "those I can tackle just fine."

As the O'Malleys ate their mid-morning treat, Mack said, "I had a call while you were gone. Bristol's."

"You didn't!" she exclaimed, her coffee mug hitting the countertop harder than she'd meant it to. Her eyes widened. "Already? We only sent the photos to them an *hour* ago."

"It wasn't the same man I'd spoken to originally, but someone from their book department."

"Well, what did he say?"

Mack swallowed a bite of his buttercream blueberry batwing popover and some coffee. "He recognized the little lion label. Seems that it and the inventory numbers on each mean that they were from a world-famous rare book auction back in the nineteen-fifties over in London. It was a Bristol's sale, too, if you can believe it."

"What are the odds?" she asked, shaking her head and blinking in surprise.

"The label wasn't a Bristol's label, though. The books were once part of a collection with connections to Richard Heber, somehow. There is, apparently, a list of books sold at the nineteen-fifties sale, and the man on the phone was able to assure us that the descriptions and photos and lion label number match their records."

"Incredible!"

"They probably changed hands at least once since the London auction, and with books, there's usually no way to know. It doesn't matter. They'll look at the catalog descriptions of that auction to see if the illustrator or illustrators were attributed to anyone at that time, based on the research done then."

"Richard Heber … why does that name sound familiar?"

Mack crinkled his bag and threw it in the trash can. He walked to the restroom to wash his hands. "He was an important, maniacal book collector back in the earlier part of the nineteenth century. He bought and bought, filling house after house with his purchases throughout England and Europe. He was one of the founders of the famous Roxburghe Club of bibliophiles back in 1812. Heber left piles and heaps of books behind in locations in Paris, Germany, the Netherlands—all over. I suppose that nearly all the great libraries around the world are home to at least a few of the books that he had once purchased. And now we likely have some, too."

"Oh, Mack! Really?" She put her unfinished rocky road cocoa dreampuff on her napkin and went to wash the sugar from her hands as Mack was leaving the restroom. "I'm so excited that I can't even *eat.*"

"Should I finish it for you?" he teased.

She replied blankly, "Yes. I don't want it."

"Wow—you *are* in shock," he said, laughing as he turned on the monitor. "But put it back in your bag. You'll probably feel like munching on it later."

Eventually, Mrs. O'Malley joined Haiku on the sofa. She absentmindedly ran her fingers through the cat's long, brown fur for a full minute before she came out of her fog and noticed the cat. "Haiku! You're leaving us today. Mack, did you realize that?"

"I'd forgotten, too." He rose to glance at the cat over the top of the monitor. "Any idea when Allison's sister will be here?"

"No. We'll hear from the shelter first, probably. They usually call to tell us that an adoption is all set." She picked up the oversized cat and settled him partially on her lap. "He wasn't here very many days at all. I feel like we never got to know him like we do most of the ones we foster. I just assumed we'd have more time." She then spoke directly to Haiku: "Now you'll be going to your new home, and you'll have new windows to sleep in and a new sofa to climb to the top of."

Buglit heard Mrs. O'Malley cooing and went to investigate.

"Bug, another friend is going away. You've done a wonderful job of taking care of him while he stayed with us." She sighed. "Mack? Why do we do this? Why put ourselves through this time after time? I miss every cat that we've fostered. I feel like a glutton for punishment."

Mack took off his glasses and rubbed his eyelids. "We do it because it feels so much better than not doing it." He put his glasses back on. "Caring for anyone or anything feels better than *not* loving and caring for them."

Buglit leaped to the sofa. She sniffed Haiku's nose and ears before rubbing her cheek on his head.

Mrs. O'Malley felt herself relaxing as she watched the cats interact. "Yes," she said after a while.

They heard knocking on one of the large show windows. Danny and Lucille waved at them as if they were going to walk by and not pop in for a visit. Mrs. O'Malley motioned for them to come in, but they didn't. A few seconds later, Lucille returned alone.

"Lucille," said Mrs. O'Malley, surprised. "I didn't know you were back in town."

"Dan went over to see Jack and Darla for a bit," she said. "Yes, I got here about half an hour ago. We're going to look for a retail location that's big enough to set up his workshop and mine in some part of the building, or in an adjoining building. And one that maybe has an apartment, too. Many of these downtown stores were built so the business owner's family could live upstairs or in the back. That's what we'd like, too. I know that even the record shop has an apartment upstairs."

Mack rolled his shirt sleeves. "Have you talked to any real estate agents yet?"

"No," she said, hesitating. She pulled her long, brown hair over a shoulder. Her voice softened, and her eyes met Mrs. O'Malley's. "Honestly, I've been thinking and thinking over this whole Danny and me situation so thoroughly that it was only last night that I made the final decision to move here and to try to make a go with him again. The building and business feel like such a minor part of what I've been thinking about and feeling. There's been a flood of water under our bridge, you know. Well, you don't know, I guess." She paused. "Let's just say that I'm older and wiser, and Dan's older and a different sort of man at heart. He had dreams that were constantly getting flattened when we were together. It hurt him over and over again. Now he has dreams that fit, and a hand that fits mine—better than ever." She looked directly at Mrs. O'Malley. "Quainty accused me of reaching back. I don't know if she told *you* that she doesn't think that we could possibly work out, but she sure told *me* all about it on the phone a couple of days ago. Well, I don't feel like I'm reaching back. We're a good fit now. It's comfortable and exciting, both." She relaxed and took a breath. "Dan told me something surprising the other night. He said that I am the only woman he has ever loved."

"How is that possible?" Mrs. O'Malley asked.

"I know. He could have had anyone before me. During our marriage, even. And in all these years since."

Mrs. O'Malley looked skeptical.

"He said that when he first saw me, his heart recognized mine. We were instantly attracted to each other. When we moved out west, he thought he could get into the movies easily. When he did get auditions based on his looks, his dyslexia held him back. I tried to help him learn lines, but he was too proud to let me. With each failure, he sewed another hem on the edge of his heart. I could see that it was ruining him from the inside, and it ruined us, too. He wanted me, but he wanted to succeed, too. After we split up, he almost gave up on living for a long time. He wouldn't call Quainty because she would mention my name and he'd be sick for days afterward, he said."

"Oh, dear," said Mrs. O'Malley, frowning.

"Developing his woodworking skills changed everything. He can read a piece of wood like a conductor reads a score, practically hearing its beauty and seeing its potential. I feel like we can read each like that, too."

"Did you tell my sister any of this?"

Lucille nodded and swallowed. "I talked with Quainty so long that we both revealed things that should have been said ages ago. I feel a lot better about my relationship with her now, too. I'm only sorry that we never talked with each other like that before."

Danny opened the door. "Hi, folks." He looked at their faces, feeling as though he'd interrupted something.

"We were just catching up with Lucy," Mrs. O'Malley said. "Sounds like your plans are coming together."

Danny nodded. He then said to the O'Malleys, "Did Kris tell you two he was in my studio yesterday?"

"Yes," Mack said, sitting again at the computer.

Danny shook his head. "Man oh, man—what a speech."

"What do you mean?" asked Mrs. O'Malley, putting Haiku to one side and standing.

Danny looked across the room and then at his sister. "I'll just say that by the time he'd finished talking, I realized that I'll never again feel as happy to give away another one of my pieces."

"I'm glad he went to talk to you," Mrs. O'Malley said. "He'll never forget what you've given him, and neither will we."

Danny nodded, and everyone was silent for a while, listening to the stereo's violin music.

"Oh, I almost forgot to tell you what I found out today," said Mack.

"Danny and Lucy! Wait until you hear what a man in the rare book department at Bristol's auction house in New York told Mack," said Mrs. O'Malley, urging Mack to relay the details.

Mack had barely begun to tell his story when the phone rang.

Mrs. O'Malley answered the call from Doris at the cat shelter. She listened for a while, before saying, "We're fine, thanks. Plenty of supplies here. Did you know that Stephanie Cooper is Allison's sister? She's the one who adopted Regular and Aussie last year. Really? She did? Oh, I'm glad. We'll talk more about taking in another foster cat another time. Thanks for the call, Doris."

"I've never heard such a cool story," said Danny to Mack. When he saw that his sister was off the phone, he said, "I'd say that it was mighty fortuitous that the last owner of those books left the lion labels alone."

"Very," Mrs. O'Malley agreed, nodding. She turned. "Mack? Stephanie will be here soon for Haiku. She also told me that Allison adopted another cat while she was there. I guess he'd been at the shelter for several months."

"Well, we need to leave," said Danny, reaching to shake Mack's hand. "I'll let you know if we find anything suitable or if we'll have to wait until a good place becomes available." He looked at Lucille. "So, are you ready to start hunting for a place?"

She looked at him, almost as if seeing him for the first time. "You know what? I am."

"Bye, you two," said Mrs. O'Malley. She hugged Lucille. "I'm *glad* you're moving to town."

Lucille nodded. "I'm swinging the world by a cloud, ready to turn over a new chapter."

"We have *got* to work on those mixed metaphors of yours, Luce," Danny said.

Thirty minutes later, Allison and Stephanie entered the shop. Stephanie was carrying a green soft-sided case similar to the one from the night before that had held Regular.

"We're here for Haiku," said Allison cheerfully. Her face was as bright and sunny as the morning.

"Hello, ladies. Allison, Doris at the shelter called to tell me that *you* picked up a new feline friend, as well. That's *wonderful*. What's your new cat like?"

"Catnip and tuna, I suppose," Stephanie replied for her sister.

Mrs. O'Malley raised an eyebrow. "I meant—"

"She knows what you meant. She's a goofball," Allison said, taking the case from her sister's hand and putting it on the floor at the end of the sofa. "I adopted a silky fellow named Shigi. That's spelled S-h-i-g-i but pronounced 'shy guy.' He's pure black with large, golden eyes. He's about nine or ten years old, they said. I don't know *what* people have against adopting black beauties. Shigi's in my car, waiting for me to take him home, and that's what I'm going to do. I'll stay home for the rest of the day to make sure Reggie and Aussie feel comfortable while they get to know their new brother. My cousin and our new summer helper can manage the bakery alone. Todd has a meeting at the college today."

"Your cousin?" asked Mrs. O'Malley. "You don't mean Roger?"

Allison nodded. "Yes. He still thinks he wants to sell pasties. If he likes working for me in general, then I guess we'll talk about pasties. Personally, I think he'd rather go back to being retired. I purposely have him in the shop before dawn to work the mixing machines before I get there. So far I don't think he exactly loves rising with the dough again."

"Are you married, Stephanie?" Mrs. O'Malley couldn't help but ask.

"Mavis!" scolded Mack.

Stephanie laughed. "I'm seeing someone. Someone *very* nice."

"Oh," said Mrs. O'Malley.

"She's disappointed that she can't set you up," Mack said, pushing the power button on the computer's printer.

"Oh, that's not true," Mrs. O'Malley protested. Her face reddened. "Much."

Stephanie laughed. "Well, I'll keep you in mind if things don't work out with David."

Kris came into the shop then, a lunch sack in his hand. He saw the cat carrier. "Oh, yeah. Haiku."

"Are you sad I'm taking him?" asked Stephanie.

"No. I know he's going to be happy. I'll miss him, though."

"Me, too," commiserated Mrs. O'Malley. "But that's the circle of life around here." She looked at the sofa and around the main room. "Where *is* Haiku, anyway?"

Kris found him behind the mini refrigerator again.

"Cats like snug spots," Mrs. O'Malley said.

Kris lifted Haiku into a hug, nuzzling the cat's neck. "Aw, Ku. I'll miss you, but this lady'll take real good care of you." He brought Haiku to Stephanie.

"I sure will. And to start our relationship on the right foot, I've written a haiku poem in your honor. Ready?"

Allison interrupted her long enough to explain, "Remember how I wrote a poem about little paw prints last year for Reggie? Steph thought that was a cute idea."

Everyone nodded, waiting.

Stephanie paused to recall what she'd memorized. "Here goes: My poetic cat / is slinky soft and handsome / Haiku's eyes see into my heart."

"Seems like too many syllables for a true haiku," said Allison.

"Well, *I* think it's perfect," said Mrs. O'Malley.

"Haiku liked it, too," said Kris.

"He *is* purring," said Stephanie, hugging the cat closer.

Allison petted the cat's neck. "Well, I'm off. Shigi is probably wondering what's going on. Have a wonderful day, everyone. Oh, and I hope you and Mack liked your pastries, Mavis. I heard you stopped by."

"They were heaven. I couldn't eat all of mine, though. I'm saving the other half for this afternoon."

After Allison left, Stephanie said, "I've got his adoption form with me. I was told to hand it to you for your file." She gave the cat back to Kris, then put the carrying case on the sofa. "Kris, will you put Haiku inside? I don't want to scare him since he doesn't know me."

"Sure. Come on, Ku. In ya go. That's a good kitty." After placing him in the carrier, Kris reached inside and scratched the cat's ears. "I'll miss saying 'Hi, Ku' to you. You always took my pun well and never rolled your eyes when I said it. Be good for Stephanie. Have a great life." His face had turned sorrowful by the time he'd finished his goodbye.

As the cat was getting settled—without fussing or fighting—Buglit stepped onto the sofa cushion and stood near the carrier. She put her head inside and licked Haiku's forehead goodbye.

"Buglit is a very good nanny and friend to the foster cats. She seems to understand that this shop is a temporary home for them," Mrs. O'Malley said, stepping closer to pet Haiku's head and neck after Bug had hopped to the top of the sofa.

Mack said, "See ya, Haiku."

When Stephanie and Haiku had left, Kris let out a long, sorrowful sigh. "I don't know how you get used to it."

"We don't, really," said Mrs. O'Malley. "Mack helps me to see the bigger picture."

"Yeah. I know. Still ..."

Mack went to sit at the computer again where he printed out a FedEx label. "I have some cool news that might cheer you up."

"Oh, *yes,* Mack. Tell him," Mrs. O'Malley said, retrieving the other half of her pastry from its bag and pouring herself a little more coffee from the thermos.

Mr. O'Malley repeated the story of the phone call from Bristol's.

Kris listened with interest. "What's next?"

"Next, I need to retrieve one of the books. In the same email as the mailing label, I got detailed instructions on how to pack the book to their strict standards. First, though, I'm going to look over the photos of the books again on the computer before I go to the bank. I'll choose a book here so I don't waste any time in the vault."

"Choose the pretty one," Mrs. O'Malley said after finishing her coffee.

Mack looked at her from over the top of his glasses.

"You know—the one with the swoops and doohickeys."

He looked back at the monitor, scrolling through the photos. "You do realize that I have absolutely zero idea which one you mean from that description, right? They all have those swirls."

She stood behind him. After a few moments, she finally pointed and said, "There. *That* one. See? Doohickeys."

Mack jotted down the book's title on a scrap of paper. He stood, putting the paper in his pocket. "I'll be back in a minute."

Kris and Mrs. O'Malley waited, staring through the windows.

Mr. O'Malley returned ten minutes later, holding a book. "Nothing anyone does at the bank is ever done quickly." He put the book under the countertop on the part of a shelf Buglit never slept on and sat at the computer. "Now, where is that email from Bristol's? Okay. Here it is."

A wave of customers entered the shop. Kris and Mrs. O'Malley waited on them so Mack wouldn't have to leave the rare book unattended.

Mack packed the leatherbound volume in layer after layer of padding, in a waterproof plastic bag, and in one cardboard box inside of another. He secured it with both packaging and filament tape. "Done. Okay. I'm heading over to the shipping center. Want me to get lunch on the way back?"

Mrs. O'Malley sheepishly pointed at her empty pastry bag. "Maybe I'll get a sandwich later. You go ahead and eat, though."

After Mack had been gone a few minutes, Kris stopped neatening the main room shelves to talk to Mrs. O'Malley, who was picking dead leaves from the hanging potted plants and on the floor below. "Last night, I read Dontae one of the books you gave him. I know he's not that old, but I think he should be farther along with reading on his own than he is. He doesn't know some pretty simple words."

"Oh, that's a shame. I wonder if all his surgeries and such interrupted his school time."

Kris hadn't thought of that. "Geez. Yeah, maybe. Even though he doesn't know a lot of words, I was able to teach him new ones without much trouble. I can tell he's smart. I hope when he goes to school this fall that he can catch up. I'm worried they won't let him go into the second grade."

Mrs. O'Malley paused. "Even if he is held back a grade, he can always advance later."

"I guess, but I think I might try to help him over the summer. I don't know when he'll be tested to get into the same school that my other brothers go to, but if it's later this summer, maybe I'll have enough time to help him read better."

She sighed, putting her fists on her hips, the plastic bag of dead leaves hanging from one wrist. "You're doing the mother hen thing again, Kris. Tell your mom and dad. They're with him all day this summer. It can be a family project. I think it's a great idea, but I don't know why you think you have to handle teaching him alone."

Kris shrugged.

"When you go home later, talk to your parents. Tell them that you think Dontae is having reading troubles. They'll take it from there. Do we have a deal? Will you promise?"

He hesitated. "But I *want* to teach him. We have a really good time reading together."

She got back on the low stepladder. "Well, keep reading to him, then. But talk to your folks so they can do most of the teaching."

"Okay. I promise. I'll talk to them."

A woman with brown hair and a pert nose entered the shop. "Hello, Mavis!"

"Hello! Good to see you again, Suzie. How is your hardware shop doing?"

Suzie shrugged. "The same as always. Yolandaville's a tiny town. I sell a hammer, sell some screws, make a key or two, cut some PVC pipe, and go home to my dogs." She had a snappy, quick way of speaking that seemed always to be an inch away from a laugh.

Mrs. O'Malley walked to the front. "Can I help you?"

Suzie nodded after scanning the room from front to back. "Wow. *Tons* of books in here. This is a good-looking building, outside and in. Sturdy construction a hundred years ago, that's for sure." She looked back at Mrs. O'Malley. "My dad and my granddad and his brother all owned and worked in what's now my hardware. I decided the other day that I'm sick to the top of my teeth of the nineteen-fifties metal desk that's in the office. I found a new desk that I love, but it's a big corner piece that will need wall space. That means that what's on my walls needs to go. I've cleared most of it out. There were several old hand tools that I never use, so I brought those to Quainty to buy. The books are boxed, and I have them in my van. Can I interest you in looking at them? Most are hardcover hardware catalogs from long ago, and books on wiring, plumbing, and that sort of thing. The higher up on the shelves they'd sat the better condition they're in. On the top shelf were some that my grandma must have had. Cookbooks, Grace Livingston Hill novels, and some books on sewing and knitting. Any interest?"

"Sure. Let's bring them on in. I'll have Mack look at them and give you a price. He should be back by the time we have them inside. Kris, will you help us ladies?"

When Suzie's nine boxes of books were stacked behind the sofa, Mrs. O'Malley looked at the clock. "Still no Mack. Can you wait a bit longer?"

Suzie nodded. "I'll have a sit here on this couch if you don't mind. Read a magazine. Pretend I'm a lady of leisure for a change. My brother's son is watching the store for me. When I'm done here, I'm going to go and pay for my new desk and hope they deliver. This is a landmark day, let me tell you. Maybe next week I'll splurge on a new office chair."

Mrs. O'Malley and Kris went back to the far end of the shop so she could continue taking care of the plants. Reaching to the next plant from the step stool, she said to

Kris, "Did I tell you that Darla's parents are going to open a business together here in town?"

"No. Really? Wait. Who *is* Darla's mom? Do I know her?"

"Her name is Lucille. She was also at the Cumbers' grand opening party. She had her long, brown hair in a ponytail. She's very pretty and kind of short. Slender."

Kris thought. "Nope. I don't remember seeing anyone like that. I don't remember Darla ever talking about her, either. Why haven't I seen her at the record shop or anything?"

"She lives in Ohio. She and Danny got divorced when Darla was a young girl."

Kris raised an eyebrow. "If they're *divorced,* and if she lives in *Ohio,* then how ..."

"They're getting back together, it seems. She's moving here. Danny's going to do his woodworking, and she's going to make her art glass. They'll have a retail store attached to a workspace. Lucy's in town again today, and she and Danny are out looking for a place to set up shop." Mrs. O'Malley stepped to the floor again, wiping her brow with the back of her hand as an older man came into the shop with a box in his arms. He put it on the countertop and walked back to the door. Mrs. O'Malley called, "Are those for sale or trade?"

"Neither, madam," he said. "They are for you, for free. I must run now, as I'm very late for a doctor's appointment. Thank you, and have a nice afternoon." As soon as he had finished speaking, he went through the door again.

Mrs. O'Malley put her bag of dead leaves in the wastebasket on her way to look at the man's box.

"Mew!"

"Merwew!"

"Mew!"

"What on Earth?!" exclaimed Mrs. O'Malley. She quickly opened the flaps of the medium-sized box and looked inside. "Kris! *Kittens!"*

333

At the sound of such appealing, desperate mewing, Buglit scrambled from somewhere and urgently hopped onto the countertop. Like a meerkat, she stood on her rear legs and peered over the edge of the box, mewing in reply with her ears laid back, looking from Mrs. O'Malley to the kittens, confused and concerned.

Kris was beside the box in an instant. "Why did he drop them off like that? Should I try to find him?"

"No. He must have wanted to be rid of them, and knew we would see that they were taken care of. He must know that we foster cats for the shelter."

Kris looked at her, torn for a moment. "I guess you have a good point." He lifted a gray-and-brown-striped kitten from the box and held it to his chest. "Oh, just *look* at them!"

Suzie put down her magazine and stood to better see the little bit of fuzziness Kris was holding.

Buglit leaped into the box and immediately started to lick their heads and faces, trying to calm them so they wouldn't cry.

"Good girl, Buggy," said Mrs. O'Malley, petting the cat. "You play mama until I can get Doris to come to pick them up. Don't get yourself all attached now, okay?" She then looked at Kris, who was melting. "That goes for you, too."

"But they're so *little*. And stripey."

"My dogs are gonna know if I even *touch* one, and then they'll have hurt feelings all night," Suzie said, resisting.

Katrina stepped into the shop then, and within two seconds, she was dancing around at the mere sight of the kitten in Kris' hands. "Oh, Kris! Where did he *come* from?"

"This box," said Kris, pointing. "There are more."

She went to the box and looked in, confused. "Did Buglit have kittens?"

Kris and Mrs. O'Malley laughed.

"No, Kat. Bug is ... unable," Mrs. O'Malley said. "She jumped in there to make sure they weren't scared and alone.

Some older man dropped them off here a minute ago but then skedaddled. I thought he was giving us a box of books."

Mr. O'Malley was the next one to walk into the shop. He was more than a little surprised to see a kitten in his wife's hands, in Kris' hands, and in Katrina's hands.

"Look what we have! Babies!" Mrs. O'Malley said, holding hers—a gray and white one—aloft.

Mack shook his head. "So, I see. Do I want to know why?"

"You do. They're not staying."

"Oh, but *why-y?*" moaned Katrina, lifting her own striped kitten to her face.

"Yeah, Mrs. O. Why? They can stay. There's plenty of room in here," Kris said, trying to sound convincing.

"For the same reason that last year your mother didn't go and fetch the kittens Bijay saw behind the grocery store. She called the shelter, instead. They need to be checked by a vet, they need to be older to get spayed or neutered, they need their shots, and *then* they can be adopted. Sorry, but I *have* to call Doris."

"I'm having a hard time keeping my hands away from that box of cuteness," complained Suzie, sitting back on the sofa. "Yes, do call for reinforcements! Take them away!"

Mack peered into the box, and when he saw Buglit inside playing babysitter, he cracked up laughing. "There are more! And Bug thinks she's a mom."

"Look at this one's little tail, Katrina," said Kris. "Have you ever seen anything so little?"

She grinned, examining the tail on her own kitten, her blue eyes widening even more. "Oh, and those feet! And those tiny toes with their teensy tiny tippy toenails!"

"Doris!" Mrs. O'Malley said into the phone after she had handed her kitten to Mack. "We have a cat-related emergency. No, Haiku is fine and with Stephanie, and Bug is fine. However, Buglit is currently playing nursemaid to a box of six kittens. Yes! Little. Very little. They should still be nursing from a mother, but instead, here they are, in a box in our shop. Some man said we could have them for free, then he tore on out of here before I knew he'd left us with his kittens. Will you come, or can you send someone to get them? Okay. Thank you, dear. What would we do without you?"

"Melt," complained Suzie from the sofa. She snapped the magazine open for emphasis.

Katrina lifted her kitten to eye level. "And their noses! Look at their big, dark eyes ... and look at their noses! And whiskers!" She looked at Mrs. O'Malley, pleading, "I *want* him."

"I'll answer for your mother. No," said Mrs. O'Malley firmly. "They are in no way ready to go home with anyone except for their—pardon me, Buglit—original mother, who would have milk for them. Since we don't know where their mom is, volunteers at the shelter will have to bottle feed them and keep them warm. Unless I'm wrong about their age, that is. It's been a long, long time since I've had anything to do with actual kittens."

Mack smiled. "Aww. Look at them." He then attempted to compose himself by putting his kitten back into the box. "Here you go, Bug." He put his hands in his pants pockets. "I don't suppose she's actually had a litter herself."

Mrs. O'Malley shook her head. "Probably not. She sure does have a knack for calming them down, though. Poor things, looking for milk."

"Is Doris coming?" he asked.

"She is, but she warned me that it might be a little while. Let's put them in the cats-only room. Miss Bug can ride along in the box with them." She looked at Kat and Kris, who were still practically whimpering over how cute the kittens were that they were still holding. "Okay, kids. Hand them over."

"Ohhh," they both complained.

Mack carried Bug and the kittens away. When he returned to the main room, he took a slip of paper from his

336

wallet and sat at the computer. "I'll record the FedEx tracking number, even though Bristol's has it already."

"Bristol's? As in Bristol's auction house?" asked Katrina. She looked from person to person for answers.

Mack shook his head, indicating that it was a story to tell when they were alone in the shop. He looked at the sofa where Suzie was waving for his attention. "Hello," he said. "I think I know you from somewhere."

"I own the Yolandaville hardware. I brought you a bunch of books. Care to look?" She pointed over her head and down. "These are them."

Mrs. O'Malley pulled Katrina into the rare book room and told her the story, and Kris came into the room behind to hear more details.

"I didn't know you'd already decided what you're going to do with the books. This feels so fast." Katrina said. "What if other auction houses write or call?"

"We made our choice. It was first come, first to the books," Mrs. O'Malley said.

Katrina glanced through the doorway. "I wish it could be first come, first one to get to take home a kitten. I think Browser wouldn't mind a kitten." She sighed. "They're *adorable.*" She looked at Kris, then started to walk toward the hallway.

He grinned, and soon the two of them were speed-walking toward the cats-only room.

"Kids! I'm warning you for your own sake—don't get attached," Mrs. O'Malley called, still standing in the rare book room.

Kris and Katrina closed the door behind them before sitting cross-legged on the floor near the box that held Buglit and "her" kittens. Neither of them held a kitten this time. They watched as the whole boxful gradually went to sleep. The only light in the room was from a dim nightlight above their heads and the square of light that shone through the door's cutout cat entrance. The kids listened to each other breathe and to Buglit's loud purring.

Katrina thought about her talks with her brother and Mrs. O'Malley. They didn't want her to ruin a true friendship by pressing a romance with Kris. She remembered times that she and Kris had laughed together over the past two years. The classes they had together, eating lunch together with their other friends, and so many other experiences that she was glad that they'd shared. She didn't want to take a chance that their relationship might change. She didn't want to ruin what they had now and what they could have in the future.

"Kris?" Katrina said softly.

"Yeah?"

"I want to tell you something, okay. Don't laugh or anything."

He folded his arms and rested them against the top edges of the box, his head on his arms. "No guarantees."

She waited until she felt able to speak again. "I had a crush on you. By accident."

His heart hammered in his chest. He didn't move. He didn't look at her.

She said, "But don't worry. I'm over it now. I only wanted to tell you in case you thought I liked you in that way. I guess I did, but I'm back to liking you as a friend again. Or, in the way you said you like me—as a brother."

He didn't say anything.

Katrina uncrossed her legs and went on, "It must have been a reaction to all the excitement we've had lately. I was worried about you after you got hit. And I was working in the shop, getting to see what you love about being here with the O'Malleys. Don't think that I was feeling this way last year when you were with Taty. I would never do that to her, or to you." She had made her voice louder, trying her best to sound convincing. "Anyway, I wanted to tell you that I *did* have a crush on you ... but now I don't."

Kris turned his head, his eyes pressing against his forearm still on the edge of the box. He felt rejected and hurt and relieved all at once. He hated her ... he wanted her ... he was afraid of her. He couldn't think of a thing he could possibly say.

Katrina stood. She paused behind his back for a few moments. When she left the room, she closed the door behind her but left it slightly ajar.

Kris sat without moving for a long time, too many varying emotions rushing through him until he felt tired of feeling them.

When the door opened again, it was Doris, coming into the room to get the kittens.

Chapter Twenty-two

Kris stayed in his bed over an hour after Dontae had gotten up. He wasn't asleep, but he couldn't seem to lift his head from his pillow. He stared at his filled bookcase and listened to his own breathing, to the birds, to the few louder sounds he could hear. He heard the television and his brothers as they ate and talked about what to do next. He made himself listen only to the unique set of basketball-playing sounds: dribbling, shoes squeaking on the pavement, laughing, self-congratulations, groaning, and the sound of the ball hitting the backboard. He tried ignoring anything else his brain wanted to think about. Like Katrina.

"She doesn't like me in a boyfriend-girlfriend way anymore." That was the first thing he let past his brain's guards. "I'm glad," was the second. The third thought was, "Yeah, right." That thought came out in a sarcastic voice. Then more and more thoughts burst out after he'd pulled his pillow from under his head to use it to cover his face.

He rode wave after wave of contradictory emotions as his brain's guards gave up in exhaustion. After a full twenty minutes, he had had enough. He'd come to a decision: Katrina was right. Whatever she was trying to do—whether she was telling the truth or not—she had done the right thing as they'd sat on the floor next to the box of kittens. They weren't ready to be anything other than friends. *He* wasn't, anyway. Maybe she knew that, and she'd only said those things to let him off the hook. They could go back to laughing and working together at the bookshop, nothing more or less than good friends. It was enough. Wasn't it?

The phone rang in the hallway. A few seconds later, his mother knocked.

"Kris? Are you awake? That girl Josie is calling for you. Will you speak to her?" she asked through the door.

"Yes," he called.

He walked around Dontae's bed and through the bedroom door, taking the phone from his mother. She tried to run her fingers through his very messy hair while he talked, but he sidestepped her, walking away to sit at the dining table.

"Josie? This is Kris. Three-thirty? I didn't think it would be that early. Oh, yeah. Dinner first. I'll eat just about anything, so anyplace your family had in mind to go is fine with me. Wait! What kind of clothes should I wear? A suit? I don't have a suit. How about tan or brown pants and a long-sleeved dress shirt? Oh, and I might have a tie. Is that going to be good enough? Are you sure? I guess I didn't think about all this when I said yes. No—I still want to go. Okay. I'll see you later, then. Tell your parents that I said thank you, please. Thanks to you, too. Bye."

After he had hung up, he dialed the bookshop. "Mrs. O? I won't be in at all today. I didn't realize I'd be leaving so early to head to Lamarr with Josie and her parents. We're going out to eat before the play starts. I'm still sleepy. I might eat and take another nap. No. I'm okay—regular tired, not conked-on-the-head tired. Have a good day. I'll see you tomorrow when we go to the Cumbers. You *forgot* about that again? Okay. Tell Mack hello, and I'll see you tomorrow. Bye."

Kris ate an extra-large bowl of wheat cereal as he sat on the patio. His father joined him, sitting on a chair opposite him with a glass of tea and the newspaper. Kris couldn't get used to seeing his usually-formally-dressed father wearing shorts and a t-shirt every day since he'd taken a break from teaching for a whole semester. Kris hadn't realized that his father owned more than two pairs of shorts.

"Not going to the bookshop today?" Mr. Dehlvi asked, opening the newspaper and scanning the front page.

"No. I have that ... date thing tonight. I thought I'd hang around here until I leave this afternoon."

His father looked up from the paper, his face unreadable. "So, tell me about this girl."

Kris munched and swallowed. He stared shyly at the tube-shaped birdfeeder on the top of the fence nearby and said, "I guess you'd call Josie friendly. Outgoing. She's smart—I know that—and easy to like."

"You are also smart, friendly, and easy to like. You will have a good time tonight, then. However, when her parents come here, I would like to meet them before you get in their car." He shook out the newspaper, making it an order.

Kris looked momentarily horrified, but then he went back to eating, realizing there was no arguing with his father about that sort of thing.

After he'd finished his cereal, Kris said, "Dad? I think Dontae—"

"Kris Dehlvi. Please do not parent again."

Kris paused, thinking about what he had planned on saying. "I'm not," he said earnestly. "I wanted to tell you that I might know something you might not. I think it's important. Okay?"

Mr. Dehlvi lowered the paper. "I am listening."

Kris pushed his bowl away from his chest. "I was reading to Dontae before bed, and I noticed he can barely read words that aren't super simple. I taught him some new words, and he learned them right away. I wonder if he missed some school during his operations that made him fall behind. I was hoping that we all could play word games and read together over the summer. That might help him before school starts again."

Mr. Dehlvi placed his elbows on his newspaper. "I am very glad that you have told me this. Seven is still very young. He can start over with the basics, if necessary." He looked at his paper again. "You are a good brother."

Kris pushed away from the table, taking his bowl and spoon. "Mrs. O'Malley said that I try to take your job from you too often. I can't seem to help it, though."

His father looked at him, and then at the group of his sons coming to the back yard through the patio door. "Maybe that is not a bad thing, hey? We will all adjust together over time."

"Dad, will you take us to the lake?" asked Bijay. He was at Mr. Dehlvi's side, tugging on his arm, pleading with his eyes.

"Yeah, Dad," said Dev. "We're hot."

"Please, Dad?" asked Dontae, going around to the side of the man not occupied by Bijay.

It was the first time that Kris had heard Dontae say the word "dad" to their father, and apparently the first time Mr. Dehlvi had heard it, too. His face changed from somber to smiling.

"Oh, yes, my boys. But you should eat lunch first. Where is your mama? Go and tell her you have a plan for the day. See if she wants to join us, too, where she may sit on a beach chair with her toes in the water."

The three younger boys ran into the house, talking happily and cheering.

"Will you come along, Kris?" asked Mr. Dehlvi.

Kris shook his head, still standing and holding his bowl. "I'm groggy. I think I'm going to take a nap. Then I'll shower and find some of my better clothes to put on. Stuff like that. If you want to meet Josie's parents, she said they'll be here at three-thirty."

His father looked at his watch. "That gives you four hours to sleep and get ready. We will be back perhaps by three."

Once everyone else had gone to the lake, Kris stood in the empty hallway, unsure if he wanted to nap on the sofa in front of the TV or in his bedroom after reading for a while. The longer he stood there, the less he felt like being alone in the house where it felt strangely quiet. A few minutes later, while he still stood in the hallway thinking about too many things at once, he no longer wanted to go to the play. He wanted to be at the lake, sitting on a beach towel after swimming with his brothers. He didn't want to be with Josie, dressed up and eating in a fancy restaurant. He didn't want to ride for hours in a car with strangers, seeing a play with strangers. Nothing about a trip to Lamarr seemed like fun anymore.

He leaned against the back of the sofa, staring through the screen door to the front porch. Memories of Katrina and Tatyana floated atop the floorboards. He tried to imagine Josie climbing the porch steps to him, but she wouldn't appear. Sighing, he decided to take a walk around the block.

The warmth of the sun made him realize that he'd been slightly chilly in the house. He shuddered, lifted a small fallen branch from the sidewalk, and then walked slower, unsure where he wanted to go.

Dogs barked from behind doors or back yards. Trees shaded him, and clearings warmed him again. Lawns needed mowing or were neatly trimmed. All the familiar sights of his neighborhood met his eyes as he started along the sidewalk. Until he saw it: the one thing that he had never seen before, and that stopped him in his tracks: Tatyana's house now had a for sale sign in front of it. She wasn't coming back.

He crossed the street to stand in front of the house he'd come to know very well. He remembered the sweep of the staircase. He could picture the bathrooms, the large kitchen, the laundry room, the basement game room, and the garage, and the backyard with its flowerbeds and small basketball court. All of it, he realized with longing, he would likely never see again now that Taty was never returning to live in that house.

Kris turned for home. He kept picturing the inside of Tatyana's house, almost as if memorizing the things he'd never see again. He then imagined Tatyana in the living room, looking up from her schoolwork to smile at him when he visited. He'd probably never see that welcoming smile again, either.

At home, he went to stand in the kitchen, wondering if he should have a snack. The silence was strange, especially since he hadn't had the house to himself in weeks. The phone rang. He didn't recognize the name displayed on the digital readout, but he answered it anyway. It was Josie, canceling their date.

Kris hung up the phone, feeling free as a bird. He went into his bedroom and changed into swimming shorts, a white t-shirt, and his old sneakers. He grabbed the largest towel and headed for the lake.

He jogged most of the half mile. When he got to the lake, he spent a few minutes locating the other Dehlvis in the crowd. He waved, and Dev waved back.

"Kris!" they all said when he was close.

The younger boys were in the wet sand at the edge of the water, playing with cups in the sand to make a castle.

He smiled and slid the towel from his overheated neck. "I'm not going to the play tonight," he said to his parents. "Josie's dad is sick with the stomach flu; they canceled their plans." He inhaled slowly, staring at the shimmering waters of the bright blue lake. Seagulls called as if they were glad he had come.

Kris left his towel, shoes, and shirt with his parents and splashed into the water until it was waist deep. He dove under, entering a cold, brown-gray world that supported him with every kick of his legs. Surfacing, he headed toward shore, swimming with his head above water.

"You look joyful," his mother said, watching him towel dry before spreading that towel next to her chair on the beach.

Kris shook the water out of his ears. "Yep."

Mr. Dehlvi said, "No book today?"

Kris hadn't even thought about grabbing a book. He sat on the towel, watching his brothers. "I can read at home." He smiled at the castle taking shape at the edge of the lake. "Nice foundation, guys!" he called. "Don't forget to put in a moat."

Dontae asked, "What's that?"

"You'll have to go over and put in a moat, little Kris," said his mother, pulling her large summery hat lower over her face. "I'm going to move my chair to the water."

Kris stayed where he was, letting the sun and breeze dry him. Remembering what he'd seen earlier, the smile on his face and in his heart vanished. "The Amos' house is for sale." He swallowed, shifting positions. "That must mean Tatyana's not coming back. I thought she'd write to tell me, but I guess that for sale sign says it all."

"Oh, that is so sad, Kris," said Mrs. Dehlvi. "But I can imagine that she and her parents and family there in Africa are very pleased to be all together again. But maybe she will come back for college."

Kris shrugged. "I walked to her house today before I came here. I loved that place. I wonder who's going to buy it. It's got everything! Four big bedrooms, a garage, basketball court, game room in the basement, a huge kitchen, gardens, two big bathrooms and an extra shower in the basement—you name it."

Mr. Dehlvi put down his magazine and sat straighter in his lawn chair. "We have all been inside. It is solid and handsome." He looked at his young sons and back at his wife. "Daya," he said louder.

"Yes," she answered as she gathered her things before moving to the water's edge. She brushed sand from her sleeveless, short terrycloth robe and tried to fold her uncooperative chair.

"*We* should buy that house."

346

She stopped fighting with her chair to stare at him. "What?"

Kris asked the same thing.

Mr. Dehlvi stood up. He motioned to his sons, calling, "Boys! Boys! Come." When they were all together, their father said, "How would you like to stay in our own nice neighborhood, but move a little way down the street to a fine, big house with many rooms?"

"Falak! Do not *say* such things. How *could* we?" Mrs. Dehlvi asked, shocked at his repeated suggestion.

"Yes!" said Bijay.

"Yes, yes, *yes!*" said Dontae, dancing around the circle of his family.

"What?" asked Dev, not understanding.

"The Amos' house is for sale," explained Kris.

"Since *when?*" asked Dev, brushing his damp, sandy hands on his shorts. He seemed upset at the news.

"I saw the for sale sign before I came here. I guess Taty's not coming back."

"It wasn't there yesterday. I'm sure of it," said Dev, frowning. "Oh, that's too bad. You liked her. *I* liked her. She was always kind to Bij and me."

"Falak, how could we?" Mrs. Dehlvi asked again, still holding her chair.

"We would sell our own house, of course, and get a loan for the rest. I have a good job. Daya, there is the offer your father is always making to us. We could take him up on it at last, since we would be able to stay in our neighborhood as we always swore we would. So. There you are: a newer, larger house for the Dehlvi family, soon to be plus one." He nodded at her stomach.

"Yay!" shouted Bijay, his eyes wild and excited.

Dontae pulled on Dev's arm, asking him questions about the house. Kris bit his lower lip, suddenly hopeful and excited, too.

Mr. Dehlvi shook out the towel that had been draped over his beach chair. "We should go home to call the real estate agent who has the house. Get a price, yes?"

"Arey!" said Mrs. Dehlvi. She took off her hat, pushed strands of her brown hair behind her ears, then put the hat on again. Her eyes appeared worried the whole time she did this. But then, in a flash as if lightning had struck, her face lit up. "I hope it won't be too expensive to hire a truck to move our things four houses away."

On the drive from the lake, Mr. Dehlvi went beyond their own house to the Amos'. He parked in front, looking at it with fresh eyes. "It needs some paint. Perhaps it will cost less to buy the house since it needs to be painted."

To Kris, it looked well cared for, its light brown color familiar and welcoming. The little boys had their heads out of the windows of the SUV, pointing. "That's my room," said Dev.

"I want the one by the bathroom," said Bijay. "If there *is* a bathroom up there."

"Your mother and I will get the one near the bathroom. If it is the largest room, of course," said Mr. Dehlvi, already planning.

When they were home, Mrs. Dehlvi called to find out the asking price of the house, and some of its particulars. She wrote down a number and handed it to her husband.

His eyebrows went up, but he whispered, "When can we see inside?"

She covered the phone with her hand and asked, "Are you quite sure?"

He nodded, and an arrangement was made for the next day, in the early afternoon.

"I can't believe this might happen," said Kris, flopping onto the sofa.

"The lady on the phone said that the price she told to me includes the furniture, appliances, dishes, bedding—

everything that the family left behind. They don't want to bother selling the house and contents separately, she said. Oh, but Kris ... this means they definitely do not plan to return." She sat next to him, still in her short terrycloth robe and sandals. She frowned. "Will it be too sad for you to live in the Amos' house?"

He put his head on the back of the sofa. "I've loved that place since the first time I went inside with Taty. There are only good memories there. So ... no. Not at all."

The three younger boys were in the back yard, running around, shouting, hopping and, in Dontae's case, doing karate moves and kicks. Dontae stopped when he saw Pip in the yard, sitting at the edge of the patio on the bricks. He stepped cautiously closer and closer to the white cat as if stalking a mouse. Pip sat very still. Bijay and Dev saw what was happening and they held still, too.

In the house, Mr. and Mrs. Dehlvi and Kris watched through the sliding glass door as Dontae gently lifted Pip into his arms. He grinned in amazement at himself when he realized he was hugging a real, live cat.

～～～～～

At the bookshop, Mrs. O'Malley finally got around to opening a tube-shaped package that had come in the mail hours earlier. Mack was at an art supply store buying the glue he used to repair books. As he stepped into the shop again, he was met with a new decal affixed to their door.

Mack asked, "Hey, isn't that the same design of a cat reading a book that's on our return address stamp?"

She nodded, pleased with the way it looked, even from its reverse side.

"Did you order only one?"

"Yes. I can get more if you like, though."

He went back outside after putting his shopping bag on the countertop. Mrs. O'Malley could see him walking up and down in front of the display windows before coming back inside.

"Maybe get three more. Can they be bigger?" he asked, putting his receipt under the money drawer.

"They can be nearly any size, I guess. I'll order them now." She admired the decal again. "I'd forgotten to tell you about it. Katrina saw our stamp and suggested we put the logo on our door. That girl is *full* of good ideas."

Mr. O'Malley raised an eyebrow.

"What?" she asked, folding her arms and sitting on her computer chair.

"I think she must have done something to Kris yesterday. I don't know what happened in the cats' room, but did you see his face after Doris came here for the kittens?"

"They're going through a period of adjustment. I've had a couple of talks with Katrina lately. She likes Kris, but I told her that now is not the right time. They're both young. The more we talked, the more she agreed that I was right about waiting. I wonder if she kind of pushed him away from her while they were looking at the kittens."

"Hmm," said Mack, not knowing what to say.

Mrs. O'Malley let out an audible breath. "I just hope she didn't push him too hard. Matt, Kat, and Kris have gotten close, especially this summer, what with so much mystery, intrigue and criminal activity going on."

"I remember when *I* was his age—"

"Oh, you do *not!*"

Mack winked. "Well, maybe not accurately."

She stood and walked to him, reaching for a hug. "If we had been around each other at their age, I would have had such a mad, fierce crush on you. I would have scared you off."

"Probably," he joked.

"Hey, do you think that's really what's going on? Do you think Kat is scaring Kris? I don't think he had real romantic feelings for Tatyana. I think they were friends, but I don't think it was more, even though Taty tried. Do you think Kris is scared because he *does* have real feelings this time around?"

Mack shrugged. "Real feelings scared the pants off me when it happened the first time. Not literally, mind you. I always wore a belt."

She smiled and playfully tugged on his belt. "Have you always been thin?"

"Always. When I was little my doctor tried lots of different things to get me to gain weight—I'm sure I've told you about it. When I hit my teen years, I bulked up a little and grew muscles."

"I like your muscles. They're very good for hugging."

He pulled her closer and laid his head over the top of hers.

"You two are the cutest," said Lucille as she and Danny came into the shop.

Mrs. O'Malley stayed where she was, saying, "Yes, we most certainly are."

Danny and Lucille hugged, too, thinking that it looked like a good idea. "Guess what," he said.

"Did you find a place for your shop?" asked Mrs. O'Malley.

"We *did*," said Lucille.

Danny said, "Remember the carpeting store that went out of business a few months ago?"

Mrs. O'Malley nodded, her face brightening. "Oh, my gosh! That's just around the corner from us, and from Jack and Darla. But I heard an antique shop was going in there."

"Nope. Their deal fell through last week. I guess they were constantly complaining about the floor layout, wanting to tear down walls and this and that. The owner of the building didn't want to alter anything that would jeopardize the structural integrity. Enter Danny and Lucy and—bam! We got the lease."

"That's wonderful, you two," said Mrs. O'Malley. "I can't even begin to say how wonderful that bit of news is."

Mack shook Danny's hand and said congratulatory things before asking, "Who owns that building?"

"The people who had the carpet store. They've retired. They aren't opposed to selling it, so maybe after we've rented and all goes well, we'll try to buy it," Danny said, putting an arm around Lucille again. "I'll talk to the lumberyard next and let them know I'll be moving this month."

"What about you, Lucy?" asked Mrs. O'Malley.

"I guess I'll head back to Ohio to pack and put my home on the market. When it sells, that money will come in handy when we're ready for decorating, remodeling, and creating."

Mack wiped his glasses on his shirttail before setting them on the printer. "Do the owners of the building know what kind of work you'll be doing in there?"

Danny nodded. "They do. We've discussed most of the particulars. The back rooms have concrete floors and walls. Lucy's kiln uses a hundred and twenty volts, so it's very safe. My power tools should be fine to work with in the other concrete room. We'll have to have an air cleaner or filter going all the time, though, so my sawdust doesn't contaminate her works or drift out into the retail area."

"The building sure does have plenty of sales space, which is great, and it has a spacious apartment upstairs. The upstairs rooms haven't been used for anything except storage for many years. We'll have to put some money into furnishings and paint or wallpaper. The building is just about perfect," Lucille said, tossing her long ponytail behind her back. After a second, she grabbed her hair again, bringing it over her shoulder to look at it. She sighed. "This thing has got to go, Dan. I don't want all this hair in my way when I'll be devoting so much of my time to glass and a kiln."

"But it's so thick and lovely," protested Mrs. O'Malley.

Danny held the ponytail, letting the strands run through his open fingers. "Want to donate it to charity? For cancer patient wigs?"

"I've actually been thinking about that for a while, now." She paused, watching Danny's hand in her hair. "I always say that when you no longer have a use for something, find someone who does. I'll do it."

Danny tugged her ponytail playfully and put it behind her back as if saying goodbye to it. To the O'Malleys, he said, "We stopped in next door to tell them, first, but Jack said that Darla's been gone all day. He was vague about where she went, for some reason. He has the baby with him. He said if he gets swamped with customers, he may ask if he can bring L.P. over here. I said I'd let you know. If you are too busy, he'll call his folks."

"It's not like Darla to leave Jack alone on a Saturday. There must have been an important reason," Mrs. O'Malley said.

"He said he knew where she went, but he didn't want to talk about it. Anyway, we're going back to our building—*our* building, can you believe it?—to start planning. Lucy's heading home again on Monday."

Lucille nodded. "This will be one big task. I'll be setting up a home, business, and shop here, and packing things back in Ohio. I'll probably have to hire someone to help with the house so I can be here, primarily. I don't know when I'll have time to actually connect with Danny on any sort of personal level, let alone eat and ... *think.*"

Mrs. O'Malley said, "We used to have much longer business hours, but it got so hectic that I could barely do the laundry and cooking, let alone do anything like bowling or reading. You'll eventually figure out how to balance everything. These next months will be the hardest."

Danny backed to the door, saying, "We'll still be working in the carpet shop after you close. Come on over for a look around if you'd like. There are a lot of carpet remnants and miscellaneous odds and ends all over the front room that haven't been cleared out, but at least we can give you some idea of what we have planned for the place."

Mack and Mrs. O'Malley glanced at each other, and both nodded.

Mrs. O'Malley said, "We'd love to, thanks! We'll be over after our closing time."

When they were alone, Mrs. O'Malley sat on the chair near the front door, her hands under her thighs.

Mack put his glasses back on. "What's wrong?"

She looked at the clock. "Kris is on his way to Lamarr by now. With that other girl."

"You can't get involved, Mavis. I can tell from our talk earlier that you're far too involved already. Teenagers are all a little bit nuts by nature. Raging hormones, acne, strange hairs popping up all over, growth spurts .... Keep your own sanity intact. Stay on the sidelines." The phone rang. Mack looked at the caller ID. "It's Kris."

Mrs. O'Malley shook her head. "It's probably Daya. Kris is on the road."

"Hello?" Mack said into the phone. "Kris! We thought you'd be long gone to Lamarr by now. He is? Oh, that's too bad, kiddo. Sure. Wait one sec." He held the phone a little away from his head and said, "Kris wants you to listen in, too. Come on. I'll put it on speaker phone."

She was beside Mack in a flash, her eyes worried. "Kris? Are you okay? Is anyone sick or hurt? Oh, Josie's dad is. That's too bad. Is that what you wanted me to hear? No? You're *what?* The Amos' house? Oh, Kris! *Really?* Is it for sure already? Oh, well of course you'll have to have a tour and talk over all the fine details. I hope no one else is interested. So many of the larger houses are bought for student rentals. Just today? Well, that was a quick decision. I hope you get it, Kris."

Mack said, "Good luck, and let us know what happens. Oh, and I'll be at your place around four tomorrow. Will you be done with the home tour by then? Good. We're very, very happy for you all, Kris. See you soon. Bye, now." Mack hung up the phone. "Well, what do you think about *that?* Fate is sure a funny thing."

Four older men and two women came in together to shop, laughing and talking. One of the women turned as soon as she'd gotten inside to pull a few books out of one of the display windows. She asked how the books were priced, then nodded and placed them on the countertop, pledging to buy them.

While the group shopped, Mrs. O'Malley smiled and smiled, chatted, and helped them find categories and authors. Mack thought that her happy attitude made them want to buy more books than they would have otherwise.

After closing for the day, Mack took care of things in the cats' room, and Mrs. O'Malley shut off the computer and printed out the day's register receipts. When Mack passed her to put fresh water in a bowl for Buglit, she asked, "Did you send the book by overnight delivery?"

"No. Bristol's should have it on Monday."

"Oh." She looked at the clock again, as if it were a calendar. "Seems like you sent that book out a *month* ago already."

"We're both feeling impatient. Monday will be here before you know it."

She shook her head. "I don't know *how* I got to sleep last night."

"You snored from the moment your head hit the pillow."

"Did I? Well, I must have been sleep-worrying, then."

Mack delivered the cat water and rejoined his wife. "When is your next bowling night?"

"Tomorrow, but we're going to Quainty's, so I bowed out again. I haven't gone bowling in over a month. Maybe even over two months. I don't miss it. Sometimes I get tired of hearing the same old stories about the ladies' grandkids. I love those friends of mine, but I don't feel like I fit into their lives like I used to. When I brag about Kris, they look at me strangely because he isn't family. In *their* eyes, not mine, you understand."

"I'd think you'd want to get together now that you've got all this huge news to tell them."

She looked at him. "You mean about the books?"

He nodded.

"They won't want to hear it. I can never bring up anything about our books with them. They get bored."

"Well, this is hardly your typical book story. This one is a thrill a minute."

"I guess I'll try to tell them next time it's bowling night. Seems like they'll at least be interested to know how much they're worth. If we ever find out, that is," she said. That was another complaint about how long it was taking, even though it had only been a single day. She had another thought. "Mack—I wonder if it wouldn't be better to keep our major book find to ourselves. Sell them anonymously, and don't make it public to our other friends and the customers. It would change things too much, and I don't want that. If we're not going to retire, then there's no reason to shake things up. We'll put the money into our bank account and sit on it until we're ready to ... do whatever we're going to do in our old age."

"I agree." He rubbed his chin with his palm. "It's too late to keep it a secret absolutely, but I don't think we should broadcast this news."

"Speaking of money," she said, but didn't finish her sentence.

"I was thinking the same thing."

"You were?"

"Yes. Matt and Kris, right?" he asked, crossing his arms.

"How much, do you think?"

"Ten percent. Five percent to each. We always pay a finder's fee to anyone who gives us a lead on a good book or a collection that we purchase. No reason the boys shouldn't get their cut."

She nodded. "Don't tell them yet. When the time comes, and when we know how much our auction earnings will be, then we can tell Mrs. Karlsson and Kris' folks."

Mrs. O'Malley admired her new decal again as Mack locked the front door behind them. They'd had compliments on it from all their regular customers, and even from one or two who were new to the shop.

They walked arm-in-arm down their block and around the corner, both feeling that a weight had been lifted from their shoulders since they'd mutually decided against retiring.

"This might even be bigger than our building," Mack said as they stood in front of the former carpet shop. Colorful vintage signs were still attached to the face of the brick building, but large sheets of paper covered the display windows from the inside, making it obvious that the carpet store was out of business. He knocked on the glass door, also covered with newspapers.

"It's open!" shouted Lucille from inside. "Come on in."

Mack opened the door. "Is this the same building? I don't remember it being this huge."

"I think that's because it was full of carpet and linoleum samples, and sales desks and other furniture, Mack," said Mrs. O'Malley, stepping over a long roll of gray carpet padding.

The white-painted metal tile ceilings were high and had large fans hanging from them, churning the stale air. A single floor lamp with a sepia shade near the entrance to the back rooms gave everything a hollow feel. Posters hung on the walls, advertising fabric treatments, rug cleaners, and carpeting brands.

"Come on over here, Maisie," Danny said. "This is where I'll put my studio. The wiring is nearly new, and there are plenty of outlets here and in Lucy's studio in the next room."

The back rooms were more spacious than Mrs. O'Malley thought they would be, allowing both Danny and Lucille plenty of room for their projects. There were lamps in each room, but they weren't lit because early-evening sunlight still streamed through the small windows in both workrooms.

"My kiln will go right here," Lucille said, pointing to the corner where she stood. "I'll have a long workbench here, and shelves and cabinets. I already have nearly everything I'll need back in Ohio, so I shouldn't have to buy much to get my side ready to use. Danny has what he needs for his work already, too. The main expenses will come when we're ready to establish the retail space out front and furnish our apartment upstairs. The building's owners will get rid of any of the remnants and such that we don't want to keep for free. They have a lot of cutting and carpet-installation tools they no longer want, so Dan and I will look those over in case we can use them." She nodded at Danny as she walked back to the dividing point between the workrooms and the front room. "I think we know what we want to do—we just need to get it all moved in and get busy."

"Yes, we do." Danny paused, looking tenderly at Lucille. "We do."

Mack tugged his wife's arm, sensing something had shifted in Danny's mood. "We need to get busy, too. We wish you all the luck in the world." He met Danny's eyes, seeming to mean what he'd said in more than one way.

Mrs. O'Malley was surprised that she was being pulled toward the door so soon, but then assumed that Mack must be hungry or tired.

Chapter Twenty-three

On Sunday morning, the Dehlvis were all awake early, excited that they would be looking inside the Amos' house that afternoon.

At the breakfast table, Mr. Dehlvi cautioned, "Remember, we have only recently started to think of moving to a larger house. This will likely only be our first such home tour. We may not buy this one. Understand? Also, we may stay in this house and not move at all. Do not go running and shouting up the staircase and out to the basketball court. You are properly-behaving boys, and I want you to act as such, not miscreants."

Dontae stopped eating his breakfast of crepes spread with peanut butter and fruit to ask, "Who is Miss Creants?"

"I thought *you* knew her," said Bijay.

Dev and Kris burst out laughing, and Mrs. Dehlvi *tsk-tsk-tsk*'d at them for being silly at the family table.

Mr. Dehlvi said, "I only mean, my sons, that I do not want you to get your heart set on this house. We should have an open mind. Just because we are very contented in this neighborhood, and just because the house is one that is in this neighborhood and it is a very handsome, spacious house does not mean that we should rush out to sign papers to buy it. There are considerations."

"Think of the *kitchen,* though, Falak," Mrs. Dehlvi said, clapping her hands together once. "Oh! And the gardens, and the large rooms for the boys, and two or three bathrooms, and a study for you, and a sewing room for me, and a game room in the basement for the boys on rainy days. The cats—they will like it too."

The phone rang, startling them all that someone was calling early on a Sunday morning.

"It must be an emergency," Mr. Dehlvi said, standing. "Yes? This is the Dehlvi residence. Oh, hello. How are you this morning? We are all quite, quite fine here. Yes, I'm sure he will want to talk. Just a moment, please." He held out the phone. "Dontae—this is a call for you."

Everyone at the table was surprised, but most surprised of all was Dontae, himself, as he walked toward his father's outstretched hand.

"Hello? Hello! Mrs. Stornburger, how did you think to call me? I was dreaming of you when I woke up today. The clouds outside were your favorite kind, with pink icing on them and little ripples. I dreamed you'd found my missing red sock. Did you ever find it? Oh, well. I have other socks. I have new shoes now, and a new bed, and a new dresser that looks like a pile of suitcases, and my bed looks like it has an old-time sailing ship on it, and I have brothers, and I have Mom and Dad, and I have lots of fun! Kris is my oldest brother. He works in a bookshop, and he's teaching me to read better, along with Mom and Dad, too. And there's Bijay, who is funny, and Dev, who is very nice. Uh-huh. And guess what, Mrs. S. My mom is going to have another baby. A *new* one, this time, from her *stomach.* No, they don't bother me now. Better every day now since my pinky toe came off with the last operation. How is Fritz? Has he remembered where his yellow ball went yet? Mrs. S? I *miss* you, Mrs. S. I know. I know. I am. I am. I promise. I feel good. I smile now, you know. I don't worry about smiling because of my teeth, I just do it now, whenever I feel like it. Tell Fritz hi for me, okay? Oh, and we might move to a bigger house. I don't know if we'll have this phone number. I don't know how that stuff works. Find me if I move, okay. I mean call me. Okay. Me, too. Yep. I will. Okay. Bye."

When Dontae went back to the table to finish his breakfast, Mrs. Dehlvi put her hand on his, feeling the ridges of his fused fingers and feeling him grip her in return. She looked into his dark eyes that held a trace of homesickness. "Dontae, you know you may talk about your Mrs. Stornburger any time you wish to. Don't feel shy. Miss Valentine said it would be better for her to wait a week before calling so we would have some time to adjust to each other, but now I think it would be fine if you call her, too. She was a big part of your life. She went through so much with you, didn't she? Yes." She knelt on the floor, hugging him as he squeezed her neck tightly.

The afternoon eventually arrived, and at one o'clock, the Dehlvis left their house to walk together to admire the craftsman home where the Amos family had lived only weeks ago.

After a few minutes, a red-haired woman driving a silver Cadillac pulled into the paved driveway.

"Hello, Dehlvi family. I'm Della, and I'll be showing you the Amos house today. How are all you?" She smiled and extended her hand to Mrs. Dehlvi and then to Mr. Dehlvi. She then shook each of the boys' hands, getting everyone's name, and didn't react at all when she took Dontae's except to give him a special wink of kindness. "Here is my card." She took it from her briefcase and gave it to Kris, who was closest to her. "Shall we go in and look around?"

She unlocked and opened the extra-wide front door, and Kris walked behind her. He almost gasped at the cold, empty feeling it gave him to be inside Tatyana's house now that her family had moved. Many personal items were still everywhere: photos, a knitted throw on the back of a recliner, Mrs. Amos' collection of classic and foreign movies, their many mementos from Africa, and their books. Everything seemed to be waiting for a family who would never return. Seeing the abandoned house made Kris feel as if there had been a sudden death.

Behind him, the boys were having an entirely different reaction to the home. "Whoa!" said Dontae, spinning in a slow circle to take it all in. "This is a *huge* house."

"Wow! Look at that TV! It must be a thousand feet big," said Bijay, pointing.

"Why are they selling the contents with the house?" Kris asked, a shiver of fear running down his spine.

Della said, "I don't exactly know, but I was told that there was a family emergency. We were asked to sell the house and contents as one lot."

"Even the photos? Even all the personal stuff all over the house?" Kris asked, his voice rising. "Do you know what that emergency was? Was anyone hurt? Does it say in your papers?"

"I'm afraid I don't know any details. There has only been impersonal contact between my agency and Mr. Amos. I only know that there were no requests to have us pack and ship any of what was left behind." She turned to smile at Mr. and Mrs. Dehlvi. "Shall I show you around? I know you said that you're familiar with the home, but when you're looking at it as a buyer, you're going to be looking with different eyes. Feel free to search high and low. Examine the bathrooms, attic, basement, bedrooms, and kitchen. It's all here for you to explore. I've only been inside once since you're my first showing, but I have notes on some of the technicalities and specifics. I'm here to answer questions about the house, the land, property taxes, and the legalities."

Mrs. Dehlvi pulled Mr. Dehlvi around the L-shaped sofa and oak console table, where shriveled white roses sagged in a tall, orange vase. She kept tugging him until they stood in the kitchen. She pointed out the marble-topped island that had a deep double sink at its center, and copper-bottomed pots and pans hanging above. The etched doors of the cabinets revealed dishes, glasses, bowls, and more cookware. It had modern details and lighting, all in a black and white theme with bursts of primary colors and African-patterned tiles.

Kris watched as his brothers left the plush chairs in front of the TV and ran up the sweeping staircase to check out the bedrooms. He walked into the living room and sat on a wooden chair beside a grandfather clock, folding his hands on his lap.

Della went to look through the dining room windows that faced the back yard. She wrote in a notebook and took out her cell phone to check her emails.

Kris took advantage of the moment alone to close his eyes. "Dear Lord," he prayed silently, *"please* don't let anything be wrong with Tatyana and her family. Please let them all be fine, and please make whatever emergency kept them in Botswana be over and done with and okay now." He kept his eyes shut, repeating his prayer a second time before ending it.

Mr. Dehlvi left his wife in the kitchen while she further explored it, the pantry, and laundry room. He found Kris just as he was opening his eyes again.

"Are you feeling ill?"

"No, Dad." Kris stood as Della joined them.

"How are you doing?" she asked. "Would you like to see the upstairs, too?"

"Sure," answered Kris. "Dad, have you ever been upstairs?"

"No. I have only seen the living room, I think, and what can be seen from there, on the few times I've come on an errand. This is a very attractive staircase, especially as the intricate waving pattern of the steps' woodwork overflows onto the floor at its base. It reminds me of a passage in our Hindu literature: 'a sea-clothed earth.'" As he started up the stairs, he repeated it. "'A sea-clothed earth.'"

When they reached the next floor and Della had stepped into the closest bedroom, Kris held his father back to say,

"I'm worried about Taty and her family. I've said a prayer. Please say one, too, that they are all okay."

Mr. Dehlvi held Kris' eyes. He nodded, saying, "I will do that again since you have asked. I have included them in my prayers twice already. I did not like hearing that the price of the house included all the contents."

"Here's the largest bedroom of the four," Della was saying from within the room to the right. "All of the bedrooms are nearly the same in size, but this one also has a larger closet with a secondary access to the attic via a pull-down ladder. The main attic staircase is at the opposite end of this floor, and there is a third access from the outside if you use the fire escape through a window. The upstairs bathroom is the room at the top of the stairs, and a linen closet is to the left of the bathroom door. I'll let you two look around. I'll see how Mrs. Dehlvi is doing in the kitchen."

"We'll call the Amos' tonight," said Mr. Dehlvi when he and Kris were alone again. "I still have Mr. Amos' cell phone number in my contacts."

Kris sat on the edge of the bed. "I didn't even think of calling Mr. Amos. Africa is so far away." He sighed. "Thanks, Dad. I'll feel a lot better if I know something terrible hasn't happened."

They looked at the bathroom and three other bedrooms, only one of which was still furnished as a place to sleep. It was Tatyana's old room. Kris couldn't bear to do more than glance through the open door. He had never seen her room before, but, almost immediately, he got a sense of her from what he could see.

Downstairs, Kris saw that his brothers were outside. Bijay was doing a poorly executed cartwheel, and Dev and Dontae were sitting on top of the burgundy-painted picnic table near a fire pit.

"Remember that night we came over here with you for the marshmallow roast?" asked Dev when Kris stepped through the door from the dining room. "Mr. Amos and Taty sang African songs, and he played that weird instrument. We could roast marshmallows if we lived here."

Kris sat beside them on the tabletop, putting his feet on the bench seat. "I remember. We'd miss our old house, though."

Dev raised his eyebrows. "It's crowded. I hate that we have only one bathroom. Even if Dad puts in a toilet in the basement, we'll still be crowded." With a determined look on his face and in his large eyes, he said, "I want this house."

"Dad warned us that even if we decide to get a bigger house, it probably won't be this one. This is only the first one we've looked at."

"I know," Dev said, "but it's on our same street. Who wants to move to some part of town where we don't even know anyone? I like it here. We're close to downtown, and the lake, and the park, and you're close to the bookshop. I think we should move here."

"Me, too," said Bijay, giving up on cartwheeling. He was out of breath as he climbed onto the table to join them.

"Me, too," echoed Dontae, smiling. "I like that tree. That could be *our* tree."

The back door opened again, and Mr. and Mrs. Dehlvi and Della walked through.

"How are you doing out here, boys?" asked Della.

"We're looking at the tree and stuff," answered Dontae.

"That is a very nice oak. And I see that a young tulip tree is coming along nicely. The Amos' took exceedingly good care of their gardens and lawn, as well as their home."

"I could not ask for better," Mrs. Dehlvi said.

Kris noticed that his mother's stance seemed determined. She wanted this house, too.

"Shall we go now, boys?" their mother asked. "We have taken up quite enough of Della's time for today."

Back home, Mr. and Mrs. Dehlvi talked together in their bedroom with the door closed so they wouldn't be influenced by any begging or opinions on the matter at hand. At one point, Kris heard his mother speaking louder than usual, and partially in a different language and with bursts of laughter. He realized that she was probably talking on the phone.

When his parents came into the living room, Mrs. Dehlvi sat on the sofa with Kris, who was holding Stomper on his lap.

"Where are your brothers?" Mr. Dehlvi asked.

"They went to play with Tommy and Opal so Dontae could meet them. Want me to go over there?" Kris asked as his father took a seat in his recliner.

"Maybe later. We have decided to put in a bid on the house."

Kris stared at his father in disbelief. "You have?" He then looked at his mother, who smiled. "I mean, I thought you might eventually go back to it when you'd looked at other houses, but I didn't think you'd definitely decide on the Amos house today."

His mother shifted to make herself more comfortable. "We know what we want. We can be very happy there. The price is high for us, even if we sell this house right away. My father said he will send us fifty thousand dollars by bank transfer on Monday. He has always wanted us to have a better house and has often offered his help. Now we will take it and try to pay him back a little at a time when we can." She shrugged. Her eyes suddenly widened. "Oh, and Kris— you have never met my mama and papa. They are going to come for a visit here in America this winter when we are settled. But first we must get settled, hey Falak?"

"They're coming all the way here from India? Wow! That's really great!" Kris said, sitting straighter.

Mr. Dehlvi inhaled. "There will be no costly vacation this summer since we are to buy the house. There is plenty to do in this part of our state, though." He yawned. "I think we should now call Mr. Amos. I am sorry that I do not know his first name. Do you, Kris?"

"Um ... it might be Oba, but maybe that's what Taty's mom called him as, like, a nickname." He shook his head and scratched Stomper under his chin. "I don't know for sure, sorry."

"Oba," his father repeated. "Now that you say that, I think you are right. I have his number written down. I will call." He pointed to the phone in the hallway. "Please?"

Kris stood and retrieved the phone, saying on the way, "I'm worried."

"That is why we are calling."

Kris gave him the phone and took a seat beside his mother again. "I hope it isn't too late there for us to call."

His father looked at his watch. "I am thinking it may be either eight-thirty or nine-thirty."

"Try, then," Mrs. Dehlvi said with an encouraging wave of her hands.

"Mr. Amos? Oba? Yes? This is Falak Dehlvi, Kris' father, here in America. Hello! Very far, yes. I am calling for two reasons today. Firstly, Kris and Daya and I are concerned for you and your family. We are praying that you are not ill or hurt and that your family is well. I see. I see. Oh, *dear* ... oh, no. When was this that it happened? How is she now? Still? And is that why you are staying in Botswana? Oh, I see. I'm happy for *that,* yes. Will she be long in recovering?" He looked at Kris blankly, not revealing how bad the news was. "Will you be returning for your household things? That leads me to the second reason I am calling you. Hello? Are you there? I am here, yes. Can you hear me? Mr. Amos, today myself, my wife, and my boys all went to your home to look it over. We would very much like to purchase your house. I am.

Perfectly serious. We have discussed it, and this is what we would like to do. We have a new baby on the way, and we have Kris and now little Dontae, our new adopted son. Thank you. Yes, but now we do not fit in our house that we have here. Would you be happy if we arranged this purchase with your agent? I am not calling to talk about the financial arrangements. I want for you and your family to be fine with the Dehlvi family living in your home. Yes. Thank you. And if we do this, Daya would like to pack your most personal things and send them to you. She does not want you to have left them behind. We want to do this, yes. And Kris is here in the room with us. Is your daughter nearby? Will she speak to Kris?" He paused, waiting. "Is that Tatyana? Hello. Kris would like to speak to you. I heard from your daddy what has happened. Kris does not know yet. I'll let him hear it from you, okay, Tatyana? We pray for a quick recovery. Yes. Here's Kris now. Hang on."

Mr. Dehlvi leaned forward, and Mrs. Dehlvi took the phone from him to give it to Kris, who looked stricken even though he didn't know what had happened. He talked to her longer than he felt he should have since it was a very long-distance call and to a cell phone. Before he hung up, he stood and walked along the hallway for some privacy. "I'll always remember what you said to me the night before you left. I miss you, but I know you want to be where your extended family lives. Me, too. Yep. And Taty, don't let that imaginary letter you recited to me be your last one. Our house number is two two six. Write to me. Okay. I'll say goodbye now. Yes. To them, too. Goodbye."

Kris disconnected. He listened as his father told Mrs. Dehlvi about how Mrs. Amos had fallen down a concrete staircase and had broken her leg in two places, an arm, and three ribs. The recovery would take longer than the short time they had planned to be in Africa. The accident was enough to convince them to make a change of life again and to be near their families.

"They will stay in Botswana?" she asked, concern darkening her eyes.

"Yes. And so, if we are to live in their home, we will box and send them their personal items."

Mrs. Dehlvi shook and hung her head. "I know that Mrs. Amos will be fine someday, but what a thing for her to endure. I will miss Tatyana. I can see her now, Kris, her smile wide, linking your arm with hers. Her long legs running here or running back home. We will pray that her mother will fully recover."

"What about the house?" asked Mr. Dehlvi. "Mr. Amos was pleased with our decision."

She wiped her eyes, still shaking her head. She swallowed. "I think that we should call the agent right away."

"Yes. I do not think I need to consult with the boys. They all have their hearts set on the house, even though I had warned them against getting attached too soon. Mr. Amos said that he will let the real estate agent know that he will not consider offers other than ours. His mind is on his wife, of course."

Kris reached into his back pocket and pulled out Della's business card. He handed it and the phone back to his mother, who gave them to his father.

"Is this Miss Della? This is Falak Dehlvi. We would like to buy the house, please. Yes. When should we meet?"

When Kris, Mack, and Mrs. O'Malley pulled into the Cumbers' driveway, they saw Danny's truck parked under the small tree at the edge of the paved area.

"Did you know Danny was coming today?" asked Mack as he stepped from the van.

370

"No," she answered. "I wonder if he came out to tell El and Quainty their big news in person."

"*What* big news?" asked Kris. He'd been talking to them about the Amos' house and about Mrs. Amos' accident on the drive to the farm.

"Well, now that Dan's here, why not wait to find out directly from him?" asked Mack, closing the van door after Kris had gotten out. "Mavis, that means 'don't tell Kris anything,' by the way."

"Hmph," she said, following them to the house.

Danny, Lucille, Elwood, and Quaintance stepped onto the porch to greet them. Danny stood behind Lucille and wrapped his long arms around her as they all called greetings to each other.

Quaintance said, "Dinner is ready when you are, folks. I have a big batch of everything."

"Ooh, my favorite," laughed Danny.

"Hey! I thought *I* was your favorite," protested Lucille playfully. Her long hair was loose and lightly curled at the ends. She had on makeup and a short, light blue dress and white sandals. Danny whispered in her ear. She laughed and pulled out of his arms to hug Mrs. O'Malley hello.

"I didn't know you two were going to be here for the painting-picking-out party tonight. I'm glad," Mrs. O'Malley said. "Are you still planning on leaving for home tomorrow?"

They all stepped into the house through the new screen door. Kris was the last one inside. Only partially listening to the others talk, he looked around at the front room. The Cumber house had gotten many renovations and improvements since they'd sold the antique cars and a lot of the other valuable items that had been in their barn for decades. He stood looking at the room that only last year had held countless old books. Now it had new windows and curtains, new lighting, and new furniture. The bookcases that had lined the walls had been taken to the barn to be used for the antique shop. Beyond was a closed door that he knew led to the downstairs bedroom where there used to be a sitting room.

He looked at the wall, beyond the carving Danny had done as a boy on the door's frame. A glass-encased reprint of a very rare booklet by Edgar Allan Poe hung there, instantly reminding him of events and feelings from the summer before. He went into the kitchen and leaned against the sink, his face too somber for the occasion.

"What's the matter, there, kid?" asked Quaintance from near the stove where a pot of coffee was perking. Her pink hair stood out against the white cupboards behind her.

Kris put his hands into his shorts' pockets. "I was thinking about last summer. The house was different then. I don't mean to sound like I don't like the changes, but I think I miss that old house."

"I know how you feel. But it's safer for Elwood and me now. We don't have to be climbing up and down the stairs like we used to, and housework's easier for me to handle. I can do the stairs quicker now that I've lost weight, but I still have my troubles." Quaintance turned off the burner under the coffee and faced the group, who were already sitting around the table. "Let's dish up, folks. I'm starved." She took dinner plates out of a cupboard.

Bowls and platters of all sorts of hot and cold food were set out along the kitchen counter. The group served themselves before settling in again around the large, round table. The screen door to the back porch let in cooling air.

Once they were all eating, Kris asked, "So, what's the big news, Mr. Kinonen? Seems like everyone knows but me."

Danny said, "First off, call me Dan or Danny." He took a bite of potato salad, his blue eyes twinkling. He swallowed. "My big news, Kris, is that I popped the question to Lucy yesterday."

"Popped what question?" Kris asked.

"I have found the chain for my ball."

"Huh?"

"I have plighted my troth."

"You did *what?*"

Elwood cracked up, folding his arms across his chest, sending everyone else at the table except Kris into fits and giggles.

Lucille was the first to regain control. "Danny asked me to marry him yesterday."

Kris was amazed. "But I just heard that you two were *divorced.*" He glanced at her bare fingers. "Did you say yes?"

Lucille looked at Danny, who was still slightly laughing. "I certainly did. I mean, who could say no to that face, those eyes, that smile, and that loving heart of his?" She kissed his cheek. "Again, I mean."

Everyone laughed at that, too, then went back to eating the dinner that Mrs. Cumber had made all day long while Mr. Cumber waited on customers in their Barntiques.

Kris then talked about Mrs. Amos' fall, and about the house and how they might buy it.

"Dad and Mom are meeting with the agent tomorrow to talk over the details. Boy, if you could have seen Dev's face, and Bijay's face, and Dontae's face, Mrs. O! They were *so* super happy."

"I'll bet!" Mrs. O'Malley said, smiling herself.

Kris said, "I love that house. Now there will be five of us kids—once the baby comes, I mean." He swallowed some milk. "Hey, D-Danny," he said, trying to remember to say that instead of Mr. K or Mr. Kinonen, "did you tell Darla and Jack yet about how you're going to get married?"

"I did," he said, standing to get more beans and seven-layer salad. "We went to their shop about two this afternoon, and I think we were there talking until after three o'clock. The baby spit up on Lucy's dress; she went back to her motel room to wash and change. Then we came out here for the smorgasborg."

"Smorgasbord," Lucille corrected.

"Are you sure?" asked Danny. "Is that right?" he asked, looking around the table.

"I always say it with a 'g' on the end," said Elwood. "But I'm not the Scandinavian in the family. Quainty?"

"I think it has a 'd' on the end," Quaintance said. "More coffee, anyone?" she asked, standing up.

Danny raised an eyebrow but didn't argue again. He held out his coffee cup, and his sister poured him a refill.

"Wait? That's it?" asked Lucille, turning in her chair to look at Danny. "Where's the argument? How come you're giving in already?"

Danny took her hand, his eyes filled with affection. "Because not a thing in this world is worth being said if it puts me at odds with you."

Mrs. Cumber and Mrs. O'Malley both said, "Oh-h-h!" in delight, but Lucille pulled her hand from his and scowled. "No, no, no! Are you *kidding* me? Listen, Dan ... are you listening?"

"Yes, dear," he said.

"I'll put up with enough of that kind of behavior to keep the peace between us, but I will not live the rest of my life with a man who won't defend what he believes. I don't want fussing and fighting, arguing and throwing things, of course, but I do *not* want the sort of thing you just tried to pull, mister."

"No, my love?" he asked, trying to hug her, smiling wryly.

"Absolutely, positively *not.* Now. Let's go back to our former discussion. D or g?"

"I forget."

She huffed. She clinked her fork on the edge of her plate. And then she gave up. "Well, *whatever* this gargantuan feast is called, it's delicious, Quainty."

Nearly an hour later, after dinner, dessert, more dessert, and more coffee and lots of talking and laughing, and after the dishes were washed and put away, Mrs. Cumber suggested that they head upstairs to start selecting their favorite artworks for her exhibition.

"I think I hear a car," said Mack, pushing his chair under the table.

Kris went to the porch door. "It's Jack and Darla."

"Jack and Darla?" asked Quaintance, coming to look through the screen door while wiping her damp hands on a white dishtowel. "I didn't think they were coming out here tonight." She went out to stand at the edge of the porch. "Dar-baby! Good you came. I have a regular smorgas-something for you two to eat up."

"We came here after we ate. I decided after dinner to drive out. Dad said he and Mom would be here, but I wasn't sure if we'd be too tired after work and eating to join you, so I made no promises." Darla gave L.P. in her carrier to Jack as they climbed the porch steps. She hugged and kissed her mother and two aunts as Patrick, their brown and black dog, romped in the yard, his tongue hanging out in happy excitement. He knew to stay far away from the chickens and that whole part of the farm. "We've come to help with your art, Aunty Q."

Quaintance kissed the baby's cheek. "Well, that's a good thing. There are plenty of paintings to go through. We'll need everyone's opinions of what I should take to my show." Inside, she put a bowl of water on the floor for Patrick and said, "Have some dessert, anyhow. I've got brownies, toffee bars, and a little banana cake left. There's coffee, too."

"Maybe later. I'm anxious to get to work. Lead the way," Darla said, stowing the baby's diaper bag and bottles under the table.

Patrick sniffed and tail-wagged hello to everyone before slurping up half his water. He then circled the floor near the back porch screen door before settling for a nap where it was cool.

On the way up the stairs behind Lucille, Darla said, "Mom and Dad, together again. Who'd a thunk it?"

L.P. started to cry.

"Well, it isn't as bad as all that, Lila Pearl," joked Danny as he started along the upstairs hallway.

"She'll get used to the idea, like the rest of us," Darla said, elbowing her father at the doorway to one of the two bedrooms. She then took L.P. from Jack to soothe her with small bounces and pats.

"Should we divide ourselves between the two rooms, Quainty?" asked Jack.

"Yes. Most of them are still in my painting room, but maybe about a quarter were moved to the other bedroom. Now I wish I'd kept my selections all separate. I was so sure I'd lost my chance with a gallery or any kind of a show that I didn't pay any attention to which ones I was putting where. I know my picked-out pieces should be in front of the others, but I've had a new thought. With all you here, everybody choose your own favorites. Put them lined along the hall, as many as you'd like. In the end, we'll all vote on each until we get about forty we agree are the best."

"What about the dresses?" Kris asked. "Do you plan to bring one or more of those?"

She ran her fingers through her pink hair and leaned against the doorway, looking at the bed where the painted dresses were sleeping. "I might. I'll decide that later, on my own. Okay. Let's get to it, folks."

A single pedestal fan in the room where Quaintance did her painting wasn't helping cool most of the second floor. Kris looked up. "Mrs. C? Can I turn on this ceiling fan?"

"Oh, yes, my boy," she said, standing straighter after starting to look through the colorful canvases near her painting room windows. "I should have thought to bring the other box fans up here earlier. Will you fetch them for me? They're out in the barn. El, give Kris the key for the shop. There's one fan by the cash register, and the other is at the back. Do you know where the light switches are?"

Kris nodded as he took the keychain from Elwood. "Need anything else?"

"Nope, I don't think so. Thank you. You're a good boy. I sure wish I had you around here all the time." She then pointed to the painting in front of her legs. "Looks like Patrick a little, don't it?"

Kris crossed the yard to take the path that led to the barn, enjoying the early evening air. As he walked, listening to the sounds of the countryside, smelling grass and cows and the chicken house, and watching a few fireflies glow and dim in the distant bushes, he wished he could be there more often, too. He again had a feeling of being split nearly in half between his two worlds: the Dehlvis; and the group of O'Malleys, Cumbers, Jacksons, Danny, and even the Karlsssons. During the months that weren't late spring to early autumn, he felt firmly like a Dehlvi, going to school, doing homework, playing with his brothers, eating and talking with his home family. Once school let out for summer vacation, he got infected with a fever for the bookshop and his other family.

He thought ahead a few years to when he would be graduating from high school. He couldn't see himself as an adult. He couldn't imagine leaving both of his families and going to another town or living a different way. Would he go to college? Would it be the one in Anders Lake, or somewhere else? What would he major in? What would he do for a job? How could he leave all he loved behind? How could he leave his mother and father with four children and without his help?

It occurred to him that he would only spend three years in the new house if he didn't go to the local college. He wouldn't get to watch his baby brother or sister grow up day by day.

Did every teenager feel this way? It didn't seem fair. He was sure that everything he could ever possibly love and want to do was part of the life he was living now.

As he unlocked and opened the antique shop door and switched on a single row of lights, another thought occurred to him: what about Ricki? What if she *was* his mother, and what if there was a natural father somewhere, too? Would they try to take him away immediately if he went to social services with the story Darla had told him? Would they have a legal right?

He found the fans, locked the shop, and hurried back into the house and up the stairs, apologizing for taking so long.

"What do you think about this one?" asked Darla in the hallway, holding a painting of a woman sitting alone at a restaurant table. She wore a red dress, hat, and ribbon at her neck. Her face was starkly white.

"Lonely," Kris answered. "I feel like she's caught between waiting for someone and giving up on someone."

"Very insightful. You have a poet's way of condensing and interpreting what you see."

He felt his face heat from the compliment. He stepped into the room across from Quaintance's art room. Mack and Mrs. O'Malley and Jack were there, bent over the canvases. He plugged in one of the fans and set it to its highest level.

"Oh, that feels *great,*" said Mrs. O'Malley, turning around. "I didn't realize how hot it had gotten up here." She went to stand in front of the fan. "I'm going to plug it in below the windowsill to suck in air from outside."

Kris then walked to a corner near the closet, away from where the others had been going through the artworks. The first painting he saw he really liked. It was full of color and geometrical designs. At the center was a man-like bird wearing shoes. With one bird hand, he seemed to be pushing away a city street scene, and with the other, he was pushing away rain, snow, or another substance falling from the sky. It didn't make sense, but Kris liked it. He carried it into the hallway and leaned it against the wall next to the painting of the white-faced woman.

Mack was right behind him. He put a painting next to Kris' selection. It was smaller, done on a thick wooden board. "How does that one grab you?"

Kris hesitated. He whispered, "I like it, but *wow*. What is it supposed to be?"

"Well, it looks sort of like those old nineteen-fifties science fiction paperback covers. That might be an alien, and the woman in the white dress might be a queen or princess he's going to attack, right after she's dropped her tennis racket."

"She should have held onto her tennis racket," observed Danny, strolling into the hall with L.P. in his arms. "Looks like she's going to need it."

Darla joined them, leaning her selection on the wall opposite the alien painting. "I like this one, don't you? It's not exactly like her others, but it is, in a way. Aunty Q had so many different styles over the decades."

"It reminds me of the nineteen-sixties or 'seventies," said Danny. "Look at those hot pinks and electric blue, that big hair and humongous eyes with spidery-long lashes."

Quaintance then carried her own selections into the hallway and had Mack and Kris put them in open spots along the walls.

"Look, Kris," said Darla as she pointed to one Mack had put next to the alien painting. "Books and a cat in a bookshop window."

"I did that one last year. I'm getting a little less steady with the brush these past months."

"I disagree," said Elwood, joining them in the crowded hallway. "Every year or two, just about, I saw a different style coming from your easel. This, Quainty, is your style now."

Darla nodded. "Writers change their styles all the time, too. Poems I wrote a few years ago are very different from what I write today. Musicians, dancers—all artists change over time. That's what makes them interesting. Who wants to listen to the same tune over and over with each album from a musician? I love what you're doing now. I love every one of your styles."

Quaintance scanned the paintings in the hallway as if reviewing segments of her life. She pointed at one, started to say something, but then remained silent.

"Forty-four," Mrs. Cumber said when they were all back downstairs in the kitchen. "Plus a dress or two, maybe." She poured hot water into Mrs. O'Malley's cup and handed her a tea bag. "I can't thank you all enough. That is a load off my mind. I'll start wrapping them on my off-hours tomorrow. I have plenty of time for that since you folks all helped me choose the paintings tonight. The gallery owner wants me to get to his place as soon as possible."

Patrick sat at Elwood's feet, sampling some of the table's offerings secretly being given to him under cover of the John Deere tablecloth.

"Are you getting excited, Quainty?" asked Jack. He was holding a sleeping L.P. in one arm, the cake on his plate untouched.

She poured out more water in other cups and placed a dish of tea bags at the center of the table. "I can't think too much about it, truth be told. When I close my eyes at night, I want it to go both ways. I want to be a big hit, but I also want to get to the gallery and find that no one showed up to see my paintings."

"I can understand that, Aunty Q," said Darla. She blew on her tea and took a sip. "I don't submit my poetry anywhere because I don't want to find out—once and for all—if it is publishable or it isn't. It's a fear either way. If it is publishable, and at least some people other than family and friends like it, then I've gone years and years holding onto my writings that could have been alive in the world for all that time. But if they're rejected, then ... that would hurt in a different way." She sipped more tea. "You've had these wonderful, quirky paintings stored upstairs for decades, never really showing them to anyone, and now you'll be offering them to strangers. If they're a hit, then you'll feel terrible that you waited this long. If they're rejected, then that will hurt like heck. I understand exactly."

Mrs. Cumber stood in front of the sink, reaching behind her to hold onto its edge. Her face reddened, and her lips trembled. "I shouldn't do it."

Darla pushed her chair from the table and went to her aunt. Taking one of her hands and looking into her eyes, she said, "Yes, you most certainly, certainly, absolutely, positively *should.*"

Quaintance frowned as she looked at her niece. "Then, Dar-baby, so should you."

"Fair is fair, Darla," said Jack, gently bouncing the newly awake Lila Pearl.

"Fah-ah-ah!" nearly echoed L.P. She then threw a little piece of cake onto the table like a comedian throwing confetti after telling a joke they thought was hilarious.

Patrick barked his encouragement from under the table, his tail thumping against Mack's chair legs.

"You should try, Darla," said Kris. "I love your poems. Everyone who hears you read them loves them."

"I don't have a fancy degree or anything. No poetry journal would even look at what I submit," Darla said, her eyes on the floor.

"Take those poems out of your pockets and share them," said Mack. "As the baby said, 'fah-ah-ah.'"

Darla laughed a little, then stepped to Jack to lift L.P. into her arms. She tugged on the baby's yellow collar and tickled her once under the chin. "I might, babykins. I might."

"I actually do feel better now, Dar," said Quaintance. "Thanks, sweetie."

As the group was settling in for more tea and dessert, Darla gave the baby to Mack and pulled Kris out onto the porch. "I need to talk to you for a little bit, okay?"

Kris nodded as he stood with her in the near dark. "Is this about Ricki?"

She swallowed. "Yes, Kris. I went back to the restaurant where I used to work. The owner is now an old man, but he still runs the place. He didn't remember me—I wasn't there that long—but he knows Ricki well. He said he almost considers her a second daughter. He knows what happened back then."

Kris sat on the porch railing, holding onto the thick column at his side.

"Where'd you go, Kris?" asked Mrs. O'Malley from the kitchen.

"Darla and I need a minute to talk out here, okay?" he called.

"Oh, okay," she said. "Shout when you're ready to go."

Darla sat beside Kris. "Listen to me; Ricki had a daughter. You aren't her baby. I got her address from the old man and went to see her yesterday. Ricki said that she was desperate when she was pregnant. She put an ad in a paper saying she was looking for a loving couple to adopt her baby, but what she basically wanted was money. She kept meeting with couples who offered her more and more money. She doesn't remember your parents, Kris, because they were just one of the dozen or more couples she talked to. Ricki wasn't well for a long time when she was expecting, but I didn't

382

know it. She wasn't taking care of herself, and she wasn't getting prenatal care. The man who owned the restaurant made her stop working one day and made her rest in the back of the kitchen. She admitted to him what she'd been doing—the scam she'd been trying to pull. He took her to a doctor, then to the family of the young man who had gotten her pregnant. That family took her in and cared for her, and when the baby was born, Ricki married that young man. They're all fine now. Struggling, but fine." She looked through the screen door to the kitchen, watching Jack with their baby. "I don't know why she decided not to go with your folks. There's a story there we'll likely never know. And since Ricki isn't your mom, I don't know how you came to be in the world. Did your mom and dad find another baby to adopt? Did they have you on their own? I don't know. I feel … I feel *terrible* that I said anything about it now, to you and to the others who know." She stood, facing the driveway. "We have to assume your parents *are* your parents, after all. We'll leave it at that."

"I can't, though," said Kris weakly.

Darla wiped her eyes with her hands. The sound of laughter from inside the house felt out of place.

Kris looked at her. "What if I *am* someone else's kid? What if they tried again with some other pregnant lady? Shouldn't I find out? Why don't I know the families of my parents? Why didn't they visit or call? Something strange happened back then. I can't just relax and forget what you told me, Darla. I *can't.*"

"We don't have to talk about it anymore tonight. I basically only wanted you to know what I found out. Please, though—forget it if you can. Think about your adopted family and their feelings."

Kris stood from the porch railing. "Thanks for doing what you did … for finding out about Ricki and her baby. I'm glad it all ended up okay for that family." He hugged her. "I still have this big question pounding in my brain and chest, though."

She didn't hug him in return, feeling drained. "There's no simple way to find out more. If you're going to try, at least wait until you're older. Be a Dehlvi for now. They need you. All your families need you, Kris."

"But what if there's another family who needs me, too?"

Darla swallowed, facing him again. "There's a whole lot of need everywhere. Let *us* have you. Let *us* be the ones you give your life to, for now. That sounds weird, maybe, but I can't think of how else to say it."

Kris exhaled. His voice dropped lower as he said, "I already told my social worker that I want to talk to her later this summer, even though I didn't say why. I'd have to lie if she contacts me." He started to say one thing, but then changed his mind. "I'll have to think."

She wiped her eyes again. "We all love you, Kris. Think about *that,* too."

The sounds from the kitchen grew quieter, or else his mind was blotting them out. "I'm going to try to find my grandparents. I'll use the internet. There has to be a record of them, either on Mom's side or Dad's. I know my mom's name before she got married. I won't ask for help through social services. I'll find out what I can on my own. I'll ask at Round Theater for photos and ask if anyone remembers my parents. There might be some answers waiting for me right downtown. But I'm not going to do it now, okay? I won't do anything now. It will be a project for some other ... year, maybe. Some other time in my life. I promise."

Darla exhaled as if she'd been waiting for Kris to make that promise. "Can you be content until then?"

He nodded. "I still feel guilty, though."

Darla inhaled. "Think about it this way, Kris. You're worried that there's a remote, infinitesimal chance that someone you're related to might possibly need your kidney or a blood transfusion. If that's the case, why aren't you donating blood constantly or registering for organ donation? Giving plasma? Delivering meals door-to-door?"

"I'm only fourteen. I don't think I'm allowed to do any of those things."

She huffed. "That's beside the point. No one can carry that sort of a burden. You have to devote your energy to what you need to right now—your family, your schooling, your friends, and your own growing up."

"I feel guilty."

"I feel more guilt than you do, kid. Me and my big mouth."

Kris shook his head. "I'm glad you told me about Ricki."

"Liar."

He laughed lightly. "I mean it. Someday this big puzzle is all going to fit together. I think there's a good reason we know each other now, and that you went with me to look at the news article on my parents. I just can't see what that reason is yet."

"So, you'll definitely wait a while?"

"I'll wait."

Darla drew in another deep breath and then exhaled slowly.

Kris cleared his throat and called into the house. "I'm ready."

Everyone shook hands, hugged, kissed, or did some combination of those things while the baby vented her tiredness. Quaintance and Elwood stood on the porch waving to them, watching a row of taillights pull from the driveway onto the gravel road. A half-moon sailed the silver nightclouds above as Elwood slid an arm around his wife's waist. They stood there alone with the sounds and scents of darkness for a few more minutes before opening their screen door once again.

Chapter Twenty-four

"There's a message on our machine from the auction house," announced Mack the next morning.

"There *is?*" Mrs. O'Malley asked, almost squealing.

Mack crossed his arms over his chest, uncrossed them, then finally pushed the play button.

"Mr. O'Malley, we've received your book early this morning, and our expert is examining it now. He has asked me to phone you to find out more details on this group of books. Please call his line directly when you can." The caller then went on with phone numbers and an extension, and the expert's name, Mr. Haley.

"Oh, Macky! What do you suppose this means?"

"I suppose it means he wants to talk to me," he said calmly. "There's the mail if you want to grab it." He waved at the postman, and Mrs. O'Malley went to take the mail.

She held the envelopes without looking through them. "Okay. Call! Call!"

He picked up the phone and held it. "I almost don't want to, now."

She sighed, sitting where she could face him. "If I can handle it, you can handle it. It's not like we're calling about *bad* news, right?"

"Let's hope." He read the number from the scrap of paper as he dialed. "Is this Mr. Haley? This is Michael O'Malley calling about the fore-edge painting book I sent you."

Mrs. O'Malley couldn't stand to listen in. She went into the bathroom, closed the door, and sat on the towel hamper. She hummed to herself so she couldn't accidentally hear anything Mack said on the phone.

After a few minutes, he knocked. "Why didn't you stay with me? That's not like you. Come on out, now, Mavis."

She emerged, her eyes worried. "How did it go?"

"He is ... blown away."

"Oh, Mack! What did he say?"

"He thinks the artist is none other than Rodolfo Himzala-Vega, otherwise known as The Spanish Rareza."

"Why does that seem familiar? The nickname more than his real one."

"He was known for painting on strange items and surfaces like rocks that were common roadside markers, on town walls, small clay scraps that he used like currency, eggshells, animal skins, and fabrics that he made himself. He would cut the outer layers of bark off a tree, let the interior layer dry, and paint faces there, making it look as though the tree were giving birth to a large rabbit or squirrel. He was sometimes called mad, sometimes a genius. And—most importantly to us—he was also known to paint on the edges of books."

"Oh, *wowsers*, as Katrina would say."

Mack grinned, inelegantly raising one thigh onto the top of the counter and leaning forward, his foot dangling. "Since the other books' paintings are very similar to the one we shipped to Bristol's, it seems likely that they're all by that same artist. Mr. Haley said that Himzala-Vega had a distinct painting style, with loops and spirals that contain little animal faces, women, trees, flowers, and other things, all within the lines of the spirals and loops and swirls. He said it was as if the artist had been dropped back in time from the twentieth or twenty-first century. Or from another planet."

Buglit leaped to the back of the sofa and then down onto her person's lap. Mrs. O'Malley shook her head, petting the cat. "What do we do next?"

"Mr. Haley told me that he'll call their Lamarr office shortly with details. I'm to pack our books carefully—not doing any sort of restoration work on them myself—and drive them to Bristol's in Lamarr. They'll be my responsibility until I hand them off. From that point, Bristol's will be financially responsible for the books and will assume liability. They'll be protected by their insurance. They'll be inspected and taken to New York. There, they'll be researched, appraised, restored to some degree, photographed, and advertised for their auction. None of this is at our expense except for the gas and time it takes me to bring them to Lamarr."

"Do we have a date for the sale yet?"

"In January. They'll be a part of a small auction—our books and some others that are from a collector in Milwaukee. I don't know anything about that other group. The fact that there will only be our twenty-two books plus the Milwaukee group probably means they expect at least ours to bring a whopping load of money. He said that he's going to set the pre-sale estimate on the one book we sent at—are you ready for this? And I should add that this is because of the artist, not because the books beneath the paintings are valuable. He said they're going to estimate this single volume at around *fifteen thousand dollars.*"

Mrs. O'Malley set Buglit carefully aside. She took in a breath and closed her eyes. "I was expecting that amount. I was. I knew what the letter from Charles said. I was mentally prepared. But, Mack!"

The phone rang. It was Kris calling to say that he wouldn't be in until later. He was watching his brothers while his parents met with the bank and real estate agency. Mrs. O'Malley mouthed and whispered to Mack that he shouldn't tell Kris about the books over the phone.

"Okay, kiddo. We'll see you when we see you. Have a good one. Bye." He disconnected. "Why couldn't I tell him on the phone?"

"I want you to tell him in person. I'll have Darla come over then, too."

Mack sat on the computer chair. "There are twenty-two of them. Times even *five* thousand each would be fantastic. I know how this works. The pre-sale estimate is always fairly low at Bristol's, especially for unique and exciting items. Mavis, it could be that Charles was right. We *could* be looking at a check next year for about a half million dollars!"

Darla pushed into the shop carrying Lila Pearl.

"Good morning, girls," said Mrs. O'Malley cheerfully. She had to shake herself free of visions of swirls and squirrel faces before her eyes. "Don't you look pretty, Miss Lila? Oh, what a lovely little dress."

"Grandma Lucy got it for her. She brought it over to our house before she left early this morning. We're gonna miss Grandma, aren't we, L.P.? Yes. But she'll be back in a week or two, and then we can all be together to watch you grow up." She smiled at her aunt. "Dad is going to be hard to deal with while Mom's back in Ohio. I can tell already. I told him he'll be fine since he'll be busy working on their new store, but I'm not so sure. Which is kind of weird, since they've been divorced for years and years."

"The heart is a funny thing," said Mrs. O'Malley, reaching for L.P., who hugged the woman around her neck.

Mack winked at the baby and went to count the money in the register.

"Did Kris talk to you on the drive home from Aunty Q's last night?" Darla asked, adjusting her blouse.

The Mary twins arrived before Mrs. O'Malley could answer. They greeted each other and Mack told the ladies a group of Betty Neels paperbacks was waiting for them on the romance shelves.

"Yes," Mrs. O'Malley said softly to Darla. She shook her head, remembering the details. "I'm glad it turned out well for Ricki and her daughter, though. And now we know Kris isn't hers. But even so …."

Darla frowned. "I asked Kris to wait until he's older to find out more. He promised to wait until next year, at least."

Mrs. O'Malley nodded. She then smiled as L.P. waved at Mack. "We have some more news, but I'm waiting until Kris gets here to tell it."

"Mavis!" said Mack.

"Well, can't I at least say *that?*"

"No. Now you *have* to tell her."

Darla laughed, glad for a change of topic. "I can wait. I have a lot of records to list online, and Jack wants me in the shop to wait on customers while he makes a couple of calls to dealers." She took L.P. into her arms and helped the baby wave goodbye. "Say bye-bye to Aunty Mavis!"

"Bah bah!" L.P. said. She giggled and hid her face in Darla's neck.

"We're getting there with talking, aren't we baby? We're getting there. Okay. I'll see you later when Kris is here."

Mr. and Mrs. Dehlvi pulled into their driveway a few minutes after noon. They sat in the car, talking before going into the house.

"Mommy! Daddy! What happened?" asked Bijay, jumping up and down in the living room.

"We are officially going to have a new house soon, little one," said his mother. She knelt and opened her arms, and the three younger boys ran to her for a group hug.

Kris stepped around them and hugged his father, something he didn't do much, he realized. "Oh, Dad," he said. "I'm glad."

Bijay and Dontae were squealing. They left the group hug to run around and around the sofa, coffee table, and dining table. Dev had one hand on his forehead in the same gesture of disbelief that he'd seen his father make.

"Go and run around like sillies outside, boys. We don't want to mess up the house now that we'll have to show it to buyers, hey?" their mother said. She stood, one hand on her stomach and went to the dining room. "I think I need to eat, Falak. I will sit here at the table. Can you find me some food?"

"I'll get it, Mom," offered Kris. "Are you sick?"

"The baby is hungry. I should remember to pack a snack when we will be gone. The meetings felt very long to me. I should have eaten an hour ago."

Kris made her a flatbread sandwich and filled a plate with pretzels and homemade spiced dip. He sat with her as she ate, and they watched the boys and Mr. Dehlvi in the back yard through the patio door.

"Happy?" Kris asked her.

"Let me eat. I cannot talk of any feelings other than the one in my stomach. I waited too long."

"I didn't want to talk about this when I came home last night, but now I think I should. Let me call Dad inside to hear this, too."

She nodded, chewing. "Some water or tea first, please."

He poured her some lemon drink and brought it to her. She quickly drank half of it, so he poured her a refill. At the patio door, Kris called, "Dad? Can I talk to you in here?"

When the three of them were seated at the table, Kris said, "Darla told me that on Saturday she went back to the restaurant where she worked as a teenager. She said that the owner remembered Ricki very well." Kris held a breath, frowning for a few seconds before he said more. "She had a daughter, and Ricki married the baby's father."

Mrs. Dehlvi burst into relieved tears.

Mr. Dehlvi reached under the table to take her hand. He took off his glasses with his free hand. For a moment, he stared through the patio door at the other boys, breathing loudly. "So, that means Ricki was not your biological parent."

Kris shook his head, feeling a renewed relief, himself. "I might never know what happened back then—if my first parents had their own baby—me, or if they found another lady to carry a baby for them."

Mr. Dehlvi looked at the tabletop. "This is a mystery. Will it be solved? I do not know. Will you try? I do not know. I leave it to you, my son. I leave it to you. Daya, what say you?"

She shook her head, a hand covering her face. "Where is the sense to this?" she asked mournfully. "How is it better to know or to not know?"

Kris and his father looked at each other. "I want to think," Kris said. "I don't want to do anything for now. I promised Darla and the O'Malleys that I would wait a year or more to try to find out my answers. But there's another thing I should probably tell you. When we went to get Dontae, I spoke to Miss Valentine. I told her that I want to talk to her later this summer. If I don't meet with her, or at least call, will she come here to find out what I meant to say?"

"She is very conscientious. She will likely call or come here," Mr. Dehlvi said, putting on his glasses. "No matter. By that time, you'll have decided either to tell her the full story or to say you wanted only to speak to her about how wonderful your adoptive parents are."

Kris smiled. "I could do the second choice. Easily."

An hour later, after the Dehlvi family had eaten their lunches, Kris walked to the bookshop. Half the time along the way he was elated, and half the time he was depressed. So much of his life and his heart felt split down the middle, he thought. He then realized he should have talked to Josie again. Even though he hadn't gone with her to the play in Lamarr, there was no reason for her to assume that he wouldn't do something else with her soon. And then there was Tatyana and how she had sounded on the phone—familiar and yet far away, without a song in her voice for him.

He wouldn't let himself think about Katrina. He had too much else on his mind to try to figure out if they were still friends.

He finally reached the rose-colored door. The decal on that door made him smile. Cats and books, just like on the shop's address stamp, and very much like what was waiting inside.

"Nice," he said, pointing.

Mrs. O'Malley looked pleased. "We're getting larger ones for a few of the display windows. Mack asked me to—he likes this one that much."

"Wait a minute before you start, Mavis," Mack said as he came from the hallway. "Two left in the kids' room."

Kris seemed confused.

"Mavis. Just *wait,*" Mack warned.

"Okay! I'm waiting," she grumped before going to sit on her computer chair. "I have internet book orders to take care of, anyway. One of them is going over to India. Kris, have you ever thought about traveling there?"

"No, I guess not. At least not without the family." He still looked puzzled. "Um, what are we waiting for, exactly?"

"Oh, yes. I need to call Darla. I said we'd have her come over to hear the news when you got here," Mrs. O'Malley said, reaching for the phone. She dialed, then spoke into it. "Kris is here. Okay. Bye."

A father and daughter came from the hallway to pay for several books. As soon as the sale was complete, Darla stepped into the shop. She held the door open for the two customers.

"Anyone else in here, Mack?" Mrs. O'Malley asked.

"No. Go ahead."

"What is going on?" asked Kris.

"It might be about the rare books, I think," Darla said, sitting on the center cushion of the sofa.

"Is it about the books?" Kris asked, sitting, too.

"I think it is," Darla said, starting to laugh at their jesting. "I do believe they're going to tell us about the books."

"Do you think it has anything to do with the auction books?" asked Kris, suppressing a smile.

"I am pretty sure that you two ought to just sit there quietly so I can tell you about them." Mrs. O'Malley put her hands firmly on her hips, a line of irritation between her eyebrows.

"Have you told them about the books yet?" asked Mack.

"Everybody! Stop!" Mrs. O'Malley yelled.

Kris whispered to Darla, "This must be when she's going to tell us about the books."

Darla snorted. "Sorry, Aunty Mavis. We had a case of the goofies."

Matt and Katrina appeared at the door, but Katrina hesitated when she saw Kris inside. Then she noticed the decal. "Hey! Look!" she said to Matt while still outside.

Mrs. O'Malley waved them in. "You're right on time. I haven't started telling the latest bit of news because Kris and Darla have been carrying on, being annoyingly silly."

"There's news?" Katrina asked, strategically standing behind the sofa. "Did you hear from Bristol's already?"

Matt sat on the other side of Darla, giving Katrina an excuse to stay behind Kris instead of where he could easily see her.

"Yes. Mack? Why don't you tell them what the man said?"

Mack explained how Mr. Haley could identify the artist, and who he was and what he was known for, and his nickname. He told them about the collection the books had been a part of a long time ago, that they once likely belonged to Richard Heber, a very famous bibliophile, and that the lion label inside the rear cover of each proved it.

Mrs. O'Malley said, "Now. Are you sitting down for this next piece of news? Katrina, how come you're still standing? Here, sit next to Kris. Okay. Ready?" she asked after pulling

Katrina around the sofa and squeezing her beside Kris after the others had moved to make some room. "That one book Mack sent has a pre-sale estimate of ... are you ready? Fifteen *thousand* dollars."

Kris darted forward to hug Mrs. O'Malley and high-five Mack, leaving Katrina behind in an awkward tilt on the edge of the cushion.

"So, when's the next auction?" asked Matt, standing, too.

Everyone laughed.

"They aren't all like that, you understand," said Mack. "In fact, I don't expect to *ever* meet up with fantastic rarities like those books again. Never have before, either. Unless you count finding my Mavis, of course."

She smiled at the compliment. "And us finding Quainty, too, and finding that I had a whole, lovely family I never knew about. *That* was the find of our lifetime. *That* will never be topped."

Kris was no longer smiling. He left the others and pushed through the door to stand outside. He plucked a leaf from the sidewalk tree and examined its veins, its connections.

"What's wrong?" asked Matt, following him out.

"Kris?" asked Katrina as she left the shop. "What happened? Tell us."

Kris didn't look back. He walked past the record shop and sat on the bus-stop bench, and there Katrina and Matt sat on either side of him. "It's hard to explain."

"Want to try?" Katrina asked softly, resisting the urge to touch his arm.

Kris picked at a wood sliver at the edge of the bench. "Darla went to the restaurant where she used to work a long time ago when she knew Ricki."

"Oh?"

"Yeah. Turns out the owner of the place did remember Ricki. She had a daughter and kept it, then married the baby's dad. So ... she definitely isn't my biological mom. But now I still don't know anything other than that Ricki isn't in the picture. What Mrs. O just said threw me—that finding Quainty meant that she also found a lot of family members she never knew about and who she now loves. How do I know that finding my biological parents would be a *bad* thing? And … I don't even know that my biological parents weren't the ones I thought they were, the ones killed in the car accident." He threw his leaf into the street. "I'm trapped. There's some weird thing going on, but I don't know what it is."

Matt raised his foot onto the bench to pull the strap on his sandal tighter. "What do you mean?"

"I have never, ever met my grandparents on either side of the family. No aunts, uncles, cousins. No one. And no one came forward to take me in when I was all alone."

"That *is* weird," agreed Matt. He lowered his foot before asking, "What're you gonna do?"

"Decide. In a while. Or not. Right now, I'm split in two. I feel happy one second, then crazy upset the next. There's so much cool stuff going on now. Like, we're buying Taty's house, and—"

"You're *what?*" shouted Katrina, hitting him on his arm. "When were you going to tell us? *Geez*, Kris. Is it a done deal?"

"Yeah. I saw a for sale sign in the yard on Saturday. We toured it with this real estate lady yesterday, and my parents have the purchase practically finalized already."

She grinned. "I love that house! Oh, wowsers! I've been in it about ten times. It's the best ever. And now you guys are buying it? That is *too* crazy!"

"I've never been inside, but Kat has pointed it out when we've been by there. It looks nice, all right," said Matt. "Does it have a pool?"

"No, but it has a pool *table* in the basement."

"What? Oh, I am definitely staying your best friend forever, now."

"Was there some question about that?" Kris asked, finally smiling again.

Josie waved to them from across Main Street.

"Hey, look who's coming. Want us to give you some privacy?" asked Matt, a hint of teasing in his voice.

Kris didn't answer, watching as the girl came closer. She was sunny, he thought. Friendly and cute and pretty. Her brown hair practically danced around her head, and her ruby red lips formed the sweetest smile on the planet.

"Hi, guys," she said cheerily. She looked past Kris. "Matt? Can I talk to you for a min?"

"Me?" Matt asked, confused.

"Yes, please."

He got up without looking back at Kris and Katrina to follow Josie.

Kris watched them go, curious but happy that she hadn't asked to see *him* alone. "Let's go back, Katrina. Mrs. O is probably standing at the window having a cow." And as they stood, he added, "Hey ... thanks for breaking my heart on Friday. Highlight of my month, you should know."

"Any time. Happy to help." She knew she hadn't made her voice sound as casual as she'd wanted to. "You like Josie now anyway, right? And you didn't say—how was the play?"

"She called and canceled since her dad was sick."

"Oh, that's too bad." She nervously tugged at the hem of her shorts. "Well, you can take her somewhere else."

Kris didn't know what to say to that. Taking Josie out didn't interest him at all. He liked her—it was almost impossible not to—but she wasn't .... He didn't let himself finish the thought.

"I wonder why Josie wanted to talk to Matt."

Kris shrugged, but then he stopped walking at the corner of the bookshop as he remembered what they'd found out when they called Mr. Amos. Kris took a step down the alley and put his back against the wall of the bookshop. Looking straight ahead at the white-painted bricks of the record shop, he said, "Kat, I forgot to tell you and Matt something else major that happened. Dad called Botswana to talk to Mr. Amos about the house, and to ask why they listed it for sale so soon after leaving the country. And to find out why they were selling not only the house, but the contents. Her dad said that Mrs. Amos had a bad accident."

"What? Oh, God! Is she okay? Oh, no, Kris!"

"I think she will be. Eventually. Right now, though, she's not doing well at all. She fell down some stairs and broke a leg in two places, and she broke three ribs and an arm."

Matt had come back to find them, but he only heard the tail end of what Kris had said. "Who broke ribs and an arm?"

"Taty's mom," Kris said to Matt. "And her leg in two places. It's going to take a long time to heal. I talked to Taty. She didn't sound good. She sounded like somebody else entirely. They're never leaving Botswana, she said. I don't know if they'll feel the same way once her mom heals up, but that's what Mr. Amos said, too."

"Crud!" said Matt, kicking a stone.

Katrina linked an arm through her brother's, needing to hold onto someone. "How can I write to her or call her?"

"I told her to write to me, so I'll have her address. Dad has their phone number, but it's her father's cell. I think that's all they might have right now."

They were silent for several seconds.

Katrina finally looked at her brother. "What did Josie want?"

Matt shrugged. "She ... um ..."

Kris said, "She ... um ... what?"

Matt turned slightly red. "She wants me to join the color guard. That way we can hang out together all summer."

"Oh, geez," said Kris. He wasn't sure if he was hurt or relieved.

"Well?" asked Katrina.

Matt shrugged, looking guilty. "I'm going to. Band camp is next month."

His sister put her hands on her hips. "I thought you liked Keylee? Why are you going to hang around all summer with some other girl?"

Matt looked at his elbow for no real reason. "I do," he said. "I don't know. Josie's hard to say no to. You're not mad, are you, buddy?" he asked, looking at Kris.

Kris shook his head, meaning it and not meaning it at the same time. He felt stomped on again by a second girl within a few days.

They silently walked the several feet back into the bookshop.

"What happened to the cheerful bunch we had in the shop a few minutes ago?" asked Mack.

"I told them about Taty's mom, and about their house. And about Ricki," Kris said, playing with the pens and pencils in Elephant Gerald's vase back.

"I heard about Mrs. Amos while we were all picking out paintings last night. That's terrible," said Darla. She patted the cushion next to her while looking at Kris.

He sat next to her at the far end of the sofa, his whole face as sad as a hound dog's.

"Is there something else wrong?" asked Mrs. O'Malley. "You all went out of here as if I'd said something hurtful."

Kris met her eyes. "I'll talk to you about it sometime. It wasn't anything you did or said. Not really."

"Mavis tells me you've got a new *girl*friend now," Darla said, nudging his arm playfully.

Kris shrugged, slouching. He then sighed and shook his head. "I'm *done* with Josie. In fact, I'm done with girls in general. *Done!*"

Darla stood. In one swift move, she grabbed Katrina by the arm and tossed her onto the sofa next to Kris.

Without thinking, Katrina took Kris' face in her hands. Holding him, she waited as the expression in his eyes changed from surprise to happiness to yearning. She closed her eyes and kissed him delicately on his lips, then more firmly as he kissed her in return and hugged her waist to bring her even closer.

She pulled away to smile at him, shaking. Without a word, she stood and left the shop.

Matt laughed and laughed, walking out after his sister.

Kris flopped face-first onto the cushions. Dead, it seemed to the assembled trio of Mr. and Mrs. O'Malley and Darla.

"He's *done* with girls," said Darla. "Yep."

"Have we any oxygen tanks handy?" asked Mack.

Mrs. O'Malley was as speechless as Kris.

Darla grinned, satisfied with her accomplishment. "Well, you two make the funeral arrangements. I need to get back to work. Bye, all. And it was nice knowing you, Kris."

Danny came in just as Darla left.

Kris moaned into the cushion.

"Is he all right?" asked Danny, pointing to the back of Kris' head.

"Katrina kissed him. A good one," said Mack.

Danny raised Kris a few inches by his shoulder to see if anything else was wrong. Smiling, he said, "I've seen worse effects. It probably wasn't his first kiss ever. Those are the *really* deadly ones."

"Yeah, but this one happened in public. We saw the whole thing," Mack said as if discussing a medical case to a colleague. "It may also have been true love's first kiss."

"Hmm. That *is* more serious than I thought. We may need to call the paramedics."

Kris moaned again, louder. He finally managed to sit upright, looking around at who was left in the room. "What was *that?*" he asked, dazed.

"Long overdue, I'd say," said Mack.

Kris staggered to the door. "Bye."

"Bye, kiddo," said Mack.

"Are we going to move in right away?" Kris asked at the dinner table. He'd been smiling at odd moments since he'd gotten home, barely noticing the world around him, barely eating.

"No. There are things to settle legally and with our financing. It is nearly ours, though," his father said.

"We have another announcement," said Mrs. Dehlvi.

"What?" asked Bijay, swinging his legs.

"A surprise," said their father.

"What?" asked Dev and Dontae together.

"Well, since we have some time before we have to be busy moving, we're going to take a short vacation. Nothing that costs much money, after our recent expenditures, but we should go on a fun trip together, since it is summer and since I am not teaching until the fall."

"Yes," said Mrs. Dehlvi. "How would you boys like to go on a museum tour?"

"Ugh," said Dontae.

Kris laughed. "Don't you like museums, D?"

Dontae shrugged.

"Have you been to a museum?" asked Mr. Dehlvi.

"Nope. But I thought a family vacation was like in the commercials. Big water slides and roller coasters or running on a beach. Or, on a cruise ship with Mickey Mouse and all that stuff."

"I saw a commercial for a museum a few days ago, D," said Kris. "If we go to the one they were showing, there are these huge, toothy dinosaurs. Rawr! And ancient Egyptian stuff, and you can go to this one exhibit where you shrink to the size of a penny to see what's underground where the worms and bugs are."

Dontae sat straighter as he seemed to quote another commercial. "That sounds like family-friendly *fun.*"

Mr. Dehlvi blinked at Kris, thanking him silently. "There are three museums we could go to on our trip. One does have dinosaurs, one has all sorts of history items from our own state, and one has exhibits from India, where your mama and I are from before we moved here. Dontae, I am a teacher at the college, a professor of all things having to do with the religions, traditions, and folklore of India, in case you did not know. When we go to the museum, I can answer questions about their collections and displays. Or, I may come home feeling pretty dumb. We shall see."

Dontae laughed. "I already know you're smart, Dad."

"He already knows?" Mr. Dehlvi looked around the table. "Who told him?" he teased.

"I know 'cause I listen to you. *Every*body knows just from listening to you," Dontae said, picking up his fork again. He accidentally dropped it, but picked it up again, never letting a smile leave his face.

"So, we're going, then?" asked Kris.

"We are. We will pack and plan tonight and tomorrow. Mama has her doctor's appointment tomorrow morning. We will be seeing the baby on the screen for the first time with what is called an ultrasound. I will need everyone's help to plan the trip. Kris, will you stay home with the boys while I take your mama to see her doctor?"

"Sure. We'll draw dinos to get all psyched up for the trip."

"What's that mean?" asked Bijay, his large, brown eyes confused.

"Psyched up means ... excited. We'll draw dinos and get excited to see them."

Dontae's voice dropped an octave as he held his fork in the air dramatically. "We're gettin' psyched u-u-u-p!"

"Oh, no. Another new word," said Dev, rolling his eyes to the ceiling.

"Dontae? Are you going to write commercials for TV when you grow up?" Kris asked.

"Nope."

"What, then?"

"I'm gonna write books."

"Very admirable," said Mr. Dehlvi with an approving nod. "What sorts of books will you write?"

"Books about museums. After we go to these ones, probably."

The next morning Kris unfolded the state map he'd gotten out of the car's glove compartment before his parents went to the doctor. He wrote down mileages and driving directions while his brothers drew prehistoric beasts and Egyptian mummies.

When his parents had pulled into the driveway, he stood and stretched, wondering if there were leftovers in the fridge in case his mother was hungry.

The phone rang. It was Miss Valentine, calling far too soon for Kris to have decided about anything he wanted to say to her. He debated avoiding the call, but on the fourth ring, he finally answered.

"Hi. Miss Valentine, I'm glad you called. Um, I only wanted to tell you how great of a job I think you do. I love it here. I love my new family, and we're all *so* super happy to have Dontae now, too. Oh, and we're going to have a new baby next year. Mom's going to have one. You know—from scratch. Yes. She's surprised too. Dad is, too. We *all* are. Oh, and we're going to move soon, right down the street. It's a much bigger house. We'll need it since there's going to be seven of us. Hold on, please—Mom is trying to tell me something. What, Mom? *What?* Miss Valentine! Oh, my gosh! She just said to tell you that we're going to be a family of *eight.*"

Kris was so excited at the news that his mother was going to have twins and was so distracted by the ultrasound image she was showing him that he almost didn't hear Miss Valentine ask to speak to one of his parents.

"What?" asked Kris. "Mom or Dad? Okay. Hang on."

Kris traded his mother the phone for the ultrasound. He took the black and white print to the sofa and sat as his brothers gathered around him, asking him where the babies were in all the shadowy blobs.

Mrs. Dehlvi pulled at her husband's arm to lead him into their bedroom. She closed the door and sat on her bed, still listening to Miss Valentine on the phone.

"What do we tell our little Kris, then? What is to be said?" she asked.

Mr. Dehlvi, never one to interrupt a phone call, couldn't help himself. "Daya! Tell me what you are hearing."

Mrs. Dehlvi asked Miss Valentine to wait a moment. To her husband, she said, "Miss Valentine is saying that the parents of Kris who were killed were his *adoptive* parents."

Mr. Dehlvi, more from shock than rudeness, took the phone. "Miss Valentine, this is Falak Dehlvi. I think you have confused my wife." He listened for a full minute, his face reddening moment by moment. "How can that be? And what does this mean?"

After he hung up, the couple sat together on their bed. Sounds of the boys laughing and talking were muffled by the door, but still filled every corner of the house.

"This is shocking, Daya. And yet it is not."

Mrs. Dehlvi looked at the phone in her husband's hands. "So, he will never have answers. He will not be taken from us, be he will never have answers."

Mr. Dehlvi stood and turned the knob on the door. "Kris? Come and talk to us, please."

All of the boys ran along the hallway to their parents' bedroom. They hugged and laughed, hopped and hugged some more, all the while Mrs. Dehlvi silently shed emotional tears from her seat on the edge of the bed.

"That is enough silliness for now. We will celebrate later. Go out for now and let us talk to Kris for a few minutes," Mr. Dehlvi said. He closed the door again when the younger boys had left the room.

Kris stood near the end of the bed, still smiling brightly. "Twins! I never even thought that you might be having twins. Wow!" He stopped talking when he realized that his mother was openly crying and that his father's eyes were downcast. "Oh, Mom! Dad! Is there something wrong with the baby? I mean babies?"

Mrs. Dehlvi shook her head, reaching for a tissue from the box on the end table. She couldn't find her voice.

"Dad? What *is* it?"

Mr. Dehlvi looked at Kris. "We continued to speak to Miss Valentine after you had left the call. She told to us something that we were not told when we took you in, and also not when we finalized your adoption."

Kris sat near his father, turning sideways with one knee pointed to the side. "I don't care. Don't tell me. Don't tell me, Dad." He shook his head, staying as calm as he could. "Don't. I'm not leaving you."

"I think though, that of all the things Miss Valentine could have told us since we heard Darla's story, this is the best possible news, little Kris," his father said. "Let us tell you now."

Kris stood and walked to the window, pushing back the curtain to look at the front yard garden. "How *could* there be good news?"

Mrs. Dehlvi wiped her eyes. "You are only ours, Kris. No one will come to take you. No one is looking for you. Miss Valentine was curious about what you may have wanted to speak to her about. She finally decided to look into your file.

She was not expecting to find what she did today. That is why she called."

Mr. Dehlvi said, "You were adopted by the parents who were killed in the car accident. Your dad had been hurt in a previous accident, and he could not make a baby with your mother as a result of his injuries. They adopted you. And Kris—that adoption is a closed one. Your records are sealed."

Kris struggled to take in all this information. He dropped to the floor, sitting against the wall. He thought about his childhood. He remembered sitting with his father in a shopping mall, where there was a large mirror across the way from where they'd sat waiting for his mother to buy shoes. Kris remembered comparing his face to his father's, telling him how much they looked alike, and that his father had agreed. "Why didn't they *tell* me?" he cried, not looking at his parents. "Why didn't they ever ...." He eventually turned to look at Mr. Dehlvi. "And you didn't know?"

"We did not," his father said. "This is the very first we have heard such information."

"What a sloppy mess," Kris said, his face in his hands. After a few moments, he lowered his hands to look at his mother's back. "And how is this *good* news? Dad—how can you say that this is *good?*"

"Come here. Sit with us. Please," Mr. Dehlvi said, holding out his hand.

Kris shook his head, staying on the floor.

Mrs. Dehlvi walked around the bed and moved a chair near Kris. She sat, saying, "This is good news because it means that no one is looking for you. I do not say that to be cruel. Your biological mother, or mother and father, wished never to have contact with you or your first adoptive parents. We won't know the reason, but ... that is a fact. You will never be anyone's child but mine and Falak's for all time. Your first adoptive parents will always be missed, and important, and special, and loved by you. But now that they have left you to us, we will be happy to have you forevermore a Dehlvi."

Kris let himself relax and think about what she was telling him.

Mr. Dehlvi left the room to be with the younger boys, but he closed the door behind him again.

"So," said Kris, looking at his shoes, at his mother's shoes, at her stomach, and then up to her eyes. "This is the end."

"I believe it is the end, yes. You are safe in our family. There is no danger hanging over our heads."

Kris took in a deep breath and held it for a long time before letting it out to kneel in front of his mother's chair. "You are always right, Mom. This *is* good news." He stood and hugged her while she stayed sitting. "Would you and the twins like something to eat? We've got to get ready for our family trip now, too. Dontae's got research to do for his first book."

She burst into tears again, this time loudly, laughing and crying in turns.

Weeks later on a Saturday afternoon, the Dehlvis walked into the Garnerette Gallery in Lamarr, housed in a stately building that had been a funeral home for a century. A vinyl banner over the door outside reproduced a few of the colorful characters from Quaintance's artwork, along with the dates and times of the show. The largest lettering proclaimed:

"Fresh Greens: A first look at Q. Cumber"

Inside, everything was dark wood and gray marble, with spotlights on the walls above Mrs. Cumber's paintings.

"You made it," said Mrs. O'Malley as she walked to meet them. She wore a black pants suit with a yellow blouse, and black shoes with a bit of a heel to them, to Kris' surprise. She had on makeup, and her hair was cut and styled. She almost seemed like a different person. Mack was wearing a pair of tan slacks, a white shirt, and a brown tie.

"We did, Mavis," Mr. Dehlvi said, bowing slightly. "This is all *very* nice. Have the crowds been this congested since the show opened?"

"More, even. Quainty's sold several paintings already today, and the show only opened an hour ago. Do you see that man and woman—the ones holding cameras? They're from a Chicago gallery, and they want to host a show for Quainty in two months up *there*. She's practically a *star* now."

Kris looked around the rooms for a pink-haired woman. In the back of the gallery, he found Danny and Lucille talking to Darla and Jack, so he left Mrs. O'Malley to join them. A woman in a gold dress turned and was hugging Kris before he realized that it was Mrs. Cumber. He pulled back to look at her. "Where's your pink hair?"

"That last pinking-up was a temporary dye, thankfully. I decided not to clash with my art. Good to see you, Kris. I haven't clapped eyes on you since my picking-out-paintings party."

Kris nodded. "Lots to do at home. We've been packing and moving across the street from morning until night since we got back from vacation. I haven't even been to the bookshop. We're finally done and settled into the new house, thanks to a moving company who hauled our furniture and the bigger boxes. Our old house is already on the market." He glanced around. "This is so *cool*, Mrs. C! Your own show in a real gallery."

"I'm not used to it yet. It feels like a dream. People here *like* my silly paintings, can you imagine? Even the ones on door halves with house paint on them. Even the dress. I'm over the moon, but scared I'll fall off when the cow jumps up there, too."

Kris paused, trying to figure out exactly what she was trying to say.

"How's your mom?" Danny asked after sipping from a champagne glass. He was wearing a gray suit, looking like he was ready to walk down a church aisle to get married.

"Good. She's here. We're all here." Kris noticed that Lucille's hair wasn't in a ponytail down her back. It fell in waves to her neckline. "You cut your hair!"

"I did. I donated it all away. Like it?" she asked.

"I kinda do. You look younger."

"Oh, *no!*" complained Danny, making a horrified face. "*Just* what I wanted to hear."

The group laughed, and Lucille wrapped her arms around Danny's arm, grinning. Kris looked at Lucille's ring finger on her left hand. On it was an intricately carved wooden engagement ring with a mirror at the center shaped like a diamond.

Kris left them to walk along the walls of exhibited paintings. He was amazed to see that each one looked very different while hanging on a gallery wall under spotlights. Some had round blue stickers next to them on the wall where the price was on others. They must have sold, Kris concluded.

The first painting he stepped closer to was one that he and Mack had brought to the college the summer before so an art professor could look at examples of Quaintance's work. It was of talking questionfish, a mermaid, and an orange octopus. Next was the forest scene he had found the first day he'd been upstairs at the Cumbers' home. It had glued-on pine needles and bits of leaves, and above the tree line were names spelled out in yarn and string. Kris pictured himself again in the Cumbers' kitchen, listening to Quaintance's sad story about those names.

Kris then came to a large glass box-frame taller than he was. Inside was one of the painted dresses. It looked magnificent in an upright position with a blown-up sepia photo of Quaintance as a young girl in the background. On the dress were painted oddly shaped dogs, singing cats, alligators, a jump rope, a green farm tractor, and toys.

Everywhere Kris looked were primary colors in bursts and swirls made into imaginary creatures, crude-looking people done in strange flesh tones, and farm life scenes with alien crops and giant grasshoppers.

He strolled to what would have been the first painting seen if he had started his tour at the main entrance. As soon as he saw it, he glanced all around for anyone he knew. Seeing no one, he looked back at the image. It was a faintly smiling young man with dark blonde hair and electric blue eyes who was holding a rusty-colored rooster in his arms. A red barn was behind the boy, and stacks of books sat near a white rocking chair on the farmhouse lawn. A cat was on its seat.

While still staring at the painting, he felt a hand on his shoulder.

"She's done you a good likeness. Billy, too," said Mr. Cumber.

Kris looked at Elwood, who was almost unrecognizable in a gray suit and short haircut. "But ..." was all Kris could say.

"He found it," announced Quaintance from somewhere behind them in the crowd.

Kris stood still, waiting to see her when roving people in between them moved aside. When he did see Mrs. Cumber again, she was grinning.

"Like it?" she asked, joining her husband. "I know it's not exactly a prize portrait, but I think it looks like the Kris I have in my heart. I'm doing a painting of Dar and L.P., too, but that one wasn't ready for the show. That's a Danny frame, you know. Made special. I think he did *fine.*"

Mr. and Mrs. O'Malley arrived beside the Cumbers, then Danny and Lucille. Darla and Jack shouldered their way closer. The Dehlvis had spotted the group and were making their way over. Soon everyone was pointing to or talking about the painting, but Kris couldn't think what to do or say. He noticed then that a little white sticker stating "Not for sale" was at the edge of the painting's description card.

"So nice that it will always be hanging in our apartment," said Mack. "When he's a grown man, he can visit us and point to it, telling his kids about a time way back in the olden days when he knew a famous artist who was just starting out."

"Just starting *out?*" said Quaintance, flabbergasted. "Mr. Bookstore, you have no idea how many long years I've been slapping paint on all manner of things." She crossed her arms and looked at Kris. When she did so, she resembled her farm-wife self far more than her dressed-up exhibited-artist self. "And besides, he won't have to point at that painting to tell his kids about me. He'll have been bringing them out to me at the farm right along since they were babes."

Mack pulled his earlobe. "Well, then I'll restate that. How about: just starting along the road to worldwide fame. Better?"

She smiled and uncrossed her arms. "We'll have to get together again to choose another bunch of paintings for my next show. And it turns out they're making a booklet for that show, which probably means picking out a whole lot more for them to photograph. The man says he wants to interview me, too. Lordy, who's gonna want to read *that?*"

"*I* will," said Kris. They were the first real words he'd spoken since seeing the painting of himself and Billy.

411

Quaintance hugged Kris. A group farther into the room was laughing and talking loudly as she whispered into his ear, "Like it, boy?"

He hugged her in return, noticing that it was strange to hug her and feel cold, metallic discs under his hands and forearms. She usually wore soft, lived-in materials. "I love it. I … I love you, too."

Quaintance kissed his cheek and turned away. Kris saw her reaching toward a tray of cheese cubes.

"I had a long discussion on the phone with your mother," Mrs. O'Malley said, pulling Kris aside where it was a little quieter. "She wanted the painting, too, of course. I told her that since she gets to have you from autumn through spring, I should get to have your likeness. Quainty said she'll do another painting of you and your brothers that can hang in your new home."

"You know I'm in your shop all year round, Mrs. O. But not as much, I guess." He walked with her outside onto the broad steps. The sunny day was starting to cool for the early evening. "I feel like I haven't seen you for five years, even though it's only been weeks. Everyone looks different all dressed up. It's like the world has gone on without me, and no one really missed me at all."

"Oh, that is so not true!" she said, shaking her head. "Mack and I spent half of our days wondering what you were up to and missing seeing your face." She paused, seeming to wonder if she should say what she had in mind. "Kat's been a big help to us while you were on your vacation and moving house. She's put nearly every rare book's dustjacket into a sleeve now, and quite a lot of the mysteries, too. I'm learning more on the computer from her, and she's helping me to wrap books that need to be mailed out."

Kris glanced at his new leather shoes and adjusted his dress shirt as if he couldn't get comfortable. "That's good."

412

"Nice to have added another member to our bookshop family, and such a lovely, fun girl, too." She waited until he looked at her to say, "I've always been able to see why you like her. She's becoming very special to us, too."

He looked down at his black slacks. "I suppose that means you don't need me for much now."

"Kris! No one could just waltz into the shop and take your place ... in any way. You sound jealous. Isn't there room for both you and Kat at No Page Unturned? *I* think there is." She waited for him to reply. When he didn't, she said, "I'm paying her for her work, and we're going to pay you now, too. We can afford it. All those books *are* by Rodolfo Himzala-Vega, did we tell you? We got confirmation about that. All of them! After the expert studied them, the presale estimate is ..." She looked around and lowered her voice, *"four hundred grand.* That's not even close to what they actually expect to get for the group." She shook her head and swallowed, still not used to the idea of that much money. "We're not retiring, even so. It's not like we're old people or anything, right?"

He looked at the street, at the leafy trees and parked cars. "You've always paid me, really. Giving me free books, buying me dinners and lunches, that sort of thing." He met her eyes. "And there's never going to be enough money to equal what I've gotten from you and Mack." He frowned. "Remember how scared and shy I was, and how lonely I was when I first started out at your shop? I didn't have a friend in the world, and I didn't feel I had a real family, either. Mom and Dad were gone, and no one came for me except these people I didn't know who were so different from what I was used to." He went to stand beside her, letting another group of people by him into the gallery. "Please, don't pay me. I won't feel the same way about the shop if you do. Pay Kat, but not me. I can pretend that I'm one of the O'Malleys when I'm with you, like all three of us are taking in money for the family when customers buy our books. I can pretend that I'm shelving books that are partially mine, fixing books for our customers when I help Mack and neatening the shop and shelves for our browsers and friends."

She put an arm through his and exhaled slowly. "I see exactly how you're feeling." She smiled to herself. "And I don't know if you realize this, but you pumped up my heart to three times its former size." She sniffled and pulled a tissue from her small, black purse. "Mack and I feel precisely the same as you said. You're *our* boy when you're with us, at least partially. We ... we couldn't possibly love you more if you *were* our own flesh and blood. But we *are* going to pay you. Indulge us in that, all right?"

He nodded, putting his head against hers.

She inhaled, bracing herself. "Let's go back inside and look at those paintings some more. Don't they look like jewels on a wall with those lights on 'em?"

Kris didn't move, his eyes downcast. "Everything's changing."

She kept her arm through his as she led him into the gallery, still wiping her eyes carefully so she wouldn't smear her makeup. "And they're staying the same, too. Just like every other day on this planet for everyone. You'll see: tomorrow we'll have our regular clothes on, and we'll look like our old selves. You'll come to the bookshop and Mack will point to a tall stack of books and ask you to shelve them. The Marys will come in, and they'll say how much taller you've gotten over the last few weeks. Darla will pop into the shop with L.P., and maybe she'll have written a new poem about this exhibition, saying that she finally sent out some of her writings to try to get published. You'll see the new foster cat, Mischief. He's ginger and white, and he loves to rip around like he's at a racetrack. Our windows have new decals now, and you'll stand outside for a while admiring them. Mack will show you a flyer about a class on fine book repairing at the college that he thinks you should take next summer. It's open to high school kids, too. I'll look at you, and you'll look at me, and we'll laugh because it will be *exactly* as I said it would be as we're standing here today."

He lowered his hand to squeeze hers as they became a part of the crowd inside the gallery. Danny waved at them to join him and the others from Kris' several families.

"That sounds perfect, Mrs. O," Kris said, looking from face to face at the people who were coming closer, binding them together. "I can hardly wait."

Jenny Kalahar lives in central Indiana with her husband, Patrick, and their pets in an old schoolhouse full of used books. She is the author of novels, stories, and poems, and has been published in several anthologies, in literary journals, and had a humor column in Tails Magazine. She has one of the numerous forms of ectodermal dysplasia. She and Patrick previously owned and operated bookshops in Michigan and Ohio, and they now sell books via the internet. They are active in the poetry community of Indiana. Jenny is the publisher for the Poetry Society of Indiana, she is the founder and leader of Last Stanza Poetry Association and is the president of the Youth Poetry Society of Indiana. She was twice nominated for a Pushcart Prize in poetry and has won writing contests. When not writing, reading, or working with old books, she loves expeditions through flea markets and playing piano and percussion.

Made in the USA
Las Vegas, NV
29 June 2021